THE LILY OF THE VALLEY

Honoré de Balzac
1799-1850
Translated by
Katharine Prescott Wormeley

The Echo Library
2005

Published by
The Echo Library
Paperbackshop Ltd
Cockrup Farm House
Coln St Aldwyn
Cirencester GL7 5AZ
www.echo-library.com

ISBN 1-84637-814-1

DEDICATION

To Monsieur J. B. Nacquart,   Member of the Royal Academy of Medicine.

Dear Doctor—Here is one of the most carefully hewn stones in the second course of the foundation of a literary edifice which I have   slowly and laboriously constructed. I wish to inscribe your name   upon it, as much to thank the man whose science once saved me as   to honor the friend of my daily life.

De Balzac.

THE LILY OF THE VALLEY

ENVOI

Felix de Vandenesse to Madame la Comtesse Natalie de Manerville:

I yield to your wishes. It is the privilege of the women whom we   love more than they love us to make the men who love them ignore   the ordinary rules of common-sense. To smooth the frown upon their   brow, to soften the pout upon their lips, what obstacles we   miraculously overcome! We shed our blood, we risk our future!

You exact the history of my past life; here it is. But remember   this, Natalie; in obeying you I crush under foot a reluctance   hitherto unconquerable. Why are you jealous of the sudden reveries   which overtake me in the midst of our happiness? Why show the   pretty anger of a petted woman when silence grasps me? Could you   not play upon the contradictions of my character without inquiring into the causes of them? Are there secrets in your heart which   seek absolution through a knowledge of mine? Ah! Natalie, you have   guessed mine; and it is better you should know the whole truth.   Yes, my life is shadowed by a phantom; a word evokes it; it hovers   vaguely above me and about me; within my soul are solemn memories,   buried in its depths like those marine productions seen in calmest weather and which the storms of ocean cast in fragments on the   shore.

The mental labor which the expression of ideas necessitates has   revived the old, old feelings which give me so much pain when they   come suddenly; and if in this confession of my past they break   forth in a way that wounds you, remember that you threatened to   punish me if I did not obey your wishes, and do not, therefore,   punish my obedience. I would that this, my confidence, might increase your love.

Until we meet,

Felix.

CHAPTER I
TWO CHILDHOODS

To what genius fed on tears shall we some day owe that most touching of all elegies,—the tale of tortures borne silently by souls whose tender roots find stony ground in the domestic soil, whose earliest buds are torn apart by rancorous hands, whose flowers are touched by frost at the moment of their blossoming? What poet will sing the sorrows of the child whose lips must suck a bitter breast, whose smiles are checked by the cruel fire of a stern eye? The tale that tells of such poor hearts, oppressed by beings placed about them to promote the development of their natures, would contain the true history of my childhood.

What vanity could I have wounded,—I a child new-born? What moral or physical infirmity caused by mother's coldness? Was I the child of duty, whose birth is a mere chance, or was I one whose very life was a reproach? Put to nurse in the country and forgotten by my family for over three years, I was treated with such indifference on my return to the parental roof that even the servants pitied me. I do not know to what feeling or happy accident I owed my rescue from this first neglect; as a child I was ignorant of it, as a man I have not discovered it. Far from easing my lot, my brother and my two sisters found amusement in making me suffer. The compact in virtue of which children hide each other's peccadilloes, and which early teaches them the principles of honor, was null and void in my case; more than that, I was often punished for my brother's faults, without being allowed to prove the injustice. The fawning spirit which seems instinctive in children taught my brother and sisters to join in the persecutions to which I was subjected, and thus keep in the good graces of a mother whom they feared as much as I. Was this partly the effect of a childish love of imitation; was it from a need of testing their powers; or was it simply through lack of pity? Perhaps these causes united to deprive me of the sweets of fraternal intercourse.

Disinherited of all affection, I could love nothing; yet nature had made me loving. Is there an angel who garners the sighs of feeling hearts rebuffed incessantly? If in many such hearts the crushed feelings turn to hatred, in mine they condensed and hollowed a depth from which, in after years, they gushed forth upon my life. In many characters the habit of trembling relaxes the fibres and begets fear, and fear ends in submission; hence, a weakness which emasculates a man, and makes him more or less a slave. But in my case these perpetual tortures led to the development of a certain strength, which increased through exercise and predisposed my spirit to the habit of moral resistance. Always in expectation of some new grief—as the martyrs expected some fresh blow—my whole being expressed, I doubt not, a sullen resignation which smothered the grace and gaiety of childhood, and gave me an appearance of idiocy which seemed to justify my mother's threatening prophecies. The certainty of injustice prematurely roused my pride—that fruit of reason—and thus, no doubt, checked the evil tendencies which an education like mine encouraged.

Though my mother neglected me I was sometimes the object of her solicitude; she occasionally spoke of my education and seemed desirous of attending to it herself. Cold chills ran through me at such times when I thought of the torture a daily intercourse with her would inflict upon me. I blessed the neglect in which I lived, and rejoiced that I could stay alone in the garden and play with the pebbles and watch the insects and gaze into the blueness of the sky. Though my loneliness naturally led me to reverie, my liking for contemplation was first aroused by an incident which will give you an idea of my early troubles. So little notice was taken of me that the governess occasionally forgot to send me to bed. One evening I was peacefully crouching under a fig-tree, watching a star with that passion of curiosity which takes possession of a child's mind, and to which my precocious melancholy gave a sort of sentimental intuition. My sisters were playing about and laughing; I heard their distant chatter like an accompaniment to my thoughts. After a while the noise ceased and darkness fell. My mother happened to notice my absence. To escape blame, our governess, a terrible Mademoiselle Caroline, worked upon my mother's fears,—told her I had a horror of my home and would long ago have run away if she had not watched me; that I was not stupid but sullen; and that in all her experience of children she had never known one of so bad a disposition as mine. She pretended to search for me. I answered as soon as I was called, and she came to the fig-tree, where she very well knew I was. "What are you doing there?" she asked. "Watching a star." "You were not watching a star," said my mother, who was listening on her balcony; "children of your age know nothing of astronomy." "Ah, madame," cried Mademoiselle Caroline, "he has opened the faucet of the reservoir; the garden is inundated!" Then there was a general excitement. The fact was that my sisters had amused themselves by turning the cock to see the water flow, but a sudden spurt wet them all over and frightened them so much that they ran away without closing it. Accused and convicted of this piece of mischief and told that I lied when I denied it, I was severely punished. Worse than all, I was jeered at for my pretended love of the stars and forbidden to stay in the garden after dark.

Such tyrannical restrains intensify a passion in the hearts of children even more than in those of men; children think of nothing but the forbidden thing, which then becomes irresistibly attractive to them. I was often whipped for my star. Unable to confide in my kind, I told it all my troubles in that delicious inward prattle with which we stammer our first ideas, just as once we stammered our first words. At twelve years of age, long after I was at school, I still watched that star with indescribable delight,—so deep and lasting are the impressions we receive in the dawn of life.

My brother Charles, five years older than I and as handsome a boy as he now is a man, was the favorite of my father, the idol of my mother, and consequently the sovereign of the house. He was robust and well-made, and had a tutor. I, puny and even sickly, was sent at five years of age as day pupil to a school in the town; taken in the morning and brought back at night by my father's valet. I was sent with a scanty lunch, while my school-fellows brought plenty of good food. This trifling contrast between my privations and their prosperity made me suffer deeply. The famous potted pork prepared at Tours and called "rillettes" and "rillons" was the chief feature of their mid-day meal, between the early breakfast and the parent's dinner, which was ready when we returned from school. This preparation of meat, much prized by certain gourmands, is seldom seen at Tours on aristocratic tables; if I had ever heard of it before I went to school, I certainly had never had the happiness of seeing that brown mess spread on slices of bread and butter. Nevertheless, my desire for those "rillons" was so great that it grew to be a fixed idea, like the longing of an elegant Parisian duchess for the stews cooked by a porter's wife,—longings which, being a woman, she found means to satisfy. Children guess each other's covetousness, just as you are able to read a man's love, by the look in the eyes; consequently I became an admirable butt for ridicule. My comrades, nearly all belonging to the lower bourgeoisie, would show me their "rillons" and ask if I knew how they were made and where they were sold, and why it was that I never had any. They licked their lips as they talked of them—scraps of pork pressed in their own fat and looking like cooked truffles; they inspected my lunch-basket, and finding nothing better than Olivet cheese or dried fruits, they plagued me with questions: "Is that all you have? have you really nothing else?"— speeches which made me realize the difference between my brother and myself.

This contrast between my own abandonment and the happiness of others nipped the roses of my childhood and blighted my budding youth. The first time that I, mistaking my comrades' actions for generosity, put forth my hand to take the dainty I had so long coveted and which was now hypocritically held out to me, my tormentor pulled back his slice to the great delight of his comrades who were expecting that result. If noble and distinguished minds are, as we often find them, capable of vanity, can we blame the child who weeps when despised and jeered at? Under such a trial many boys would have turned into gluttons and cringing beggars. I fought to escape my persecutors. The courage of despair made me formidable; but I was hated, and thus had no protection against treachery. One evening as I left school I was struck in the back by a handful of small stones tied in a handkerchief. When the valet, who punished the perpetrator, told this to my mother she exclaimed: "That dreadful child! he will always be a torment to us."

Finding that I inspired in my schoolmates the same repulsion that was felt for me by my family, I sank into a horrible distrust of myself. A second fall of snow checked the seeds that were germinating in my soul. The boys whom I most liked were notorious scamps; this fact roused my pride and I held aloof. Again I was shut up within myself and had no vent for the feelings with which my heart was full. The master of the school, observing that I was gloomy, disliked by my comrades, and always alone, confirmed the family verdict as to my sulky temper. As soon as I could read and write, my mother transferred me to Pont-le-Voy, a school in charge of Oratorians who took boys of my age into a form called the "class of the Latin steps" where dull lads with torpid brains were apt to linger.

There I remained eight years without seeing my family; living the life of a pariah,—partly for the following reason. I received but three francs a month pocket-money, a sum barely sufficient to buy the pens, ink, paper, knives, and rules which we were forced to supply ourselves. Unable to buy stilts or skipping-ropes, or any of the things that were used in the playground, I was driven out of the games; to gain admission on suffrage I should have had to toady the rich and flatter the strong of my division. My heart rose against either of these meannesses, which, however, most children readily employ. I lived under a tree, lost in dejected thought, or reading the books distributed to us monthly by the librarian. How many griefs were in the shadow of that solitude; what genuine anguish filled my neglected life! Imagine what my sore heart felt when, at the first distribution of prizes,—of which I obtained the two most valued, namely, for theme and for translation,—

neither my father nor my mother was present in the theatre when I came forward to receive the awards amid general acclamations, although the building was filled with the relatives of all my comrades. Instead of kissing the distributor, according to custom, I burst into tears and threw myself on his breast. That night I burned my crowns in the stove. The parents of the other boys were in town for a whole week preceding the distribution of the prizes, and my comrades departed joyfully the next day; while I, whose father and mother were only a few miles distant, remained at the school with the "outremers,"—a name given to scholars whose families were in the colonies or in foreign countries.

You will notice throughout how my unhappiness increased in proportion as the social spheres on which I entered widened. God knows what efforts I made to weaken the decree which condemned me to live within myself! What hopes, long cherished with eagerness of soul, were doomed to perish in a day! To persuade my parents to come and see me, I wrote them letters full of feeling, too emphatically worded, it may be; but surely such letters ought not to have drawn upon me my mother's reprimand, coupled with ironical reproaches for my style. Not discouraged even then, I implored the help of my sisters, to whom I always wrote on their birthdays and fete-days with the persistence of a neglected child; but it was all in vain. As the day for the distribution of prizes approached I redoubled my entreaties, and told of my expected triumphs. Misled by my parents' silence, I expected them with a beating heart. I told my schoolfellows they were coming; and then, when the old porter's step sounded in the corridors as he called my happy comrades one by one to receive their friends, I was sick with expectation. Never did that old man call my name!

One day, when I accused myself to my confessor of having cursed my life, he pointed to the skies, where grew, he said, the promised palm for the "Beati qui lugent" of the Saviour. From the period of my first communion I flung myself into the mysterious depths of prayer, attracted to religious ideas whose moral fairyland so fascinates young spirits. Burning with ardent faith, I prayed to God to renew in my behalf the miracles I had read of in martyrology. At five years of age I fled to my star; at twelve I took refuge in the sanctuary. My ecstasy brought dreams unspeakable, which fed my imagination, fostered my susceptibilities, and strengthened my thinking powers. I have often attributed those sublime visions to the guardian angel charged with moulding my spirit to its divine destiny; they endowed my soul with the faculty of seeing the inner soul of things; they prepared my heart for the magic craft which makes a man a poet when the fatal power is his to compare what he feels within him with reality,—the great things aimed for with the small things gained. Those visions wrote upon my brain a book in which I read that which I must voice; they laid upon my lips the coal of utterance.

My father having conceived some doubts as to the tendency of the Oratorian teachings, took me from Pont-le-Voy, and sent me to Paris to an institution in the Marais. I was then fifteen. When examined as to my capacity, I, who was in the rhetoric class at Pont-le-Voy, was pronounced worthy of the third class. The sufferings I had endured in my family and in school were continued under another form during my stay at the Lepitre Academy. My father gave me no money; I was to be fed, clothed, and stuffed with Latin and Greek, for a sum agreed on. During my school life I came in contact with over a thousand comrades; but I never met with such an instance of neglect and indifference as mine. Monsieur Lepitre, who was fanatically attached to the Bourbons, had had relations with my father at the time when all devoted royalists were endeavoring to bring about the escape of Marie Antoinette from the Temple. They had lately renewed acquaintance; and Monsieur Lepitre thought himself obliged to repair my father's oversight, and to give me a small sum monthly. But not being authorized to do so, the amount was small indeed.

The Lepitre establishment was in the old Joyeuse mansion where, as in all seignorial houses, there was a porter's lodge. During a recess, which preceded the hour when the man-of-all-work took us to the Charlemagne Lyceum, the well-to-do pupils used to breakfast with the porter, named Doisy. Monsieur Lepitre was either ignorant of the fact or he connived at this arrangement with Doisy, a regular smuggler whom it was the pupils' interest to protect,—he being the secret guardian of their pranks, the safe confidant of their late returns and their intermediary for obtaining forbidden books. Breakfast on a cup of "cafe-au-lait" is an aristocratic habit, explained by the high prices to which colonial products rose under Napoleon. If the use of sugar and coffee was a luxury to our parents, with us it was the sign of self-conscious superiority. Doisy gave credit, for he reckoned on the sisters and aunts of the pupils, who made it a point of honor to pay their debts. I resisted the blandishments of his place for a long time. If my judges knew the strength of its seduction, the heroic efforts I made after stoicism, the repressed desires of my long resistance, they would pardon my final overthrow. But, child as I was, could I have the grandeur of soul that scorns the scorn of others? Moreover, I may have felt the promptings of several social vices whose power was increased by my longings.

About the end of the second year my father and mother came to Paris. My brother had written me the day of their arrival. He lived in Paris, but had never been to see me. My sisters, he said, were of the party; we were all to see Paris together. The first day we were to dine in the Palais-Royal, so as to be near the Theatre-Francais. In spite of the intoxication such a programme of unhoped-for delights excited, my joy was dampened by the wind of a coming storm, which those who are used to unhappiness apprehend instinctively. I was forced to own a debt of a hundred francs to the Sieur Doisy, who threatened to ask my parents himself for the money. I bethought me of making my brother the emissary of Doisy, the mouth-piece of my repentance and the mediator of pardon. My father inclined to forgiveness, but my mother was pitiless; her dark blue eye froze me; she fulminated cruel prophecies: "What should I be later if at seventeen years of age I committed such follies? Was I really a son of hers? Did I mean to ruin my family? Did I think myself the only child of the house? My brother Charles's career, already begun, required large outlay, amply deserved by his conduct which did honor to the family, while mine would always disgrace it. Did I know nothing of the value of money, and what I cost them? Of what use were coffee and sugar to my education? Such conduct was the first step into all the vices."

After enduring the shock of this torrent which rasped my soul, I was sent back to school in charge of my brother. I lost the dinner at the Freres Provencaux, and was deprived of seeing Talma in Britannicus. Such was my first interview with my mother after a separation of twelve years.

When I had finished school my father left me under the guardianship of Monsieur Lepitre. I was to study the higher mathematics, follow a course of law for one year, and begin philosophy. Allowed to study in my own room and released from the classes, I expected a truce with trouble. But, in spite of my nineteen years, perhaps because of them, my father persisted in the system which had sent me to school without food, to an academy without pocket-money, and had driven me into debt to Doisy. Very little money was allowed to me, and what can you do in Paris without money? Moreover, my freedom was carefully chained up. Monsieur Lepitre sent me to the law school accompanied by a man-of-all-work who handed me over to the professor and fetched me home again. A young girl would have been treated with less precaution than my mother's fears insisted on for me. Paris alarmed my parents, and justly. Students are secretly engaged in the same occupation which fills the minds of young ladies in their boarding-schools. Do what you will, nothing can prevent the latter from talking of lovers, or the former of women. But in Paris, and especially at this particular time, such talk among young lads was influenced by the oriental and sultanic atmosphere and customs of the Palais-Royal.

The Palais-Royal was an Eldorado of love where the ingots melted away in coin; there virgin doubts were over; there curiosity was appeased. The Palais-Royal and I were two asymptotes bearing one towards the other, yet unable to meet. Fate miscarried all my attempts. My father had presented me to one of my aunts who lived in the Ile St. Louis. With her I was to dine on Sundays and Thursdays, escorted to the house by either Monsieur or Madame Lepitre, who went out themselves on those days and were to call for me on their way home. Singular amusement for a young lad! My aunt, the Marquise de Listomere, was a great lady, of ceremonious habits, who would never have dreamed of offering me money. Old as a cathedral, painted like a miniature, sumptuous in dress, she lived in her great house as though Louis XV. were not dead, and saw none but old women and men of a past day, —a fossil society which made me think I was in a graveyard. No one spoke to me and I had not the courage to speak first. Cold and alien looks made me ashamed of my youth, which seemed to annoy them. I counted on this indifference to aid me in certain plans; I was resolved to escape some day directly after dinner and rush to the Palais-Royal. Once seated at whist my aunt would pay no attention to me. Jean, the footman, cared little for Monsieur Lepitre and would have aided me; but on the day I chose for my adventure that luckless dinner was longer than usual,—either because the jaws employed were worn out or the false teeth more imperfect. At last, between eight and nine o'clock, I reached the staircase, my heart beating like that of Bianca Capello on the day of her flight; but when the porter pulled the cord I beheld in the street before me Monsieur Lepitre's hackney-coach, and I heard his pursy voice demanding me!

Three times did fate interpose between the hell of the Palais-Royal and the heaven of my youth. On the day when I, ashamed at twenty years of age of my own ignorance, determined to risk all dangers to put an end to it, at the very moment when I was about to run away from Monsieur Lepitre as he got into the coach,—a difficult process, for he was as fat as Louis XVIII. and club-footed,—well, can you believe it, my mother arrived in a post-chaise! Her glance arrested me; I stood still, like a bird before a snake. What fate had brought her there? The simplest thing in the world. Napoleon was then making his last efforts. My father, who foresaw the return of the Bourbons, had come to Paris with my mother to advise my brother, who was employed in the imperial diplomatic service. My mother was to take me back with her, out of the way of dangers which seemed, to those who followed the march of events intelligently, to threaten the capital. In a few minutes, as it were, I was taken out of Paris, at the very moment when my life there was about to become fatal to me.

The tortures of imagination excited by repressed desires, the weariness of a life depressed by constant privations had driven me to study, just as men, weary of fate, confine themselves in a cloister. To me, study had become a passion, which might even be fatal to my health by imprisoning me at a period of life when young men ought to yield to the bewitching activities of their springtide youth.

This slight sketch of my boyhood, in which you, Natalie, can readily perceive innumerable songs of woe, was needful to explain to you its influence on my future life. At twenty years of age, and affected by many morbid elements, I was still small and thin and pale. My soul, filled with the will to do, struggled with a body that seemed weakly, but which, in the words of an old physician at Tours, was undergoing its final fusion into a temperament of iron. Child in body and old in mind, I had read and thought so much that I knew life metaphysically at its highest reaches at the moment when I was about to enter the tortuous difficulties of its defiles and the sandy roads of its plains. A strange chance had held me long in that delightful period when the soul awakes to its first tumults, to its desires for joy, and the savor of life is fresh. I stood in the period between puberty and manhood,—the one prolonged by my excessive study, the other tardily developing its living shoots. No young man was ever more thoroughly prepared to feel and to love. To understand my history, let your mind dwell on that pure time of youth when the mouth is innocent of falsehood; when the glance of the eye is honest, though veiled by lids which droop from timidity contradicting desire; when the soul bends not to worldly Jesuitism, and the heart throbs as violently from trepidation as from the generous impulses of young emotion.

I need say nothing of the journey I made with my mother from Paris to Tours. The coldness of her behavior repressed me. At each relay I tried to speak; but a look, a word from her frightened away the speeches I had been meditating. At Orleans, where we had passed the night, my mother complained of my silence. I threw myself at her feet and clasped her knees; with tears I opened my heart. I tried to touch hers by the eloquence of my hungry love in accents that might have moved a stepmother. She replied that I was playing comedy. I complained that she had abandoned me. She called me an unnatural child. My whole nature was so wrung that at Blois I went upon the bridge to drown myself in the Loire. The height of the parapet prevented my suicide.

When I reached home, my two sisters, who did not know me, showed more surprise than tenderness. Afterwards, however, they seemed, by comparison, to be full of kindness towards me. I was given a room on the third story. You will understand the extent of my hardships when I tell you that my mother left me, a young man of twenty, without other linen than my miserable school outfit, or any other outside clothes than those I had long worn in Paris. If I ran from one end of the room to the other to pick up her handkerchief, she took it with the cold thanks a lady gives to her footman. Driven to watch her to find if there were any soft spot where I could fasten the rootlets of affection, I came to see her as she was,—a tall, spare woman, given to cards, egotistical and insolent, like all the Listomeres, who count insolence as part of their dowry. She saw nothing in life except duties to be fulfilled. All cold women whom I have known made, as she did, a religion of duty; she received our homage as a priest receives the incense of the mass. My elder brother appeared to absorb the trifling sentiment of maternity which was in her nature. She stabbed us constantly with her sharp irony,—the weapon of those who have no heart,—and which she used against us, who could make her no reply.

Notwithstanding these thorny hindrances, the instinctive sentiments have so many roots, the religious fear inspired by a mother whom it is dangerous to displease holds by so many threads, that the sublime mistake—if I may so call it—of our love for our mother lasted until the day, much later in our lives, when we judged her finally. This terrible despotism drove from my mind all thoughts of the voluptuous enjoyments I had dreamed of finding at Tours. In despair I took refuge in my father's library, where I set myself to read every book I did not know. These long periods of hard study saved me from contact with my mother; but they aggravated the dangers of my moral condition. Sometimes my eldest sister—she who afterwards married our cousin, the Marquis de Listomere—tried to comfort me, without, however, being able to calm the irritation to which I was a victim. I desired to die.

Great events, of which I knew nothing, were then in preparation. The Duc d'Angouleme, who had left Bordeaux to join Louis XVIII. in Paris, was received in every town through which he passed with ovations inspired by the enthusiasm felt throughout old France at the return of the Bourbons. Touraine was aroused for its legitimate princes; the town itself was in a flutter, every window decorated, the inhabitants in their Sunday clothes, a festival in preparation, and that nameless excitement in the air which intoxicates, and which gave me a strong desire to be present at the ball given by the duke. When I summoned courage to make this request of my mother, who was too ill to go herself, she became extremely angry. "Had I come from Congo?" she inquired. "How could I suppose that our family would not be represented at the ball? In the absence of my father and brother, of course it was my duty to be present. Had I no mother? Was she not always thinking of the welfare of her children?"

In a moment the semi-disinherited son had become a personage! I was more dumfounded by my importance than by the deluge of ironical reasoning with which my mother received my request. I questioned my sisters, and then discovered that my mother, who liked such theatrical plots, was already attending to my clothes. The tailors in Tours were fully occupied by the sudden demands of their regular customers, and my mother was forced to employ her usual seamstress, who—according to provincial custom—could do all kinds of sewing. A bottle-blue coat had been secretly made for me, after a fashion, and silk stockings and pumps provided; waistcoats were then worn short, so that I could wear one of my father's; and for the first time in my life I had a shirt with a frill, the pleatings of which puffed out my chest and were gathered in to the knot of my cravat. When dressed in this apparel I looked so little like myself that my sister's compliments nerved me to face all Touraine at the ball. But it was a bold enterprise. Thanks to my slimness I slipped into a tent set up in the gardens of the Papion house, and found a place close to the armchair in which the duke was seated. Instantly I was suffocated by the heat, and dazzled by the lights, the scarlet draperies, the gilded ornaments, the dresses, and the diamonds of the first public ball I had ever witnessed. I was pushed hither and thither by a mass of men and women, who hustled each other in a cloud of dust. The brazen clash of military music was drowned in the hurrahs and acclamations of "Long live the Duc d'Angouleme! Long live the King! Long live the Bourbons!" The ball was an outburst of pent-up enthusiasm, where each man endeavored to outdo the rest in his fierce haste to worship the rising sun,—an exhibition of partisan greed which left me unmoved, or rather, it disgusted me and drove me back within myself.

Swept onward like a straw in the whirlwind, I was seized with a childish desire to be the Duc d'Angouleme himself, to be one of these princes parading before an awed assemblage. This silly fancy of a Tourangean lad roused an ambition to which my nature and the surrounding circumstances lent dignity. Who would not envy such worship?—a magnificent repetition of which I saw a few months later, when all Paris rushed to the feet of the Emperor on his return from Elba. The sense of this dominion exercised over the masses, whose feelings and whose very life are thus merged into one soul, dedicated me then and thenceforth to glory, that priestess who slaughters the Frenchmen of to-day as the Druidess once sacrificed the Gauls.

Suddenly I met the woman who was destined to spur these ambitious desires and to crown them by sending me into the heart of royalty. Too timid to ask any one to dance,—fearing, moreover, to confuse the figures,—I naturally became very awkward, and did not know what to do with my arms and legs. Just as I was suffering severely from the pressure of the crowd an officer stepped on my feet, swollen by the new leather of my shoes as well as by the heat. This disgusted me with the whole affair. It was impossible to get away; but I took refuge in a corner of a room at the end of an empty bench, where I sat with fixed eyes, motionless and sullen. Misled by my puny appearance, a woman—taking me for a sleepy child—slid softly into the place beside me, with the motion of a bird as she drops upon her nest. Instantly I breathed the woman-atmosphere, which irradiated my soul as, in after days, oriental poesy has shone there. I looked at my neighbor, and was more dazzled by that vision than I had been by the scene of the fete.

If you have understood this history of my early life you will guess the feelings which now welled up within me. My eyes rested suddenly on white, rounded shoulders where I would fain have laid my head, —shoulders faintly rosy, which seemed to blush as if uncovered for the first time; modest shoulders, that possessed a soul, and reflected light from their satin surface as from a silken texture. These shoulders were parted by a line along which my eyes wandered. I raised myself to see the bust and was spell-bound by the beauty of the bosom, chastely covered with gauze, where blue-veined globes of perfect outline were softly hidden in waves of lace. The slightest details of the head were each and all enchantments which awakened infinite delights within me; the brilliancy of the hair laid smoothly above a neck as soft and velvety as a child's, the white lines drawn by the comb where my imagination ran as along a dewy path,—all these things put me, as it were, beside myself. Glancing round to be sure that no one saw me, I threw myself upon those shoulders as a child upon the breast of its mother, kissing them as I laid my head there. The woman uttered a piercing cry, which the noise of the music drowned; she turned, saw me, and exclaimed, "Monsieur!" Ah! had she said, "My little lad, what possesses you?" I might have killed her; but at the word "Monsieur!" hot tears fell from my eyes. I was petrified by a glance of saintly anger, by a noble face crowned with a diadem of golden hair in harmony with the shoulders I adored. The crimson of offended modesty glowed on her cheeks, though already it was appeased by the pardoning instinct of a woman who comprehends a frenzy which she inspires, and divines the infinite adoration of those repentant tears. She moved away with the step and carriage of a queen.

I then felt the ridicule of my position; for the first time I realized that I was dressed like the monkey of a barrel organ. I was ashamed. There I stood, stupefied,—tasting the fruit that I had stolen, conscious of the warmth upon my lips, repenting not, and following with my eyes the woman who had come down to me from heaven. Sick with the first fever of the heart I wandered through the rooms, unable to find mine Unknown, until at last I went home to bed, another man.

A new soul, a soul with rainbow wings, had burst its chrysalis. Descending from the azure wastes where I had long admired her, my star had come to me a woman, with undiminished lustre and purity. I loved, knowing naught of love. How strange a thing, this first irruption of the keenest human emotion in the heart of a man! I had seen pretty women in other places, but none had made the slightest impression upon me. Can there be an appointed hour, a conjunction of stars, a union of circumstances, a certain woman among all others to awaken an exclusive passion at the period of life when love includes the whole sex?

The thought that my Elect lived in Touraine made the air I breathed delicious; the blue of the sky seemed bluer than I had ever yet seen it. I raved internally, but externally I was seriously ill, and my mother had fears, not unmingled with remorse. Like animals who know when danger is near, I hid myself away in the garden to think of the kiss that I had stolen. A few days after this memorable ball my mother attributed my neglect of study, my indifference to her tyrannical looks and sarcasms, and my gloomy behavior to the condition of my health. The country, that perpetual remedy for ills that doctors cannot cure, seemed to her the best means of bringing me out of my apathy. She decided that I should spend a few weeks at Frapesle, a chateau on the Indre midway between Montbazon and Azay-le-Rideau, which belonged to a friend of hers, to whom, no doubt, she gave private instructions.

By the day when I thus for the first time gained my liberty I had swum so vigorously in Love's ocean that I had well-nigh crossed it. I knew nothing of mine unknown lady, neither her name, nor where to find her; to whom, indeed, could I speak of her? My sensitive nature so exaggerated the inexplicable fears which beset all youthful hearts at the first approach of love that I began with the melancholy which often ends a hopeless passion. I asked nothing better than to roam about the country, to come and go and live in the fields. With the courage of a child that fears no failure, in which there is something really chivalrous, I determined to search every chateau in Touraine, travelling on foot, and saying to myself as each old tower came in sight, "She is there!"

Accordingly, of a Thursday morning I left Tours by the barrier of Saint-Eloy, crossed the bridges of Saint-Sauveur, reached Poncher whose every house I examined, and took the road to Chinon. For the first time in my life I could sit down under a tree or walk fast or slow as I pleased without being dictated to by any one. To a poor lad crushed under all sorts of despotism (which more or less does weigh upon all youth) the first employment of freedom, even though it be expended upon nothing, lifts the soul with irrepressible buoyancy. Several reasons combined to make that day one of enchantment. During my school years I had never been taken to walk more than two or three miles from a city; yet there remained in my mind among the earliest recollections of my childhood that feeling for the beautiful which the scenery about Tours inspires. Though quite untaught as to the poetry of such a landscape, I was, unknown to myself, critical upon it, like those who imagine the ideal of art without knowing anything of its practice.

To reach the chateau of Frapesle, foot-passengers, or those on horseback, shorten the way by crossing the Charlemagne moors, —uncultivated tracts of land lying on the summit of the plateau which separates the valley of the Cher from that of the Indre, and over which there is a cross-road leading to Champy. These moors are flat and sandy, and for more than three miles are dreary enough until you reach, through a clump of woods, the road to Sache, the name of the township in which Frapesle stands. This road, which joins that of Chinon beyond Ballan, skirts an undulating plain to the little hamlet of Artanne. Here we come upon a valley, which begins at Montbazon, ends at the Loire, and seems to rise and fall,—to bound, as it were, —beneath the chateaus placed on its double hillsides,—a splendid emerald cup, in the depths of which flow the serpentine lines of the river Indre. I gazed at this scene with ineffable delight, for which the gloomy moor-land and the fatigue of the sandy walk had prepared me.

"If that woman, the flower of her sex, does indeed inhabit this earth, she is here, on this spot."

Thus musing, I leaned against a walnut-tree, beneath which I have rested from that day to this whenever I return to my dear valley. Beneath that tree, the confidant of my thoughts, I ask myself what changes there are in me since last I stood there.

My heart deceived me not—she lived there; the first castle that I saw on the slope of a hill was the dwelling that held her. As I sat beneath my nut-tree, the mid-day sun was sparkling on the slates of her roof and the panes of her windows. Her cambric dress made the white line which I saw among the vines of an arbor. She was, as you know already without as yet knowing anything, the Lily of this valley, where she grew for heaven, filling it with the fragrance of her virtues. Love, infinite love, without other sustenance than the vision, dimly seen, of which my soul was full, was there, expressed to me by that long ribbon of water flowing in the sunshine between the grass-green banks, by the lines of the poplars adorning with their mobile laces that vale of love, by the oak-woods coming down between the vineyards to the shore, which the river curved and rounded as it chose, and by those dim varying horizons as they fled confusedly away.

If you would see nature beautiful and virgin as a bride, go there of a spring morning. If you would still the bleeding wounds of your heart, return in the last days of autumn. In the spring, Love beats his wings beneath the broad blue sky; in the autumn, we think of those who are no more. The lungs diseased breathe in a blessed purity; the eyes will rest on golden copses which impart to the soul their peaceful stillness. At this moment, when I stood there for the first time, the mills upon the brooksides gave a voice to the quivering valley; the poplars were laughing as they swayed; not a cloud was in the sky; the birds sang, the crickets chirped,—all was melody. Do not ask me again why I love Touraine. I love it, not as we love our cradle, not as we love the oasis in a desert; I love it as an artist loves art; I love it less than I love you; but without Touraine, perhaps I might not now be living.

Without knowing why, my eyes reverted ever to that white spot, to the woman who shone in that garden as the bell of a convolvulus shines amid the underbrush, and wilts if touched. Moved to the soul, I descended the slope and soon saw a village, which the superabounding poetry that filled my heart made me fancy without an equal. Imagine three mills placed among islands of graceful outline crowned with groves of trees and rising from a field of water,—for what other name can I give to that aquatic vegetation, so verdant, so finely colored, which carpeted the river, rose above its surface and undulated upon it, yielding to its caprices and swaying to the turmoil of the water when the mill-wheels lashed it. Here and there were mounds of gravel, against which the wavelets broke in fringes that shimmered in the sunlight. Amaryllis, water-lilies, reeds, and phloxes decorated the banks with their glorious tapestry. A trembling bridge of rotten planks, the abutments swathed with flowers, and the hand-rails green with perennials and velvet mosses drooping to the river but not falling to it; mouldering boats, fishing-nets; the monotonous sing-song of a shepherd; ducks paddling among the islands or preening on the "jard,"—a name given to the coarse sand which the Loire brings down; the millers, with their caps over one ear, busily loading their mules,—all these details made the scene before me one of primitive simplicity. Imagine, also, beyond the bridge two or three farm-houses, a dove-cote, turtle-doves, thirty or more dilapidated cottages, separated by gardens, by hedges of honeysuckle, clematis, and jasmine; a dunghill beside each door, and cocks and hens about the road. Such is the village of Pont-de-Ruan, a picturesque little hamlet leading up to an old church full of character, a church of the days of the Crusades, such a one as painters desire for their pictures. Surround this scene with ancient walnut-trees and slim young poplars with their pale-gold leaves; dot graceful buildings here and there along the grassy slopes where sight is lost beneath the vaporous, warm sky, and you will have some idea of one of the points of view of this most lovely region.

I followed the road to Sache along the left bank of the river, noticing carefully the details of the hills on the opposite shore. At length I reached a park embellished with centennial trees, which I knew to be that of Frapesle. I arrived just as the bell was ringing for breakfast. After the meal, my host, who little suspected that I had walked from Tours, carried me over his estate, from the borders of which I saw the valley on all sides under its many aspects,—here through a vista, there to its broad extent; often my eyes were drawn to the horizon along the golden blade of the Loire, where the sails made fantastic figures among the currents as they flew before the wind. As we mounted a crest I came in sight of the chateau d'Azay, like a diamond of many facets in a setting of the Indre, standing on wooden piles concealed by flowers. Farther on, in a hollow, I saw the romantic masses of the chateau of Sache, a sad retreat though full of harmony; too sad for the superficial, but dear to a poet with a soul in pain. I, too, came to love its silence, its great gnarled trees, and the nameless mysterious influence of its solitary valley. But now, each time that we reached an opening towards the neighboring slope which gave to view the pretty castle I had first noticed in the morning, I stopped to look at it with pleasure.

"Hey!" said my host, reading in my eyes the sparkling desires which youth so ingenuously betrays, "so you scent from afar a pretty woman as a dog scents game!"

I did not like the speech, but I asked the name of the castle and of its owner.

"It is Clochegourde," he replied; "a pretty house belonging to the Comte de Mortsauf, the head of an historic family in Touraine, whose fortune dates from the days of Louis XI., and whose name tells the story to which they owe their arms and their distinction. Monsieur de Mortsauf is descended from a man who survived the gallows. The family bear: Or, a cross potent and counter-potent sable, charged with a fleur-de-lis or; and 'Dieu saulve le Roi notre Sire,' for motto. The count settled here after the return of the emigration. The estate belongs to his wife, a demoiselle de Lenoncourt, of the house of Lenoncourt-Givry which is now dying out. Madame de Mortsauf is an only daughter. The limited fortune of the family contrasts strangely with the distinction of their names; either from pride, or, possibly, from necessity, they never leave Clochegourde and see no company. Until now their attachment to the Bourbons explained this retirement, but the return of the king has not changed their way of living. When I came to reside here last year I paid them a visit of courtesy; they returned it and invited us to dinner; the winter separated us for some months, and political events kept me away from Frapesle until recently. Madame de Mortsauf is a woman who would hold the highest position wherever she might be."

"Does she often come to Tours?"

"She never goes there. However," he added, correcting himself, "she did go there lately to the ball given to the Duc d'Angouleme, who was very gracious to her husband."

"It was she!" I exclaimed.

"She! who?"

"A woman with beautiful shoulders."

"You will meet a great many women with beautiful shoulders in Touraine," he said, laughing. "But if you are not tired we can cross the river and call at Clochegourde and you shall renew acquaintance with those particular shoulders."

I agreed, not without a blush of shame and pleasure. About four o'clock we reached the little chateau on which my eyes had fastened from the first. The building, which is finely effective in the landscape, is in reality very modest. It has five windows on the front; those at each end of the facade, looking south, project about twelve feet,—an architectural device which gives the idea of two towers and adds grace to the structure. The middle window serves as a door from which you descend through a double portico into a terraced garden which joins the narrow strip of grass-land that skirts the Indre along its whole course. Though this meadow is separated from the lower terrace, which is shaded by a double line of acacias and Japanese ailanthus, by the country road, it nevertheless appears from the house to be a part of the garden, for the road is sunken and hemmed in on one side by the terrace, on the other side by a Norman hedge. The terraces being very well managed put enough distance between the house and the river to avoid the inconvenience of too great proximity to water, without losing the charms of it. Below the house are the stables, coach-house, green-houses, and kitchen, the various openings to which form an arcade. The roof is charmingly rounded at the angles, and bears mansarde windows with carved mullions and leaden finials on their gables. This roof, no doubt much neglected during the Revolution, is stained by a sort of mildew produced by lichens and the reddish moss which grows on houses exposed to the sun. The glass door of the portico is surmounted by a little tower which holds the bell, and on which is carved the escutcheon of the Blamont-Chauvry family, to which Madame de Mortsauf belonged, as follows: Gules, a pale vair, flanked quarterly by two hands clasped or, and two lances in chevron sable. The motto, "Voyez tous, nul ne touche!" struck me greatly. The supporters, a griffin and dragon gules, enchained or, made a pretty effect in the carving. The Revolution has damaged the ducal crown and the crest, which was a palm-tree vert with fruit or. Senart, the secretary of the committee of public safety was bailiff of Sache before 1781, which explains this destruction.

These arrangements give an elegant air to the little castle, dainty as a flower, which seems to scarcely rest upon the earth. Seen from the valley the ground-floor appears to be the first story; but on the other side it is on a level with a broad gravelled path leading to a grass-plot, on which are several flower-beds. To right and left are vineyards, orchards, and a few acres of tilled land planted with chestnut-trees which surround the house, the ground falling rapidly to the Indre, where other groups of trees of variegated shades of green, chosen by Nature herself, are spread along the shore. I admired these groups, so charmingly disposed, as we mounted the hilly road which borders Clochegourde; I breathed an atmosphere of happiness. Has the moral nature, like the physical nature, its own electrical communications and its rapid changes of temperature? My heart was beating at the approach of events then unrevealed which were to change it forever, just as animals grow livelier when foreseeing fine weather.

This day, so marked in my life, lacked no circumstance that was needed to solemnize it. Nature was adorned like a woman to meet her lover. My soul heard her voice for the first time; my eyes worshipped her, as fruitful, as varied as my imagination had pictured her in those school-dreams the influence of which I have tried in a few unskilful words to explain to you, for they were to me an Apocalypse in which my life was figuratively foretold; each event, fortunate or unfortunate, being mated to some one of these strange visions by ties known only to the soul.

We crossed a court-yard surrounded by buildings necessary for the farm work,—a barn, a wine-press, cow-sheds, and stables. Warned by the barking of the watch-dog, a servant came to meet us, saying that Monsieur le comte had gone to Azay in the morning but would soon return, and that Madame la comtesse was at home. My companion looked at me. I fairly trembled lest he should decline to see Madame de Mortsauf in her husband's absence; but he told the man to announce us. With the eagerness of a child I rushed into the long antechamber which crosses the whole house.

"Come in, gentlemen," said a golden voice.

Though Madame de Mortsauf had spoken only one word at the ball, I recognized her voice, which entered my soul and filled it as a ray of sunshine fills and gilds a prisoner's dungeon. Thinking, suddenly, that she might remember my face, my first impulse was to fly; but it was too late,—she appeared in the doorway, and our eyes met. I know not which of us blushed deepest. Too much confused for immediate speech she returned to her seat at an embroidery frame while the servant placed two chairs, then she drew out her needle and counted some stitches, as if to explain her silence; after which she raised her head, gently yet proudly, in the direction of Monsieur de Chessel as she asked to what fortunate circumstance she owed his visit. Though curious to know the secret of my unexpected appearance, she looked at neither of us,—her eyes were fixed on the river; and yet you could have told by the way she listened that she was able to recognize, as the blind do, the agitations of a neighboring soul by the imperceptible inflexions of the voice.

Monsieur de Chessel gave my name and biography. I had lately arrived at Tours, where my parents had recalled me when the armies threatened Paris. A son of Touraine to whom Touraine was as yet unknown, she would find me a young man weakened by excessive study and sent to Frapesle to amuse himself; he had already shown me his estate, which I saw for the first time. I had just told him that I had walked from Tours to Frapesle, and fearing for my health—which was really delicate—he had stopped at Clochegourde to ask her to allow me to rest there. Monsieur de Chessel told the truth; but the accident seemed so forced that Madame de Mortsauf distrusted us. She gave me a cold, severe glance, under which my own eyelids fell, as much from a sense of humiliation as to hide the tears that rose beneath them. She saw the moisture on my forehead, and perhaps she guessed the tears; for she offered me the restoratives I needed, with a few kind and consoling words, which gave me back the power of speech. I blushed like a young girl, and in a voice as tremulous as that of an old man I thanked her and declined.

"All I ask," I said, raising my eyes to hers, which mine now met for the second time in a glance as rapid as lightning,—"is to rest here. I am so crippled with fatigue I really cannot walk farther."

"You must not doubt the hospitality of our beautiful Touraine," she said; then, turning to my companion, she added: "You will give us the pleasure of your dining at Clochegourde?"

I threw such a look of entreaty at Monsieur de Chessel that he began the preliminaries of accepting the invitation, though it was given in a manner that seemed to expect a refusal. As a man of the world, he recognized these shades of meaning; but I, a young man without experience, believed so implicitly in the sincerity between word and thought of this beautiful woman that I was wholly astonished when my host said to me, after we reached home that evening, "I stayed because I saw you were dying to do so; but if you do not succeed in making it all right, I may find myself on bad terms with my neighbors." That expression, "if you do not make it all right," made me ponder the matter deeply. In other words, if I pleased Madame de Mortsauf, she would not be displeased with the man who introduced me to her. He evidently thought I had the power to please her; this in itself gave me that power, and corroborated my inward hope at a moment when it needed some outward succor.

"I am afraid it will be difficult," he began; "Madame de Chessel expects us."

"She has you every day," replied the countess; "besides, we can send her word. Is she alone?"

"No, the Abbe de Quelus is there."

"Well, then," she said, rising to ring the bell, "you really must dine with us."

This time Monsieur de Chessel thought her in earnest, and gave me a congratulatory look. As soon as I was sure of passing a whole evening under that roof I seemed to have eternity before me. For many miserable beings to-morrow is a word without meaning, and I was of the number who had no faith in it; when I was certain of a few hours of happiness I made them contain a whole lifetime of delight.

Madame de Mortsauf talked about local affairs, the harvest, the vintage, and other matters to which I was a total stranger. This usually argues either a want of breeding or great contempt for the stranger present who is thus shut out from the conversation, but in this case it was embarrassment. Though at first I thought she treated me as a child and I envied the man of thirty to whom she talked of serious matters which I could not comprehend, I came, a few months later, to understand how significant a woman's silence often is, and how many thoughts a voluble conversation masks. At first I attempted to be at my ease and take part in it, then I perceived the advantages of my situation and gave myself up to the charm of listening to Madame de Mortsauf's voice. The breath of her soul rose and fell among the syllables as sound is divided by the notes of a flute; it died away to the ear as it quickened the pulsation of the blood. Her way of uttering the terminations in "i" was like a bird's song; the "ch" as she said it was a kiss, but the "t's" were an echo of her heart's despotism. She thus extended, without herself knowing that she did so, the meaning of her words, leading the soul of the listener into regions above this earth. Many a time I have continued a discussion I could easily have ended, many a time I have allowed myself to be unjustly scolded that I might listen to those harmonies of the human voice, that I might breathe the air of her soul as it left her lips, and strain to my soul that spoken light as I would fain have strained the speaker to my breast. A swallow's song of joy it was when she was gay!—but when she spoke of her griefs, a swan's voice calling to its mates!

Madame de Mortsauf's inattention to my presence enabled me to examine her. My eyes rejoiced as they glided over the sweet speaker; they kissed her feet, they clasped her waist, they played with the ringlets of her hair. And yet I was a prey to terror, as all who, once in their lives, have experienced the illimitable joys of a true passion will understand. I feared she would detect me if I let my eyes rest upon the shoulder I had kissed, and the fear sharpened the temptation. I yielded, I looked, my eyes tore away the covering; I saw the mole which lay where the pretty line between the shoulders started, and which, ever since the ball, had sparkled in that twilight which seems the region of the sleep of youths whose imagination is ardent and whose life is chaste.

I can sketch for you the leading features which all eyes saw in Madame de Mortsauf; but no drawing, however correct, no color, however warm, can represent her to you. Her face was of those that require the unattainable artist, whose hand can paint the reflection of inward fires and render that luminous vapor which defies science and is not revealable by language—but which a lover sees. Her soft, fair hair often caused her much suffering, no doubt through sudden rushes of blood to the head. Her brow, round and prominent like that of Joconda, teemed with unuttered thoughts, restrained feelings—flowers drowning in bitter waters. The eyes, of a green tinge flecked with brown, were always wan; but if her children were in question, or if some keen condition of joy or suffering (rare in the lives of all resigned women) seized her, those eyes sent forth a subtile gleam as if from fires that were consuming her,—the gleam that wrung the tears from mine when she covered me with her contempt, and which sufficed to lower the boldest eyelid. A Grecian nose, designed it might be by Phidias, and united by its double arch to lips that were gracefully curved, spiritualized the face, which was oval with a skin of the texture of a white camellia colored with soft rose-tints upon the cheeks. Her plumpness did not detract from the grace of her figure nor from the rounded outlines which made her shape beautiful though well developed. You will understand the character of this perfection when I say that where the dazzling treasures which had so fascinated me joined the arm there was no crease or wrinkle. No hollow disfigured the base of her head, like those which make the necks of some women resemble trunks of trees; her muscles were not harshly defined, and everywhere the lines were rounded into curves as fugitive to the eye as to the pencil. A soft down faintly showed upon her cheeks and on the outline of her throat, catching the light which made it silken. Her little ears, perfect in shape, were, as she said herself, the ears of a mother and a slave. In after days, when our hearts were one, she would say to me, "Here comes Monsieur de Mortsauf"; and she was right, though I, whose hearing is remarkably acute, could hear nothing.

Her arms were beautiful. The curved fingers of the hand were long, and the flesh projected at the side beyond the finger-nails, like those of antique statues. I should displease you, I know, if you were not yourself an exception to my rule, when I say that flat waists should have the preference over round ones. The round waist is a sign of strength; but women thus formed are imperious, self-willed, and more voluptuous than tender. On the other hand, women with flat waists are devoted in soul, delicately perceptive, inclined to sadness, more truly woman than the other class. The flat waist is supple and yielding; the round waist is inflexible and jealous.

You now know how she was made. She had the foot of a well-bred woman, —the foot that walks little, is quickly tired, and delights the eye when it peeps beneath the dress. Though she was the mother of two children, I have never met any woman so truly a young girl as she. Her whole air was one of simplicity, joined to a certain bashful dreaminess which attracted others, just as a painter arrests our steps before a figure into which his genius has conveyed a world of sentiment. If you recall the pure, wild fragrance of the heath we gathered on our return from the Villa Diodati, the flower whose tints of black and rose you praised so warmly, you can fancy how this woman could be elegant though remote from the social world, natural in expression, fastidious in all things which became part of herself,—in short, like the heath of mingled colors. Her body had the freshness we admire in the unfolding leaf; her spirit the clear conciseness of the aboriginal mind; she was a child by feeling, grave through suffering, the mistress of a household, yet a maiden too. Therefore she charmed artlessly and unconsciously, by her way of sitting down or rising, of throwing in a word or keeping silence. Though habitually collected, watchful as the sentinel on whom the safety of others depends and who looks for danger, there were moments when smiles would wreathe her lips and betray the happy nature buried beneath the saddened bearing that was the outcome of her life. Her gift of attraction was mysterious. Instead of inspiring the gallant attentions which other women seek, she made men dream, letting them see her virginal nature of pure flame, her celestial visions, as we see the azure heavens through rifts in the clouds. This involuntary revelation of her being made others thoughtful. The rarity of her gestures, above all, the rarity of her glances—for, excepting her children, she seldom looked at any one—gave a strange solemnity to all she said and did when her words or actions seemed to her to compromise her dignity.

On this particular morning Madame de Mortsauf wore a rose-colored gown patterned in tiny stripes, a collar with a wide hem, a black belt, and little boots of the same hue. Her hair was simply twisted round her head, and held in place by a tortoise-shell comb. Such, my dear Natalie, is the imperfect sketch I promised you. But the constant emanation of her soul upon her family, that nurturing essence shed in floods around her as the sun emits its light, her inward nature, her cheerfulness on days serene, her resignation on stormy ones,—all those variations of expression by which character is displayed depend, like the effects in the sky, on unexpected and fugitive circumstances, which have no connection with each other except the background against which they rest, though all are necessarily mingled with the events of this history,—truly a household epic, as great to the eyes of a wise man as a tragedy to the eyes of the crowd, an epic in which you will feel an interest, not only for the part I took in it, but for the likeness that it bears to the destinies of so vast a number of women.

Everything at Clochegourde bore signs of a truly English cleanliness. The room in which the countess received us was panelled throughout and painted in two shades of gray. The mantelpiece was ornamented with a clock inserted in a block of mahogany and surmounted with a tazza, and two large vases of white porcelain with gold lines, which held bunches of Cape heather. A lamp was on a pier-table, and a backgammon board on legs before the fireplace. Two wide bands of cotton held back the white cambric curtains, which had no fringe. The furniture was covered with gray cotton bound with a green braid, and the tapestry on the countess's frame told why the upholstery was thus covered. Such simplicity rose to grandeur. No apartment, among all that I have seen since, has given me such fertile, such teeming impressions as those that filled my mind in that salon of Clochegourde, calm and composed as the life of its mistress, where the conventual regularity of her occupations made itself felt. The greater part of my ideas in science or politics, even the boldest of them, were born in that room, as perfumes emanate from flowers; there grew the mysterious plant that cast upon my soul its fructifying pollen; there glowed the solar warmth which developed my good and shrivelled my evil qualities. Through the windows the eye took in the valley from the heights of Pont-de-Ruan to the chateau d'Azay, following the windings of the further shore, picturesquely varied by the towers of Frapesle, the church, the village, and the old manor-house of Sache, whose venerable pile looked down upon the meadows.

In harmony with this reposeful life, and without other excitements to emotion than those arising in the family, this scene conveyed to the soul its own serenity. If I had met her there for the first time, between the count and her two children, instead of seeing her resplendent in a ball dress, I should not have ravished that delirious kiss, which now filled me with remorse and with the fear of having lost the future of my love. No; in the gloom of my unhappy life I should have bent my knee and kissed the hem of her garment, wetting it with tears, and then I might have flung myself into the Indre. But having breathed the jasmine perfume of her skin and drunk the milk of that cup of love, my soul had acquired the knowledge and the hope of human joys; I would live and await the coming of happiness as the savage awaits his hour of vengeance; I longed to climb those trees, to creep among the vines, to float in the river; I wanted the companionship of night and its silence, I needed lassitude of body, I craved the heat of the sun to make the eating of the delicious apple into which I had bitten perfect. Had she asked of me the singing flower, the riches buried by the comrades of Morgan the destroyer, I would have sought them, to obtain those other riches and that mute flower for which I longed.

When my dream, the dream into which this first contemplation of my idol plunged me, came to an end and I heard her speaking of Monsieur de Mortsauf, the thought came that a woman must belong to her husband, and a raging curiosity

possessed me to see the owner of this treasure. Two emotions filled my mind, hatred and fear,—hatred which allowed of no obstacles and measured all without shrinking, and a vague, but real fear of the struggle, of its issue, and above all of _ *her_*
.

"Here is Monsieur de Mortsauf," she said.

I sprang to my feet like a startled horse. Though the movement was seen by Monsieur de Chessel and the countess, neither made any observation, for a diversion was effected at this moment by the entrance of a little girl, whom I took to be about six years old, who came in exclaiming, "Here's papa!"

"Madeleine?" said her mother, gently.

The child at once held out her hand to Monsieur de Chessel, and looked attentively at me after making a little bow with an air of astonishment.

"Are you more satisfied about her health?" asked Monsieur de Chessel.

"She is better," replied the countess, caressing the little head which was already nestling in her lap.

The next question of Monsieur de Chessel let me know that Madeleine was nine years old; I showed great surprise, and immediately the clouds gathered on the mother's brow. My companion threw me a significant look,—one of those which form the education of men of the world. I had stumbled no doubt upon some maternal wound the covering of which should have been respected. The sickly child, whose eyes were pallid and whose skin was white as a porcelain vase with a light within it, would probably not have lived in the atmosphere of a city. Country air and her mother's brooding care had kept the life in that frail body, delicate as a hot-house plant growing in a harsh and foreign climate. Though in nothing did she remind me of her mother, Madeleine seemed to have her soul, and that soul held her up. Her hair was scanty and black, her eyes and cheeks hollow, her arms thin, her chest narrow, showing a battle between life and death, a duel without truce in which the mother had so far been victorious. The child willed to live,—perhaps to spare her mother, for at times, when not observed, she fell into the attitude of a weeping-willow. You might have thought her a little gypsy dying of hunger, begging her way, exhausted but always brave and dressed up to play her part.

"Where have you left Jacques?" asked the countess, kissing the white line which parted the child's hair into two bands that looked like a crow's wings.

"He is coming with papa."

Just then the count entered, holding his son by the hand. Jacques, the image of his sister, showed the same signs of weakness. Seeing these sickly children beside a mother so magnificently healthy it was impossible not to guess at the causes of the grief which clouded her brow and kept her silent on a subject she could take to God only. As he bowed, Monsieur de Mortsauf gave me a glance that was less observing than awkwardly uneasy,—the glance of a man whose distrust grows out of his inability to analyze. After explaining the circumstances of our visit, and naming me to him, the countess gave him her place and left the room. The children, whose eyes were on those of their mother as if they drew the light of theirs from hers, tried to follow her; but she said, with a finger on her lips, "Stay dears!" and they obeyed, but their eyes filled. Ah! to hear that one word "dears" what tasks they would have undertaken!

Like the children, I felt less warm when she had left us. My name seemed to change the count's feeling toward me. Cold and supercilious in his first glance, he became at once, if not affectionate, at least politely attentive, showing me every consideration and seeming pleased to receive me as a guest. My father had formerly done devoted service to the Bourbons, and had played an important and perilous, though secret part. When their cause was lost by the elevation of Napoleon, he took refuge in the quietude of the country and domestic life, accepting the unmerited accusations that followed him as the inevitable reward of those who risk all to win all, and who succumb after serving as pivot to the political machine. Knowing nothing of the fortunes, nor of the past, nor of the future of my family, I was unaware of this devoted service which the Comte de Mortsauf well remembered. Moreover, the antiquity of our name, the most precious quality of a man in his eyes, added to the warmth of his greeting. I knew nothing of these reasons until later; for the time being the sudden transition to cordiality put me at my ease. When the two children saw that we were all three fairly engaged in conversation, Madeleine slipped her head from her father's hand, glanced at the open door, and glided away like an eel, Jacques following her. They rejoined their mother, and I heard their voices and their movements, sounding in the distance like the murmur of bees about a hive.

I watched the count, trying to guess his character, but I became so interested in certain leading traits that I got no further than a superficial examination of his personality. Though he was only forty-five years old, he seemed nearer sixty, so much had the great shipwreck at the close of the eighteenth century aged him. The crescent of hair which monastically fringed the back of his head, otherwise completely bald, ended at the ears in little tufts of gray mingled with black. His face bore a vague resemblance to that of a white wolf with blood about its muzzle, for his nose was inflamed and gave signs of a life poisoned at its springs and vitiated by diseases of long standing. His flat forehead, too broad for the face beneath it, which ended in a point, and transversely wrinkled in crooked lines, gave signs of a life in the open air, but not of any mental activity; it also showed the burden of constant misfortunes, but not of any efforts made to surmount them. His cheekbones, which were brown and prominent amid the general pallor of his skin, showed a physical structure which was likely to ensure him a long life. His hard, light-yellow eye fell upon mine like a ray of wintry sun, bright without warmth, anxious without thought, distrustful without conscious cause. His mouth was violent and domineering, his chin flat and long. Thin and very tall, he had the bearing of a gentleman who relies upon the conventional value of his caste, who knows himself above others by right, and beneath them in fact. The carelessness of country life had made him neglect his external appearance. His dress was that of a country-man whom peasants and neighbors no longer considered except for his territorial worth. His brown and wiry hands showed that he wore no gloves unless he mounted a horse, or went to church, and his shoes were thick and common.

Though ten years of emigration and ten years more of farm-life had changed his physical condition, he still retained certain vestiges of nobility. The bitterest liberal (a term not then in circulation) would readily have admitted his chivalric loyalty and the imperishable convictions of one who puts his faith to the "Quotidienne"; he would have felt respect for the man religiously devoted to a cause, honest in his political antipathies, incapable of serving his party but very capable of injuring it, and without the slightest real knowledge of the affairs of France. The count was in fact one of those upright men who are available for nothing, but stand obstinately in the way of all; ready to die under arms at the post assigned to them, but preferring to give their life rather than to give their money.

During dinner I detected, in the hanging of his flaccid cheeks and the covert glances he cast now and then upon his children, the traces of some wearing thought which showed for a moment upon the surface. Watching him, who could fail to understand him? Who would not have seen that he had fatally transmitted to his children their weakly bodies in which the principle of life was lacking. But if he blamed himself he denied to others the right to judge him. Harsh as one who knows himself in fault, yet without greatness of soul or charm to compensate for the weight of misery he had thrown into the balance, his private life was no doubt the scene of irascibilities that were plainly revealed in his angular features and by the incessant restlessness of his eye. When his wife returned, followed by the children who seemed fastened to her side, I felt the presence of unhappiness, just as in walking over the roof of a vault the feet become in some way conscious of the depths below. Seeing these four human beings together, holding them all as it were in one glance, letting my eye pass from one to the other, studying their countenances and their respective attitudes, thoughts steeped in sadness fell upon my heart as a fine gray rain dims a charming landscape after the sun has risen clear.

When the immediate subject of conversation was exhausted the count told his wife who I was, and related certain circumstances connected with my family that were wholly unknown to me. He asked me my age. When I told it, the countess echoed my own exclamation of surprise at her daughter's age. Perhaps she had thought me fifteen. Later on, I discovered that this was still another tie which bound her strongly to me. Even then I read her soul. Her motherhood quivered with a tardy ray of hope. Seeing me at over twenty years of age so slight and delicate and yet so nervously strong, a voice cried to her, "They too will live!" She looked at me searchingly, and in that moment I felt the barriers of ice melting between us. She seemed to have many questions to ask, but uttered none.

"If study has made you ill," she said, "the air of our valley will soon restore you."

"Modern education is fatal to children," remarked the count. "We stuff them with mathematics and ruin their health with sciences, and make them old before their time. You must stay and rest here," he added, turning to me. "You are crushed by the avalanche of ideas that have rolled down upon you. What sort of future will this universal education bring upon us unless we prevent its evils by replacing public education in the hands of the religious bodies?"

These words were in harmony with a speech he afterwards made at the elections when he refused his support to a man whose gifts would have done good service to the royalist cause. "I shall always distrust men of talent," he said.

Presently the count proposed that we should make the tour of the gardens.

"Monsieur—" said his wife.

"Well, what, my dear?" he said, turning to her with an arrogant harshness which showed plainly enough how absolute he chose to be in his own home.

"Monsieur de Vandenesse walked from Tours this morning and Monsieur de Chessel, not aware of it, has already taken him on foot over Frapesle."

"Very imprudent of you," the count said, turning to me; "but at your age—" and he shook his head in sign of regret.

The conversation was resumed. I soon saw how intractable his royalism was, and how much care was needed to swim safely in his waters. The man-servant, who had now put on his livery, announced dinner. Monsieur de Chessel gave his arm to Madame de Mortsauf, and the count gaily seized mine to lead me into the dining-room, which was on the ground-floor facing the salon.

This room, floored with white tiles made in Touraine, and wainscoted to the height of three feet, was hung with a varnished paper divided into wide panels by wreaths of flowers and fruit; the windows had cambric curtains trimmed with red, the buffets were old pieces by Boulle himself, and the woodwork of the chairs, which were covered by hand-made tapestry, was carved oak. The dinner, plentifully supplied, was not luxurious; family silver without uniformity, Dresden china which was not then in fashion, octagonal decanters, knives with agate handles, and lacquered trays beneath the wine-bottles, were the chief features of the table, but flowers adorned the porcelain vases and overhung the gilding of their fluted edges. I delighted in these quaint old things. I thought the Reveillon paper with its flowery garlands beautiful. The sweet content that filled my sails hindered me from perceiving the obstacles which a life so uniform, so unvarying in solitude of the country placed between her and me. I was near her, sitting at her right hand, serving her with wine. Yes, unhoped-for joy! I touched her dress, I ate her bread. At the end of three hours my life had mingled with her life! That terrible kiss had bound us to each other in a secret which inspired us with mutual shame. A glorious self-abasement took possession of me. I studied to please the count, I fondled the dogs, I would gladly have gratified every desire of the children, I would have brought them hoops and marbles and played horse with them; I was even provoked that they did not already fasten upon me as a thing of their own. Love has intuitions like those of genius; and I dimly perceived that gloom, discontent, hostility would destroy my footing in that household.

The dinner passed with inward happiness on my part. Feeling that I was there, under her roof, I gave no heed to her obvious coldness, nor to the count's indifference masked by his politeness. Love, like life, has an adolescence during which period it suffices unto itself. I made several stupid replies induced by the tumults of passion, but no one perceived their cause, not even SHE, who knew nothing of love. The rest of my visit was a dream, a dream which did not cease until by moonlight on that warm and balmy night I recrossed the Indre, watching the white visions that embellished meadows, shores, and hills, and listening to the clear song, the matchless note, full of deep melancholy and uttered only in still weather, of a tree-frog whose scientific name is unknown to me. Since that solemn evening I have never heard it without infinite delight. A sense came to me then of the marble wall against which my feelings had hitherto dashed themselves. Would it be always so? I fancied myself under some fatal spell; the unhappy events of my past life rose up and struggled with the purely personal pleasure I had just enjoyed. Before reaching Frapesle I turned to look at Clochegourde and saw beneath its windows a little boat, called in Touraine a punt, fastened to an ash-tree and swaying on the water. This punt belonged to Monsieur de Mortsauf, who used it for fishing.

"Well," said Monsieur de Chessel, when we were out of ear-shot. "I needn't ask if you found those shoulders; I must, however, congratulate you on the reception Monsieur de Mortsauf gave you. The devil! you stepped into his heart at once."

These words followed by those I have already quoted to you raised my spirits. I had not as yet said a word, and Monsieur de Chessel may have attributed my silence to happiness.

"How do you mean?" I asked.

"He never, to my knowledge, received any one so well."

"I will admit that I am rather surprised myself," I said, conscious of a certain bitterness underlying my companion's speech.

Though I was too inexpert in social matters to understand its cause, I was much struck by the feeling Monsieur de Chessel betrayed. His real name was Durand, but he had had the weakness to discard the name of a worthy father, a merchant who had made a large fortune under the Revolution. His wife was sole heiress of the Chessels, an old parliamentary family under Henry IV., belonging to the middle classes, as did most of the Parisian magistrates. Ambitious of higher flights Monsieur de Chessel endeavored to smother the original Durand. He first called himself Durand de Chessel, then D. de Chessel, and that made him Monsieur de Chessel. Under the Restoration he entailed an estate with the title of count in virtue of letters-patent from Louis XVIII. His children reaped the fruits of his audacity without knowing what it cost him in sarcastic comments. Parvenus are like monkeys, whose cleverness they possess; we watch them climbing, we admire their agility, but once at the summit we see only their absurd and contemptible parts. The reverse side of my host's character was made up of pettiness with the addition of envy. The peerage and he were on diverging lines. To have an ambition and gratify it shows merely the insolence of strength, but to live below one's avowed ambition is a constant source of ridicule to petty minds. Monsieur de Chessel did not advance with the straightforward step of a strong man. Twice elected deputy, twice defeated; yesterday director-general, to-day nothing at all, not even prefect, his successes and his defeats had injured his nature, and given him the sourness of invalided ambition. Though a brave man and a witty one and capable of great things, envy, which is the root of existence in Touraine, the inhabitants of which employ their native genius in jealousy of all things, injured him in upper social circles, where a dissatisfied man, frowning at the success of others, slow at compliments and ready at epigram, seldom succeeds. Had he sought less he might perhaps have obtained more; but unhappily he had enough genuine superiority to make him wish to advance in his own way.

At this particular time Monsieur de Chessel's ambition had a second dawn. Royalty smiled upon him, and he was now affecting the grand manner. Still he was, I must say, most kind to me, and he pleased me for the very simple reason that with him I had found peace and rest for the first time. The interest, possibly very slight, which he showed in my affairs, seemed to me, lonely and rejected as I was, an image of paternal love. His hospitable care contrasted so strongly with the neglect to which I was accustomed, that I felt a childlike gratitude to the home where no fetters bound me and where I was welcomed and even courted.

The owners of Frapesle are so associated with the dawn of my life's happiness that I mingle them in all those memories I love to revive. Later, and more especially in connection with his letters-patent, I had the pleasure of doing my host some service. Monsieur de Chessel enjoyed his wealth with an ostentation that gave umbrage to certain of his neighbors. He was able to vary and renew his fine horses and elegant equipages; his wife dressed exquisitely; he received on a grand scale; his servants were more numerous than his neighbors approved; for all of which he was said to be aping princes. The Frapesle estate is immense. Before such luxury as this the Comte de Mortsauf, with one family cariole,—which in Touraine is something between a coach without springs and a post-chaise,—forced by limited means to let or farm Clochegourde, was Tourangean up to the time when royal favor restored the family to a distinction possibly unlooked for. His greeting to me, the younger son of a ruined family whose escutcheon dated back to the Crusades, was intended to show contempt for the large fortune and to belittle the possessions, the woods, the arable lands, the meadows, of a neighbor who was not of noble birth. Monsieur de Chessel fully understood this. They always met politely; but there was none of that daily intercourse or that agreeable intimacy which ought to have existed between Clochegourde and Frapesle, two estates separated only by the Indre, and whose mistresses could have beckoned to each other from their windows.

Jealousy, however, was not the sole reason for the solitude in which the Count de Mortsauf lived. His early education was that of the children of great families,—an incomplete and superficial instruction as to knowledge, but supplemented by the training of society, the habits of a court life, and the exercise of important duties under the crown or in eminent offices. Monsieur de Mortsauf had emigrated at the very moment when the second stage of his education was about to begin, and accordingly that training was lacking to him. He was one of those who believed in the immediate restoration of the monarchy; with that conviction in his mind, his exile was a long and miserable period of idleness. When the army of Conde, which his courage led him to join with the utmost devotion, was disbanded, he expected to find some other post under the white flag, and never sought, like other emigrants, to take up an industry. Perhaps he had not the sort of courage that could lay aside his name and earn his living in the sweat of a toil he despised. His hopes, daily postponed to the morrow, and possibly a scruple of honor, kept him from offering his services to foreign powers. Trials undermined his courage. Long tramps afoot on insufficient nourishment, and above all, on hopes betrayed, injured his health and discouraged his mind. By degrees he became utterly destitute. If to some men misery is a tonic, on others it acts as a dissolvent; and the count was of the latter.

Reflecting on the life of this poor Touraine gentleman, tramping and sleeping along the highroads of Hungary, sharing the mutton of Prince Esterhazy's shepherds, from whom the foot-worn traveller begged the food he would not, as a gentleman, have accepted at the table of the master, and refusing again and again to do service to the enemies of France, I never found it in my heart to feel bitterness against him, even when I saw him at his worst in after days. The natural gaiety of a Frenchman and a Tourangean soon deserted him; he became morose, fell ill, and was charitably cared for in some German hospital. His disease was an inflammation of the mesenteric membrane, which is often fatal, and is liable, even if cured, to change the constitution and produce hypochondria. His love affairs, carefully buried out of sight and which I alone discovered, were low-lived, and not only destroyed his health but ruined his future.

After twelve years of great misery he made his way to France, under the decree of the Emperor which permitted the return of the emigrants. As the wretched wayfarer crossed the Rhine and saw the tower of Strasburg against the evening sky, his strength gave way. "'France! France!' I cried. 'I see France!'" (he said to me) "as a child cries 'Mother!' when it is hurt." Born to wealth, he was now poor; made to command a regiment or govern a province, he was now without authority and without a future; constitutionally healthy and robust, he returned infirm and utterly worn out. Without enough education to take part among men and affairs, now broadened and enlarged by the march of events, necessarily without influence of any kind, he lived despoiled of everything, of his moral strength as well as his physical. Want of money made his name a burden. His unalterable opinions, his antecedents with the army of Conde, his trials, his recollections, his wasted health, gave him susceptibilities which are but little spared in France, that land of jest and sarcasm. Half dead he reached Maine, where, by some accident of the civil war, the revolutionary government had forgotten to sell one of his farms of considerable extent, which his farmer had held for him by giving out that he himself was the owner of it.

When the Lenoncourt family, living at Givry, an estate not far from this farm, heard of the arrival of the Comte de Mortsauf, the Duc de Lenoncourt invited him to stay at Givry while a house was being prepared for him. The Lenoncourt family were nobly generous to him, and with them he remained some months, struggling to hide his sufferings during that first period of rest. The Lenoncourts had themselves lost an immense property. By birth Monsieur de Mortsauf was a suitable husband for their daughter. Mademoiselle de Lenoncourt, instead of rejecting a marriage with a feeble and worn-out man of thirty-five, seemed satisfied to accept it. It gave her the opportunity of living with her aunt, the Duchesse de Verneuil, sister of the Prince de Blamont-Chauvry, who was like a mother to her.

Madame de Verneuil, the intimate friend of the Duchesse de Bourbon, was a member of the devout society of which Monsieur Saint-Martin (born in Touraine and called the Philosopher of Mystery) was the soul. The disciples of this philosopher practised the virtues taught them by the lofty doctrines of mystical illumination. These doctrines hold the key to worlds divine; they explain existence by reincarnations through which the human spirit rises to its sublime destiny; they liberate duty from its legal degradation, enable the soul to meet the trials of life with the unalterable serenity of the Quaker, ordain contempt for the sufferings of this life, and inspire a fostering care of that angel within us who allies us to the divine. It is stoicism with an immortal future. Active prayer and pure love are the elements of this faith, which is born of the Roman Church but returns to the Christianity of the primitive faith. Mademoiselle de Lenoncourt remained, however, in the Catholic communion, to which her aunt was equally bound. Cruelly tried by revolutionary horrors, the Duchesse de Verneuil acquired in the last years of her life a halo of passionate piety, which, to use the phraseology of Saint-Martin, shed the light of celestial love and the chrism of inward joy upon the soul of her cherished niece.

After the death of her aunt, Madame de Mortsauf received several visits at Clochegourde from Saint-Martin, a man of peace and of virtuous wisdom. It was at Clochegourde that he corrected his last books, printed at Tours by Letourmy. Madame de Verneuil, wise with the wisdom of an old woman who has known the stormy straits of life, gave Clochegourde to the young wife for her married home; and with the grace of old age, so perfect where it exists, the duchess yielded everything to her niece, reserving for herself only one room above the one she had always occupied, and which she now fitted up for the countess. Her sudden death threw a gloom over the early days of the marriage, and connected Clochegourde with ideas of sadness in the sensitive mind of the bride. The first period of her settlement in Touraine was to Madame de Mortsauf, I cannot say the happiest, but the least troubled of her life.

After the many trials of his exile, Monsieur de Mortsauf, taking comfort in the thought of a secure future, had a certain recovery of mind; he breathed anew in this sweet valley the intoxicating essence of revived hope. Compelled to husband his means, he threw himself into agricultural pursuits and began to find some happiness in life. But the birth of his first child, Jacques, was a thunderbolt which ruined both the past and the future. The doctor declared the child had not vitality enough to live. The count concealed this sentence from the mother; but he sought other advice, and received the same fatal answer, the truth of which was confirmed at the subsequent birth of Madeleine. These events and a certain inward consciousness of the cause of this disaster increased the diseased tendencies of the man himself. His name doomed to extinction, a pure and irreproachable young woman made miserable beside him and doomed to the anguish of maternity without its joys—this uprising of his former into his present life, with its growth of new sufferings, crushed his spirit and completed its destruction.

The countess guessed the past from the present, and read the future. Though nothing is so difficult as to make a man happy when he knows himself to blame, she set herself to that task, which is worthy of an angel. She became stoical. Descending into an abyss, whence she still could see the sky, she devoted herself to the care of one man as the sister of charity devotes herself to many. To reconcile him with himself, she forgave him that for which he had no forgiveness. The count grew miserly; she accepted the privations he imposed. Like all who have known the world only to acquire its suspiciousness, he feared betrayal; she lived in solitude and yielded without a murmur to his mistrust. With a woman's tact she made him will to do that which was right, till he fancied the ideas were his own, and thus enjoyed in his own person the honors of a superiority that was never his. After due experience of married life, she came to the resolution of never leaving Clochegourde; for she saw the hysterical tendencies of the count's nature, and feared the outbreaks which might be talked of in that gossipping and jealous neighborhood to the injury of her children. Thus, thanks to her, no one suspected Monsieur de Mortsauf's real incapacity, for she wrapped his ruins in a mantle of ivy. The fickle, not merely discontented but embittered nature of the man found rest and ease in his wife; his secret anguish was lessened by the balm she shed upon it.

This brief history is in part a summary of that forced from Monsieur de Chessel by his inward vexation. His knowledge of the world enabled him to penetrate several of the mysteries of Clochegourde. But the prescience of love could not be misled by the sublime attitude with which Madame de Mortsauf deceived the world. When alone in my little bedroom, a sense of the full truth made me spring from my bed; I could not bear to stay at Frapesle when I saw the lighted windows of Clochegourde. I dressed, went softly down, and left the chateau by the door of a tower at the foot of a winding stairway. The coolness of the night calmed me. I crossed the Indre by the bridge at the Red Mill, took the ever-blessed punt, and rowed in front of Clochegourde, where a brilliant light was streaming from a window looking towards Azay.

Again I plunged into my old meditations; but they were now peaceful, intermingled with the love-note of the nightingale and the solitary cry of the sedge-warbler. Ideas glided like fairies through my mind, lifting the black veil which had hidden till then the glorious future. Soul and senses were alike charmed. With what passion my thoughts rose to her! Again and again I cried, with the repetition of a madman, "Will she be mine?" During the preceding days the universe had enlarged to me, but now in a single night I found its centre. On her my will and my ambition henceforth fastened; I desired to be all in all to her, that I might heal and fill her lacerated heart.

Beautiful was that night beneath her windows, amid the murmur of waters rippling through the sluices, broken only by a voice that told the hours from the clock-tower of Sache. During those hours of darkness bathed in light, when this sidereal flower illumined my existence, I betrothed to her my soul with the faith of the poor Castilian knight whom we laugh at in the pages of Cervantes,—a faith, nevertheless, with which all love begins.

At the first gleam of day, the first note of the waking birds, I fled back among the trees of Frapesle and reached the house; no one had seen me, no one suspected by absence, and I slept soundly until the bell rang for breakfast. When the meal was over I went down, in spite of the heat, to the meadow-lands for another sight of the Indre and its isles, the valley and its slopes, of which I seemed so passionate an admirer. But once there, thanks to a swiftness of foot like that of a loose horse, I returned to my punt, the willows, and Clochegourde. All was silent and palpitating, as a landscape is at midday in summer. The still foliage lay sharply defined on the blue of the sky; the insects that live by light, the dragon-flies, the cantharides, were flying among the reeds and the ash-trees; cattle chewed the cud in the shade, the ruddy earth of the vineyards glowed, the adders glided up and down the banks. What a change in the sparkling and coquettish landscape while I slept! I sprang suddenly from the boat and ran up the road which went round Clochegourde for I fancied that I saw the count coming out. I was not mistaken; he was walking beside the hedge, evidently making for a gate on the road to Azay which followed the bank of the river.

"How are you this morning, Monsieur le comte?"

He looked at me pleasantly, not being used to hear himself thus addressed.

"Quite well," he answered. "You must love the country, to be rambling about in this heat!"

"I was sent here to live in the open air."

"Then what do you say to coming with me to see them cut my rye?"

"Gladly," I replied. "I'll own to you that my ignorance is past belief; I don't know rye from wheat, nor a poplar from an aspen; I know nothing of farming, nor of the various methods of cultivating the soil."

"Well, come and learn," he cried gaily, returning upon his steps. "Come in by the little gate above."

The count walked back along the hedge, he being within it and I without.

"You will learn nothing from Monsieur de Chessel," he remarked; "he is altogether too fine a gentleman to do more than receive the reports of his bailiff."

The count then showed me his yards and the farm buildings, the pleasure-grounds, orchards, vineyards, and kitchen garden, until we finally came to the long alley of acacias and ailanthus beside the river, at the end of which I saw Madame de Mortsauf sitting on a bench, with her children. A woman is very lovely under the light and quivering shade of such foliage. Surprised, perhaps, at my prompt visit, she did not move, knowing very well that we should go to her. The count made me admire the view of the valley, which at this point is totally different from that seen from the heights above. Here I might have thought myself in a corner of Switzerland. The meadows, furrowed with little brooks which flow into the Indre, can be seen to their full extent till lost in the misty distance. Towards Montbazon the eye ranges over a vast green plain; in all other directions it is stopped by hills, by masses of trees, and rocks. We quickened our steps as we approached Madame de Mortsauf, who suddenly dropped the book in which Madeleine was reading to her and took Jacques upon her knees, in the paroxysms of a violent cough.

"What's the matter?" cried the count, turning livid.

"A sore throat," answered the mother, who seemed not to see me; "but it is nothing serious."

She was holding the child by the head and body, and her eyes seemed to shed two rays of life into the poor frail creature.

"You are so extraordinarily imprudent," said the count, sharply; "you expose him to the river damps and let him sit on a stone bench."

"Why, papa, the stone is burning hot," cried Madeleine.

"They were suffocating higher up," said the countess.

"Women always want to prove they are right," said the count, turning to me.

To avoid agreeing or disagreeing with him by word or look I watched Jacques, who complained of his throat. His mother carried him away, but as she did so she heard her husband say:—

"When they have brought such sickly children into the world they ought to learn how to take care of them."

Words that were cruelly unjust; but his self-love drove him to defend himself at the expense of his wife. The countess hurried up the steps and across the portico, and I saw her disappear through the glass door. Monsieur de Mortsauf seated himself on the bench, his head bowed in gloomy silence. My position became annoying; he neither spoke nor looked at me. Farewell to the walk he had proposed, in the course of which I had hoped to fathom him. I hardly remember a more unpleasant moment. Ought I to go away, or should I not go? How many painful thoughts must have arisen in his mind, to make him forget to follow Jacques and learn how he was! At last however he rose abruptly and came towards me. We both turned and looked at the smiling valley.

"We will put off our walk to another day, Monsieur le comte," I said gently.

"No, let us go," he replied. "Unfortunately, I am accustomed to such scenes—I, who would give my life without the slightest regret to save that of the child."

"Jacques is better, my dear; he has gone to sleep," said a golden voice. Madame de Mortsauf suddenly appeared at the end of the path. She came forward, without bitterness or ill-will, and bowed to me.

"I am glad to see that you like Clochegourde," she said.

"My dear, should you like me to ride over and fetch Monsieur Deslandes?" said the count, as if wishing her to forgive his injustice.

"Don't be worried," she said. "Jacques did not sleep last night, that's all. The child is very nervous; he had a bad dream, and I told him stories all night to keep him quiet. His cough is purely nervous; I have stilled it with a lozenge, and he has gone to sleep."

"Poor woman!" said her husband, taking her hand in his and giving her a tearful look, "I knew nothing of it."

"Why should you be troubled when there is no occasion?" she replied. "Now go and attend to the rye. You know if you are not there the men will let the gleaners of the other villages get into the field before the sheaves are carried away."

"I am going to take a first lesson in agriculture, madame," I said to her.

"You have a very good master," she replied, motioning towards the count, whose mouth screwed itself into that smile of satisfaction which is vulgarly termed a "bouche en coeur."

Two months later I learned she had passed that night in great anxiety, fearing that her son had the croup; while I was in the boat, rocked by thoughts of love, imagined that she might see me from her window adoring the gleam of the candle which was then lighting a forehead furrowed by fears! The croup prevailed at Tours, and was often fatal. When we were outside the gate, the count said in a voice of emotion, "Madame de Mortsauf is an angel!" The words staggered me. As yet I knew but little of the family, and the natural conscience of a young soul made me exclaim inwardly: "What right have I to trouble this perfect peace?"

Glad to find a listener in a young man over whom he could lord it so easily, the count talked to me of the future which the return of the Bourbons would secure to France. We had a desultory conversation, in which I listened to much childish nonsense which positively amazed me. He was ignorant of facts susceptible of proof that might be called geometric; he feared persons of education; he rejected superiority, and scoffed, perhaps with some reason, at progress. I discovered in his nature a number of sensitive fibres which it required the utmost caution not to wound; so that a conversation with him of any length was a positive strain upon the mind. When I had, as it were, felt of his defects, I conformed to them with the same suppleness that his wife showed in soothing him. Later in life I should certainly have made him angry, but now, humble as a child, supposing that I knew nothing and believing that men in their prime knew all, I was genuinely amazed at the results obtained at Clochegourde by this patient agriculturist. I listened admiringly to his plans; and with an involuntary flattery which won his good-will, I envied him the estate and its outlook—a terrestrial paradise, I called it, far superior to Frapesle.

"Frapesle," I said, "is a massive piece of plate, but Clochegourde is a jewel-case of gems,"—a speech which he often quoted, giving credit to its author.

"Before we came here," he said, "it was desolation itself."

I was all ears when he told of his seed-fields and nurseries. New to country life, I besieged him with questions about prices, means of preparing and working the soil, etc., and he seemed glad to answer all in detail.

"What in the world do they teach you in your colleges?" he exclaimed at last in astonishment.

On this first day the count said to his wife when he reached home, "Monsieur Felix is a charming young man."

That evening I wrote to my mother and asked her to send my clothes and linen, saying that I should remain at Frapesle. Ignorant of the great revolution which was just taking place, and not perceiving the influence it was to have upon my fate, I expected to return to Paris to resume my legal studies. The Law School did not open till the first week in November; meantime I had two months and a half before me.

The first part of my stay, while I studied to understand the count, was a period of painful impressions to me. I found him a man of extreme irascibility without adequate cause; hasty in action in hazardous cases to a degree that alarmed me. Sometimes he showed glimpses of the brave gentleman of Conde's army, parabolic flashes of will such as may, in times of emergency, tear through politics like bomb-shells, and may also, by virtue of honesty and courage, make a man condemned to live buried on his property an Elbee, a Bonchamp, or a Charette. In presence of certain ideas his nostril contracted, his forehead cleared, and his eyes shot lightnings, which were soon quenched. Sometimes I feared he might detect the language of my eyes and kill me. I was young then and merely tender. Will, that

force that alters men so strangely, had scarcely dawned within me. My p
desires shook me with an emotion that was like the throes of fear. Death I feared
not, but I would not die until I knew the happiness of mutual love—But how tell of
what I felt! I was a prey to perplexity; I hoped for some fortunate chance; I
watched; I made the children love me; I tried to identify myself with the family.

Little by little the count restrained himself less in my presence. I came to
know his sudden outbreaks of temper, his deep and ceaseless melancholy, his
flashes of brutality, his bitter, cutting complaints, his cold hatreds, his impulses of
latent madness, his childish moans, his cries of a man's despair, his unexpected fury.
The moral nature differs from the physical nature inasmuch as nothing is absolute
in it. The force of effects is in direct proportion to the characters or the ideas which
are grouped around some fact. My position at Clochegourde, my future life,
depended on this one eccentric will.

I cannot describe to you the distress that filled my soul (as quick in those
days to expand as to contract), whenever I entered Clochegourde, and asked myself,
"How will he receive me?" With what anxiety of heart I saw the clouds collecting on
that stormy brow. I lived in a perpetual "qui-vive." I fell under the dominion of that
man; and the sufferings I endured taught me to understand those of Madame de
Mortsauf. We began by exchanging looks of comprehension; tried by the same fire,
how many discoveries I made during those first forty days! —of actual bitterness, of
tacit joys, of hopes alternately submerged and buoyant. One evening I found her
pensively watching a sunset which reddened the summits with so ravishing a glow
that it was impossible not to listen to that voice of the eternal Song of Songs by
which Nature herself bids all her creatures love. Did the lost illusions of her
girlhood return to her? Did the woman suffer from an inward comparison? I
fancied I perceived a desolation in her attitude that was favorable to my first appeal,
and I said, "Some days are hard to bear."

"You read my soul," she answered; "but how have you done so?"

"We touch at many points," I replied. "Surely we belong to the small
number of human beings born to the highest joys and the deepest sorrows; whose
feeling qualities vibrate in unison and echo each other inwardly; whose sensitive
natures are in harmony with the principle of things. Put such beings among
surroundings where all is discord and they suffer horribly, just as their happiness
mounts to exaltation when they meet ideas, or feelings, or other beings who are
congenial to them. But there is still a third condition, where sorrows are known
only to souls affected by the same distress; in this alone is the highest fraternal
comprehension. It may happen that such souls find no outlet either for good or
evil. Then the organ within us endowed with expression and motion is exercised in
a void, expends its passion without an object, utters sounds without melody, and
cries that are lost in solitude,—terrible defeat of a soul which revolts against the
inutility of nothingness. These are struggles in which our strength oozes away
without restraint, as blood from an inward wound. The sensibilities flow to waste
and the result is a horrible weakening of the soul; an indescribable melancholy for
which the confessional itself has no ears. Have I not expressed our mutual
sufferings?"

She shuddered, and then without removing her eyes from the setting sun, she said, "How is it that, young as you are, you know these things? Were you once a woman?"

"Ah!" I replied, "my childhood was like a long illness—"

"I hear Madeleine coughing," she cried, leaving me abruptly.

The countess showed no displeasure at my constant visits, and for two reasons. In the first place she was pure as a child, and her thoughts wandered into no forbidden regions; in the next I amused the count and made a sop for that lion without claws or mane. I found an excuse for my visits which seemed plausible to every one. Monsieur de Mortsauf proposed to teach me backgammon, and I accepted; as I did so the countess was betrayed into a look of compassion, which seemed to say, "You are flinging yourself into the jaws of the lion." If I did not understand this at the time, three days had not passed before I knew what I had undertaken. My patience, which nothing exhausts, the fruit of my miserable childhood, ripened under this last trial. The count was delighted when he could jeer at me for not putting in practice the principles or the rules he had explained; if I reflected before I played he complained of my slowness; if I played fast he was angry because I hurried him; if I forgot to mark my points he declared, making his profit out of the mistake, that I was always too rapid. It was like the tyranny of a schoolmaster, the despotism of the rod, of which I can really give you no idea unless I compare myself to Epictetus under the yoke of a malicious child. When we played for money his winnings gave him the meanest and most abject delight.

A word from his wife was enough to console me, and it frequently recalled him to a sense of politeness and good-breeding. But before long I fell into the furnace of an unexpected misery. My money was disappearing under these losses. Though the count was always present during my visits until I left the house, which was sometimes very late, I cherished the hope of finding some moment when I might say a word that would reach my idol's heart; but to obtain that moment, for which I watched and waited with a hunter's painful patience, I was forced to continue these weary games, during which my feelings were lacerated and my money lost. Still, there were moments when we were silent, she and I, looking at the sunlight on the meadows, the clouds in a gray sky, the misty hills, or the quivering of the moon on the sandbanks of the river; saying only, "Night is beautiful!"

"Night is woman, madame."

"What tranquillity!"

"Yes, no one can be absolutely wretched here."

Then she would return to her embroidery frame. I came at last to hear the inward beatings of an affection which sought its object. But the fact remained—without money, farewell to these evenings. I wrote to my mother to send me some. She scolded me and sent only enough to last a week. Where could I get more? My life depended on it. Thus it happened that in the dawn of my first great happiness I found the same sufferings that assailed me elsewhere; but in Paris, at college, at school I evaded them by abstinence; there my privations were negative, at Frapesle they were active; so active that I was possessed by the impulse to theft, by visions of crime, furious desperations which rend the soul and must be subdued under pain of losing our self-respect. The memory of what I suffered through my mother's parsimony taught me that indulgence for young men which one who has stood upon the brink of the abyss and measured its depths, without falling into them, must inevitably feel. Though my own rectitude was strengthened by those moments when life opened and let me see the rocks and quicksands beneath the surface, I have never known that terrible thing called human justice draw its blade through the throat of a criminal without saying to myself: "Penal laws are made by men who have never known misery."

At this crisis I happened to find a treatise on backgammon in Monsieur de Chessel's library, and I studied it. My host was kind enough to give me a few lessons; less harshly taught by the count I made good progress and applied the rules and calculations I knew by heart. Within a few days I was able to beat Monsieur de Mortsauf, but no sooner had I done so and won his money for the first time than his temper became intolerable; his eyes glittered like those of tigers, his face shrivelled, his brows knit as I never saw brows knit before or since. His complainings were those of a fretful child. Sometimes he flung down the dice, quivered with rage, bit the dice-box, and said insulting things to me. Such violence, however, came to an end. When I had acquired enough mastery of the game I played it to suit me; I so managed that we were nearly equal up to the last moment; I allowed him to win the first half and made matters even during the last half. The end of the world would have surprised him less than the rapid superiority of his pupil; but he never admitted it. The unvarying result of our games was a topic of discourse on which he fastened.

"My poor head," he would say, "is fatigued; you manage to win the last of the game because by that time I lose my skill."

The countess, who knew backgammon, understood my manoeuvres from the first, and gave me those mute thanks which swell the heart of a young man; she granted me the same look she gave to her children. From that ever-blessed evening she always looked at me when she spoke. I cannot explain to you the condition I was in when I left her. My soul had annihilated my body; it weighed nothing; I did not walk, I flew. That look I carried within me; it bathed me with light just as her last words, "Adieu, monsieur," still sounded in my soul with the harmonies of "O filii, o filioe" in the paschal choir. I was born into a new life, I was something to her! I slept on purple and fine linen. Flames darted before my closed eyelids, chasing each other in the darkness like threads of fire in the ashes of burned paper. In my dreams her voice became, though I cannot describe it, palpable, an atmosphere of light and fragrance wrapping me, a melody enfolding my spirit. On the morrow her greeting expressed the fulness of feelings that remained unuttered, and from that moment I was initiated into the secrets of her voice.

That day was to be one of the most decisive of my life. After dinner we walked on the heights across a barren plain where no herbage grew; the ground was stony, arid, and without vegetable soil of any kind; nevertheless a few scrub oaks and thorny bushes straggled there, and in place of grass, a carpet of crimped mosses, illuminated by the setting sun and so dry that our feet slipped upon it. I held Madeleine by the hand to keep her up. Madame de Mortsauf was leading

Jacques. The count, who was in front, suddenly turned round and striking the earth with his cane said to me in a dreadful tone: "Such is my life! —but before I knew you," he added with a look of penitence at his wife. The reparation was tardy, for the countess had turned pale; what woman would not have staggered as she did under the blow?

"But what delightful scenes are wafted here, and what a view of the sunset!" I cried. "For my part I should like to own this barren moor; I fancy there may be treasures if we dig for them. But its greatest wealth is that of being near you. Who would not pay a great cost for such a view?—all harmony to the eye, with that winding river where the soul may bathe among the ash-trees and the alders. See the difference of taste! To you this spot of earth is a barren waste; to me, it is paradise."

She thanked me with a look.

"Bucolics!" exclaimed the count, with a bitter look. "This is no life for a man who bears your name." Then he suddenly changed his tone —"The bells!" he cried, "don't you hear the bells of Azay? I hear them ringing."

Madame de Mortsauf gave me a frightened look. Madeleine clung to my hand.

"Suppose we play a game of backgammon?" I said. "Let us go back; the rattle of the dice will drown the sound of the bells."

We returned to Clochegourde, conversing by fits and starts. Once in the salon an indefinable uncertainty and dread took possession of us. The count flung himself into an armchair, absorbed in reverie, which his wife, who knew the symptoms of his malady and could foresee an outbreak, was careful not to interrupt. I also kept silence. As she gave me no hint to leave, perhaps she thought backgammon might divert the count's mind and quiet those fatal nervous susceptibilities, the excitements of which were killing him. Nothing was ever harder than to make him play that game, which, however, he had a great desire to play. Like a pretty woman, he always required to be coaxed, entreated, forced, so that he might not seem the obliged person. If by chance, being interested in the conversation, I forgot to propose it, he grew sulky, bitter, insulting, and spoiled the talk by contradicting everything. If, warned by his ill-humor, I suggested a game, he would dally and demur. "In the first place, it is too late," he would say; "besides, I don't care for it." Then followed a series of affectations like those of women, which often leave you in ignorance of their real wishes.

On this occasion I pretended a wild gaiety to induce him to play. He complained of giddiness which hindered him from calculating; his brain, he said, was squeezed into a vice; he heard noises, he was choking; and thereupon he sighed heavily. At last, however, he consented to the game. Madame de Mortsauf left us to put the children to bed and lead the household in family prayers. All went well during her absence; I allowed Monsieur de Mortsauf to win, and his delight seemed to put him beside himself. This sudden change from a gloom that led him to make the darkest predictions to the wild joy of a drunken man, expressed in a crazy laugh and without any adequate motive, distressed and alarmed me. I had never seen him in quite so marked a paroxysm. Our intimacy had borne fruits in the fact that he no longer restrained himself before me. Day by day he had endeavored to bring me under his tyranny, and obtain fresh food, as it were, for his evil temper; for it really seems as though moral diseases were creatures with appetites and instincts, seeking to enlarge the boundaries of their empire as a landowner seeks to increase his domain.

Presently the countess came down, and sat close to the backgammon table, apparently for better light on her embroidery, though the anxiety which led her to place her frame was ill-concealed. A piece of fatal ill-luck which I could not prevent changed the count's face; from gaiety it fell to gloom, from purple it became yellow, and his eyes rolled. Then followed worse ill-luck, which I could neither avert nor repair. Monsieur de Mortsauf made a fatal throw which decided the game. Instantly he sprang up, flung the table at me and the lamp on the floor, struck the chimney-piece with his fist and jumped, for I cannot say he walked, about the room. The torrent of insults, imprecations, and incoherent words which rushed from his lips would have made an observer think of the old tales of satanic possession in the Middle Ages. Imagine my position!

"Go into the garden," said the countess, pressing my hand.

I left the room before the count could notice my disappearance. On the terrace, where I slowly walked about, I heard his shouts and then his moans from the bedroom which adjoined the dining-room. Also I heard at intervals through that tempest of sound the voice of an angel, which rose like the song of a nightingale as the rain ceases. I walked about under the acacias in the loveliest night of the month of August, waiting for the countess to join me. I knew she would come; her gesture promised it. For several days an explanation seemed to float between us; a word would suffice to send it gushing from the spring, overfull, in our souls. What timidity had thus far delayed a perfect understanding between us? Perhaps she loved, as I did, these quiverings of the spirit which resembled emotions of fear and numbed the sensibilities while we held our life unuttered within us, hesitating to unveil its secrets with the modesty of the young girl before the husband she loves. An hour passed. I was sitting on the brick balustrade when the sound of her footsteps blending with the undulating ripple of her flowing gown stirred the calm air of the night. These are sensations to which the heart suffices not.

"Monsieur de Mortsauf is sleeping," she said. "When he is thus I give him an infusion of poppies, a cup of water in which a few poppies have been steeped; the attacks are so infrequent that this simple remedy never loses its effect— Monsieur," she continued, changing her tone and using the most persuasive inflexion of her voice, "this most unfortunate accident has revealed to you a secret which has hitherto been sedulously kept; promise me to bury the recollection of that scene. Do this for my sake, I beg of you. I don't ask you to swear it; give me your word of honor and I shall be content."

"Need I give it to you?" I said. "Do we not understand each other?"

"You must not judge unfavorably of Monsieur de Mortsauf; you see the effects of his many sufferings under the emigration," she went on. "To-morrow he will entirely forget all that he has said and done; you will find him kind and excellent as ever."

"Do not seek to excuse him, madame," I replied. "I will do all you wish. I would fling myself into the Indre at this moment if I could restore Monsieur de Mortsauf's health and ensure you a happy life. The only thing I cannot change is my opinion. I can give you my life, but not my convictions; I can pay no heed to what he says, but can I hinder him from saying it? No, in my opinion Monsieur de Mortsauf is—"

"I understand you," she said, hastily interrupting me; "you are right. The count is as nervous as a fashionable woman," she added, as if to conceal the idea of madness by softening the word. "But he is only so at intervals, once a year, when the weather is very hot. Ah, what evils have resulted from the emigration! How many fine lives ruined! He would have been, I am sure of it, a great soldier, an honor to his country—"

"I know," I said, interrupting in my turn to let her see that it was useless to attempt to deceive me.

She stopped, laid one hand lightly on my brow, and looked at me. "Who has sent you here," she said, "into this home? Has God sent me help, a true friendship to support me?" She paused, then added, as she laid her hand firmly upon mine, "For you are good and generous—" She raised her eyes to heaven, as if to invoke some invisible testimony to confirm her thought, and then let them rest upon me. Electrified by the look, which cast a soul into my soul, I was guilty, judging by social laws, of a want of tact, though in certain natures such indelicacy really means a brave desire to meet danger, to avert a blow, to arrest an evil before it happens; oftener still, an abrupt call upon a heart, a blow given to learn if it resounds in unison with ours. Many thoughts rose like gleams within my mind and bade me wash out the stain that blotted my conscience at this moment when I was seeking a complete understanding.

"Before we say more," I said in a voice shaken by the throbbings of my heart, which could be heard in the deep silence that surrounded us, "suffer me to purify one memory of the past."

"Hush!" she said quickly, touching my lips with a finger which she instantly removed. She looked at me haughtily, with the glance of a woman who knows herself too exalted for insult to reach her. "Be silent; I know of what you are about to speak,—the first, the last, the only outrage ever offered to me. Never speak to me of that ball. If as a Christian I have forgiven you, as a woman I still suffer from your act."

"You are more pitiless than God himself," I said, forcing back the tears that came into my eyes.

"I ought to be so, I am more feeble," she replied.

"But," I continued with the persistence of a child, "listen to me now if only for the first, the last, the only time in your life."

"Speak, then," she said; "speak, or you will think I dare not hear you."

Feeling that this was the turning moment of our lives, I spoke to her in the tone that commands attention; I told her that all women whom I had ever seen were nothing to me; but when I met her, I, whose life was studious, whose nature was not bold, I had been, as it were, possessed by a frenzy that no one who once felt it could condemn; that never heart of man had been so filled with the passion which no being can resist, which conquers all things, even death—

"And contempt?" she asked, stopping me.

"Did you despise me?" I exclaimed.

"Let us say no more on this subject," she replied.

"No, let me say all!" I replied, in the excitement of my intolerable pain. "It concerns my life, my whole being, my inward self; it contains a secret you must know or I must die in despair. It also concerns you, who, unawares, are the lady in whose hand is the crown promised to the victor in the tournament!"

Then I related to her my childhood and youth, not as I have told it to you, judged from a distance, but in the language of a young man whose wounds are still bleeding. My voice was like the axe of a woodsman in the forest. At every word the dead years fell with echoing sound, bristling with their anguish like branches robbed of their foliage. I described to her in feverish language many cruel details which I have here spared you. I spread before her the treasure of my radiant hopes, the virgin gold of my desires, the whole of a burning heart kept alive beneath the snow of these Alps, piled higher and higher by perpetual winter. When, bowed down by the weight of these remembered sufferings, related as with the live coal of Isaiah, I awaited the reply of the woman who listened with a bowed head, she illumined the darkness with a look, she quickened the worlds terrestrial and divine with a single sentence.

"We have had the same childhood!" she said, turning to me a face on which the halo of the martyrs shone.

After a pause, in which our souls were wedded in the one consoling thought, "I am not alone in suffering," the countess told me, in the voice she kept for her little ones, how unwelcome she was as a girl when sons were wanted. She showed me how her troubles as a daughter bound to her mother's side differed from those of a boy cast out upon the world of school and college life. My desolate neglect seemed to me a paradise compared to that contact with a millstone under which her soul was ground until the day when her good aunt, her true mother, had saved her from this misery, the ever-recurring pain of which she now related to me; misery caused sometimes by incessant faultfinding, always intolerable to high-strung natures which do not shrink before death itself but die beneath the sword of Damocles; sometimes by the crushing of generous impulses beneath an icy hand, by the cold rebuffal of her kisses, by a stern command of silence, first imposed and then as often blamed; by inward tears that dared not flow but stayed within the heart; in short, by all the bitterness and tyranny of convent rule, hidden to the eyes of the world under the appearance of an exalted motherly devotion. She gratified her mother's vanity before strangers, but she dearly paid in private for this homage. When, believing that by obedience and gentleness she had softened her mother's heart, she opened hers, the tyrant only armed herself with the girl's confidence. No spy was ever more traitorous and base. All the pleasures of girlhood, even her fete days, were dearly purchased, for she was scolded for her gaiety as much as for her faults. No teaching and no training for her position had been given in love, always with sarcastic irony. She was not angry against her mother; in fact she blamed herself for feeling more terror than love for her. "Perhaps," she said, dear angel, "these severities were needful; they had certainly prepared her for her present life." As I listened it seemed to me that the harp of Job, from which I had drawn such savage sounds, now touched by the Christian fingers gave forth the litanies of the Virgin at the foot of the cross.

"We lived in the same sphere before we met in this," I said; "you coming from the east, I from the west."

She shook her head with a gesture of despair.

"To you the east, to me the west," she replied. "You will live happy, I must die of pain. Life is what we make of it, and mine is made forever. No power can break the heavy chain to which a woman is fastened by this ring of gold—the emblem of a wife's purity."

We knew we were twins of one womb; she never dreamed of a half-confidence between brothers of the same blood. After a short sigh, natural to pure hearts when they first open to each other, she told me of her first married life, her deceptions and disillusions, the rebirth of her childhood's misery. Like me, she had suffered under trifles; mighty to souls whose limpid substance quivers to the least shock, as a lake quivers on the surface and to its utmost depths when a stone is flung into it. When she married she possessed some girlish savings; a little gold, the fruit of happy hours and repressed fancies. These, in a moment when they were needed, she gave to her husband, not telling him they were gifts and savings of her own. He took no account of them, and never regarded himself her debtor. She did not even obtain the glance of thanks that would have paid for all. Ah! how she went from trial to trial! Monsieur de Mortsauf habitually neglected to give her money for the household. When, after a struggle with her timidity, she asked him for it, he seemed surprised and never once spared her the mortification of petitioning for necessities. What terror filled her mind when the real nature of the ruined man's disease was revealed to her, and she quailed under the first outbreak of his mad anger! What bitter reflections she had made before she brought herself to admit that her husband was a wreck! What horrible calamities had come of her bearing children! What anguish she felt at the sight of those infants born almost dead! With what courage had she said in her heart: "I will breathe the breath of life into them; I will bear them anew day by day!" Then conceive the bitterness of finding her greatest obstacle in the heart and hand from which a wife should draw her greatest succor! She saw the untold disaster that threatened him. As each difficulty was conquered, new deserts opened before her, until the day when she thoroughly understood her husband's condition, the constitution of her children, and the character of the neighborhood in which she lived; a day when (like the child taken by Napoleon from a tender home) she taught her feet to trample through mud and snow, she trained her nerves to bullets and all her being to the passive obedience of a soldier.

These things, of which I here make a summary, she told me in all their dark extent, with every piteous detail of conjugal battles lost and fruitless struggles.

"You would have to live here many months," she said, in conclusion, "to understand what difficulties I have met with in improving Clochegourde; what persuasions I have had to use to make him do a thing which was most important to his interests. You cannot imagine the childish glee he has shown when anything that I advised was not at once successful. All that turned out well he claimed for himself. Yes, I need an infinite patience to bear his complaints when I am half-exhausted in the effort to amuse his weary hours, to sweeten his life and smooth the paths which he himself has strewn with stones. The reward he gives me is that awful cry: 'Let me die, life is a burden to me!' When visitors are here and he enjoys them, he forgets his gloom and is courteous and polite. You ask me why he cannot be so to his family. I cannot explain that want of loyalty in a man who is truly chivalrous. He is quite capable of riding at full speed to Paris to buy me a set of ornaments, as he did the other day before the ball. Miserly in his household, he would be lavish upon me if I wished it. I would it were reversed; I need nothing for myself, but the wants of the household are many. In my strong desire to make him happy, and not reflecting that I might be a mother, I began my married life by letting him treat me as a victim, I, who at that time by using a few caresses could have led him like a child— but I was unable to play a part I should have thought disgraceful. Now, however, the welfare of my family requires me to be as calm and stern as the figure of Justice —and yet, I too have a heart that overflows with tenderness."

"But why," I said, "do you not use this great influence to master him and govern him?"

"If it concerned myself only I should not attempt either to overcome the dogged silence with which for days together he meets my arguments, nor to answer his irrational remarks, his childish reasons. I have no courage against weakness, any more than I have against childhood; they may strike me as they will, I cannot resist. Perhaps I might meet strength with strength, but I am powerless against those I pity. If I were required to coerce Madeleine in some matter that would save her life, I should die with her. Pity relaxes all my fibres and unstrings my nerves. So it is that the violent shocks of the last ten years have broken me down; my feelings, so often battered, are numb at times; nothing can revive them; even the courage with which I once faced my troubles begins to fail me. Yes, sometimes I am beaten. For want of rest—I mean repose—and sea-baths by which to recover my nervous strength, I shall perish. Monsieur de Mortsauf will have killed me, and he will die of my death."

"Why not leave Clochegourde for a few months? Surely you could take your children and go to the seashore."

"In the first place, Monsieur de Mortsauf would think he were lost if I left him. Though he will not admit his condition he is well aware of it. He is both sane and mad, two natures in one man, a contradiction which explains many an irrational action. Besides this, he would have good reason for objecting. Nothing would go right here if I were absent. You may have seen in me the mother of a family watchful to protect her young from the hawk that is hovering over them; a weighty task, indeed, but harder still are the cares imposed upon me by Monsieur de Mortsauf, whose constant cry, as he follows me about is, 'Where is Madame?' I am Jacques' tutor and Madeleine's governess; but that is not all, I am bailiff and steward too. You will understand what that means when you come to see, as you will, that the working of an estate in these parts is the most fatiguing of all employments. We get small returns in money; the farms are cultivated on shares, a system which needs the closest supervision. We are obliged ourselves to sell our own produce, our cattle and harvests of all kinds. Our competitors in the markets are our own farmers, who meet consumers in the wine-shops and determine prices by selling first. I should weary you if I explained the many difficulties of agriculture in this region. No matter what care I give to it, I cannot always prevent our tenants from putting our manure upon their ground, I cannot be ever on the watch lest they take advantage of us in the division of the crops; neither can I always know the exact moment when sales should be made. So, if you think of Monsieur de Mortsauf's defective memory, and the difficulty you have seen me have in persuading him to attend to business, you can understand the burden that is on my shoulders, and the impossibility of my laying it down for a single day. If I were absent we should be ruined. No one would obey Monsieur de Mortsauf. In the first place his orders are conflicting; then no one likes him; he finds incessant fault, and he is very domineering. Moreover, like all men of feeble mind, he listens too readily to his inferiors. If I left the house not a servant would be in it in a week's time. So you see I am attached to Clochegourde as those leaden finals are to our roof. I have no reserves with you. The whole country-side is still ignorant of the secrets of this house, but you know them, you have seen them. Say nothing but what is kind and friendly, and you shall have my esteem —my gratitude," she added in a softer voice. "On those terms you are welcome at Clochegourde, where you will find friends."

"Ah!" I exclaimed, "I see that I have never really suffered, while you—"

"No, no!" she exclaimed, with a smile, that smile of all resigned women which might melt a granite rock. "Do not be astonished at my frank confidence; it shows you life as it is, not as your imagination pictures it. We all have our defects and our good qualities. If I had married a spendthrift he would have ruined me. If I had given myself to an ardent and pleasure-loving young man, perhaps I could not have retained him; he might have left me, and I should have died of jealousy. For I am jealous!" she said, in a tone of excitement, which was like the thunderclap of a passing storm. "But Monsieur de Mortsauf loves me as much as he is capable of loving; all that his heart contains of affection he pours at my feet, like the Magdalen's cup of ointment. Believe me, a life of love is an exception to the laws of this earth; all flowers fade; great joys and emotions have a morrow of evil—if a morrow at all. Real life is a life of anguish; its image is in that nettle growing there at the foot of the wall,—no sun can reach it and it keeps green. Yet, here, as in parts of the North, there are smiles in the sky, few to be sure, but they compensate for many a grief. Moreover, women who are naturally mothers live and love far more through sacrifices than through pleasures. Here I draw upon myself the storms I fear may break upon my children or my people; and in doing so I feel a something I cannot explain, which gives me secret courage. The resignation of the night carries me through the day that follows. God does not leave me comfortless. Time was when the condition of my children filled me with despair; to-day as they advance in life they grow healthier and stronger. And then, after all, our home is improved and beautified, our means are improving also. Who knows but Monsieur de Mortsauf's old age may be a blessing to me? Ah, believe me! those who stand before the Great

Judge with palms in their hands, leading comforted to Him the beings who cursed their lives, they, they have turned their sorrows into joy. If my sufferings bring about the happiness of my family, are they sufferings at all?"

"Yes," I said, "they are; but they were necessary, as mine have been, to make us understand the true flavor of the fruit that has ripened on our rocks. Now, surely, we shall taste it together; surely we may admire its wonders, the sweetness of affection it has poured into our souls, that inward sap which revives the searing leaves—Good God! do you not understand me?" I cried, falling into the mystical language to which our religious training had accustomed us. "See the paths by which we have approached each other; what magnet led us through that ocean of bitterness to these springs of running water, flowing at the foot of those hills above the shining sands and between their green and flowery meadows? Have we not followed the same star? We stand before the cradle of a divine child whose joyous carol will renew the world for us, teach us through happiness a love of life, give to our nights their long-lost sleep, and to the days their gladness. What hand is this that year by year has tied new cords between us? Are we not more than brother and sister? That which heaven has joined we must not keep asunder. The sufferings you reveal are the seeds scattered by the sower for the harvest already ripening in the sunshine. Shall we not gather it sheaf by sheaf? What strength is in me that I dare address you thus! Answer, or I will never again recross that river!"

"You have spared me the word

*love_*

," she said, in a stern voice, "but you have spoken of a sentiment of which I know nothing and which is not permitted to me. You are a child; and again I pardon you, but for the last time. Endeavor to understand, Monsieur, that my heart is, as it were, intoxicated with motherhood. I love Monsieur de Mortsauf neither from social duty nor from a calculated desire to win eternal blessings, but from an irresistible feeling which fastens all the fibres of my heart upon him. Was my marriage a mistake? My sympathy for misfortune led to it. It is the part of women to heal the woes caused by the march of events, to comfort those who rush into the breach and return wounded. How shall I make you understand me? I have felt a selfish pleasure in seeing that you amused him; is not that pure motherhood? Did I not make you see by what I owned just now, the _

*three_*

children to whom I am bound, to whom I shall never fail, on whom I strive to shed a healing dew and the light of my own soul without withdrawing or adulterating a single particle? Do not embitter the mother's milk! though as a wife I am invulnerable, you must never again speak thus to me. If you do not respect this command, simple as it is, the door of this house will be closed to you. I believed in pure friendship, in a voluntary brotherhood, more real, I thought, than the brotherhood of blood. I was mistaken. I wanted a friend who was not a judge, a friend who would listen to me in those moments of weakness when reproof is killing, a sacred friend from whom I should have nothing to fear. Youth is noble, truthful, capable of sacrifice, disinterested; seeing your persistency in coming to us, I believed, yes, I will admit that I believed in some divine purpose; I thought I should find a soul that would be mine, as the priest is the soul of all; a heart in which to pour my troubles when they deluged mine, a friend to hear my cries when if I continued to smother them they would strangle me. Could I but have this friend, my life, so precious to these children, might be prolonged until Jacques had grown to manhood. But that is selfish! The Laura of Petrarch cannot be lived again. I must die at my post, like a soldier, friendless. My confessor is harsh, austere, and—my aunt is dead."

Two large tears filled her eyes, gleamed in the moonlight, and rolled down her cheeks; but I stretched my hand in time to catch them, and I drank them with an avidity excited by her words, by the thought of those ten years of secret woe, of wasted feelings, of constant care, of ceaseless dread—years of the lofty heroism of her sex. She looked at me with gentle stupefaction.

"It is the first communion of love," I said. "Yes, I am now a sharer of your sorrows. I am united to your soul as our souls are united to Christ in the sacrament. To love, even without hope, is happiness. Ah! what woman on earth could give me a joy equal to that of receiving your tears! I accept the contract which must end in suffering to myself. I give myself to you with no ulterior thought. I will be to you that which you will me to be—"

She stopped me with a motion of her hand, and said in her deep voice, "I consent to this agreement if you will promise never to tighten the bonds which bind us together."

"Yes," I said; "but the less you grant the more evidence of possession I ought to have."

"You begin by distrusting me," she replied, with an expression of melancholy doubt.

"No, I speak from pure happiness. Listen; give me a name by which no one calls you; a name to be ours only, like the feeling which unites us."

"That is much to ask," she said, "but I will show you that I am not petty. Monsieur de Mortsauf calls me Blanche. One only person, the one I have most loved, my dear aunt, called me Henriette. I will be Henriette once more, to you."

I took her hand and kissed it. She left it in mine with the trustfulness that makes a woman so far superior to men; a trustfulness that shames us. She was leaning on the brick balustrade and gazing at the river.

"Are you not unwise, my friend, to rush at a bound to the extremes of friendship? You have drained the cup, offered in all sincerity, at a draught. It is true that a real feeling is never piecemeal; it must be whole, or it does not exist. Monsieur de Mortsauf," she added after a short silence, "is above all things loyal and brave. Perhaps for my sake you will forget what he said to you to-day; if he has forgotten it to-morrow, I will myself tell him what occurred. Do not come to Clochegourde for a few days; he will respect you more if you do not. On Sunday, after church, he will go to you. I know him; he will wish to undo the wrong he did, and he will like you all the better for treating him as a man who is responsible for his words and actions."

"Five days without seeing you, without hearing your voice!"

"Do not put such warmth into your manner of speaking to me," she said.

We walked twice round the terrace in silence. Then she said, in a tone of command which proved to me that she had taken possession of my soul, "It is late; we will part."

I wished to kiss her hand; she hesitated, then gave it to me, and said in a voice of entreaty: "Never take it unless I give it to you; leave me my freedom; if not, I shall be simply a thing of yours, and that ought not to be."

"Adieu," I said.

I went out by the little gate of the lower terrace, which she opened for me. Just as she was about to close it she opened it again and offered me her hand, saying: "You have been truly good to me this evening; you have comforted my whole future; take it, my friend, take it."

I kissed her hand again and again, and when I raised my eyes I saw the tears in hers. She returned to the upper terrace and I watched her for a moment from the meadow. When I was on the road to Frapesle I again saw her white robe shimmering in a moonbeam; then, a few moments later, a light was in her bedroom.

"Oh, my Henriette!" I cried, "to you I pledge the purest love that ever shone upon this earth."

I turned at every step as I regained Frapesle. Ineffable contentment filled my mind. A way was open for the devotion that swells in all youthful hearts and which in mine had been so long inert. Like the priest who by one solemn step enters a new life, my vows were taken; I was consecrated. A simple "Yes" had bound me to keep my love within my soul and never to abuse our friendship by leading this woman step by step to love. All noble feelings were awakened within me, and I heard the murmur of their voices. Before confining myself within the narrow walls of a room, I stopped beneath the azure heavens sown with stars, I listened to the ring-dove plaints of my own heart, I heard again the simple tones of that ingenuous confidence, I gathered in the air the emanations of that soul which henceforth must ever seek me. How grand that woman seemed to me, with her absolute forgetfulness of self, her religion of mercy to wounded hearts, feeble or suffering, her declared allegiance to her legal yoke. She was there, serene upon her pyre of saint and martyr. I adored her face as it shone to me in the darkness. Suddenly I fancied I perceived a meaning in her words, a mysterious significance which made her to my eyes sublime. Perhaps she longed that I should be to her what she was to the little world around her. Perhaps she sought to draw from me her strength and consolation, putting me thus within her sphere, her equal, or perhaps above her. The stars, say some bold builders of the universe, communicate to each other light and motion. This thought lifted me to ethereal regions. I entered once more the heaven of my former visions; I found a meaning for the miseries of my childhood in the illimitable happiness to which they had led me.

Spirits quenched by tears, hearts misunderstood, saintly Clarissa Harlowes forgotten or ignored, children neglected, exiles innocent of wrong, all ye who enter life through barren ways, on whom men's faces everywhere look coldly, to whom ears close and hearts are shut, cease your complaints! You alone can know the infinitude of joy held in that moment when one heart opens to you, one ear listens, one look answers yours. A single day effaces all past evil. Sorrow, despondency, despair, and melancholy, passed but not forgotten, are links by which the soul then fastens to its mate. Woman falls heir to all our past, our sighs, our lost illusions, and gives them back to us ennobled; she explains those former griefs as payment claimed by destiny for joys eternal, which she brings to us on the day our souls are wedded. The angels alone can utter the new name by which that sacred love is called, and none but women, dear martyrs, truly know what Madame de Mortsauf now became to me—to me, poor and desolate.

CHAPTER II
FIRST LOVE

This scene took place on a Tuesday. I waited until Sunday and did not cross the river. During those five days great events were happening at Clochegourde. The count received his brevet as general of brigade, the cross of Saint Louis, and a pension of four thousand francs. The Duc de Lenoncourt-Givry, made peer of France, recovered possession of two forests, resumed his place at court, and his wife regained all her unsold property, which had been made part of the imperial crown lands. The Comtesse de Mortsauf thus became an heiress. Her mother had arrived at Clochegourde, bringing her a hundred thousand francs economized at Givry, the amount of her dowry, still unpaid and never asked for by the count in spite of his poverty. In all such matters of external life the conduct of this man was proudly disinterested. Adding to this sum his own few savings he was able to buy two neighboring estates, which would yield him some nine thousand francs a year. His son would of course succeed to the grandfather's peerage, and the count now saw his way to entail the estate upon him without injury to Madeleine, for whom the Duc de Lenoncourt would no doubt assist in promoting a good marriage.

These arrangements and this new happiness shed some balm upon the count's sore mind. The presence of the Duchesse de Lenoncourt at Clochegourde was a great event to the neighborhood. I reflected gloomily that she was a great lady, and the thought made me conscious of the spirit of caste in the daughter which the nobility of her sentiments had hitherto hidden from me. Who was I— poor, insignificant, and with no future but my courage and my faculties? I did not then think of the consequences of the Restoration either for me or for others. On Sunday morning, from the private chapel where I sat with Monsieur and Madame de Chessel and the Abbe de Quelus, I cast an eager glance at another lateral chapel occupied by the duchess and her daughter, the count and his children. The large straw hat which hid my idol from me did not tremble, and this unconsciousness of my presence seemed to bind me to her more than all the past. This noble Henriette de Lenoncourt, my Henriette, whose life I longed to garland, was praying earnestly; faith gave to her figure an abandonment, a prosternation, the attitude of some religious statue, which moved me to the soul.

According to village custom, vespers were said soon after mass. Coming out of church Madame de Chessel naturally proposed to her neighbors to pass the intermediate time at Frapesle instead of crossing the Indre and the meadows twice in the great heat. The offer was accepted. Monsieur de Chessel gave his arm to the duchess, Madame de Chessel took that of the count. I offered mine to the countess, and felt, for the first time, that beautiful arm against my side. As we walked from the church to Frapesle by the woods of Sache, where the light, filtering down through the foliage, made those pretty patterns on the path which seem like painted silk, such sensations of pride, such ideas took possession of me that my heart beat violently.

"What is the matter?" she said, after walking a little way in a silence I dared not break. "Your heart beats too fast—"

"I have heard of your good fortune," I replied, "and, like all others who love truly, I am beset with vague fears. Will your new dignities change you and lessen your friendship?"

"Change me!" she said; "oh, fie! Another such idea and I shall—not despise you, but forget you forever."

I looked at her with an ecstasy which should have been contagious.

"We profit by the new laws which we have neither brought about nor demanded," she said; "but we are neither place-hunters nor beggars; besides, as you know very well, neither Monsieur de Mortsauf nor I can leave Clochegourde. By my advice he has declined the command to which his rank entitled him at the Maison Rouge. We are quite content that my father should have the place. This forced modesty," she added with some bitterness, "has already been of service to our son. The king, to whose household my father is appointed, said very graciously that he would show Jacques the favor we were not willing to accept. Jacques' education, which must now be thought of, is already being discussed. He will be the representative of two houses, the Lenoncourt and the Mortsauf families. I can have no ambition except for him, and therefore my anxieties seem to have increased. Not only must Jacques live, but he must be made worthy of his name; two necessities which, as you know, conflict. And then, later, what friend will keep him safe for me in Paris, where all things are pitfalls for the soul and dangers for the body? My friend," she said, in a broken voice, "who could not see upon your brow and in your eyes that you are one who will inhabit heights? Be some day the guardian and sponsor of our boy. Go to Paris; if your father and brother will not second you, our family, above all my mother, who has a genius for the management of life, will help you. Profit by our influence; you will never be without support in whatever career you choose; put the strength of your desires into a noble ambition—"

"I understand you," I said, interrupting her; "ambition is to be my mistress. I have no need of that to be wholly yours. No, I will not be rewarded for my obedience here by receiving favors there. I will go; I will make my own way; I will rise alone. From you I would accept everything, from others nothing."

"Child!" she murmured, ill-concealing a smile of pleasure.

"Besides, I have taken my vows," I went on. "Thinking over our situation I am resolved to bind myself to you by ties that never can be broken."

She trembled slightly and stopped short to look at me.

"What do you mean?" she asked, letting the couples who preceded us walk on, and keeping the children at her side.

"This," I said; "but first tell me frankly how you wish me to love you."

"Love me as my aunt loved me; I gave you her rights when I permitted you to call me by the name which she chose for her own among my others."

"Then I am to love without hope and with an absolute devotion. Well, yes; I will do for you what some men do for God. I shall feel that you have asked it. I will enter a seminary and make myself a priest, and then I will educate your son. Jacques shall be myself in his own form; political conceptions, thoughts, energy, patience, I will give him all. In that way I shall live near to you, and my love, enclosed in religion as a silver image in a crystal shrine, can never be suspected of evil. You will not have to fear the undisciplined passions which grasp a man and by which already I have allowed myself to be vanquished. I will consume my own being in the flame, and I will love you with a purified love."

She turned pale and said, hurrying her words: "Felix, do not put yourself in bonds that might prove an obstacle to our happiness. I should die of grief for having caused a suicide like that. Child, do you think despairing love a life's vocation? Wait for life's trials before you judge of life; I command it. Marry neither the Church nor a woman; marry not at all,—I forbid it. Remain free. You are twenty-one years old—My God! can I have mistaken him? I thought two months sufficed to know some souls."

"What hope have you?" I cried, with fire in my eyes.

"My friend, accept our help, rise in life, make your way and your fortune and you shall know my hope. And," she added, as if she were whispering a secret, "never release the hand you are holding at this moment."

She bent to my ear as she said these words which proved her deep solicitude for my future.

"Madeleine!" I exclaimed "never!"

We were close to a wooden gate which opened into the park of Frapesle; I still seem to see its ruined posts overgrown with climbing plants and briers and mosses. Suddenly an idea, that of the count's death, flashed through my brain, and I said, "I understand you."

"I am glad of it," she answered in a tone which made me know I had supposed her capable of a thought that could never be hers.

Her purity drew tears of admiration from my eyes which the selfishness of passion made bitter indeed. My mind reacted and I felt that she did not love me enough even to wish for liberty. So long as love recoils from a crime it seems to have its limits, and love should be infinite. A spasm shook my heart.

"She does not love me," I thought.

To hide what was in my soul I stooped over Madeleine and kissed her hair.

"I am afraid of your mother," I said to the countess presently, to renew the conversation.

"So am I," she answered with a gesture full of childlike gaiety. "Don't forget to call her Madame la duchesse, and to speak to her in the third person. The young people of the present day have lost these polite manners; you must learn them; do that for my sake. Besides, it is such good taste to respect women, no matter what their age may be, and to recognize social distinctions without disputing them. The respect shown to established superiority is guarantee for that which is due to you. Solidarity is the basis of society. Cardinal Della Rovere and Raffaelle were two powers equally revered. You have sucked the milk of the Revolution in your academy and your political ideas may be influenced by it; but as you advance in life you will find that crude and ill-defined principles of liberty are powerless to create the happiness of the people. Before considering, as a Lenoncourt, what an aristocracy ought to be, my common-sense as a woman of the people tells me that societies can exist only through a hierarchy. You are now at a turning-point in your life, when you must choose wisely. Be on our side,—especially now," she added, laughing, "when it triumphs."

I was keenly touched by these words, in which the depth of her political feeling mingled with the warmth of affection,—a combination which gives to women so great a power of persuasion; they know how to give to the keenest arguments a tone of feeling. In her desire to justify all her husband's actions Henriette had foreseen the criticisms that would rise in my mind as soon as I saw the servile effects of a courtier's life upon him. Monsieur de Mortsauf, king in his own castle and surrounded by an historic halo, had, to my eyes, a certain grandiose dignity. I was therefore greatly astonished at the distance he placed between the duchess and himself by manners that were nothing less than obsequious. A slave has his pride and will only serve the greatest despots. I confess I was humiliated at the degradation of one before whom I trembled as the power that ruled my love. This inward repulsion made me understand the martyrdom of women of generous souls yoked to men whose meannesses they bury daily. Respect is a safeguard which protects both great and small alike; each side can hold its own. I was respectful to the duchess because of my youth; but where others saw only a duchess I saw the mother of my Henriette, and that gave sanctity to my homage.

We reached the great court-yard of Frapesle, where we found the others. The Comte de Mortsauf presented me very gracefully to the duchess, who examined me with a cold and reserved air. Madame de Lenoncourt was then a woman fifty-six years of age, wonderfully well preserved and with grand manners. When I saw the hard blue eyes, the hollow temples, the thin emaciated face, the erect, imposing figure slow of movement, and the yellow whiteness of the skin (reproduced with such brilliancy in the daughter), I recognized the cold type to which my own mother belonged, as quickly as a mineralogist recognizes Swedish iron. Her language was that of the old court; she pronounced the "oit" like "ait," and said "frait" for "froid," "porteux" for "porteurs." I was not a courtier, neither was I stiff-backed in my manner to her; in fact I behaved so well that as I passed the countess she said in a low voice, "You are perfect."

The count came to me and took my hand, saying: "You are not angry with me, Felix, are you? If I was hasty you will pardon an old soldier? We shall probably stay here to dinner, and I invite you to dine with us on Thursday, the evening before the duchess leaves. I must go to Tours to-morrow to settle some business. Don't neglect Clochegourde. My mother-in-law is an acquaintance I advise you to cultivate. Her salon will set the tone for the faubourg St. Germain. She has all the traditions of the great world, and possesses an immense amount of social knowledge; she knows the blazon of the oldest as well as the newest family in Europe."

The count's good taste, or perhaps the advice of his domestic genius, appeared under his altered circumstances. He was neither arrogant nor offensively polite, nor pompous in any way, and the duchess was not patronizing. Monsieur and Madame de Chessel gratefully accepted the invitation to dinner on the following Thursday. I pleased the duchess, and by her glance I knew she was examining a man of whom her daughter had spoken to her. As we returned from vespers she questioned me about my family, and asked if the Vandenesse now in diplomacy was my relative. "He is my brother," I replied. On that she became almost affectionate. She told me that my great-aunt, the old Marquise de Listomere, was a Grandlieu. Her manners were as cordial as those of Monsieur de Mortsauf the day he saw me for the first time; the haughty glance with which these sovereigns of the earth make you measure the distance that lies between you and them disappeared. I knew almost nothing of my family. The duchess told me that my great-uncle, an old abbe whose very name I did not know, was to be member of the privy council, that my brother was already promoted, and also that by a provision of the Charter, of which I had not yet heard, my father became once more Marquis de Vandenesse.

"I am but one thing, the serf of Clochegourde," I said in a low voice to the countess.

The transformation scene of the Restoration was carried through with a rapidity which bewildered the generation brought up under the imperial regime. To me this revolution meant nothing. The least word or gesture from Madame de Mortsauf were the sole events to which I attached importance. I was ignorant of what the privy council was, and knew as little of politics as of social life; my sole ambition was to love Henriette better than Petrarch loved Laura. This indifference made the duchess take me for a child. A large company assembled at Frapesle and we were thirty at table. What intoxication it is for a young man unused to the world to see the woman he loves more beautiful than all others around her, the centre of admiring looks; to know that for him alone is reserved the chaste fire of those eyes, that none but he can discern in the tones of that voice, in the words it utters, however gay or jesting they may be, the proofs of unremitting thought. The count, delighted with the attentions paid to him, seemed almost young; his wife looked hopeful of a change; I amused myself with Madeleine, who, like all children with bodies weaker than their minds, made others laugh with her clever observations, full of sarcasm, though never malicious, and which spared no one. It was a happy day. A word, a hope awakened in the morning illumined nature. Seeing me so joyous, Henriette was joyful too.

"This happiness smiling on my gray and cloudy life seems good," she said to me the next day.

That day I naturally spent at Clochegourde. I had been banished for five days, I was athirst for life. The count left at six in the morning for Tours. A serious disagreement had arisen between mother and daughter. The duchess wanted the countess to move to Paris, where she promised her a place at court, and where the count, reconsidering his refusal, might obtain some high position. Henriette, who was thought happy in her married life, would not reveal, even to her mother, her tragic sufferings and the fatal incapacity of her husband. It was to hide his condition from the duchess that she persuaded him to go to Tours and transact business with his notaries. I alone, as she had truly said, knew the dark secret of Clochegourde. Having learned by experience how the pure air and the blue sky of the lovely valley calmed the excitements and soothed the morbid griefs of the diseased mind, and what beneficial effect the life at Clochegourde had upon the health of her children, she opposed her mother's desire that she should leave it with reasons which the overbearing woman, who was less grieved than mortified by her daughter's bad marriage, vigorously combated.

Henriette saw that the duchess cared little for Jacques and Madeleine, —a terrible discovery! Like all domineering mothers who expect to continue the same authority over their married daughters that they maintained when they were girls, the duchess brooked no opposition; sometimes she affected a crafty sweetness to force her daughter to compliance, at other times a cold severity, intending to obtain by fear what gentleness had failed to win; then, when all means failed, she displayed the same native sarcasm which I had often observed in my own mother. In those ten days Henriette passed through all the contentions a young woman must endure to establish her independence. You, who for your happiness have the best of mothers, can scarcely comprehend such trials. To gain a true idea of the struggle between that cold, calculating, ambitious woman and a daughter abounding in the tender natural kindness that never faileth, you must imagine a lily, to which my heart has always compared her, bruised beneath the polished wheels of a steel car. That mother had nothing in common with her daughter; she was unable even to imagine the real difficulties which hindered her from taking advantage of the Restoration and forced her to continue a life of solitude. Though families bury their internal dissensions with the utmost care, enter behind the scenes, and you will find in nearly all of them deep, incurable wounds, which lessen the natural affections. Sometimes these wounds are given by passions real and most affecting, rendered eternal by the dignity of those who feel them; sometimes by latent hatreds which slowly freeze the heart and dry all tears when the hour of parting comes. Tortured yesterday and to-day, wounded by all, even by the suffering children who were guiltless of the ills they endured, how could that poor soul fail to love the one human being who did not strike her, who would fain have built a wall of defence around her to guard her from storms, from harsh contacts and cruel blows? Though I suffered from a knowledge of these debates, there were moments when I was happy in the sense that she rested upon my heart; for she told me of these new troubles. Day by day I learned more fully the meaning of her words, —"Love me as my aunt loved me."

"Have you no ambition?" the duchess said to me at dinner, with a stern air.

"Madame," I replied, giving her a serious look, "I have enough in me to conquer the world; but I am only twenty-one, and I am all alone."

She looked at her daughter with some astonishment. Evidently she believed that Henriette had crushed my ambition in order to keep me near her. The visit of

Madame de Lenoncourt was a period of unrelieved constraint. The countess begged me to be cautious; she was frightened by the least kind word; to please her I wore the harness of deceit. The great Thursday came; it was a day of wearisome ceremonial,—one of those stiff days which lovers hate, when their chair is no longer in its place, and the mistress of the house cannot be with them. Love has a horror of all that does not concern itself. But the duchess returned at last to the pomps and vanities of the court, and Clochegourde recovered its accustomed order.

My little quarrel with the count resulted in making me more at home in the house than ever; I could go there at all times without hindrance; and the antecedents of my life inclined me to cling like a climbing plant to the beautiful soul which had opened to me the enchanting world of shared emotions. Every hour, every minute, our fraternal marriage, founded on trust, became a surer thing; each of us settled firmly into our own position; the countess enfolded me with her nurturing care, with the white draperies of a love that was wholly maternal; while my love for her, seraphic in her presence, seared me as with hot irons when away from her. I loved her with a double love which shot its arrows of desire, and then lost them in the sky, where they faded out of sight in the impermeable ether. If you ask me why, young and ardent, I continued in the deluding dreams of Platonic love, I must own to you that I was not yet man enough to torture that woman, who was always in dread of some catastrophe to her children, always fearing some outburst of her husband's stormy temper, martyrized by him when not afflicted by the illness of Jacques or Madeleine, and sitting beside one or the other of them when her husband allowed her a little rest. The mere sound of too warm a word shook her whole being; a desire shocked her; what she needed was a veiled love, support mingled with tenderness,—that, in short, which she gave to others. Then, need I tell you, who are so truly feminine? this situation brought with it hours of delightful languor, moments of divine sweetness and content which followed by secret immolation. Her conscience was, if I may call it so, contagious; her self-devotion without earthly recompense awed me by its persistence; the living, inward piety which was the bond of her other virtues filled the air about her with spiritual incense. Besides, I was young,—young enough to concentrate my whole being on the kiss she allowed me too seldom to lay upon her hand, of which she gave me only the back, and never the palm, as though she drew the line of sensual emotions there. No two souls ever clasped each other with so much ardor, no bodies were ever more victoriously annihilated. Later I understood the cause of this sufficing joy. At my age no worldly interests distracted my heart; no ambitions blocked the stream of a love which flowed like a torrent, bearing all things on its bosom. Later, we love the woman in a woman; but the first woman we love is the whole of womanhood; her children are ours, her interests are our interests, her sorrows our greatest sorrow; we love her gown, the familiar things about her; we are more grieved by a trifling loss of hers than if we knew we had lost everything. This is the sacred love that makes us live in the being of another; whereas later, alas! we draw another life into ours, and require a woman to enrich our pauper spirit with her young soul.

I was now one of the household, and I knew for the first time an infinite sweetness, which to a nature bruised as mine was like a bath to a weary body; the soul is refreshed in every fibre, comforted to its very depths. You will hardly understand me, for you are a woman, and I am speaking now of a happiness women give but do not receive. A man alone knows the choice happiness of being, in the midst of a strange household, the privileged friend of its mistress, the secret centre of her affections. No dog barks at you; the servants, like the dogs, recognize your rights; the children (who are never misled, and know that their power cannot be lessened, and that you cherish the light of their life), the children possess the gift of divination, they play with you like kittens and assume the friendly tyranny they show only to those they love; they are full of intelligent discretion and come and go on tiptoe without noise. Every one hastens to do you service; all like you, and smile upon you. True passions are like beautiful flowers all the more charming to the eye when they grow in a barren soil.

But if I enjoyed the delightful benefits of naturalization in a family where I found relations after my own heart, I had also to pay some costs for it. Until then Monsieur de Mortsauf had more or less restrained himself before me. I had only seen his failings in the mass; I was now to see the full extent of their application and discover how nobly charitable the countess had been in the account she had given me of these daily struggles. I learned now all the angles of her husband's intolerable nature; I heard his perpetual scolding about nothing, complaints of evils of which not a sign existed; I saw the inward dissatisfaction which poisoned his life, and the incessant need of his tyrannical spirit for new victims. When we went to walk in the evenings he selected the way; but whichever direction we took he was always bored; when we reached home he blamed others; his wife had insisted on going where she wanted; why was he governed by her in all the trifling things of life? was he to have no will, no thought of his own? must he consent to be a cipher in his own house? If his harshness was to be received in patient silence he was angry because he felt a limit to his power; he asked sharply if religion did not require a wife to please her husband, and whether it was proper to despise the father of her children? He always ended by touching some sensitive chord in his wife's mind; and he seemed to find a domineering pleasure in making it sound. Sometimes he tried gloomy silence and a morbid depression, which always alarmed his wife and made her pay him the most tender attentions. Like petted children, who exercise their power without thinking of the distress of their mother, he would let her wait upon him as upon Jacques and Madeleine, of whom he was jealous.

I discovered at last that in small things as well as in great ones the count acted towards his servants, his children, his wife, precisely as he had acted to me about the backgammon. The day when I understood, root and branch, these difficulties, which like a rampant overgrowth repressed the actions and stifled the breathing of the whole family, hindered the management of the household and retarded the improvement of the estate by complicating the most necessary acts, I felt an admiring awe which rose higher than my love and drove it back into my heart. Good God! what was I? Those tears that I had taken on my lips solemnized my spirit; I found happiness in wedding the sufferings of that woman. Hitherto I had yielded to the count's despotism as the smuggler pays his fine; henceforth I was a voluntary victim that I might come the nearer to her. The countess understood me, allowed me a place beside her, and gave me permission to share her sorrows; like the repentant apostate, eager to rise to heaven with his brethren, I obtained the favor of dying in the arena.

"Were it not for you I must have succumbed under this life," Henriette said to me one evening when the count had been, like the flies on a hot day, more stinging, venomous, and persistent than usual.

He had gone to bed. Henriette and I remained under the acacias; the children were playing about us, bathed in the setting sun. Our few exclamatory words revealed the mutuality of the thoughts in which we rested from our common sufferings. When language failed silence as faithfully served our souls, which seemed to enter one another without hindrance; together they luxuriated in the charms of pensive languor, they met in the undulations of the same dream, they plunged as one into the river and came out refreshed like two nymphs as closely united as their souls could wish, but with no earthly tie to bind them. We entered the unfathomable gulf, we returned to the surface with empty hands, asking each other by a look, "Among all our days on earth will there be one for us?"

In spite of the tranquil poetry of evening which gave to the bricks of the balustrade their orange tones, so soothing and so pure; in spite of the religious atmosphere of the hour, which softened the voices of the children and wafted them towards us, desire crept through my veins like the match to the bonfire. After three months of repression I was unable to content myself with the fate assigned me. I took Henriette's hand and softly caressed it, trying to convey to her the ardor that invaded me. She became at once Madame de Mortsauf, and withdrew her hand; tears rolled from my eyes, she saw them and gave me a chilling look, as she offered her hand to my lips.

"You must know," she said, "that this will cause me grief. A friendship that asks so great a favor is dangerous."

Then I lost my self-control; I reproached her, I spoke of my sufferings, and the slight alleviation that I asked for them. I dared to tell her that at my age, if the senses were all soul still the soul had a sex; that I could meet death, but not with closed lips. She forced me to silence with her proud glance, in which I seemed to read the cry of the Mexican: "And I, am I on a bed of roses?" Ever since that day by the gate of Frapesle, when I attributed to her the hope that our happiness might spring from a grave, I had turned with shame from the thought of staining her soul with the desires of a brutal passion. She now spoke with honeyed lip, and told me that she never could be wholly mine, and that I ought to know it. As she said the words I know that in obeying her I dug an abyss between us. I bowed my head. She went on, saying she had an inward religious certainty that she might love me as a brother without offending God or man; such love was a living image of the divine love, which her good Saint-Martin told her was the life of the world. If I could not be to her somewhat as her old confessor was, less than a lover yet more than a brother, I must never see her again. She could die and take to God her sheaf of sufferings, borne not without tears and anguish.

"I gave you," she said in conclusion, "more than I ought to have given, so that nothing might be left to take, and I am punished."

I was forced to calm her, to promise never to cause her pain, and to love her at twenty-one years of age as old men love their youngest child.

The next day I went early. There were no flowers in the vases of her gray salon. I rushed into the fields and vineyards to make her two bouquets; but as I gathered the flowers, one by one, cutting their long stalks and admiring their beauty, the thought occurred to me that the colors and foliage had a poetry, a harmony, which meant something to the understanding while they charmed the eye; just as musical melodies awaken memories in hearts that are loving and beloved. If color is light organized, must it not have a meaning of its own, as the combinations of the air have theirs? I called in the assistance of Jacques and Madeleine, and all three of us conspired to surprise our dear one. I arranged, on the lower steps of the portico, where we established our floral headquarters, two bouquets by which I tried to convey a sentiment. Picture to yourself a fountain of flowers gushing from the vases and falling back in curving waves; my message springing from its bosom in white roses and lilies with their silver cups. All the blue flowers, harebells, forget-me-nots, and ox-tongues, whose tines, caught from the skies, blended so well with the whiteness of the lilies, sparkled on this dewy texture; were they not the type of two purities, the one that knows nothing, the other that knows all; an image of the child, an image of the martyr? Love has its blazon, and the countess discerned it inwardly. She gave me a poignant glance which was like the cry of a soldier when his wound is touched; she was humbled but enraptured too. My reward was in that glance; to refresh her heart, to have given her comfort, what encouragement for me! Then it was that I pressed the theories of Pere Castel into the service of love, and recovered a science lost to Europe, where written pages have supplanted the flowery missives of the Orient with their balmy tints. What charm in expressing our sensations through these daughters of the sun, sisters to the flowers that bloom beneath the rays of love! Before long I communed with the flora of the fields, as a man whom I met in after days at Grandlieu communed with his bees.

Twice a week during the remainder of my stay at Frapesle I continued the slow labor of this poetic enterprise, for the ultimate accomplishment of which I needed all varieties of herbaceous plants; into these I made a deep research, less as a botanist than as a poet, studying their spirit rather than their form. To find a flower in its native haunts I walked enormous distances, beside the brooklets, through the valleys, to the summit of the cliffs, across the moorland, garnering thoughts even from the heather. During these rambles I initiated myself into pleasures unthought of by the man of science who lives in meditation, unknown to the horticulturist busy with specialities, to the artisan fettered to a city, to the merchant fastened to his desk, but known to a few foresters, to a few woodsmen, and to some dreamers. Nature can show effects the significations of which are limitless; they rise to the grandeur of the highest moral conceptions—be it the heather in bloom, covered with the diamonds of the dew on which the sunlight dances; infinitude decked for the single glance that may chance to fall upon it:—be it a corner of the forest hemmed in with time-worn rocks crumbling to gravel and clothed with mosses overgrown with juniper, which grasps our minds as something savage, aggressive, terrifying as the cry of the kestrel issuing from it:—be it a hot and barren moor without vegetation, stony, rigid, its horizon like those of the desert, where once I gathered a sublime and solitary flower, the anemone pulsatilla, with its violet petals opening for the golden stamens; affecting image of my pure idol alone in her valley:—be it great sheets of water, where nature casts those spots of greenery, a species of transition between the plant and animal, where life makes haste to come in flowers and insects, floating there like worlds in ether:—be it a cottage with its garden of cabbages, its vineyards, its hedges overhanging a bog, surrounded by a few sparse fields of rye; true image of many humble existences: —be it a forest path like some cathedral nave, where the trees are columns and their branches arch the roof, at the far end of which a light breaks through, mingled with shadows or tinted with sunset reds athwart the leaves which gleam like the colored windows of a chancel: —then, leaving these woods so cool and branchy, behold a chalk-land lying fallow, where among the warm and cavernous mosses adders glide to their lairs, or lift their proud slim heads. Cast upon all these pictures torrents of sunlight like beneficent waters, or the shadow of gray clouds drawn in lines like the wrinkles of an old man's brow, or the cool tones of a sky faintly orange and streaked with lines of a paler tint; then listen—you will hear indefinable harmonies amid a silence which blends them all.

During the months of September and October I did not make a single bouquet which cost me less than three hours search; so much did I admire, with the real sympathy of a poet, these fugitive allegories of human life, that vast theatre I was about to enter, the scenes of which my memory must presently recall. Often do I now compare those splendid scenes with memories of my soul thus expending itself on nature; again I walk that valley with my sovereign, whose white robe brushed the coppice and floated on the green sward, whose spirit rose, like a promised fruit, from each calyx filled with amorous stamens.

No declaration of love, no vows of uncontrollable passion ever conveyed more than these symphonies of flowers; my baffled desires impelled me to efforts of expression through them like those of Beethoven through his notes, to the same bitter reactions, to the same mighty bounds towards heaven. In their presence Madame de Mortsauf was my Henriette. She looked at them constantly; they fed her spirit, she gathered all the thoughts I had given them, saying, as she raised her head from the embroidery frame to receive my gift, "Ah, how beautiful!"

Natalie, you will understand this delightful intercourse through the details of a bouquet, just as you would comprehend Saadi from a fragment of his verse. Have you ever smelt in the fields in the month of May the perfume that communicates to all created beings the intoxicating sense of a new creation; the sense that makes you trail your hand in the water from a boat, and loosen your hair to the breeze while your mind revives with the springtide greenery of the trees? A little plant, a species of vernal grass, is a powerful element in this veiled harmony; it cannot be worn with impunity; take into your hand its shining blade, striped green and white like a silken robe, and mysterious emotions will stir the rosebuds your modesty keeps hidden in the depths of your heart. Round the neck of a porcelain vase imagine a broad margin of the gray-white tufts peculiar to the sedum of the vineyards of Touraine, vague image of submissive forms; from this foundation come tendrils of the bind-weed with its silver bells, sprays of pink rest-barrow mingled with a few young shoots of oak-leaves, lustrous and magnificently colored; these creep forth prostrate, humble as the weeping-willow, timid and supplicating as prayer. Above, see those delicate threads of the purple amoret, with its flood of anthers that are nearly yellow; the snowy pyramids of the meadow-sweet, the green tresses of the wild oats, the slender plumes of the agrostis, which we call wind-ear; roseate hopes, decking love's earliest dream and standing forth against the gray surroundings. But higher still, remark the Bengal roses, sparsely scattered among the laces of the daucus, the plumes of the linaria, the marabouts of the meadow-queen; see the umbels of the myrrh, the spun glass of the clematis in seed, the dainty petals of the cross-wort, white as milk, the corymbs of the yarrow, the spreading stems of the fumitory with their black and rosy blossoms, the tendrils of the grape, the twisted shoots of the honeysuckle; in short, all the innocent creatures have that is most tangled, wayward, wild,—flames and triple darts, leaves lanceolated or jagged, stalks convoluted like passionate desires writhing in the soul. From the bosom of this torrent of love rises the scarlet poppy, its tassels about to open, spreading its flaming flakes above the starry jessamine, dominating the rain of pollen—that soft mist fluttering in the air and reflecting the light in its myriad particles. What woman intoxicated with the odor of the vernal grasses would fail to understand this wealth of offered thoughts, these ardent desires of a love demanding the happiness refused in a hundred struggles which passion still renews, continuous, unwearying, eternal!

Put this speech of the flowers in the light of a window to show its crisp details, its delicate contrasts, its arabesques of color, and allow the sovereign lady to see a tear upon some petal more expanded than the rest. What do we give to God? perfumes, light, and song, the purest expression of our nature. Well, these offerings to God, are they not likewise offered to love in this poem of luminous flowers murmuring their sadness to the heart, cherishing its hidden transports, its unuttered hopes, its illusions which gleam and fall to fragments like the gossamer of a summer's night?

Such neutral pleasures help to soothe a nature irritated by long contemplation of the person beloved. They were to me, I dare not say to her, like those fissures in a dam through which the water finds a vent and avoids disaster. Abstinence brings deadly exhaustion, which a few crumbs falling from heaven like manna in the desert, suffices to relieve. Sometimes I found my Henriette standing before these bouquets with pendant arms, lost in agitated reverie, thoughts swelling her bosom, illumining her brow as they surged in waves and sank again, leaving lassitude and languor behind them. Never again have I made a bouquet for any one. When she and I had created this language and formed it to our uses, a satisfaction filled our souls like that of a slave who escapes his masters.

During the rest of this month as I came from the meadows through the gardens I often saw her face at the window, and when I reached the salon she was ready at her embroidery frame. If I did not arrive at the hour expected (though never appointed), I saw a white form wandering on the terrace, and when I joined her she would say, "I came to meet you; I must show a few attentions to my youngest child."

The miserable games of backgammon had come to end. The count's late purchases took all his time in going hither and thither about the property, surveying, examining, and marking the boundaries of his new possessions. He had orders to give, rural works to overlook which needed a master's eye,—all of them planned and decided on by his wife and himself. We often went to meet him, the countess and I, with the children, who amused themselves on the way by running after insects, stag-beetles, darning-needles, they too making their bouquets, or to speak more truly, their bundles of flowers. To walk beside the woman we love, to take her on our arm, to guide her steps,—these are illimitable joys that suffice a lifetime. Confidence is then complete. We went alone, we returned with the "general," a title given to the count when he was good-humored. These two ways of taking the same path gave light and shade to our pleasure, a secret known only to hearts debarred from union. Our talk, so free as we went, had hidden significations as we returned, when either of us gave an answer to some furtive interrogation, or continued a subject, already begun, in the enigmatic phrases to which our language lends itself, and which women are so ingenious in composing. Who has not known the pleasure of such secret understandings in a sphere apart from those about us, a sphere where spirits meet outside of social laws?

One day a wild hope, quickly dispelled, took possession of me, when the count, wishing to know what we were talking of, put the inquiry, and Henriette answered in words that allowed another meaning, which satisfied him. This amused Madeleine, who laughed; after a moment her mother blushed and gave me a forbidding look, as if to say she might still withdraw from me her soul as she had once withdrawn her hand. But our purely spiritual union had far too many charms, and on the morrow it continued as before.

The hours, days, and weeks fled by, filled with renascent joys. Grape harvest, the festal season in Touraine, began. Toward the end of September the sun, less hot than during the wheat harvest, allows of our staying in the vineyards without danger of becoming overheated. It is easier to gather grapes than to mow wheat. Fruits of all kinds are ripe, harvests are garnered, bread is less dear; the sense of plenty makes the country people happy. Fears as to the results of rural toil, in which more money than sweat is often spent, vanish before a full granary and cellars about to overflow. The vintage is then like a gay dessert after the dinner is eaten; the skies of Touraine, where the autumns are always magnificent, smile upon it. In this hospitable land the vintagers are fed and lodged in the master's house. The meals are the only ones throughout the year when these poor people taste substantial, well-cooked food; and they cling to the custom as the children of patriarchal families cling to anniversaries. As the time approaches they flock in crowds to those houses where the masters are known to treat the laborers liberally. The house is full of people and of provisions. The presses are open. The country is alive with the coming and going of itinerant coopers, of carts filled with laughing girls and joyous husbandmen, who earn better wages than at any other time during the year, and who sing as they go. There is also another cause of pleasurable content: classes and ranks are equal; women, children, masters, and men, all that little world, share in the garnering of the divine hoard. These various elements of satisfaction explain the hilarity of the vintage, transmitted from age to age in these last glorious days of autumn, the remembrance of which inspired Rabelais with the bacchic form of his great work.

The children, Jacques and Madeleine, had never seen a vintage; I was like them, and they were full of infantine delight at finding a sharer of their pleasure; their mother, too, promised to accompany us. We went to Villaines, where baskets are manufactured, in quest of the prettiest that could be bought; for we four were to cut certain rows reserved for our scissors; it was, however, agreed that none of us were to eat too many grapes. To eat the fat bunches of Touraine in a vineyard seemed so delicious that we all refused the finest grapes on the dinner-table. Jacques made me swear I would go to no other vineyard, but stay closely at Clochegourde. Never were these frail little beings, usually pallid and smiling, so fresh and rosy and active as they were this morning. They chattered for chatter's sake, and trotted about without apparent object; they suddenly seemed, like other children, to have more life than they needed; neither Monsieur nor Madame de Mortsauf had ever seen them so before. I became a child again with them, more of a child than either of them, perhaps; I, too, was hoping for my harvest. It was glorious weather when we went to the vineyard, and we stayed there half the day. How we disputed as to who had the finest grapes and who could fill his basket quickest! The little human shoots ran to and fro from the vines to their mother; not a bunch could be cut without showing it to her. She laughed with the good, gay laugh of her girlhood when I, running up with my basket after Madeleine, cried out, "Mine too! See mine, mamma!" To which she answered: "Don't get overheated, dear child." Then passing her hand round my neck and through my hair, she added, giving me a little tap on the cheek, "You are melting away." It was the only caress she ever gave me. I looked at the pretty line of purple clusters, the hedges full of haws and blackberries; I heard the voices of the children; I watched the trooping girls, the cart loaded with barrels, the men with the panniers. Ah, it is all engraved on my memory, even to the almond-tree beside which she stood, girlish, rosy, smiling, beneath the sunshade held open in her hand. Then I busied myself in cutting the bunches and filling my basket, going forward to empty it in the vat, silently, with measured bodily movement and slow steps that left my spirit free. I discovered then the ineffable pleasure of an external labor which carries life along, and thus regulates the rush of passion, often so near, but for this mechanical motion, to kindle into flame. I learned how much wisdom is contained in uniform labor; I understood monastic discipline.

For the first time in many days the count was neither surly nor cruel. His son was so well; the future Duc de Lenoncourt-Mortsauf, fair and rosy and stained with grape-juice, rejoiced his heart. This day being the last of the vintage, he had promised a dance in front of Clochegourde in honor of the return of the Bourbons, so that our festival gratified everybody. As we returned to the house, the countess took my arm and leaned upon it, as if to let my heart feel the weight of hers,—the instinctive movement of a mother who seeks to convey her joy. Then she whispered in my ear, "You bring us happiness."

Ah, to me, who knew her sleepless nights, her cares, her fears, her former existence, in which, although the hand of God sustained her, all was barren and wearisome, those words uttered by that rich voice brought pleasures no other woman in the world could give me.

"The terrible monotony of my life is broken, all things are radiant with hope," she said after a pause. "Oh, never leave me! Do not despise my harmless superstitions; be the elder son, the protector of the younger."

In this, Natalie, there is nothing romantic. To know the infinite of our deepest feelings, we must in youth cast our lead into those great lakes upon whose shores we live. Though to many souls passions are lava torrents flowing among arid rocks, other souls there be in whom passion, restrained by insurmountable obstacles, fills with purest water the crater of the volcano.

We had still another fete. Madame de Mortsauf, wishing to accustom her children to the practical things of life, and to give them some experience of the toil by which men earn their living, had provided each of them with a source of income, depending on the chances of agriculture. To Jacques she gave the produce of the walnut-trees, to Madeleine that of the chestnuts. The gathering of the nuts began soon after the vintage,—first the chestnuts, then the walnuts. To beat Madeleine's trees with a long pole and hear the nuts fall and rebound on the dry, matted earth of a chestnut-grove; to see the serious gravity of the little girl as she examined the heaps and estimated their probable value, which to her represented many pleasures on which she counted; the congratulations of Manette, the trusted servant who alone supplied Madame de Mortsauf's place with the children; the explanations of the mother, showing the necessity of labor to obtain all crops, so often imperilled by the uncertainties of climate,—all these things made up a charming scene of innocent, childlike happiness amid the fading colors of the late autumn.

Madeleine had a little granary of her own, in which I was to see her brown treasure garnered and share her delight. Well, I quiver still when I recall the sound of each basketful of nuts as it was emptied on the mass of yellow husks, mixed with earth, which made the floor of the granary. The count bought what was needed for the household; the farmers and tenants, indeed, every one around Clochegourde, sent buyers to the Mignonne, a pet name which the peasantry give even to strangers, but which in this case belonged exclusively to Madeleine.

Jacques was less fortunate in gathering his walnuts. It rained for several days; but I consoled him with the advice to hold back his nuts and sell them a little later. Monsieur de Chessel had told me that the walnut-trees in the Brehemont, also those about Amboise and Vouvray, were not bearing. Walnut oil is in great demand in Touraine. Jacques might get at least forty sous for the product of each tree, and as he had two hundred the amount was considerable; he intended to spend it on the equipment of a pony. This wish led to a discussion with his father, who bade him think of the uncertainty of such returns, and the wisdom of creating a reserve fund for the years when the trees might not bear, and so equalizing his resources. I felt what was passing through the mother's mind as she sat by in silence; she rejoiced in the way Jacques listened to his father, the father seeming to recover the paternal dignity that was lacking to him, thanks to the ideas which she herself had prompted in him. Did I not tell you truly that in picturing this woman earthly language was insufficient to render either her character or her spirit. When such scenes occurred my soul drank in their delights without analyzing them; but now, with what vigor they detach themselves on the dark background of my troubled life! Like diamonds they shine against the settling of thoughts degraded by alloy, of bitter regrets for a lost happiness. Why do the names of the two estates purchased after the Restoration, and in which Monsieur and Madame de Mortsauf both took the deepest interest, the Cassine and the Rhetoriere, move me more than the sacred names of the Holy Land or of Greece? "Who loves, knows!" cried La Fontaine. Those names possess the talismanic power of words uttered under certain constellations by seers; they explain magic to me; they awaken sleeping forms which arise and speak to me; they lead me to the happy valley; they recreate skies and landscape. But such evocations are in the regions of the spiritual world; they pass in the silence of my own soul. Be not surprised, therefore, if I dwell on all these homely scenes; the smallest details of that simple, almost common life are ties which, frail as they may seem, bound me in closest union to the countess.

The interests of her children gave Madame de Mortsauf almost as much anxiety as their health. I soon saw the truth of what she had told me as to her secret share in the management of the family affairs, into which I became slowly initiated. After ten years' steady effort Madame de Mortsauf had changed the method of cultivating the estate. She had "put it in fours," as the saying is in those parts, meaning the new system under which wheat is sown every four years only, so as to make the soil produce a different crop yearly. To evade the obstinate unwillingness of the peasantry it was found necessary to cancel the old leases and give new ones, to divide the estate into four great farms and let them on equal shares, the sort of lease that prevails in Touraine and its neighborhood. The owner of the estate gives the house, farm-buildings, and seed-grain to tenants-at-will, with whom he divides the costs of cultivation and the crops. This division is superintended by an agent or bailiff, whose business it is to take the share belonging to the owner; a costly system, complicated by the market changes of values, which alter the character of the shares constantly. The countess had induced Monsieur de Mortsauf to cultivate a fifth farm, made up of the reserved lands about Clochegourde, as much to occupy his mind as to show other farmers the excellence of the new method by the evidence of facts. Being thus, in a hidden way, the mistress of the estate, she had slowly and with a woman's persistency rebuilt two of the farm-houses on the principle of those in Artois and Flanders. It is easy to see her motive. She wished, after the expiration of the leases on shares, to relet to intelligent and capable persons for rental in money, and thus simplify the revenues of Clochegourde. Fearing to die before her husband, she was anxious to secure for him a regular income, and to her children a property which no incapacity could jeopardize. At the present time the fruit-trees planted during the last ten years were in full bearing; the hedges, which secured the boundaries from dispute, were in good order; the elms and poplars were growing well. With the new purchases and the new farming system well under way, the estate of Clochegourde, divided into four great farms, two of which still needed new houses, was capable of bringing in forty thousand francs a year, ten thousand for each farm, not counting the yield of the vineyards, and the two hundred acres of woodland which adjoined them, nor the profits of the model home-farm. The roads to the great farms all opened on an avenue which followed a straight line from Clochegourde to the main road leading to Chinon. The distance from the entrance of this avenue to Tours was only fifteen miles; tenants would never be wanting, especially now that everybody was talking of the count's improvements and the excellent condition of his land.

The countess wished to put some fifteen thousand francs into each of the estates lately purchased, and to turn the present dwellings into two large farm-houses and buildings, in order that the property might bring in a better rent after the ground had been cultivated for a year or two. These ideas, so simple in themselves, but complicated with the thirty odd thousand francs it was necessary to expend upon them, were just now the topic of many discussions between herself and the count, sometimes amounting to bitter quarrels, in which she was sustained by the thought of her children's interests. The fear, "If I die to-morrow what will become of them?" made her heart beat. The gentle, peaceful hearts to whom anger is an impossibility, and whose sole desire is to shed on those about them their own inward peace, alone know what strength is needed for such struggles, what demands upon the spirit must be made before beginning the contest, what weariness ensues when the fight is over and nothing has been won. At this moment, just as her children seemed less anemic, less frail, more active (for the fruit season had had its effect on them), and her moist eyes followed them as they played about her with a sense of contentment which renewed her strength and refreshed her heart, the poor woman was called upon to bear the sharp sarcasms and attacks of an angry opposition. The count, alarmed at the plans she proposed, denied with stolid obstinacy the advantages of all she had done and the possibility of doing more. He replied to conclusive reasoning with the folly of a child who denies the influence of the sun in summer. The countess, however, carried the day. The victory of commonsense over insanity so healed her wounds that she forgot the battle. That day we all went to the Cassine and the Rhetoriere, to decide upon the buildings. The count walked alone in front, the children went next, and we ourselves followed slowly, for she was speaking in a low, gentle tone, which made her words like the murmur of the sea as it ripples on a smooth beach.

She was, she said, certain of success. A new line of communication between Tours and Chinon was to be opened by an active man, a carrier, a cousin of Manette's, who wanted a large farm on the route. His family was numerous; the eldest son would drive the carts, the second could attend to the business, the father living half-way along the road, at Rabelaye, one of the farms then to let, would look after the relays and enrich his land with the manure of the stables. As to the other farm, la Baude, the nearest to Clochegourde, one of their own people, a worthy, intelligent, and industrious man, who saw the advantages of the new system of agriculture, was ready to take a lease on it. The Cassine and the Rhetoriere need give no anxiety; their soil was the very best in the neighborhood; the farm-houses once built, and the ground brought into cultivation, it would be quite enough to advertise them at Tours; tenants would soon apply for them. In two years' time Clochegourde would be worth at least twenty-four thousand francs a year. Gravelotte, the farm in Maine, which Monsieur de Mortsauf had recovered after the emigration, was rented for seven thousand francs a year for nine years; his pension was four thousand. This income might not be a fortune, but it was certainly a competence. Later, other additions to it might enable her to go to Paris and attend to Jacques' education; in two years, she thought, his health would be established.

With what feeling she uttered the word "Paris!" I knew her thought; she wished to be as little separated as possible from her friend. On that I broke forth; I told her that she did not know me; that without talking of it, I had resolved to finish my education by working day and night so as to fit myself to be Jacques' tutor. She looked grave.

"No, Felix," she said, "that cannot be, any more than your priesthood. I thank you from my heart as a mother, but as a woman who loves you sincerely I can never allow you to be the victim of your attachment to me. Such a position would be a social discredit to you, and I could not allow it. No! I cannot be an injury to you in any way. You, Vicomte de Vandenesse, a tutor! You, whose motto is 'Ne se vend!' Were you Richelieu himself it would bar your way in life; it would give the utmost pain to your family. My friend, you do not know what insult women of the world, like my mother, can put into a patronizing glance, what degradation into a word, what contempt into a bow."

"But if you love me, what is the world to me?"

She pretended not to hear, and went on:—

"Though my father is most kind and desirous of doing all I ask, he would never forgive your taking so humble a position; he would refuse you his protection. I could not consent to your becoming tutor to the Dauphin even. You must accept society as it is; never commit the fault of flying in the face of it. My friend, this rash proposal of—"

"Love," I whispered.

"No, charity," she said, controlling her tears, "this wild idea enlightens me as to your character; your heart will be your bane. I shall claim from this moment the right to teach you certain things. Let my woman's eye see for you sometimes. Yes, from the solitudes of Clochegourde I mean to share, silently, contentedly, in your successes. As to a tutor, do not fear; we shall find some good old abbe, some learned Jesuit, and my father will gladly devote a handsome sum to the education of the boy who is to bear his name. Jacques is my pride. He is, however, eleven years old," she added after a pause. "But it is with him as with you; when I first saw you I took you to be about thirteen."

We now reached the Cassine, where Jacques, Madeleine, and I followed her about as children follow a mother; but we were in her way; I left her presently and went into the orchard where Martineau the elder, keeper of the place, was discussing with Martineau the younger, the bailiff, whether certain trees ought or ought not to be taken down; they were arguing the matter as if it concerned their own property. I then saw how much the countess was beloved. I spoke of it to a poor laborer, who, with one foot on his spade and an elbow on its handle, stood listening to the two doctors of pomology.

"Ah, yes, monsieur," he answered, "she is a good woman, and not haughty like those hussies at Azay, who would see us die like dogs sooner than yield us one penny of the price of a grave! The day when that woman leaves these parts the Blessed Virgin will weep, and we too. She knows what is due to her, but she knows our hardships, too, and she puts them into the account."

With what pleasure I gave that man all the money I had.

A few days later a pony arrived for Jacques, his father, an excellent horseman, wishing to accustom the child by degrees to the fatigues of such exercise. The boy had a pretty riding-dress, bought with the product of the nuts. The morning when he took his first lesson accompanied by his father and by Madeleine, who jumped and shouted about the lawn round which Jacques was riding, was a great maternal festival for the countess. The boy wore a blue collar embroidered by her, a little sky-blue overcoat fastened by a polished leather belt, a pair of white trousers pleated at the waist, and a Scotch cap, from which his fair hair flowed in heavy locks. He was charming to behold. All the servants clustered round to share the domestic joy. The little heir smiled at his mother as he passed her, sitting erect, and quite fearless. This first manly act of a child to whom death had often seemed so near, the promise of a sound future warranted by this ride which showed him so handsome, so fresh, so rosy,—what a reward for all her cares! Then too the joy of the father, who seemed to renew his youth, and who smiled for the first time in many long months; the pleasure shown on all faces, the shout of an old huntsman of the Lenoncourts, who had just arrived from Tours, and who, seeing how the boy held the reins, shouted to him, "Bravo, monsieur le vicomte!"—all this was too much for the poor mother, and she burst into tears; she, so calm in her griefs, was too weak to bear the joy of admiring her boy as he bounded over the gravel, where so often she had led him in the sunshine inwardly weeping his expected death. She leaned upon my arm unreservedly, and said: "I think I have never suffered. Do not leave us to-day."

The lesson over, Jacques jumped into his mother's arms; she caught him and held him tightly to her, kissing him passionately. I went with Madeleine to arrange two magnificent bouquets for the dinner-table in honor of the young equestrian. When we returned to the salon the countess said: "The fifteenth of October is certainly a great day with me. Jacques has taken his first riding lesson, and I have just set the last stitch in my furniture cover."

"Then, Blanche," said the count, laughing, "I must pay you for it."

He offered her his arm and took her to the first courtyard, where stood an open carriage which her father had sent her, and for which the count had purchased two English horses. The old huntsman had prepared the surprise while Jacques was taking his lesson. We got into the carriage, and went to see where the new avenue entered the main road towards Chinon. As we returned, the countess said to me in an anxious tone, "I am too happy; to me happiness is like an illness,—it overwhelms me; I fear it may vanish like a dream."

I loved her too passionately not to feel jealous,—I who could nothing! In my rage against myself I longed for some means of dying for her. She asked me to tell her the thoughts that filled my eyes, and I told her honestly. She was more touched than by all her presents; then taking me to the portico, she poured comfort into my heart. "Love me as my aunt loved me," she said, "and that will be giving me your life; and if I take it, must I not ever be grateful to you?

"It was time I finished my tapestry," she added as we re-entered the salon, where I kissed her hand as if to renew my vows. "Perhaps you do not know, Felix, why I began so formidable a piece of work. Men find the occupations of life a great resource against troubles; the management of affairs distracts their mind; but we poor women have no support within ourselves against our sorrows. To be able to smile before my children and my husband when my heart was heavy I felt the need of controlling my inward sufferings by some physical exercise. In this way I escaped the depression which is apt to follow a great strain upon the moral strength, and likewise all outbursts of excitement. The mere action of lifting my arm regularly as I drew the stitches rocked my thoughts and gave to my spirit when the tempest raged a monotonous ebb and flow which seemed to regulate its emotions. To every stitch I confided my secrets,—you understand me, do you not? Well, while doing my last chair I have thought much, too much, of you, dear friend. What you have put into your bouquets I have said in my embroidery."

The dinner was lovely. Jacques, like all children when you take notice of them, jumped into my arms when he saw the flowers I had arranged for him as a garland. His mother pretended to be jealous; ah, Natalie, you should have seen the charming grace with which the dear child offered them to her. In the afternoon we played a game of backgammon, I alone against Monsieur and Madame de Mortsauf, and the count was charming. They accompanied me along the road to Frapesle in the twilight of a tranquil evening, one of those harmonious evenings when our feelings gain in depth what they lose in vivacity. It was a day of days in this poor woman's life; a spot of brightness which often comforted her thoughts in painful hours.

Soon, however, the riding lessons became a subject of contention. The countess justly feared the count's harsh reprimands to his son. Jacques grew thin, dark circles surrounded his sweet blue eyes; rather than trouble his mother, he suffered in silence. I advised him to tell his father he was tired when the count's temper was violent; but that expedient proved unavailing, and it became necessary to substitute the old huntsman as a teacher in place of the father, who could with difficulty be induced to resign his pupil. Angry reproaches and contentions began once more; the count found a text for his continual complaints in the base ingratitude of women; he flung the carriage, horses, and liveries in his wife's face twenty times a day. At last a circumstance occurred on which a man with his nature and his disease naturally fastened eagerly. The cost of the buildings at the Cassine and the Rhetoriere proved to be half as much again as the estimate. This news was unfortunately given in the first instance to Monsieur de Mortsauf instead of to his wife. It was the ground of a quarrel, which began mildly but grew more and more embittered until it seemed as though the count's madness, lulled for a short time, was demanding its arrearages from the poor wife.

That day I had started from Frapesle at half-past ten to search for flowers with Madeleine. The child had brought the two vases to the portico, and I was wandering about the gardens and adjoining meadows gathering the autumn flowers, so beautiful, but too rare. Returning from my final quest, I could not find my little lieutenant with her white cape and broad pink sash; but I heard cries within the house, and Madeleine presently came running out.

"The general," she said, crying (the term with her was an expression of dislike), "the general is scolding mamma; go and defend her."

I sprang up the steps of the portico and reached the salon without being seen by either the count or his wife. Hearing the madman's sharp cries I first shut all the doors, then I returned and found Henriette as white as her dress.

"Never marry, Felix," said the count as soon as he saw me; "a woman is led by the devil; the most virtuous of them would invent evil if it did not exist; they are all vile."

Then followed arguments without beginning or end. Harking back to the old troubles, Monsieur de Mortsauf repeated the nonsense of the peasantry against the new system of farming. He declared that if he had had the management of Clochegourde he should be twice as rich as he now was. He shouted these complaints and insults, he swore, he sprang around the room knocking against the furniture and displacing it; then in the middle of a sentence he stopped short, complained that his very marrow was on fire, his brains melting away like his money, his wife had ruined him! The countess smiled and looked upward.

"Yes, Blanche," he cried, "you are my executioner; you are killing me; I am in your way; you want to get rid of me; you are monster of hypocrisy. She is smiling! Do you know why she smiles, Felix?"

I kept silence and looked down.

"That woman," he continued, answering his own question, "denies me all happiness; she is no more to me than she is to you, and yet she pretends to be my wife! She bears my name and fulfils none of the duties which all laws, human and divine, impose upon her; she lies to God and man. She obliges me to go long distances, hoping to wear me out and make me leave her to herself; I am displeasing to her, she hates me; she puts all her art into keeping me away from her; she has made me mad through the privations she imposes on me—for everything flies to my poor head; she is killing me by degrees, and she thinks herself a saint and takes the sacrament every month!"

The countess was weeping bitterly, humiliated by the degradation of the man, to whom she kept saying for all answer, "Monsieur! monsieur! monsieur!"

Though the count's words made me blush, more for him than for Henriette, they stirred my heart violently, for they appealed to the sense of chastity and delicacy which is indeed the very warp and woof of first love.

"She is virgin at my expense," cried the count.

At these words the countess cried out, "Monsieur!"

"What do you mean with your imperious 'Monsieur!'" he shouted. "Am I not your master? Must I teach you that I am?"

He came towards her, thrusting forward his white wolf's head, now hideous, for his yellow eyes had a savage expression which made him look like a wild beast rushing out of a wood. Henriette slid from her chair to the ground to avoid a blow, which however was not given; she lay at full length on the floor and lost consciousness, completely exhausted. The count was like a murderer who feels the blood of his victim spurting in his face; he stopped short, bewildered. I took the poor woman in my arms, and the count let me take her, as though he felt unworthy to touch her; but he went before me to open the door of her bedroom next the salon,—a sacred room I had never entered. I put the countess on her feet and held her for a moment in one arm, passing the other round her waist, while Monsieur de Mortsauf took the eider-down coverlet from the bed; then together we lifted her and laid her, still dressed, on the bed. When she came to herself she motioned to us to unfasten her belt. Monsieur de Mortsauf found a pair of scissors, and cut through it; I made her breathe salts, and she opened her eyes. The count left the room, more ashamed than sorry. Two hours passed in perfect silence. Henriette's hand lay in mine; she pressed it to mine, but could not speak. From time to time she opened her eyes as if to tell me by a look that she wished to be still and silent; then suddenly, for an instant, there seemed a change; she rose on her elbow and whispered, "Unhappy man!—ah! if you did but know —"

She fell back upon the pillow. The remembrance of her past sufferings, joined to the present shock, threw her again into the nervous convulsions I had just calmed by the magnetism of love,—a power then unknown to me, but which I used instinctively. I held her with gentle force, and she gave me a look which made me weep. When the nervous motions ceased I smoothed her disordered hair, the first and only time that I ever touched it; then I again took her hand and sat looking at the room, all brown and gray, at the bed with its simple chintz curtains, at the toilet table draped in a fashion now discarded, at the commonplace sofa with its quilted mattress. What poetry I could read in that room! What renunciations of luxury for herself; the only luxury being its spotless cleanliness. Sacred cell of a married nun, filled with holy resignation; its sole adornments were the crucifix of her bed, and above it the portrait of her aunt; then, on each side of the holy water basin, two drawings of the children made by herself, with locks of their hair when they were little. What a retreat for a woman whose appearance in the great world of fashion would have made the handsomest of her sex jealous! Such was the chamber where the daughter of an illustrious family wept out her days, sunken at this moment in anguish, and denying herself the love that might have comforted her. Hidden, irreparable woe! Tears of the victim for her slayer, tears of the slayer for his victim! When the children and waiting-woman came at length into the room I left it. The count was waiting for me; he seemed to seek me as a mediating power between himself and his wife. He caught my hands, exclaiming, "Stay, stay with us, Felix!"

"Unfortunately," I said, "Monsieur de Chessel has a party, and my absence would cause remark. But after dinner I will return."

He left the house when I did, and took me to the lower gate without speaking; then he accompanied me to Frapesle, seeming not to know what he was doing. At last I said to him, "For heaven's sake, Monsieur le comte, let her manage your affairs if it pleases her, and don't torment her."

"I have not long to live," he said gravely; "she will not suffer long through me; my head is giving way."

He left me in a spasm of involuntary self-pity. After dinner I returned for news of Madame de Mortsauf, who was already better. If such were the joys of marriage, if such scenes were frequent, how could she survive them long? What slow, unpunished murder was this? During that day I understood the tortures by which the count was wearing out his wife. Before what tribunal can we arraign such crimes? These thoughts stunned me; I could say nothing to Henriette by word of mouth, but I spent the night in writing to her. Of the three or four letters that I wrote I have kept only the beginning of one, with which I was not satisfied. Here it is, for though it seems to me to express nothing, and to speak too much of myself when I ought only to have thought of her, it will serve to show you the state my soul was in:—

To Madame de Mortsauf:

How many things I had to say to you when I reached the house! I thought of them on the way, but I forgot them in your presence. Yes, when I see you, dear Henriette, I find my thoughts no longer in keeping with the light from your soul which heightens your beauty; then, too, the happiness of being near you is so ineffable as to efface all other feelings. Each time we meet I am born into a broader life; I am like the traveller who climbs a rock and sees before him a new horizon. Each time you talk with me I add new treasures to my treasury. There lies, I think, the secret of long and inexhaustible affections. I can only speak to you of yourself when away from you. In your presence I am too dazzled to see, too happy to question my happiness, too full of you to be myself, too eloquent through you to speak, too eager in seizing the present moment to remember the past. You must think of this state of intoxication and forgive me its consequent mistakes.

When near you I can only feel. Yet, I have courage to say, dear Henriette, that never, in all the many joys you have given me, never did I taste such joy as filled my soul when, after that dreadful storm through which you struggled with superhuman courage, you came to yourself alone with me, in the twilight of your chamber where that unhappy scene had brought me. I alone know the light that shines from a woman when through the portals of death she re-enters life with the dawn of a rebirth tinting her brow. What harmonies were in your voice! How words, even your words, seemed paltry when the sound of that adored voice—in itself the echo of past pains mingled with divine consolations —blessed me with the gift of your first thought. I knew you were brilliant with all human splendor, but yesterday I found a new Henriette, who might be mine if God so willed; I beheld a spirit freed from the bodily trammels which repress the ardors of the soul. Ah! thou wert beautiful indeed in thy weakness, majestic in thy prostration. Yesterday I found something more beautiful than thy beauty, sweeter than thy voice; lights more sparkling than the   light of thine eyes, perfumes for which there are no words   —yesterday thy soul was visible and palpable. Would I could have   opened my heart and made thee live there! Yesterday I lost the respectful timidity with which thy presence inspires me; thy   weakness brought us nearer together. Then, when the crisis passed   and thou couldst bear our atmosphere once more, I knew what it was   to breathe in unison with thy breath. How many prayers rose up to   heaven in that moment! Since I did not die as I rushed through   space to ask of God that he would leave thee with me, no human creature can die of joy nor yet of sorrow. That moment has left   memories buried in my soul which never again will reappear upon   its surface and leave me tearless. Yes, the fears with which my   soul was tortured yesterday are incomparably greater than all   sorrows that the future can bring upon me, just as the joys which   thou hast given me, dear eternal thought of my life! will be   forever greater than any future joy God may be pleased to grant   me. Thou hast made me comprehend the love divine, that sure love,   sure in strength and in duration, that knows no doubt or jealousy.

Deepest melancholy gnawed my soul; the glimpse into that hidden life was agonizing to a young heart new to social emotions; it was an awful thing to find this abyss at the opening of life,—a bottomless abyss, a Dead Sea. This dreadful aggregation of misfortunes suggested many thoughts; at my first step into social life I found a standard of comparison by which all other events and circumstances must seem petty.

The next day when I entered the salon she was there alone. She looked at me for a moment, held out her hand, and said, "My friend is always too tender." Her eyes grew moist; she rose, and then she added, in a tone of desperate entreaty, "Never write thus to me again."

Monsieur de Mortsauf was very kind. The countess had recovered her courage and serenity; but her pallor betrayed the sufferings of the previous night, which were calmed, but not extinguished. That evening she said to me, as she paced among the autumn leaves which rustled beneath our footsteps, "Sorrow is infinite; joys are limited,"—words which betrayed her sufferings by the comparison she made with the fleeting delights of the previous week.

"Do not slander life," I said to her. "You are ignorant of love; love gives happiness which shines in heaven."

"Hush!" she said. "I wish to know nothing of it. The Icelander would die in Italy. I am calm and happy beside you; I can tell you all my thoughts; do not destroy my confidence. Why will you not combine the virtue of the priest with the charm of a free man."

"You make me drink the hemlock!" I cried, taking her hand and laying it on my heart, which was beating fast.

"Again!" she said, withdrawing her hand as if it pained her. "Are you determined to deny me the sad comfort of letting my wounds be stanched by a friendly hand? Do not add to my sufferings; you do not know them all; those that are hidden are the worst to bear. If you were a woman you would know the melancholy disgust that fills her soul when she sees herself the object of attentions which atone for nothing, but are thought to atone for all. For the next few days I shall be courted and caressed, that I may pardon the wrong that has been done. I could then obtain consent to any wish of mine, however unreasonable. I am humiliated by his humility, by caresses which will cease as soon as he imagines that I have forgotten that scene. To owe our master's good graces to his faults—"

"His crimes!" I interrupted quickly.

"Is not that a frightful condition of existence?" she continued, with a sad smile. "I cannot use this transient power. At such times I am like the knights who could not strike a fallen adversary. To see in the dust a man whom we ought to honor, to raise him only to enable him to deal other blows, to suffer from his degradation more than he suffers himself, to feel ourselves degraded if we profit by such influence for even a useful end, to spend our strength, to waste the vigor of our souls in struggles that have no grandeur, to have no power except for a moment when a fatal crisis comes—ah, better death! If I had no children I would let myself drift on the wretched current of this life; but if I lose my courage, what will become of them? I must live for them, however cruel this life may be. You talk to me of love. Ah! my dear friend, think of the hell into which I should fling myself if I gave that pitiless being, pitiless like all weak creatures, the right to despise me. The purity of my conduct is my strength. Virtue, dear friend, is holy water in which we gain fresh strength, from which we issue renewed in the love of God."

"Listen to me, dear Henriette; I have only another week to stay here, and I wish—"

"Ah, you mean to leave us!" she exclaimed.

"You must know what my father intends to do with me," I replied. "It is now three months—"

"I have not counted the days," she said, with momentary self-abandonment. Then she checked herself and cried, "Come, let us go to Frapesle."

She called the count and the children, sent for a shawl, and when all were ready she, usually so calm and slow in all her movements, became as active as a Parisian, and we started in a body to pay a visit at Frapesle which the countess did not owe. She forced herself to talk to Madame de Chessel, who was fortunately discursive in her answers. The count and Monsieur de Chessel conversed on business. I was afraid the former might boast of his carriage and horses; but he committed no such solecisms. His neighbor questioned him about his projected improvements at the Cassine and the Rhetoriere. I looked at the count, wondering if he would avoid a subject of conversation so full of painful memories to all, so cruelly mortifying to him. On the contrary, he explained how urgent a duty it was to better the agricultural condition of the canton, to build good houses and make the premises salubrious; in short, he glorified himself with his wife's ideas. I blushed as I looked at her. Such want of scruple in a man who, on certain occasions, could be scrupulous enough, this oblivion of the dreadful scene, this adoption of ideas against which he had fought so violently, this confident belief in himself, petrified me.

When Monsieur de Chessel said to him, "Do you expect to recover your outlay?"

"More than recover it!" he exclaimed, with a confident gesture.

Such contradictions can be explained only by the word "insanity." Henriette, celestial creature, was radiant. The count was appearing to be a man of intelligence, a good administrator, an excellent agriculturist; she played with her boy's curly head, joyous for him, happy for herself. What a comedy of pain, what mockery in this drama; I was horrified by it. Later in life, when the curtain of the world's stage was lifted before me, how many other Mortsaufs I saw without the loyalty and the religious faith of this man. What strange, relentless power is it that perpetually awards an angel to a madman; to a man of heart, of true poetic passion, a base woman; to the petty, grandeur; to this demented brain, a beautiful, sublime being; to Juana, Captain Diard, whose history at Bordeaux I have told you; to Madame de Beauseant, an Ajuda; to Madame d'Aiglemont, her husband; to the Marquis d'Espard, his wife! Long have I sought the meaning of this enigma. I have ransacked many mysteries, I have discovered the reason of many natural laws, the purport of some divine hieroglyphics; of the meaning of this dark secret I know nothing. I study it as I would the form of an Indian weapon, the symbolic construction of which is known only to the Brahmans. In this dread mystery the spirit of Evil is too visibly the master; I dare not lay the blame to God. Anguish irremediable, what power finds amusement in weaving you? Can Henriette and her mysterious philosopher be right? Does their mysticism contain the explanation of humanity?

The autumn leaves were falling during the last few days which I passed in the valley, days of lowering clouds, which do sometimes obscure the heaven of Touraine, so pure, so warm at that fine season. The evening before my departure Madame de Mortsauf took me to the terrace before dinner.

"My dear Felix," she said, after we had taken a turn in silence under the leafless trees, "you are about to enter the world, and I wish to go with you in thought. Those who have suffered much have lived and known much. Do not think that solitary souls know nothing of the world; on the contrary, they are able to judge it. Hear me: If I am to live in and for my friend I must do what I can for his heart and for his conscience. When the conflict rages it is hard to remember rules; therefore let me give you a few instructions, the warnings of a mother to her son. The day you leave us I shall give you a letter, a long letter, in which you will find my woman's thoughts on the world, on society, on men, on the right methods of meeting difficulty in this great clash of human interests. Promise me not to read this letter till you reach Paris. I ask it from a fanciful sentiment, one of those secrets of womanhood not impossible to understand, but which we grieve to find deciphered; leave me this covert way where as a woman I wish to walk alone."

"Yes, I promise it," I said, kissing her hand.

"Ah," she added, "I have one more promise to ask of you; but grant it first."

"Yes, yes!" I cried, thinking it was surely a promise of fidelity.

"It does not concern myself," she said smiling, with some bitterness. "Felix, do not gamble in any house, no matter whose it be; I except none."

"I will never play at all," I replied.

"Good," she said. "I have found a better use for your time than to waste it on cards. The end will be that where others must sooner or later be losers you will invariably win."

"How so?"

"The letter will tell you," she said, with a playful smile, which took from her advice the serious tone which might certainly have been that of a grandfather.

The countess talked to me for an hour, and proved the depth of her affection by the study she had made of my nature during the last three months. She penetrated the recesses of my heart, entering it with her own; the tones of her voice were changeful and convincing; the words fell from maternal lips, showing by their tone as well as by their meaning how many ties already bound us to each other.

"If you knew," she said in conclusion, "with what anxiety I shall follow your course, what joy I shall feel if you walk straight, what tears I must shed if you strike against the angles! Believe that my affection has no equal; it is involuntary and yet deliberate. Ah, I would that I might see you happy, powerful, respected,—you who are to me a living dream."

She made me weep, so tender and so terrible was she. Her feelings came boldly to the surface, yet they were too pure to give the slightest hope even to a young man thirsting for pleasure. Ignoring my tortured flesh, she shed the rays, undeviating, incorruptible, of the divine love, which satisfies the soul only. She rose to heights whither the prismatic pinions of a love like mine were powerless to bear me. To reach her a man must needs have won the white wings of the seraphim.

"In all that happens to me I will ask myself," I said, "'What would my Henriette say?'"

"Yes, I will be the star and the sanctuary both," she said, alluding to the dreams of my childhood.

"You are my light and my religion," I cried; "you shall be my all."

"No," she answered; "I can never be the source of your pleasures."

She sighed; the smile of secret pain was on her lips, the smile of the slave who momentarily revolts. From that day forth she was to me, not merely my beloved, but my only love; she was not IN my heart as a woman who takes a place, who makes it hers by devotion or by excess of pleasure given; but she was my heart itself,—it was all hers, a something necessary to the play of my muscles. She became to me as Beatrice to the Florentine, as the spotless Laura to the Venetian, the mother of great thoughts, the secret cause of resolutions which saved me, the support of my future, the light shining in the darkness like a lily in a wood. Yes, she inspired those high resolves which pass through flames, which save the thing in peril; she gave me a constancy like Coligny's to vanquish conquerors, to rise above defeat, to weary the strongest wrestler.

The next day, having breakfasted at Frapesle and bade adieu to my kind hosts, I went to Clochegourde. Monsieur and Madame de Mortsauf had arranged to drive with me to Tours, whence I was to start the same night for Paris. During the drive the countess was silent; she pretended at first to have a headache; then she blushed at the falsehood, and expiated it by saying that she could not see me go without regret. The count invited me to stay with them whenever, in the absence of the Chessels, I might long to see the valley of the Indre once more. We parted heroically, without apparent tears, but Jacques, who like other delicate children was quickly touched, began to cry, while Madeleine, already a woman, pressed her mother's hand.

"Dear little one!" said the countess, kissing Jacques passionately.

When I was alone at Tours after dinner a wild, inexplicable desire known only to young blood possessed me. I hired a horse and rode from Tours to Pont-de-Ruan in an hour and a quarter. There, ashamed of my folly, I dismounted, and went on foot along the road, stepping cautiously like a spy till I reached the terrace. The countess was not there, and I imagined her ill; I had kept the key of the little gate, by which I now entered; she was coming down the steps of the portico with the two children to breathe in sadly and slowly the tender melancholy of the landscape, bathed at that moment in the setting sun.

"Mother, here is Felix," said Madeleine.

"Yes," I whispered; "it is I. I asked myself why I should stay at Tours while I still could see you; why not indulge a desire that in a few days more I could not gratify."

"He won't leave us again, mother," cried Jacques, jumping round me.

"Hush!" said Madeleine; "if you make such a noise the general will come."

"It is not right," she said. "What folly!"

The tears in her voice were the payment of what must be called a usurious speculation of love.

"I had forgotten to return this key," I said smiling.

"Then you will never return," she said.

"Can we ever be really parted?" I asked, with a look which made her drop her eyelids for all answer.

I left her after a few moments passed in that happy stupor of the spirit where exaltation ends and ecstasy begins. I went with lagging step, looking back at every minute. When, from the summit of the hill, I saw the valley for the last time I was struck with the contrast it presented to what it was when I first came there. Then it was verdant, then it glowed, glowed and blossomed like my hopes and my desires. Initiated now into the gloomy secrets of a family, sharing the anguish of a Christian Niobe, sad with her sadness, my soul darkened, I saw the valley in the tone of my own thoughts. The fields were bare, the leaves of the poplars falling, the few that remained were rusty, the vine-stalks were burned, the tops of the trees were tan-colored, like the robes in which royalty once clothed itself as if to hide the purple of its power beneath the brown of grief. Still in harmony with my thoughts, the valley, where the yellow rays of the setting sun were coldly dying, seemed to me a living image of my heart.

To leave a beloved woman is terrible or natural, according as the mind takes it. For my part, I found myself suddenly in a strange land of which I knew not the language. I was unable to lay hold of things to which my soul no longer felt attachment. Then it was that the height and the breadth of my love came before me; my Henriette rose in all her majesty in this desert where I existed only through thoughts of her. That form so worshipped made me vow to keep myself spotless before my soul's divinity, to wear ideally the white robe of the Levite, like Petrarch, who never entered Laura's presence unless clothed in white. With what impatience I awaited the first night of my return to my father's roof, when I could read the letter which I felt of during the journey as a miser fingers the bank-bills he carries about him. During the night I kissed the paper on which my Henriette had manifested her will; I sought to gather the mysterious emanations of her hand, to recover the intonations of her voice in the hush of my being. Since then I have never read her letters except as I read that first letter; in bed, amid total silence. I cannot understand how the letters of our beloved can be read in any other way; yet there are men, unworthy to be loved, who read such letters in the turmoil of the day, laying them aside and taking them up again with odious composure.

Here, Natalie, is the voice which echoed through the silence of that night. Behold the noble figure which stood before me and pointed to the right path among the cross-ways at which I stood.

To Monsieur le Vicomte Felix de Vandenesse:

What happiness for me, dear friend, to gather the scattered   elements of my experience that I may arm you against the dangers   of the world, through which I pray that you pass scatheless. I   have felt the highest pleasures of maternal love as night after   night I have thought of these things. While writing this letter,   sentence by sentence, projecting my thoughts into the life you are   about to lead, I went often to my window. Looking at the towers of   Frapesle, visible in the moonlight, I said to myself, "He sleeps,   I wake for him." Delightful feelings! which recall the happiest of   my life, when I watched Jacques sleeping in his cradle and waited   till he wakened, to feed him with my milk. You are the man-child   whose soul must now be strengthened by precepts never taught in   schools, but which we women have the privilege of inculcating.   These precepts will influence your success; they prepare the way   for it, they will secure it. Am I not exercising a spiritual motherhood in giving you a standard by which to judge the actions   of your life; a motherhood comprehended, is it not, by the child?   Dear Felix, let me, even though I may make a few mistakes, let me   give to our friendship a proof of the disinterestedness which   sanctifies it.

In yielding you to the world I am renouncing you; but I love you   too well not to sacrifice my happiness to your welfare. For the   last four months you have made me reflect deeply on the laws and   customs which regulate our epoch. The conversations I have had   with my aunt, well-known to you who have replaced her, the events   of Monsieur de Mortsauf's life, which he has told me, the tales related by my father, to whom society and the court are familiar   in their greatest as well as in their smallest aspects, all these   have risen in my memory for the benefit of my adopted child at the   moment when he is about to be launched, well-nigh alone, among   men; about to act without adviser in a world where many are wrecked by their own best qualities thoughtlessly displayed, while   others succeed through a judicious use of their worst.

I ask you to ponder this statement of my opinion of society as a   whole; it is concise, for to you a few words are sufficient.

I do not know whether societies are of divine origin or whether they were invented by man. I am equally ignorant of the direction in which they tend. What I do know certainly is the fact of their existence. No sooner therefore do you enter society, instead of living a life apart, than you are bound to consider its conditions binding; a contract is signed between you. Does society in these days gain more from a man than it returns to him? I think so; but as to whether the individual man finds more cost than profit, or buys too dear the advantages he obtains, concerns the legislator only; I have nothing to say to that. In my judgment you are bound to obey in all things the general law, without discussion, whether it injures or benefits your personal interests. This principle may seem to you a very simple one, but it is difficult of application; it is like sap, which must infiltrate the smallest of the capillary tubes to stir the tree, renew its verdure, develop its flowers, and ripen fruit. Dear, the laws of society are not all written in a book; manners and customs create laws, the more important of which are often the least known. Believe me, there are neither teachers, nor schools, nor text-books for the laws that are now to regulate your actions, your language, your visible life, the manner of your presentation to the world, and your quest of fortune. Neglect those secret laws or fail to understand them, and you stay at the foot of the social system instead of looking down upon it. Even though this letter may seem to you diffuse, telling you much that you have already thought, let me confide to you a woman's ethics.

To explain society on the theory of individual happiness adroitly won at the cost of the greater number is a monstrous doctrine, which in its strict application leads men to believe that all they can secretly lay hold of before the law or society or other individuals condemn it as a wrong is honestly and fairly theirs. Once admit that claim and the clever thief goes free; the woman who violates her marriage vow without the knowledge of the world is virtuous and happy; kill a man, leaving no proof for justice, and if, like Macbeth, you win a crown you have done wisely; your selfish interests become the higher law; the only question then is how to evade, without witnesses or proof, the obstacles which law and morality place between you and your self-indulgence. To those who hold this view of society, the problem of making their fortune, my dear friend, resolves itself into playing a game where the stakes are millions or the galleys, political triumphs or dishonor. Still, the green cloth is not long enough for all the players, and a certain kind of genius is required to play the game. I say nothing of religious beliefs, nor yet of feelings; what concerns us now is the running-gear of the great machine of gold and iron, and its practical results with which men's lives are occupied. Dear child of my heart, if you share my horror at this criminal theory of the world, society will present to your mind, as it does to all sane minds, the opposite theory of duty. Yes, you will see that man owes himself to man in a thousand differing ways. To my mind, the duke and peer owe far more to the workman and the pauper than the pauper and the workman owe to the duke. The obligations of duty enlarge in proportion to the benefits which society bestows on men; in accordance with the maxim, as true in social politics as in business, that the burden of care and vigilance is everywhere in proportion to profits. Each man pays his debt in his own way. When our poor toiler at the Rhetoriere comes home weary with his day's work has he not done his duty? Assuredly he has done it better than many in the ranks above him.

If you take this view of society, in which you are about to seek a place in keeping with your intellect and your faculties, you must set before you as a generating principle and mainspring, this maxim: never permit yourself to act against either your own conscience or the public conscience. Though my entreaty may seem to you superfluous, yet I entreat, yes, your Henriette implores you to ponder the meaning of that rule. It seems simple but, dear, it means that integrity, loyalty, honor, and courtesy are the safest and surest instruments for your success. In this selfish world you will find many to tell you that a man cannot make his way by sentiments, that too much respect for moral considerations will hinder his advance. It is not so; you will see men ill-trained, ill-taught, incapable of measuring the future, who are rough to a child, rude to an old woman, unwilling to be irked by some worthy old man on the ground that they can do nothing for him; later, you will find the same men caught by the thorns which they might have rendered pointless, and missing their triumph for some trivial reason; whereas the man who is early trained to a sense of duty does not meet the same obstacles; he may attain success less rapidly, but when attained it is solid and does not crumble like that of others.

When I show you that the application of this doctrine demands in the first place a mastery of the science of manners, you may think my jurisprudence has a flavor of the court and of the training I received as a Lenoncourt. My dear friend, I do attach great importance to that training, trifling as it seems. You will find that the habits of the great world are as important to you as the wide and varied knowledge that you possess. Often they take the place of such knowledge; for some really ignorant men, born with natural gifts and accustomed to give connection to their ideas, have been known to attain a grandeur never reached by others far more worthy of it. I have studied you thoroughly, Felix, wishing to know if your education, derived wholly from schools, has injured your nature. God knows the joy with which I find you fit for that further education of which I speak.

The manners of many who are brought up in the traditions of the great world are purely external; true politeness, perfect manners, come from the heart, and from a deep sense of personal dignity. This is why some men of noble birth are, in spite of their training, ill-mannered, while others, among the middle classes, have instinctive good taste and only need a few lessons to give them excellent manners without any signs of awkward imitation. Believe a poor woman who no longer leaves her valley when she tells you that this dignity of tone, this courteous simplicity in words, in gesture, in bearing, and even in the character of the home, is a living and material poem, the charm of which is irresistible; imagine therefore what it is when it takes its inspiration from the heart. Politeness, dear, consists in seeming to forget ourselves for others; with many it is social cant, laid aside when personal self-interest shows its cloven-foot; a noble then becomes ignoble. But— and this is what I want you to practise, Felix—true politeness involves a Christian principle; it is the flower of Love, it requires that we forget ourselves   really. In memory of your Henriette, for her sake, be not a   fountain without water, have the essence and the form of true   courtesy. Never fear to be the dupe and victim of this social   virtue; you will some day gather the fruit of seeds scattered   apparently to the winds.

My father used to say that one of the great offences of sham   politeness was the neglect of promises. When anything is demanded   of you that you cannot do, refuse positively and leave no   loopholes for false hopes; on the other hand, grant at once   whatever you are willing to bestow. Your prompt refusal will make you friends as well as your prompt benefit, and your character   will stand the higher; for it is hard to say whether a promise   forgotten, a hope deceived does not make us more enemies than a   favor granted brings us friends.

Dear friend, there are certain little matters on which I may   dwell, for I know them, and it comes within my province to impart   them. Be not too confiding, nor frivolous, nor over enthusiastic,   —three rocks on which youth often strikes. Too confiding a nature   loses respect, frivolity brings contempt, and others take   advantage of excessive enthusiasm. In the first place, Felix, you   will never have more than two or three friends in the course of   your life. Your entire confidence is their right; to give it to   many is to betray your real friends. If you are more intimate with   some men than with others keep guard over yourself; be as cautious   as though you knew they would one day be your rivals, or your   enemies; the chances and changes of life require this. Maintain an   attitude which is neither cold nor hot; find the medium point at   which a man can safely hold intercourse with others without   compromising himself. Yes, believe me, the honest man is as far   from the base cowardice of Philinte as he is from the harsh virtue   of Alceste. The genius of the poet is displayed in the mind of   this true medium; certainly all minds do enjoy more the ridicule   of virtue than the sovereign contempt of easy-going selfishness   which underlies that picture of it; but all, nevertheless, are prompted to keep themselves from either extreme.

As to frivolity, if it causes fools to proclaim you a charming   man, others who are accustomed to judge of men's capacities and   fathom character, will winnow out your tare and bring you to   disrepute, for frivolity is the resource of weak natures, and   weakness is soon appraised in a society which regards its members   as nothing more than organs—and perhaps justly, for nature   herself puts to death imperfect beings. A woman's protecting   instincts may be roused by the pleasure she feels in supporting   the weak against the strong, and in leading the intelligence of   the heart to victory over the brutality of matter; but society,   less a mother than a stepmother, adores only the children who   flatter her vanity.

As to ardent enthusiasm, that first sublime mistake of youth,   which finds true happiness in using its powers, and begins by   being its own dupe before it is the dupe of others, keep it within   the region of the heart's communion, keep it for woman and for   God. Do not hawk its treasures in the bazaars of society or of politics, where trumpery will be offered in exchange for them.   Believe the voice which commands you to be noble in all things   when it also prays you not to expend your forces uselessly.   Unhappily, men will rate you according to your usefulness, and not according to your worth. To use an image which I think will strike your poetic mind, let a cipher be what it may, immeasurable in size, written in gold, or written in pencil, it is only a cipher after all. A man of our times has said, "No zeal, above all, no zeal!" The lesson may be sad, but it is true, and it saves the soul from wasting its bloom. Hide your pure sentiments, or put them in regions inaccessible, where their blossoms may be passionately admired, where the artist may dream amorously of his master-piece. But duties, my friend, are not sentiments. To do what we ought is by no means to do what we like. A man who would give his life enthusiastically for a woman must be ready to die coldly for his country.

One of the most important rules in the science of manners is that of almost absolute silence about ourselves. Play a little comedy for your own instruction; talk of yourself to acquaintances, tell them about your sufferings, your pleasures, your business, and you will see how indifference succeeds pretended interest; then annoyance follows, and if the mistress of the house does not find some civil way of stopping you the company will disappear under various pretexts adroitly seized. Would you, on the other hand, gather sympathies about you and be spoken of as amiable and witty, and a true friend? talk to others of themselves, find a way to bring them forward, and brows will clear, lips will smile, and after you leave the room all present will praise you. Your conscience and the voice of your own heart will show you the line where the cowardice of flattery begins and the courtesy of intercourse ceases.

One word more about a young man's demeanor in public. My dear friend, youth is always inclined to a rapidity of judgment which does it honor, but also injury. This was why the old system of education obliged young people to keep silence and study life in a probationary period beside their elders. Formerly, as you know, nobility, like art, had its apprentices, its pages, devoted body and soul to the masters who maintained them. To-day youth is forced in a hot-house; it is trained to judge of thoughts, actions, and writings with biting severity; it slashes with a blade that has not been fleshed. Do not make this mistake. Such judgments will seem like censures to many about you, who would sooner pardon an open rebuke than a secret wound. Young people are pitiless because they know nothing of life and its difficulties. The old critic is kind and considerate, the young critic is implacable; the one knows nothing, the other knows all. Moreover, at the bottom of all human actions there is a labyrinth of determining reasons on which God reserves for himself the final judgment. Be severe therefore to none but yourself.

Your future is before you; but no one in the world can make his way unaided. Therefore, make use of my father's house; its doors are open to you; the connections that you will create for yourself under his roof will serve you in a hundred ways. But do not yield an inch of ground to my mother; she will crush any one who gives up to her, but she will admire the courage of whoever resists her. She is like iron, which if beaten, can be fused with iron, but when cold will break everything less hard than itself. Cultivate my mother; for if she thinks well of you she will introduce you into certain houses where you can acquire the fatal science of the world, the art of listening, speaking, answering, presenting yourself to the company and taking leave of it; the precise use of language, the something—how shall I explain it?—which is no more superiority than the coat is the man, but without which the highest talent in the world will never be admitted within those portals.

I know you well enough to be quite sure I indulge no illusion when I imagine that I see you as I wish you to be; simple in manners, gentle in tone, proud without conceit, respectful to the old, courteous without servility, above all, discreet. Use your wit but never display it for the amusement of others; for be sure that if your brilliancy annoys an inferior man, he will retire from the field and say of you in a tone of contempt, "He is very amusing." Let your superiority be leonine. Moreover, do not be always seeking to please others. I advise a certain coldness in your relations with men, which may even amount to indifference; this will not anger others, for all persons esteem those who slight them; and it will win you the favor of women, who will respect you for the little consequence that you attach to men. Never remain in company with those who have lost their reputation, even though they may not have deserved to do so; for society holds us responsible for our friendships as well as for our enmities. In this matter let your judgments be slowly and maturely weighed, but see that they are irrevocable. When the men whom you have repulsed justify the repulsion, your esteem and regard will be all the more sought after; you have inspired the tacit respect which raises a man among his peers. I behold you now armed with a youth that pleases, grace which attracts, and wisdom with which to preserve your conquests. All that I have now told you can be summed up in two words, two old-fashioned words, "Noblesse oblige."

Now apply these precepts to the management of life. You will hear many persons say that strategy is the chief element of success; that the best way to press through the crowd is to set some men against other men and so take their places. That was a good system for the Middle Ages, when princes had to destroy their rivals by pitting one against the other; but in these days, all things being done in open day, I am afraid it would do you ill-service. No, you must meet your competitors face to face, be they loyal and true men, or traitorous enemies whose weapons are calumny, evil-speaking, and fraud. But remember this, you have no more powerful auxiliaries than these men themselves; they are their own enemies; fight them with honest weapons, and sooner or later they are condemned. As to the first of them, loyal men and true, your straightforwardness will obtain their respect, and the differences between you once settled (for all things can be settled), these men will serve you. Do not be afraid of making enemies; woe to him who has none in the world you are about to enter; but try to give no handle for ridicule or disparagement. I say _

*try_*

, for in Paris a man cannot always belong solely to himself; he is sometimes at the mercy of circumstances; you will not always be able to avoid the mud in the gutter nor the tile that falls from the roof. The moral world has gutters where persons of no reputation endeavor to splash the mud in which they live upon men of honor. But you can always compel respect by showing that you are, under all circumstances, immovable in your principles. In the conflict of opinions, in the midst of quarrels and cross-purposes, go straight to the point, keep resolutely to the question; never fight except for the essential thing, and put your whole strength into that. You know how Monsieur de Mortsauf hates Napoleon, how he curses him and pursues him as justice does a criminal; demanding punishment day and night for the death of the Duc d'Enghien, the only death, the only misfortune, that ever brought the tears to his eyes; well, he nevertheless admired him as the greatest of captains, and has often explained to me his strategy. May not the same tactics be applied to the war of human interests; they would economize time as heretofore they economized men and space. Think this over, for as a woman I am liable to be mistaken on such points which my sex judges only by instinct and sentiment. One point, however, I may insist on; all trickery, all deception, is certain to be discovered and to result in doing harm; whereas every situation presents less danger if a man plants himself firmly on his own truthfulness. If I may cite my own case, I can tell you that, obliged as I am by Monsieur de Mortsauf's condition to avoid litigation and to bring to an immediate settlement all difficulties which arise in the management of Clochegourde, and which would otherwise cause him an excitement under which his mind would succumb, I have invariably settled matters promptly by taking hold of the knot of the difficulty and saying to our opponents: "We will either untie it or cut it!"

It will often happen that you do a service to others and find yourself ill-rewarded; I beg you not to imitate those who complain of men and declare them to be all ungrateful. That is putting themselves on a pedestal indeed! and surely it is somewhat silly to admit their lack of knowledge of the world. But you, I trust, will not do good as a usurer lends his money; you will do it—will you not?—for good's sake. Noblesse oblige. Nevertheless, do not bestow such services as to force others to ingratitude, for if you do, they will become your most implacable enemies; obligations sometimes lead to despair, like the despair of ruin itself, which is capable of very desperate efforts. As for yourself, accept as little as you can from others. Be no man's vassal; and bring yourself out of your own difficulties.

You see, dear friend, I am advising you only on the lesser points of life. In the world of politics things wear a different aspect; the rules which are to guide your individual steps give way before the national interests. If you reach that sphere where great men revolve you will be, like God himself, the sole arbiter of your determinations. You will no longer be a man, but law, the living law; no longer an individual, you are then the Nation incarnate. But remember this, though you judge, you will yourself be judged; hereafter you will be summoned before the ages, and you know history well enough to be fully informed as to what deeds and what sentiments have led to true grandeur.

I now come to a serious matter, your conduct towards women. Wherever you visit make it a principle not to fritter yourself away in a petty round of gallantry. A man of the last century who had great social success never paid attention to more than one woman of an evening, choosing the one who seemed the most neglected. That man, my dear child, controlled his epoch. He wisely reckoned that by a given time all women would speak well of him. Many young men waste their most precious possession, namely, the time necessary to create connections which contribute more than all else to social success. Your springtime is short, endeavor to make the most of it. Cultivate influential women. Influential women are old women; they will teach you the intermarriages and the secrets of all the families of the great world; they will show you the cross-roads which will bring you soonest to your goal. They will be fond of you. The bestowal of protection is their last form of love—when they are not devout. They will do you innumerable good services; sing your praises and make you desirable to society. Avoid young women. Do not think I say this from personal self-interest. The woman of fifty will do all for you, the woman of twenty will do nothing; she wants your whole life while the other asks only a few attentions. Laugh with the young women, meet them for pastime merely; they are incapable of serious thought. Young women, dear friend, are selfish, vain, petty, ignorant of true friendship; they love no one but themselves; they would sacrifice you to an evening's success. Besides, they all want absolute devotion, and your present situation requires that devotion be shown to you; two irreconcilable needs! None of these young women would enter into your interests; they would think of themselves and not of you; they would injure you more by their emptiness and frivolity than they could serve you by their love; they will waste your time unscrupulously, hinder your advance to fortune, and end by destroying your future with the best grace possible. If you complain, the silliest of them will make you think that her glove is more precious than fortune, and that nothing is so glorious as to be her slave. They will all tell you that they bestow happiness, and thus lull you to forget your nobler destiny. Believe me, the happiness they give is transitory; your great career will endure. You know not with what perfidious cleverness they contrive to satisfy their caprices, nor the art with which they will convert your passing fancy into a love which ought to be eternal. The day when they abandon you they will tell you that the words, "I no longer love you," are a full justification of their conduct, just as the words, "I love," justified their winning you; they will declare that love is involuntary and not to be coerced. Absurd! Believe me, dear, true love is eternal, infinite, always like unto itself; it is equable, pure, without violent demonstration; white hair often covers the head but the heart that holds it is ever young. No such love is found among the women of the world; all are playing comedy; this one will interest you by her misfortunes; she seems the gentlest and least exacting of her sex, but when once she is necessary to you, you will feel the tyranny of weakness and will do her will; you may wish to be a diplomat, to go and come, and study men and interests,—no, you must stay in Paris, or at her country-place, sewn to her petticoat, and the more devotion you show the more ungrateful and exacting she will be. Another will attract you by her submissiveness; she will be your attendant, follow you romantically about, compromise herself to keep you, and be the millstone about your neck. You will drown yourself some day, but the woman will come to the surface.

The least manoeuvring of these women of the world have many nets. The silliest triumph because too foolish to excite distrust. The one to be feared least may be the woman of gallantry whom you love without exactly knowing why; she will leave you for no motive and go back to you out of vanity. All these women will injure you, either in the present or the future. Every young woman who enters society and lives a life of pleasure and of gratified vanity is semi-corrupt and will corrupt you. Among them you will not find the chaste and tranquil being in whom you may forever reign. Ah! she who loves you will love solitude; the festivals of her heart will be your glances; she will live upon your words. May she be all the world to you, for you will be all in all to her. Love her well; give her neither griefs nor rivals; do not rouse her jealousy. To be loved, dear, to be comprehended, is the greatest of all joys; I pray that you may taste it! But run no risk of injuring the flower of your soul; be sure, be very sure of the heart in which you place your affections. That woman will never be her own self; she will never think of herself, but of you. She will never oppose you, she will have no interests of her own; for you she will see a danger where you can see none and where she would be oblivious of her own. If she suffers it will be in silence; she will have no personal vanity, but deep reverence for whatever in her has won your love. Respond to such a love by surpassing it. If you are fortunate enough to find that which I, your poor friend, must ever be without, I mean a love mutually inspired, mutually felt, remember that in a valley lives a mother whose heart is so filled with the feelings you have put there that you can never sound its depths. Yes, I bear you an affection which you will never know to its full extent; before it could show itself for what it is you would have to lose your mind and intellect, and then you would be unable to comprehend the length and breadth of my devotion.

Shall I be misunderstood in bidding you avoid young women (all more or less artful, satirical, vain, frivolous, and extravagant) and attach yourself to influential women, to those imposing dowagers full of excellent good-sense, like my aunt, who will help your career, defend you from attacks, and say for you the things that you cannot say for yourself? Am I not, on the contrary, generous in bidding you reserve your love for the coming angel with the guileless heart? If the motto Noblesse oblige sums up the advice I gave you just now, my further advice on your relations to women is based upon that other motto of chivalry, "Serve all, love one!"

Your educational knowledge is immense; your heart, saved by early suffering, is without a stain; all is noble, all is well with you. Now, Felix, WILL! Your future lies in that one word, that word of great men. My child, you will obey your Henriette, will you not? You will permit her to tell you from time to time the thoughts that are in her mind of you and of your relations to the world? I have an eye in my soul which sees the future for you as for my children; suffer me to use that faculty for your benefit; it is a faculty, a mysterious gift bestowed by my lonely life; far from its growing weaker, I find it strengthened and exalted by solitude and silence.

I ask you in return to bestow a happiness on me; I desire to see   you becoming more and more important among men, without one single   success that shall bring a line of shame upon my brow; I desire   that you may quickly bring your fortunes to the level of your   noble name, and be able to tell me I have contributed to your   advancement by something better than a wish. This secret   co-operation in your future is the only pleasure I can allow   myself. For it, I will wait and hope.

I do not say farewell. We are separated; you cannot put my hand to   your lips, but you must surely know the place you hold in the   heart of your
Henriette.

As I read this letter I felt the maternal heart beating beneath my fingers which held the paper while I was still cold from the harsh greeting of my own mother. I understood why the countess had forbidden me to open it in Touraine; no doubt she feared that I would fall at her feet and wet them with my tears.

I now made the acquaintance of my brother Charles, who up to this time had been a stranger to me. But in all our intercourse he showed a haughtiness which kept us apart and prevented brotherly affection. Kindly feelings depend on similarity of soul, and there was no point of touch between us. He preached to me dogmatically those social trifles which head or heart can see without instruction; he seemed to mistrust me. If I had not had the inward support of my great love he would have made me awkward and stupid by affecting to believe that I knew nothing of life. He presented me in society under the expectation that my dulness would be a foil to his qualities. Had I not remembered the sorrows of my childhood I might have taken his protecting vanity for brotherly affection; but inward solitude produces the same effects as outward solitude; silence within our souls enables us to hear the faintest sound; the habit of taking refuge within ourselves develops a perception which discerns every quality of the affections about us. Before I knew Madame de Mortsauf a hard look grieved me, a rough word wounded me to the heart; I bewailed these things without as yet knowing anything of a life of tenderness; whereas now, since my return from Clochegourde, I could make comparisons which perfected my instinctive perceptions. All deductions derived only from sufferings endured are incomplete. Happiness has a light to cast. I now allowed myself the more willingly to be kept under the heel of primogeniture because I was not my brother's dupe.

I always went alone to the Duchesse de Lenoncourt's, where Henriette's name was never mentioned; no one, except the good old duke, who was simplicity itself, ever spoke of her to me; but by the way he welcomed me I guessed that his daughter had privately commended me to his care. At the moment when I was beginning to overcome the foolish wonder and shyness which besets a young man at his first entrance into the great world, and to realize the pleasures it could give through the resources it offers to ambition, just, too, as I was beginning to make use of Henriette's maxims, admiring their wisdom, the events of the 20th of March took place.

My brother followed the court to Ghent; I, by Henriette's advice (for I kept up a correspondence with her, active on my side only), went there also with the Duc de Lenoncourt. The natural kindness of the old duke turned to a hearty and sincere protection as soon as he saw me attached, body and soul, to the Bourbons. He himself presented me to his Majesty. Courtiers are not numerous when misfortunes are rife; but youth is gifted with ingenuous admiration and uncalculating fidelity. The king had the faculty of judging men; a devotion which might have passed unobserved in Paris counted for much at Ghent, and I had the happiness of pleasing Louis XVIII.

A letter from Madame de Mortsauf to her father, brought with despatches by an emissary of the Vendeens, enclosed a note to me by which I learned that Jacques was ill. Monsieur de Mortsauf, in despair at his son's ill-health, and also at the news of a second emigration, added a few words which enabled me to guess the situation of my dear one. Worried by him, no doubt, when she passed all her time at Jacques' bedside, allowed no rest either day or night, superior to annoyance, yet unable always to control herself when her whole soul was given to the care of her child, Henriette needed the support of a friendship which might lighten the burden of her life, were it only by diverting her husband's mind. Though I was now most impatient to rival the career of my brother, who had lately been sent to the Congress of Vienna, and was anxious at any risk to justify Henriette's appeal and become a man myself, freed from all vassalage, nevertheless my ambition, my desire for independence, the great interest I had in not leaving the king, all were of no account before the vision of Madame de Mortsauf's sad face. I resolved to leave the court at Ghent and serve my true sovereign. God rewarded me. The emissary sent by the Vendeens was unable to return. The king wanted a messenger who would faithfully carry back his instructions. The Duc de Lenoncourt knew that the king would never forget the man who undertook so perilous an enterprise; he asked for the mission without consulting me, and I gladly accepted it, happy indeed to be able to return to Clochegourde employed in the good cause.

After an audience with the king I returned to France, where, both in Paris and in Vendee, I was fortunate enough to carry out his Majesty's instructions. Towards the end of May, being tracked by the Bonapartist authorities to whom I was denounced, I was obliged to fly from place to place in the character of a man endeavoring to get back to his estate. I went on foot from park to park, from wood to wood, across the whole of upper Vendee, the Bocage and Poitou, changing my direction as danger threatened.

I reached Saumur, from Saumur I went to Chinon, and from Chinon I reached, in a single night, the woods of Nueil, where I met the count on horseback; he took me up behind him and we reached Clochegourde without passing any one who recognized me.

"Jacques is better," were the first words he said to me.

I explained to him my position of diplomatic postman, hunted like a wild beast, and the brave gentleman in his quality of royalist claimed the danger over Chessel of receiving me. As we came in sight of Clochegourde the past eight months rolled away like a dream. When we entered the salon the count said: "Guess whom I bring you?—Felix!"

"Is it possible!" she said, with pendant arms and a bewildered face.

I showed myself and we both remained motionless; she in her armchair, I on the threshold of the door; looking at each other with that hunger of the soul which endeavors to make up in a single glance for the lost months. Then, recovering from a surprise which left her heart unveiled, she rose and I went up to her.

"I have prayed for your safety," she said, giving me her hand to kiss.

She asked news of her father; then she guessed my weariness and went to prepare my room, while the count gave me something to eat, for I was dying of hunger. My room was the one above hers, her aunt's room; she requested the count to take me there, after setting her foot on the first step of the staircase, deliberating no doubt whether to accompany me; I turned my head, she blushed, bade me sleep well, and went away. When I came down to dinner I heard for the first time of the disasters at Waterloo, the flight of Napoleon, the march of the Allies to Paris, and the probable return of the Bourbons. These events were all in all to the count; to us they were nothing. What think you was the great event I was to learn, after kissing the children?—for I will not dwell on the alarm I felt at seeing the countess pale and shrunken; I knew the injury I might do by showing it and was careful to express only joy at seeing her. But the great event for us was told in the words, "You shall have ice to-day!" She had often fretted the year before that the water was not cold enough for me, who, never drinking anything else, liked it iced. God knows how many entreaties it had cost her to get an ice house built. You know better than any one that a word, a look, an inflection of the voice, a trifling attention, suffices for love; love's noblest privilege is to prove itself by love. Well, her words, her look, her pleasure, showed me her feelings, as I had formerly shown her mine by that first game of backgammon. These ingenuous proofs of her affection were many; on the seventh day after my arrival she recovered her freshness, she sparkled with health and youth and happiness; my lily expanded in beauty just as the treasures of my heart increased. Only in petty minds or in common hearts can absence lessen love or efface the features or diminish the beauty of our dear one. To ardent imaginations, to all beings through whose veins enthusiasm passes like a crimson tide, and in whom passion takes the form of constancy, absence has the same effect as the sufferings of the early Christians, which strengthened their faith and made God visible to them. In hearts that abound in love are there not incessant longings for a desired object, to which the glowing fire of our dreams gives higher value and a deeper tint? Are we not conscious of instigations which give to the beloved features the beauty of the ideal by inspiring them with thought? The past, dwelt on in all its details becomes magnified; the future teems with hope. When two hearts filled with these electric clouds meet each other, their interview is like the welcome storm which revives the earth and stimulates it with the swift lightnings of the thunderbolt. How many tender pleasures came to me when I found these thoughts and these sensations reciprocal! With what glad eyes I followed the development of happiness in Henriette! A woman who renews her life from that of her beloved gives, perhaps, a greater proof of feeling than she who dies killed by a doubt, withered on her stock for want of sap; I know not which of the two is the more touching.

The revival of Madame de Mortsauf was wholly natural, like the effects of the month of May upon the meadows, or those of the sun and of the brook upon the drooping flowers. Henriette, like our dear valley of love, had had her winter; she revived like the valley in the springtime. Before dinner we went down to the beloved terrace. There, with one hand stroking the head of her son, who walked feebly beside her, silent, as though he were breeding an illness, she told me of her nights beside his pillow.

For three months, she said, she had lived wholly within herself, inhabiting, as it were, a dark palace; afraid to enter sumptuous rooms where the light shone, where festivals were given, to her denied, at the door of which she stood, one glance turned upon her child, another to a dim and distant figure; one ear listening for moans, another for a voice. She told me poems, born of solitude, such as no poet ever sang; but all ingenuously, without one vestige of love, one trace of voluptuous thought, one echo of a poesy orientally soothing as the rose of Frangistan. When the count joined us she continued in the same tone, like a woman secure within herself, able to look proudly at her husband and kiss the forehead of her son without a blush. She had prayed much; she had clasped her hands for nights together over her child, refusing to let him die.

"I went," she said, "to the gate of the sanctuary and asked his life of God."

She had had visions, and she told them to me; but when she said, in that angelic voice of hers, these exquisite words, "While I slept my heart watched," the count harshly interrupted her.

"That is to say, you were half crazy," he cried.

She was silent, as deeply hurt as though it were a first wound; forgetting that for thirteen years this man had lost no chance to shoot his arrows into her heart. Like a soaring bird struck on the wing by vulgar shot, she sank into a dull depression; then she roused herself.

"How is it, monsieur," she said, "that no word of mine ever finds favor in your sight? Have you no indulgence for my weakness,—no comprehension of me as a woman?"

She stopped short. Already she regretted the murmur, and measured the future by the past; how could she expect comprehension? Had she not drawn upon herself some virulent attack? The blue veins of her temples throbbed; she shed no tears, but the color of her eyes faded. Then she looked down, that she might not see her pain reflected on my face, her feelings guessed, her soul wooed by my soul; above all, not see the sympathy of young love, ready like a faithful dog to spring at the throat of whoever threatened his mistress, without regard to the assailant's strength or quality. At such cruel moments the count's air of superiority was supreme. He thought he had triumphed over his wife, and he pursued her with a hail of phrases which repeated the one idea, and were like the blows of an axe which fell with unvarying sound.

"Always the same?" I said, when the count left us to follow the huntsman who came to speak to him.

"Always," answered Jacques.

"Always excellent, my son," she said, endeavoring to withdraw Monsieur de Mortsauf from the judgment of his children. "You see only the present, you know nothing of the past; therefore you cannot criticise your father without doing him injustice. But even if you had the pain of seeing that your father was to blame, family honor requires you to bury such secrets in silence."

"How have the changes at the Cassine and the Rhetoriere answered?" I asked, to divert her mind from bitter thoughts.

"Beyond my expectations," she replied. "As soon as the buildings were finished we found two excellent farmers ready to hire them; one at four thousand five hundred francs, taxes paid; the other at five thousand; both leases for fifteen years. We have already planted three thousand young trees on the new farms. Manette's cousin is delighted to get the Rabelaye; Martineau has taken the Baude. All _

*our_*

efforts have been crowned with success. Clochegourde, without the reserved land which we call the home-farm, and without the timber and vineyards, brings in nineteen thousand francs a year, and the plantations are becoming valuable. I am battling to let the home-farm to Martineau, the keeper, whose eldest son can now take his place. He offers three thousand francs if Monsieur de Mortsauf will build him a farm-house at the Commanderie. We might then clear the approach to Clochegourde, finish the proposed avenue to the main road, and have only the woodland and the vineyards to take care of ourselves. If the king returns, _

*our_*

pension will be restored; WE shall consent after clashing a little with _

*our_*

wife's common-sense. Jacques' fortune will then be permanently secured. That result obtained, I shall leave monsieur to lay by as much as he likes for Madeleine, though the king will of course dower her, according to custom. My conscience is easy; I have all but accomplished my task. And you?" she said.

I explained to her the mission on which the king had sent me, and showed her how her wise counsel had borne fruit. Was she endowed with second sight thus to foretell events?

"Did I not write it to you?" she answered. "For you and for my children alone I possess a remarkable faculty, of which I have spoken only to my confessor, Monsieur de la Berge; he explains it by divine intervention. Often, after deep meditation induced by fears about the health of my children, my eyes close to the things of earth and see into another region; if Jacques and Madeleine there appear to me as two luminous figures they are sure to have good health for a certain period of time; if wrapped in mist they are equally sure to fall ill soon after. As for you, I not only see you brilliantly illuminated, but I hear a voice which explains to me without words, by some mental communication, what you ought to do. Does any law forbid me to use this wonderful gift for my children and for you?" she asked, falling into a reverie. Then, after a pause, she added, "Perhaps God wills to take the place of their father."

"Let me believe that my obedience is due to none but you," I cried.

She gave me one of her exquisitely gracious smiles, which so exalted my heart that I should not have felt a death-blow if given at that moment.

"As soon as the king returns to Paris, go there; leave Clochegourde," she said. "It may be degrading to beg for places and favors, but it would be ridiculous to be out of the way of receiving them. Great changes will soon take place. The king needs capable and trustworthy men; don't fail him. It is well for you to enter young into the affairs of the nation and learn your way; for statesmen, like actors, have a routine business to acquire, which genius does not reveal, it must be learnt. My father heard the Duc de Choiseul say this. Think of me," she said, after a pause; "let me enjoy the pleasures of superiority in a soul that is all my own; for are you not my son?"

"Your son?" I said, sullenly.

"Yes, my son!" she cried, mocking me; "is not that a good place in my heart?"

The bell rang for dinner; she took my arm and leaned contentedly upon it.

"You have grown," she said, as we went up the steps. When we reached the portico she shook my arm a little, as if my looks were importunate; for though her eyes were lowered she knew that I saw only her. Then she said, with a charming air of pretended impatience, full of grace and coquetry, "Come, why don't you look at our dear valley?"

She turned, held her white silk sun-shade over our heads and drew Jacques closely to her side. The motion of her head as she looked towards the Indre, the punt, the meadows, showed me that in my absence she had come to many an understanding with those misty horizons and their vaporous outline. Nature was a mantle which sheltered her thoughts. She now knew what the nightingale was sighing the livelong night, what the songster of the sedges hymned with his plaintive note.

At eight o'clock that evening I was witness of a scene which touched me deeply, and which I had never yet witnessed, for in my former visits I had played backgammon with the count while his wife took the children into the dining-room before their bedtime. The bell rang twice, and all the servants of the household entered the room.

"You are now our guest and must submit to convent rule," said the countess, leading me by the hand with that air of innocent gaiety which distinguishes women who are naturally pious.

The count followed. Masters, children, and servants knelt down, all taking their regular places. It was Madeleine's turn to read the prayers. The dear child said them in her childish voice, the ingenuous tones of which rose clear in the harmonious silence of the country, and gave to the words the candor of holy innocence, the grace of angels. It was the most affecting prayer I ever heard. Nature replied to the child's voice with the myriad murmurs of the coming night, like the low accompaniment of an organ lightly touched, Madeleine was on the right of the countess, Jacques on her left. The graceful curly heads, between which rose the smooth braids of the mother, and above all three the perfectly white hair and yellow cranium of the father, made a picture which repeated, in some sort, the ideas aroused by the melody of the prayer. As if to fulfil all conditions of the unity which marks the sublime, this calm and collected group were bathed in the fading light of the setting sun; its red tints coloring the room, impelling the soul—be it poetic or superstitious—to believe that the fires of heaven were visiting these faithful servants of God as they knelt there without distinction of rank, in the equality which heaven demands. Thinking back to the days of the patriarchs my mind still further magnified this scene, so grand in its simplicity.

The children said good-night, the servants bowed, the countess went away holding a child by each hand, and I returned to the salon with the count.

"We provide you with salvation there, and hell here," he said, pointing to the backgammon-board.

The countess returned in half an hour, and brought her frame near the table.

"This is for you," she said, unrolling the canvas; "but for the last three months it has languished. Between that rose and this heartsease my poor child was ill."

"Come, come," said Monsieur de Mortsauf, "don't talk of that any more. Six—five, emissary of the king!"

When alone in my room I hushed my breathing that I might hear her passing to and fro in hers. She was calm and pure, but I was lashed with maddening ideas. "Why should she not be mine?" I thought; "perhaps she is, like me, in this whirlwind of agitation." At one o'clock, I went down, walking noiselessly, and lay before her door. With my ear pressed to a chink I could hear her equable, gentle breathing, like that of a child. When chilled to the bone I went back to bed and slept tranquilly till morning. I know not what prenatal influence, what nature within me, causes the delight I take in going to the brink of precipices, sounding the gulf of evil, seeking to know its depths, feeling its icy chill, and retreating in deep emotion. That hour of night passed on the threshold of her door where I wept with rage,—though she never knew that on the morrow her foot had trod upon my tears and kisses, on her virtue first destroyed and then respected, cursed and adored,— that hour, foolish in the eyes of many, was nevertheless an inspiration of the same mysterious impulse which impels the soldier. Many have told me they have played their lives upon it, flinging themselves before a battery to know if they could escape the shot, happy in thus galloping into the abyss of probabilities, and smoking like Jean Bart upon the gunpowder.

The next day I went to gather flowers and made two bouquets. The count admired them, though generally nothing of the kind appealed to him. The clever saying of Champcenetz, "He builds dungeons in Spain," seemed to have been made for him.

I spent several days at Clochegourde, going but seldom to Frapesle, where, however, I dined three times. The French army now occupied Tours. Though my presence was health and strength to Madame de Mortsauf, she implored me to make my way to Chateauroux, and so round by Issoudun and Orleans to Paris with what haste I could. I tried to resist; but she commanded me, saying that my guardian angel spoke. I obeyed. Our farewell was, this time, dim with tears; she feared the allurements of the life I was about to live. Is it not a serious thing to enter the maelstrom of interests, passions, and pleasures which make Paris a dangerous ocean for chaste love and purity of conscience? I promised to write to her every night, relating the events and thoughts of the day, even the most trivial. When I gave the promise she laid her head on my shoulder and said: "Leave nothing out; everything will interest me."

She gave me letters for the duke and duchess, which I delivered the second day after my return.

"You are in luck," said the duke; "dine here to-day, and go with me this evening to the Chateau; your fortune is made. The king spoke of you this morning, and said, 'He is young, capable, and trustworthy.' His Majesty added that he wished he knew whether you were living or dead, and in what part of France events had thrown you after you had executed your mission so ably."

That night I was appointed master of petitions to the council of State, and I also received a private and permanent place in the employment of Louis XVIII. himself,—a confidential position, not highly distinguished, but without any risks, a position which put me at the very heart of the government and has been the source of all my subsequent prosperity. Madame de Mortsauf had judged rightly. I now owed everything to her; power and wealth, happiness and knowledge; she guided and encouraged me, purified my heart, and gave to my will that unity of purpose without which the powers of youth are wasted. Later I had a colleague; we each served six months. We were allowed to supply each other's place if necessary; we had rooms at the Chateau, a carriage, and large allowances for travelling when absent on missions. Strange position! We were the secret disciples of a monarch in a policy to which even his enemies have since done signal justice; alone with us he gave judgment on all things, foreign and domestic, yet we had no legitimate influence; often we were consulted like Laforet by Moliere, and made to feel that the hesitations of long experience were confirmed or removed by the vigorous perceptions of youth.

In other respects my future was secured in a manner to satisfy ambition. Beside my salary as master of petitions, paid by the budget of the council of State, the king gave me a thousand francs a month from his privy purse, and often himself added more to it. Though the king knew well that no young man of twenty-three could long bear up under the labors with which he loaded me, my colleague, now a peer of France, was not appointed till August, 1817. The choice was a difficult one; our functions demanded so many capabilities that the king was long in coming to a decision. He did me the honor to ask which of the young men among whom he was hesitating I should like for an associate. Among them was one who had been my school-fellow at Lepitre's; I did not select him. His Majesty asked why.

"The king," I replied, "chooses men who are equally faithful, but whose capabilities differ. I choose the one whom I think the most able, certain that I shall always be able to get on with him."

My judgment coincided with that of the king, who was pleased with the sacrifice I had made. He said on this occasion, "You are to be the chief"; and he related these circumstances to my colleague, who became, in return for the service I had done him, my good friend. The consideration shown to me by the Duc de Lenoncourt set the tone of that which I met with in society. To have it said, "The king takes an interest in the young man; that young man has a future, the king likes him," would have served me in place of talents; and it now gave to the kindly welcome accorded to youth a certain respect that is only given to power. In the salon of the Duchesse de Lenoncourt and also at the house of my sister who had just married the Marquis de Listomere, son of the old lady in the Ile St. Louis, I gradually came to know the influential personages of the Faubourg St. Germain.

Henriette herself put me at the heart of the circle then called "le Petit Chateau" by the help of her great-aunt, the Princesse de Blamont-Chauvry, to whom she wrote so warmly in my behalf that the princess immediately sent for me. I cultivated her and contrived to please her, and she became, not my protectress but a friend, in whose kindness there was something maternal. The old lady took pains to make me intimate with her daughter Madame d'Espard, with the Duchesse de Langeais, the Vicomtesse de Beauseant, and the Duchesse de Maufrigneuse, women who held the sceptre of fashion, and who were all the more gracious to me because I made no pretensions and was always ready to be useful and agreeable to them. My brother Charles, far from avoiding me, now began to lean upon me; but my rapid success roused a secret jealousy in his mind which in after years caused me great vexation. My father and mother, surprised by a triumph so unexpected, felt their vanity flattered, and received me at last as a son. But their feeling was too artificial, I might say false, to let their present treatment have much influence upon a sore heart. Affectations stained with selfishness win little sympathy; the heart abhors calculations and profits of all kinds.

I wrote regularly to Henriette, who answered by two letters a month. Her spirit hovered over me, her thoughts traversed space and made the atmosphere around me pure. No woman could captivate me. The king noticed my reserve, and as, in this respect, he belonged to the school of Louis XV., he called me, in jest, Mademoiselle de Vandenesse; but my conduct pleased him. I am convinced that the habit of patience I acquired in my childhood and practised at Clochegourde had much to do in my winning the favor of the king, who was always most kind to me. He no doubt took a fancy to read my letters, for he soon gave up his notion of my life as that of a young girl. One day when the duke was on duty, and I was writing at the king's dictation, the latter suddenly remarked, in that fine, silvery voice of his, to which he could give, when he chose, the biting tone of epigram:—

"So that poor devil of a Mortsauf persists in living?"

"Yes," replied the duke.

"Madame de Mortsauf is an angel, whom I should like to see at my court," continued the king; "but if I cannot manage it, my chancellor here," turning to me, "may be more fortunate. You are to have six months' leave; I have decided on giving you the young man we spoke of yesterday as colleague. Amuse yourself at Clochegourde, friend Cato!" and he laughed as he had himself wheeled out of the room.

I flew like a swallow to Touraine. For the first time I was to show myself to my beloved, not merely a little less insignificant, but actually in the guise of an elegant young man, whose manners had been formed in the best salons, his education finished by gracious women; who had found at last a compensation for all his sufferings, and had put to use the experience given to him by the purest angel to whom heaven had ever committed the care of a child. You know how my mother had equipped me for my three months' visit at Frapesle. When I reached Clochegourde after fulfilling my mission in Vendee, I was dressed like a huntsman; I wore a jacket with white and red buttons, striped trousers, leathern gaiters and shoes. Tramping through underbrush had so injured my clothes that the count was obliged to lend me linen. On the present occasion, two years' residence in Paris, constant intercourse with the king, the habits of a life at ease, my completed growth, a youthful countenance, which derived a lustre from the placidity of the soul within magnetically united with the pure soul that beamed on me from Clochegourde,—all these things combined had transformed me. I was self-possessed without conceit, inwardly pleased to find myself, in spite of my years, at the summit of affairs; above all, I had the consciousness of being secretly the support and comfort of the dearest woman on earth, and her unuttered hope. Perhaps I felt a flutter of vanity as the postilions cracked their whips along the new avenue leading from the main road to Clochegourde and through an iron gate I had never seen before, which opened into a circular enclosure recently constructed. I had not written to the countess of my coming, wishing to surprise her. For this I found myself doubly in fault: first, she was overwhelmed with the excitement of a pleasure long desired, but supposed to be impossible; and secondly, she proved to me that all such deliberate surprises are in bad taste.

When Henriette saw a young man in him who had hitherto seemed but a child to her, she lowered her eyes with a sort of tragic slowness. She allowed me to take and kiss her hand without betraying her inward pleasure, which I nevertheless felt in her sensitive shiver. When she raised her face to look at me again, I saw that she was pale.

"Well, you don't forget your old friends?" said Monsieur de Mortsauf, who had neither changed nor aged.

The children sprang upon me. I saw them behind the grave face of the Abbe Dominis, Jacques' tutor.

"No," I replied, "and in future I am to have six months' leave, which will always be spent here—Why, what is the matter?" I said to the countess, putting my arm round her waist and holding her up in presence of them all.

"Oh, don't!" she said, springing away from me; "it is nothing."

I read her mind, and answered to its secret thought by saying, "Am I not allowed to be your faithful slave?"

She took my arm, left the count, the children, and the abbe, and led me to a distance on the lawn, though still within sight of the others; then, when sure that her voice could not be heard by them, she spoke.

"Felix, my dear friend," she said, "forgive my fears; I have but one thread by which to guide me in the labyrinth of life, and I dread to see it broken. Tell me that I am more than ever Henriette to you, that you will never abandon me, that nothing shall prevail against me, that you will ever be my devoted friend. I have suddenly had a glimpse into my future, and you were not there, as hitherto, your eyes shining and fixed upon me—"

"Henriette! idol whose worship is like that of the Divine,—lily, flower of my life, how is it that you do not know, you who are my conscience, that my being is so fused with yours that my soul is here when my body is in Paris? Must I tell you that I have come in seventeen hours, that each turn of the wheels gathered thoughts and desires in my breast, which burst forth like a tempest when I saw you?"

"Yes, tell me! tell me!" she cried; "I am so sure of myself that I can hear you without wrong. God does not will my death. He sends you to me as he sends his breath to his creatures; as he pours the rain of his clouds upon a parched earth,— tell me! tell me! Do you love me sacredly?"

"Sacredly."

"For ever?"

"For ever."

"As a virgin Mary, hidden behind her veil, beneath her white crown."

"As a virgin visible."

"As a sister?"

"As a sister too dearly loved."

"With chivalry and without hope?"

"With chivalry and with hope."

"As if you were still twenty years of age, and wearing that absurd blue coat?"

"Oh better far! I love you thus, and I also love you"—she looked at me with keen apprehension—"as you loved your aunt."

"I am happy! You dispel my terrors," she said, returning towards the family, who were surprised at our private conference. "Be still a child at Clochegourde— for you are one still. It may be your policy to be a man with the king, but here, let me tell you, monsieur, your best policy is to remain a child. As a child you shall be loved. I can resist a man, but to a child I can refuse nothing, nothing! He can ask for nothing I will not give him.—Our secrets are all told," she said, looking at the count with a mischievous air, in which her girlish, natural self reappeared. "I leave you now; I must go and dress."

Never for three years had I heard her voice so richly happy. For the first time I heard those swallow cries, the infantile notes of which I told you. I had brought Jacques a hunting outfit, and for Madeleine a work-box—which her mother afterwards used. The joy of the two children, delighted to show their presents to each other, seemed to annoy the count, always dissatisfied when attention was withdrawn from himself. I made a sign to Madeleine and followed her father, who wanted to talk to me of his ailments.

"My poor Felix," he said, "you see how happy and well they all are. I am the shadow on the picture; all their ills are transferred to me, and I bless God that it is so. Formerly I did not know what was the matter with me; now I know. The orifice of my stomach is affected; I can digest nothing."

"How do you come to be as wise as the professor of a medical school?" I asked, laughing. "Is your doctor indiscreet enough to tell you such things?"

"God forbid I should consult a doctor," he cried, showing the aversion most imaginary invalids feel for the medical profession.

I now listened to much crazy talk, in the course of which he made the most absurd confidences,—complained of his wife, of the servants, of the children, of life, evidently pleased to repeat his daily speeches to a friend who, not having heard them daily, might be alarmed, and who at any rate was forced to listen out of politeness. He must have been satisfied, for I paid him the utmost attention, trying to penetrate his inconceivable nature, and to guess what new tortures he had been inflicting on his wife, of which she had not written to me. Henriette presently put an end to the monologue by appearing in the portico. The count saw her, shook his head, and said to me: "You listen to me, Felix; but here no one pities me."

He went away, as if aware of the constraint he imposed on my intercourse with Henriette, or perhaps from a really chivalrous consideration for her, knowing he could give her pleasure by leaving us alone. His character exhibited contradictions that were often inexplicable; he was jealous, like all weak beings, but his confidence in his wife's sanctity was boundless. It may have been the sufferings of his own self-esteem, wounded by the superiority of that lofty virtue, which made him so eager to oppose every wish of the poor woman, whom he braved as children brave their masters or their mothers.

Jacques was taking his lessons, and Madeleine was being dressed; I had therefore a whole hour to walk with the countess alone on the terrace.

"Dear angel!" I said, "the chains are heavier, the sands hotter, the thorns grow apace."

"Hush!" she said, guessing the thoughts my conversation with the count had suggested. "You are here, and all is forgotten! I don't suffer; I have never suffered."

She made a few light steps as if to shake her dress and give to the breeze its ruches of snowy tulle, its floating sleeves and fresh ribbons, the laces of her pelerine, and the flowing curls of her coiffure a la Sevigne; I saw her for the first time a young girl,—gay with her natural gaiety, ready to frolic like a child. I knew then the meaning of tears of happiness; I knew the joy a man feels in bringing happiness to another.

"Sweet human flower, wooed by my thought, kissed by my soul, oh my lily!" I cried, "untouched, untouchable upon thy stem, white, proud, fragrant, and solitary—"

"Enough, enough," she said, smiling. "Speak to me of yourself; tell me everything."

Then, beneath the swaying arch of quivering leaves, we had a long conversation, filled with interminable parentheses, subjects taken, dropped, and retaken, in which I told her my life and my occupations; I even described my apartment in Paris, for she wished to know everything; and (happiness then unappreciated) I had nothing to conceal. Knowing thus my soul and all the details of a daily life full of incessant toil, learning the full extent of my functions, which to any one not sternly upright offered opportunities for deception and dishonest gains, but which I had exercised with such rigid honor that the king, I told her, called me

Mademoiselle de Vandenesse, she seized my hand and kissed it, and dropped a tear, a tear of joy, upon it.

This sudden transposition of our roles, this homage, coupled with the thought—swiftly expressed but as swiftly comprehended—"Here is the master I have sought, here is my dream embodied!" all that there was of avowal in the action, grand in its humility, where love betrayed itself in a region forbidden to the senses,—this whirlwind of celestial things fell on my heart and crushed it. I felt myself too small; I wished to die at her feet.

"Ah!" I said, "you surpass us in all things. Can you doubt me?—for you did doubt me just now, Henriette."

"Not now," she answered, looking at me with ineffable tenderness, which, for a moment, veiled the light of her eyes. "But seeing you so changed, so handsome, I said to myself, 'Our plans for Madeleine will be defeated by some woman who will guess the treasures in his heart; she will steal our Felix, and destroy all happiness here.'"

"Always Madeleine!" I replied. "Is it Madeleine to whom I am faithful?"

We fell into a silence which Monsieur de Mortsauf inconveniently interrupted. I was forced to keep up a conversation bristling with difficulties, in which my honest replies as to the king's policy jarred with the count's ideas, and he forced me to explain again and again the king's intentions. In spite of all my questions as to his horses, his agricultural affairs, whether he was satisfied with his five farms, whether he meant to cut the timber of the old avenue, he returned to the subject of politics with the pestering faculty of an old maid and the persistency of a child. Minds like his prefer to dash themselves against the light; they return again and again and hum about it without ever getting into it, like those big flies which weary our ears as they buzz upon the glass.

Henriette was silent. To stop the conversation, in which I feared my young blood might take fire, I answered in monosyllables, mostly acquiescent, avoiding discussion; but Monsieur de Mortsauf had too much sense not to perceive the meaning of my politeness. Presently he was angry at being always in the right; he grew refractory, his eyebrows and the wrinkles of his forehead worked, his yellow eyes blazed, his rufous nose grew redder, as it did on the day I first witnessed an attack of madness. Henriette gave me a supplicating look, making me understand that she could not employ on my behalf an authority to which she had recourse to protect her children. I at once answered the count seriously, taking up the political question, and managing his peevish spirit with the utmost care.

"Poor dear! poor dear!" she murmured two or three times; the words reaching my ear like a gentle breeze. When she could intervene with success she said, interrupting us, "Let me tell you, gentlemen, that you are very dull company."

Recalled by this conversation to his chivalrous sense of what was due to a woman, the count ceased to talk politics, and as we bored him in our turn by commonplace matters, he presently left us to continue our walk, declaring that it made his head spin to go round and round on the same path.

My sad conjectures were true. The soft landscape, the warm atmosphere, the cloudless skies, the soothing poetry of this valley, which for fifteen years had calmed the stinging fancies of that diseased mind, were now impotent. At a period of life when the asperities of other men are softened and their angles smoothed, the disposition of this man became more and more aggressive. For the last few months he had taken a habit of contradicting for the sake of contradiction, without reason, without even trying to justify his opinions; he insisted on knowing the why and the wherefore of everything; grew restless under a delay or an omission; meddled with every item of the household affairs, and compelled his wife and the servants to render him the most minute and fatiguing account of all that was done; never allowing them the slightest freedom of action. Formerly he did not lose his temper except for some special reason; now his irritation was constant. Perhaps the care of his farms, the interests of agriculture, an active out-door life had formerly soothed his atrabilious temper by giving it a field for its uneasiness, and by furnishing employment for his activity. Possibly the loss of such occupation had allowed his malady to prey upon itself; no longer exercised on matters without, it was showing itself in more fixed ideas; the moral being was laying hold of the physical being. He had lately become his own doctor; he studied medical books, fancied he had the diseases he read of, and took the most extraordinary and unheard of precautions about his health,—precautions never the same, impossible to foresee, and consequently impossible to satisfy. Sometimes he wanted no noise; then, when the countess had succeeded in establishing absolute silence, he would declare he was in a tomb, and blame her for not finding some medium between incessant noise and the stillness of La Trappe. Sometimes he affected a perfect indifference for all earthly things. Then the whole household breathed freely; the children played; family affairs went on without criticism. Suddenly he would cry out lamentably, "They want to kill me!—My dear," he would say to his wife, increasing the injustice of his words by the aggravating tones of his sharp voice, "if it concerned your children you would know very well what was the matter with them."

He dressed and re-dressed himself incessantly, watching every change of temperature, and doing nothing without consulting the barometer. Notwithstanding his wife's attentions, he found no food to suit him, his stomach being, he said, impaired, and digestion so painful as to keep him awake all night. In spite of this he ate, drank, digested, and slept, in a manner to satisfy any doctor. His capricious will exhausted the patience of the servants, accustomed to the beaten track of domestic service and unable to conform to the requirements of his conflicting orders. Sometimes he bade them keep all the windows open, declaring that his health required a current of fresh air; a few days later the fresh air, being too hot or too damp, as the case might be, became intolerable; then he scolded, quarrelled with the servants, and in order to justify himself, denied his former orders. This defect of memory, or this bad faith, call it which you will, always carried the day against his wife in the arguments by which she tried to pit him against himself. Life at Clochegourde had become so intolerable that the Abbe Dominis, a man of great learning, took refuge in the study of scientific problems, and withdrew into the shelter of pretended abstraction. The countess had no longer any hope of hiding the secret of these insane furies within the circle of her own home; the servants had witnessed scenes of exasperation without exciting cause, in which the premature old man passed the bounds of reason. They were, however, so devoted to the countess that nothing so far had transpired outside; but she dreaded daily some public outburst of a frenzy no longer controlled by respect for opinion.

Later I learned the dreadful details of the count's treatment of his wife. Instead of supporting her when the children were ill, he assailed her with dark predictions and made her responsible for all future illnesses, because she refused to let the children take the crazy doses which he prescribed. When she went to walk with them the count would predict a storm in the face of a clear sky; if by chance the prediction proved true, the satisfaction he felt made him quite indifferent to any harm to the children. If one of them was ailing, the count gave his whole mind to fastening the cause of the illness upon the system of nursing adopted by his wife, whom he carped at for every trifling detail, always ending with the cruel words, "If your children fall ill again you have only yourself to thank for it."

He behaved in the same way in the management of the household, seeing the worst side of everything, and making himself, as his old coachman said, "the devil's own advocate." The countess arranged that Jacques and Madeleine should take their meals alone at different hours from the family, so as to save them from the count's outbursts and draw all the storms upon herself. In this way the children now saw but little of their father. By one of the hallucinations peculiar to selfish persons, the count had not the slightest idea of the misery he caused. In the confidential communication he made to me on my arrival he particularly dwelt on his goodness to his family. He wielded the flail, beat, bruised, and broke everything about him as a monkey might have done. Then, having half-destroyed his prey, he denied having touched it. I now understood the lines on Henriette's forehead,—fine lines, traced as it were with the edge of a razor, which I had noticed the moment I saw her. There is a pudicity in noble minds which withholds them from speaking of their personal sufferings; proudly they hide the extent of their woes from hearts that love them, feeling a merciful joy in doing so. Therefore in spite of my urgency, I did not immediately obtain the truth from Henriette. She feared to grieve me; she made brief admissions, and then blushed for them; but I soon perceived myself the increase of trouble which the count's present want of regular occupation had brought upon the household.

"Henriette," I said, after I had been there some days, "don't you think you have made a mistake in so arranging the estate that the count has no longer anything to do?"

"Dear," she said, smiling, "my situation is critical enough to take all my attention; believe me, I have considered all my resources, and they are now exhausted. It is true that the bickerings are getting worse and worse. As Monsieur de Mortsauf and I are always together, I cannot lessen them by diverting his attention in other directions; in fact the pain would be the same to me in any case. I did think of advising him to start a nursery for silk-worms at Clochegourde, where we have many mulberry-trees, remains of the old industry of Touraine. But I reflected that he would still be the same tyrant at home, and I should have many more annoyances through the enterprise. You will learn, my dear observer, that in youth a man's ill qualities are restrained by society, checked in their swing by the play of passions, subdued under the fear of public opinion; later, a middle-aged man, living in solitude, shows his native defects, which are all the more terrible because so long repressed. Human weaknesses are essentially base; they allow of neither peace nor truce; what you yield to them to-day they exact to-morrow, and always; they fasten on concessions and compel more of them. Power, on the other hand, is merciful; it conforms to evidence, it is just and it is peaceable. But the passions born of weakness are implacable. Monsieur de Mortsauf takes an absolute pleasure in getting the better of me; and he who would deceive no one else, deceives me with delight."

One morning as we left the breakfast table, about a month after my arrival, the countess took me by the arm, darted through an iron gate which led into the vineyard, and dragged me hastily among the vines.

"He will kill me!" she cried. "And I want to live—for my children's sake. But oh! not a day's respite! Always to walk among thorns! to come near falling every instant! every instant to have to summon all my strength to keep my balance! No human being can long endure such strain upon the system. If I were certain of the ground I ought to take, if my resistance could be a settled thing, then my mind might concentrate upon it—but no, every day the attacks change character and leave me without defence; my sorrows are not one, they are manifold. Ah! my friend—" she cried, leaning her head upon my shoulder, and not continuing her confidence. "What will become of me? Oh, what shall I do?" she said presently, struggling with thoughts she did not express. "How can I resist? He will kill me! No, I will kill myself—but that would be a crime! Escape? yes, but my children! Separate from him? how, after fifteen years of marriage, how could I ever tell my parents that I will not live with him? for if my father and mother came here he would be calm, polite, intelligent, judicious. Besides, can married women look to fathers or mothers? Do they not belong body and soul to their husbands? I could live tranquil if not happy—I have found strength in my chaste solitude, I admit it; but if I am deprived of this negative happiness I too shall become insane. My resistance is based on powerful reasons which are not personal to myself. It is a crime to give birth to poor creatures condemned to endless suffering. Yet my position raises serious questions, so serious that I dare not decide them alone; I cannot be judge and party both. To-morrow I will go to Tours and consult my new confessor, the Abbe Birotteau—for my dear and virtuous Abbe de la Berge is dead," she said, interrupting herself. "Though he was severe, I miss and shall always miss his apostolic power. His successor is an angel of goodness, who pities but does not reprimand. Still, all courage draws fresh life from the heart of religion; what soul is not strengthened by the voice of the Holy Spirit? My God," she said, drying her tears and raising her eyes to heaven, "for what sin am I thus punished?—I believe, yes, Felix, I believe it, we must pass through a fiery furnace before we reach the saints, the just made perfect of the upper spheres. Must I keep silence? Am I forbidden, oh, my God, to cry to the heart of a friend? Do I love him too well?" She pressed me to her heart as though she feared to lose me. "Who will solve my doubts? My conscience does not reproach me. The stars shine from above on men;

may not the soul, the human star, shed its light upon a friend, if we go to him with pure thoughts?"

I listened to this dreadful cry in silence, holding her moist hand in mine that was still more moist. I pressed it with a force to which Henriette replied with an equal pressure.

"Where are you?" cried the count, who came towards us, bareheaded.

Ever since my return he had insisted on sharing our interviews, —either because he wanted amusement, or feared the countess would tell me her sorrows and complain to me, or because he was jealous of a pleasure he did not share.

"How he follows me!" she cried, in a tone of despair. "Let us go into the orchard, we shall escape him. We can stoop as we run by the hedge, and he will not see us."

We made the hedge a rampart and reached the enclosure, where we were soon at a good distance from the count in an alley of almond-trees.

"Dear Henriette," I then said to her, pressing her arm against my heart and stopping to contemplate her in her sorrow, "you have guided me with true knowledge along the perilous ways of the great world; let me in return give you some advice which may help you to end this duel without witnesses, in which you must inevitably be worsted, for you are fighting with unequal weapons. You must not struggle any longer with a madman—"

"Hush!" she said, dashing aside the tears that rolled from her eyes.

"Listen to me, dear," I continued. "After a single hour's talk with the count, which I force myself to endure for love of you, my thoughts are bewildered, my head heavy; he makes me doubtful of my own intellect; the same ideas repeated over and over again seem to burn themselves on my brain. Well-defined monomanias are not communicated; but when the madness consists in a distorted way of looking at everything, and when it lurks under all discussions, then it can and does injure the minds of those who live with it. Your patience is sublime, but will it not end in disordering you? For your sake, for that of your children, change your system with the count. Your adorable kindness has made him selfish; you have treated him as a mother treats the child she spoils; but now, if you want to live— and you do want it," I said, looking at her, "use the control you have over him. You know what it is; he loves you and he fears you; make him fear you more; oppose his erratic will with your firm will. Extend your power over him, confine his madness to a moral sphere just as we lock maniacs in a cell."

"Dear child," she said, smiling bitterly, "a woman without a heart might do it. But I am a mother; I should make a poor jailer. Yes, I can suffer, but I cannot make others suffer. Never!" she said, "never! not even to obtain some great and honorable result. Besides, I should have to lie in my heart, disguise my voice, lower my head, degrade my gesture—do not ask of me such falsehoods. I can stand between Monsieur de Mortsauf and his children, I willingly receive his blows that they may not fall on others; I can do all that, and will do it to conciliate conflicting interests, but I can do no more."

"Let me worship thee, O saint, thrice holy!" I exclaimed, kneeling at her feet and kissing her robe, with which I wiped my tears. "But if he kills you?" I cried.

She turned pale and said, lifting her eyes to heaven:

"God's will be done!"

"Do you know that the king said to your father, 'So that devil of a Mortsauf is still living'?"

"A jest on the lips of the king," she said, "is a crime when repeated here."

In spite of our precautions the count had tracked us; he now arrived, bathed in perspiration, and sat down under a walnut-tree where the countess had stopped to give me that rebuke. I began to talk about the vintage; the count was silent, taking no notice of the dampness under the tree. After a few insignificant remarks, interspersed with pauses that were very significant, he complained of nausea and headache; but he spoke gently, and did not appeal to our pity, or describe his sufferings in his usual exaggerated way. We paid no attention to him. When we reached the house, he said he felt worse and should go to bed; which he did, quite naturally and with much less complaint than usual. We took advantage of the respite and went down to our dear terrace accompanied by Madeleine.

"Let us get that boat and go upon the river," said the countess after we had made a few turns. "We might go and look at the fishing which is going on to-day."

We went out by the little gate, found the punt, jumped into it and were presently paddling up the Loire. Like three children amused with trifles, we looked at the sedges along the banks and the blue and green dragon-flies; the countess wondered perhaps that she was able to enjoy such peaceful pleasures in the midst of her poignant griefs; but Nature's calm, indifferent to our struggles, has a magic gift of consolation. The tumults of a love full of restrained desires harmonize with the wash of the water; the flowers that the hand of man has never wilted are the voice of his secret dreams; the voluptuous swaying of the boat vaguely responds to the thoughts that are floating in his soul. We felt the languid influence of this double poesy. Words, tuned to the diapason of nature, disclosed mysterious graces; looks were impassioned rays sharing the light shed broadcast by the sun on the glowing meadows. The river was a path along which we flew. Our spirit, no longer kept down by the measured tread of our footsteps, took possession of the universe. The abounding joy of a child at liberty, graceful in its motions, enticing in its play, is the living expression of two freed souls, delighting themselves by becoming ideally the wondrous being dreamed of by Plato and known to all whose youth has been filled with a blessed love. To describe to you that hour, not in its indescribable details but in its essence, I must say to you that we loved each other in all the creations animate and inanimate which surrounded us; we felt without us the happiness our own hearts craved; it so penetrated our being that the countess took off her gloves and let her hands float in the water as if to cool an inward ardor. Her eyes spoke; but her mouth, opening like a rose to the breeze, gave voice to no desire. You know the harmony of deep tones mingling perfectly with high ones? Ever, when I hear it now, it recalls to me the harmony of our two souls in this one hour, which never came again.

"Where do you fish?" I asked, "if you can only do so from the banks you own?"

"Near Pont-de-Ruan," she replied. "Ah! we now own the river from Pont-de-Ruan to Clochegourde; Monsieur de Mortsauf has lately bought forty acres of the meadow lands with the savings of two years and the arrearage of his pension. Does that surprise you?"

"Surprise me?" I cried; "I would that all the valley were yours." She answered me with a smile. Presently we came below the bridge to a place where the Indre widens and where the fishing was going on.

"Well, Martineau?" she said.

"Ah, Madame la comtesse, such bad luck! We have fished up from the mill the last three hours, and have taken nothing."

We landed near them to watch the drawing in of the last net, and all three of us sat down in the shade of a "bouillard," a sort of poplar with a white bark, which grows on the banks of the Danube and the Loire (probably on those of other large rivers), and sheds, in the spring of the year, a white and silky fluff, the covering of its flower. The countess had recovered her august serenity; she half regretted the unveiling of her griefs, and mourned that she had cried aloud like Job, instead of weeping like the Magdalen,—a Magdalen without loves, or galas, or prodigalities, but not without beauty and fragrance. The net came in at her feet full of fish; tench, barbels, pike, perch, and an enormous carp, which floundered about on the grass.

"Madame brings luck!" exclaimed the keeper.

All the laborers opened their eyes as they looked with admiration at the woman whose fairy wand seemed to have touched the nets. Just then the huntsman was seen urging his horse over the meadows at a full gallop. Fear took possession of her. Jacques was not with us, and the mother's first thought, as Virgil so poetically says, is to press her children to her breast when danger threatens.

"Jacques! Where is Jacques? What has happened to my boy?"

She did not love me! If she had loved me I should have seen upon her face when confronted with my sufferings that expression of a lioness in despair.

"Madame la comtesse, Monsieur le comte is worse."

She breathed more freely and started to run towards Clochegourde, followed by me and by Madeleine.

"Follow me slowly," she said, looking back; "don't let the dear child overheat herself. You see how it is; Monsieur de Mortsauf took that walk in the sun which put him into a perspiration, and sitting under the walnut-tree may be the cause of a great misfortune."

The words, said in the midst of her agitation, showed plainly the purity of her soul. The death of the count a misfortune! She reached Clochegourde with great rapidity, passing through a gap in the wall and crossing the fields. I returned slowly. Henriette's words lighted my mind, but as the lightning falls and blasts the gathered harvest. On the river I had fancied I was her chosen one; now I felt bitterly the sincerity of her words. The lover who is not everything is nothing. I loved with the desire of a love that knows what it seeks; which feeds in advance on coming transports, and is content with the pleasures of the soul because it mingles with them others which the future keeps in store. If Henriette loved, it was certain that she knew neither the pleasures of love nor its tumults. She lived by feelings only, like a saint with God. I was the object on which her thoughts fastened as bees swarm upon the branch of a flowering tree. In my mad jealousy I reproached myself that I had dared nothing, that I had not tightened the bonds of a tenderness which seemed to me at that moment more subtile than real, by the chains of positive possession.

The count's illness, caused perhaps by a chill under the walnut-tree, became alarming in a few hours. I went to Tours for a famous doctor named Origet, but was unable to find him until evening. He spent that night and the next day at Clochegourde. We had sent the huntsman in quest of leeches, but the doctor, thinking the case urgent, wished to bleed the count immediately, but had brought no lancet with him. I at once started for Azay in the midst of a storm, roused a surgeon, Monsieur Deslandes, and compelled him to come with the utmost celerity to Clochegourde. Ten minutes later and the count would have died; the bleeding saved him. But in spite of this preliminary success the doctor predicted an inflammatory fever of the worst kind. The countess was overcome by the fear that she was the secret cause of this crisis. Two weak to thank me for my exertions, she merely gave me a few smiles, the equivalent of the kiss she had once laid upon my hand. Fain would I have seen in those haggard smiles the remorse of illicit love; but no, they were only the act of contrition of an innocent repentance, painful to see in one so pure, the expression of admiring tenderness for me whom she regarded as noble while reproaching herself for an imaginary wrong. Surely she loved as Laura loved Petrarch, and not as Francesca da Rimini loved Paolo,—a terrible discovery for him who had dreamed the union of the two loves.

The countess half lay, her body bent forwards, her arms hanging, in a soiled armchair in a room that was like the lair of a wild boar. The next evening before the doctor departed he said to the countess, who had sat up the night before, that she must get a nurse, as the illness would be a long one.

"A nurse!" she said; "no, no! We will take care of him," she added, looking at me; "we owe it to ourselves to save him."

The doctor gave us both an observing look full of astonishment. The words were of a nature to make him suspect an atonement. He promised to come twice a week, left directions for the treatment with Monsieur Deslandes, and pointed out the threatening symptoms that might oblige us to send for him. I asked the countess to let me sit up the alternate nights and then, not without difficulty, I persuaded her to go to bed on the third night. When the house was still and the count sleeping I heard a groan from Henriette's room. My anxiety was so keen that I went to her. She was kneeling before the crucifix bathed in tears. "My God!" she cried; "if this be the cost of a murmur, I will never complain again."

"You have left him!" she said on seeing me.

"I heard you moaning, and I was frightened."

"Oh, I!" she said; "I am well."

Wishing to be certain that Monsieur de Mortsauf was asleep she came down with me; by the light of the lamp we looked at him. The count was weakened by the loss of blood and was more drowsy than asleep; his hands picked the counterpane and tried to draw it over him.

"They say the dying do that," she whispered. "Ah! if he were to die of this illness, that I have caused, never will I marry again, I swear it," she said, stretching her hand over his head with a solemn gesture.

"I have done all I could to save him," I said.

"Oh, you!" she said, "you are good; it is I who am guilty."

She stooped to that discolored brow, wiped the perspiration from it and laid a kiss there solemnly; but I saw, not without joy, that she did it as an expiation.

"Blanche, I am thirsty," said the count in a feeble voice.

"You see he knows me," she said giving him to drink.

Her accent, her affectionate manner to him seemed to me to take the feelings that bound us together and immolate them to the sick man.

"Henriette," I said, "go and rest, I entreat you."

"No more Henriette," she said, interrupting me with imperious haste.

"Go to bed if you would not be ill. Your children, _

*he himself_*

would order you to be careful; it is a case where selfishness becomes a virtue."

"Yes," she said.

She went away, recommending her husband to my care by a gesture which would have seemed like approaching delirium if childlike grace had not been mingled with the supplicating forces of repentance. But the scene was terrible, judged by the habitual state of that pure soul; it alarmed me; I feared the exaltation of her conscience. When the doctor came again, I revealed to him the nature of my pure Henriette's self-reproach. This confidence, made discreetly, removed Monsieur Origet's suspicions, and enabled him to quiet the distress of that noble soul by telling her that in any case the count had to pass through this crisis, and that as for the nut-tree, his remaining there had done more good than harm by developing the disease.

For fifty-two days the count hovered between life and death. Henriette and I each watched twenty-six nights. Undoubtedly, Monsieur de Mortsauf owed his life to our nursing and to the careful exactitude with which we carried out the orders of Monsieur Origet. Like all philosophical physicians, whose sagacious observation of what passes before them justifies many a doubt of noble actions when they are only the accomplishment of a duty, this man, while assisting the countess and me in our rivalry of devotion, could not help watching us, with scrutinizing glances, so afraid was he of being deceived in his admiration.

"In diseases of this nature," he said to me at his third visit, "death has a powerful auxiliary in the moral nature when that is seriously disturbed, as it is in this case. The doctor, the family, the nurses hold the patient's life in their hands; sometimes a single word, a fear expressed by a gesture, has the effect of poison."

As he spoke Origet studied my face and expression; but he saw in my eyes the clear look of an honest soul. In fact during the whole course of this distressing illness there never passed through my mind a single one of the involuntary evil thoughts which do sometimes sear the consciences of the innocent. To those who study nature in its grandeur as a whole all tends to unity through assimilation. The moral world must undoubtedly be ruled by an analogous principle. In an pure sphere all is pure. The atmosphere of heaven was around my Henriette; it seemed as though an evil desire must forever part me from her. Thus she not only stood for happiness, but for virtue; she _

*was_*

virtue. Finding us always equally careful and attentive, the doctor's words and manners took a tone of respect and even pity; he seemed to say to himself, "Here are the real sufferers; they hide their ills, and forget them." By a fortunate change, which, according to our excellent doctor, is common enough in men who are completely shattered, Monsieur de Mortsauf was patient, obedient, complained little, and showed surprising docility,—he, who when well never did the simplest thing without discussion. The secret of this submission to medical care, which he formerly so derided, was an innate dread of death; another contradiction in a man of tried courage. This dread may perhaps explain several other peculiarities in the character which the cruel years of exile had developed.

Shall I admit to you, Natalie, and will you believe me? these fifty days and the month that followed them were the happiest moments of my life. Love, in the celestial spaces of the soul is like a noble river flowing through a valley; the rains, the brooks, the torrents hie to it, the trees fall upon its surface, so do the flowers, the gravel of its shores, the rocks of the summits; storms and the loitering tribute of the crystal streams alike increase it. Yes, when love comes all comes to love!

The first great danger over, the countess and I grew accustomed to illness. In spite of the confusion which the care of the sick entails, the count's room, once so untidy, was now clean and inviting. Soon we were like two beings flung upon a desert island, for not only do anxieties isolate, but they brush aside as petty the conventions of the world. The welfare of the sick man obliged us to have points of contact which no other circumstances would have authorized. Many a time our hands, shy or timid formerly, met in some service that we rendered to the count— was I not there to sustain and help my Henriette? Absorbed in a duty comparable to that of a soldier at the pickets, she forgot to eat; then I served her, sometimes on her lap, a hasty meal which necessitated a thousand little attentions. We were like children at a grave. She would order me sharply to prepare whatever might ease the sick man's suffering; she employed me in a hundred petty ways. During the time when actual danger obscured, as it does during the battle, the subtile distinctions which characterize the facts of ordinary life, she necessarily laid aside the reserve which all women, even the most unconventional, preserve in their looks and words and actions before the world or their own family. At the first chirping of the birds she would come to relieve my watch, wearing a morning garment which revealed to me once more the dazzling treasures that in my folly I had treated as my own. Always dignified, nay imposing, she could still be familiar.

Thus it came to pass that we found ourselves unconsciously intimate, half-married as it were. She showed herself nobly confiding, as sure of me as she was of herself. I was thus taken deeper and deeper into her heart. The countess became once more my Henriette, Henriette constrained to love with increasing strength the friend who endeavored to be her second soul. Her hand unresistingly met mine at the least solicitation; my eyes were permitted to follow with delight the lines of her beauty during the long hours when we listened to the count's breathing, without driving her from their sight. The meagre pleasures which we allowed ourselves— sympathizing looks, words spoken in whispers not to wake the count, hopes and fears repeated and again repeated, in short, the thousand incidents of the fusion of two hearts long separated—stand out in bright array upon the sombre background of the actual scene. Our souls knew each other to their depths under this test, which many a warm affection is unable to bear, finding life too heavy or too flimsy in the close bonds of hourly intercourse.

You know what disturbance follows the illness of a master; how the affairs of life seem to come to a standstill. Though the real care of the family and estate fell upon Madame de Mortsauf, the count was useful in his way; he talked with the farmers, transacted business with his bailiff, and received the rents; if she was the soul, he was the body. I now made myself her steward so that she could nurse the count without neglecting the property. She accepted this as a matter of course, in fact without thanking me. It was another sweet communion to share her family cares, to transmit her orders. In the evenings we often met in her room to discuss these interests and those of her children. Such conversations gave one semblance the more to our transitory marriage. With what delight she encouraged me to take a husband's place, giving me his seat at table, sending me to talk with the bailiff,—all in perfect innocence, yet not without that inward pleasure the most virtuous woman in the world will feel when she finds a course where strict obedience to duty and the satisfaction of her wishes are combined.

Nullified, as it were, by illness, the count no longer oppressed his wife or his household, the countess then became her natural self; she busied herself with my affairs and showed me a thousand kindnesses. With what joy I discovered in her mind a thought, vaguely conceived perhaps, but exquisitely expressed, namely, to show me the full value of her person and her qualities and make me see the change that would come over her if she lived understood. This flower, kept in the cold atmosphere of such a home, opened to my gaze, and to mine only; she took as much delight in letting me comprehend her as I felt in studying her with the searching eyes of love. She proved to me in all the trifling things of daily life how much I was in her thoughts. When, after my turn of watching, I went to bed and slept late, Henriette would keep the house absolutely silent near me; Jacques and Madeleine played elsewhere, though never ordered to do so; she invented excuses to serve my breakfast herself—ah, with what sparkling pleasure in her movements, what swallow-like rapidity, what lynx-eyed perception! and then! what carnation on her cheeks, what quiverings in her voice!

Can such expansions of the soul be described in words?

Often she was wearied out; but if, at such moments of lassitude my welfare came in question, for me, as for her children, she found fresh strength and sprang up eagerly and joyfully. How she loved to shed her tenderness like sunbeams in the air! Ah, Natalie, some women share the privileges of angels here below; they diffuse that light which Saint-Martin, the mysterious philosopher, declared to be intelligent, melodious, and perfumed. Sure of my discretion, Henriette took pleasure in raising the curtain which hid the future and in showing me two women in her,—the woman bound hand and foot who had won me in spite of her severity, and the woman freed, whose sweetness should make my love eternal! What a difference. Madame de Mortsauf was the skylark of Bengal, transported to our cold Europe, mournful on its perch, silent and dying in the cage of a naturalist; Henriette was the singing bird of oriental poems in groves beside the Ganges, flying from branch to branch like a living jewel amid the roses of a volkameria that ever blooms. Her beauty grew more beautiful, her mind recovered strength. The continual sparkle of this happiness was a secret between ourselves, for she dreaded the eye of the Abbe Dominis, the representative of the world; she masked her contentment with playfulness, and covered the proofs of her tenderness with the banner of gratitude.

"We have put your friendship to a severe test, Felix; we may give you the same rights we give to Jacques, may we not, Monsieur l'abbe?" she said one day.

The stern abbe answered with the smile of a man who can read the human heart and see its purity; for the countess he always showed the respect mingled with adoration which the angels inspire. Twice during those fifty days the countess passed beyond the limits in which we held our affection. But even these infringements were shrouded in a veil, never lifted until the final hour when avowal came. One morning, during the first days of the count's illness, when she repented her harsh treatment in withdrawing the innocent privileges she had formerly granted me, I was expecting her to relieve my watch. Much fatigued, I fell asleep, my head against the wall. I wakened suddenly at the touch of something cool upon my forehead which gave me a sensation as if a rose had rested there. I opened my eyes and saw the countess, standing a few steps distant, who said, "I have just come." I rose to leave the room, but as I bade her good-bye I took her hand; it was moist and trembling.

"Are you ill?" I said.

"Why do you ask that question?" she replied.

I looked at her blushing and confused. "I was dreaming," I replied.

Another time, when Monsieur Origet had announced positively that the count was convalescent, I was lying with Jacques and Madeleine on the step of the portico intent on a game of spillikins which we were playing with bits of straw and hooks made of pins; Monsieur de Mortsauf was asleep. The doctor, while waiting for his horse to be harnessed, was talking with the countess in the salon. Monsieur Origet went away without my noticing his departure. After he left, Henriette leaned against the window, from which she watched us for some time without our seeing her. It was one of those warm evenings when the sky is copper-colored and the earth sends up among the echoes a myriad mingling noises. A last ray of sunlight was leaving the roofs, the flowers in the garden perfumed the air, the bells of the cattle returning to their stalls sounded in the distance. We were all conforming to the silence of the evening hour and hushing our voices that we might not wake the count. Suddenly, I heard the guttural sound of a sob violently suppressed; I rushed into the salon and found the countess sitting by the window with her handkerchief to her face. She heard my step and made me an imperious gesture, commanding me to leave her. I went up to her, my heart stabbed with fear, and tried to take her handkerchief away by force. Her face was bathed in tears and she fled into her room, which she did not leave again until the hour for evening prayer. When that was over, I led her to the terrace and asked the cause of her emotion; she affected a wild gaiety and explained it by the news Monsieur Origet had given her.

"Henriette, Henriette, you knew that news when I saw you weeping. Between you and me a lie is monstrous. Why did you forbid me to dry your tears? were they mine?"

"I was thinking," she said, "that for me this illness has been a halt in pain. Now that I no longer fear for Monsieur de Mortsauf I fear for myself."

She was right. The count's recovery was soon attested by the return of his fantastic humor. He began by saying that neither the countess, nor I, nor the doctor had known how to take care of him; we were ignorant of his constitution and also of his disease, we misunderstood his sufferings and the necessary remedies. Origet, infatuated with his own doctrines, had mistaken the case, he ought to have attended only to the pylorus. One day he looked at us maliciously, with an air of having guessed our thoughts, and said to his wife with a smile, "Now, my dear, if I had died you would have regretted me, no doubt, but pray admit you would have been quite resigned."

"Yes, I should have mourned you in pink and black, court mourning," she answered laughing, to change the tone of his remarks.

But it was chiefly about his food, which the doctor insisted on regulating, that scenes of violence and wrangling now took place, unlike any that had hitherto occurred; for the character of the count was all the more violent for having slumbered. The countess, fortified by the doctor's orders and the obedience of her servants, stimulated too by me, who thought this struggle a good means to teach her to exercise authority over the count, held out against his violence. She showed a calm front to his demented cries, and even grew accustomed to his insulting epithets, taking him for what he was, a child. I had the happiness of at last seeing her take the reins in hand and govern that unsound mind. The count cried out, but he obeyed; and he obeyed all the better when he had made an outcry. But in spite of the evidence of good results, Henriette often wept at the spectacle of this emaciated, feeble old man, with a forehead yellower than the falling leaves, his eyes wan, his hands trembling. She blamed herself for too much severity, and could not resist the joy she saw in his eyes when, in measuring out his food, she gave him more than the doctor allowed. She was even more gentle and gracious to him than she had been to me; but there were differences here which filled my heart with joy. She was not unwearying, and she sometimes called her servants to wait upon the count when his caprices changed too rapidly, and he complained of not being understood.

The countess wished to return thanks to God for the count's recovery; she directed a mass to be said, and asked if I would take her to church. I did so, but I left her at the door, and went to see Monsieur and Madame Chessel. On my return she reproached me.

"Henriette," I said, "I cannot be false. I will throw myself into the water to save my enemy from drowning, and give him my coat to keep him warm; I will forgive him, but I cannot forget the wrong."

She was silent, but she pressed my arm.

"You are an angel, and you were sincere in your thanksgiving," I said, continuing. "The mother of the Prince of the Peace was saved from the hands of an angry populace who sought to kill her, and when the queen asked, 'What did you do?' she answered, 'I prayed for them.' Women are ever thus. I am a man, and necessarily imperfect."

"Don't calumniate yourself," she said, shaking my arm, "perhaps you are more worthy than I."

"Yes," I replied, "for I would give eternity for a day of happiness, and you—"

"I!" she said haughtily.

I was silent and lowered my eyes to escape the lightning of hers.

"There is many an I in me," she said. "Of which do you speak? Those children," pointing to Jacques and Madeleine, "are one—Felix," she cried in a heartrending voice, "do you think me selfish? Ought I to sacrifice eternity to reward him who devotes to me his life? The thought is dreadful; it wounds every sentiment of religion. Could a woman so fallen rise again? Would her happiness absolve her? These are questions you force me to consider.—Yes, I betray at last the secret of my conscience; the thought has traversed my heart; often do I expiate it by penance; it caused the tears you asked me to account for yesterday—"

"Do you not give too great importance to certain things which common women hold at a high price, and—"

"Oh!" she said, interrupting me; "do you hold them at a lower?"

This logic stopped all argument.

"Know this," she continued. "I might have the baseness to abandon that poor old man whose life I am; but, my friend, those other feeble creatures there before us, Madeleine and Jacques, would remain with their father. Do you think, I ask you do you think they would be alive in three months under the insane dominion of that man? If my failure of duty concerned only myself—" A noble smile crossed her face. "But shall I kill my children! My God!" she exclaimed. "Why speak of these things? Marry, and let me die!"

She said the words in a tone so bitter, so hollow, that they stifled the remonstrances of my passion.

"You uttered cries that day beneath the walnut-tree; I have uttered my cries here beneath these alders, that is all," I said; "I will be silent henceforth."

"Your generosity shames me," she said, raising her eyes to heaven.

We reached the terrace and found the count sitting in a chair, in the sun. The sight of that sunken face, scarcely brightened by a feeble smile, extinguished the last flames that came from the ashes. I leaned against the balustrade and considered the picture of that poor wreck, between his sickly children and his wife, pale with her vigils, worn out by extreme fatigue, by the fears, perhaps also by the joys of these terrible months, but whose cheeks now glowed from the emotions she had just passed through. At the sight of that suffering family beneath the trembling leafage through which the gray light of a cloudy autumn sky came dimly, I felt within me a rupture of the bonds which hold the body to the spirit. There came upon me then that moral spleen which, they say, the strongest wrestlers know in the crisis of their combats, a species of cold madness which makes a coward of the bravest man, a bigot of an unbeliever, and renders those it grasps indifferent to all things, even to vital sentiments, to honor, to love—for the doubt it brings takes from us the knowledge of ourselves and disgusts us with life itself. Poor, nervous creatures, whom the very richness of your organization delivers over to this mysterious, fatal power, who are your peers and who your judges? Horrified by the thoughts that rose within me, and demanding, like the wicked man, "Where is now thy God?" I could not restrain the tears that rolled down my cheeks.

"What is it, dear Felix?" said Madeleine in her childish voice.

Then Henriette put to flight these dark horrors of the mind by a look of tender solicitude which shone into my soul like a sunbeam. Just then the old huntsman brought me a letter from Tours, at sight of which I made a sudden cry of surprise, which made Madame de Mortsauf tremble. I saw the king's signet and knew it contained my recall. I gave her the letter and she read it at a glance.

"What will become of me?" she murmured, beholding her desert sunless.

We fell into a stupor of thought which oppressed us equally; never had we felt more strongly how necessary we were to one another. The countess, even when she spoke indifferently of other things, seemed to have a new voice, as if the instrument had lost some chords and others were out of tune. Her movements were apathetic, her eyes without light. I begged her to tell me her thoughts.

"Have I any?" she replied in a dazed way.

She drew me into her chamber, made me sit upon the sofa, took a package from the drawer of her dressing-table, and knelt before me, saying: "This hair has fallen from my head during the last year; take it, it is yours; you will some day know how and why."

Slowly I bent to meet her brow, and she did not avoid my lips. I kissed her sacredly, without unworthy passion, without one impure impulse, but solemnly, with tenderness. Was she willing to make the sacrifice; or did she merely come, as I did once, to the verge of the precipice? If love were leading her to give herself could she have worn that calm, that holy look; would she have asked, in that pure voice of hers, "You are not angry with me, are you?"

I left that evening; she wished to accompany me on the road to Frapesle; and we stopped under my walnut-tree. I showed it to her, and told her how I had first seen her four years earlier from that spot. "The valley was so beautiful then!" I cried.

"And now?" she said quickly.

"You are beneath my tree, and the valley is ours!"

She bowed her head and that was our farewell; she got into her carriage with Madeleine, and I into mine alone.

On my return to Paris I was absorbed in pressing business which took all my time and kept me out of society, which for a while forgot me. I corresponded with Madame de Mortsauf, and sent her my journal once a week. She answered twice a month. It was a life of solitude yet teeming, like those sequestered spots, blooming unknown, which I had sometimes found in the depths of woods when gathering the flowers for my poems.

Oh, you who love! take these obligations on you; accept these daily duties, like those the Church imposes upon Christians. The rigorous observances of the Roman faith contain a great idea; they plough the furrow of duty in the soul by the daily repetition of acts which keep alive the sense of hope and fear. Sentiments flow clearer in furrowed channels which purify their stream; they refresh the heart, they fertilize the life from the abundant treasures of a hidden faith, the source divine in which the single thought of a single love is multiplied indefinitely.

My love, an echo of the Middle Ages and of chivalry, was known, I know not how; possibly the king and the Duc de Lenoncourt had spoken of it. From that upper sphere the romantic yet simple story of a young man piously adoring a beautiful woman remote from the world, noble in her solitude, faithful without support to duty, spread, no doubt quickly, through the faubourg St. Germain. In the salons I was the object of embarrassing notice; for retired life has advantages which if once experienced make the burden of a constant social intercourse insupportable. Certain minds are painfully affected by violent contrasts, just as eyes accustomed to soft colors are hurt by glaring light. This was my condition then; you may be surprised at it now, but have patience; the inconsistencies of the Vandenesse of to-day will be explained to you.

I found society courteous and women most kind. After the marriage of the Duc de Berry the court resumed its former splendor and the glory of the French fetes revived. The Allied occupation was over, prosperity reappeared, enjoyments were again possible. Noted personages, illustrious by rank, prominent by fortune, came from all parts of Europe to the capital of the intellect, where the merits and the vices of other countries were found magnified and whetted by the charms of French intellect.

Five months after leaving Clochegourde my good angel wrote me, in the middle of the winter, a despairing letter, telling me of the serious illness of her son. He was then out of danger, but there were many fears for the future; the doctor said that precautions were necessary for his lungs—the suggestion of a terrible idea which had put the mother's heart in mourning. Hardly had Jacques begun to convalesce, and she could breathe again, when Madeleine made them all uneasy. That pretty plant, whose bloom had lately rewarded the mother's culture, was now frail and pallid and anemic. The countess, worn-out by Jacques' long illness, found no courage, she said, to bear this additional blow, and the ever present spectacle of these two dear failing creatures made her insensible to the redoubled torment of her husband's temper. Thus the storms were again raging; tearing up by the roots the hopes that were planted deepest in her bosom. She was now at the mercy of the count; weary of the struggle, she allowed him to regain all the ground he had lost.

"When all my strength is employed in caring for my children," she wrote, "how is it possible to employ it against Monsieur de Mortsauf; how can I struggle against his aggressions when I am fighting against death? Standing here to-day, alone and much enfeebled, between these two young images of mournful fate overpowered with disgust, invincible disgust for life. What blow can I feel, to what affection can I answer, when I see Jacques motionless on the terrace, scarcely a sign of life about him, except in those dear eyes, large by emaciation, hollow as those of an old man and, oh, fatal sign, full of precocious intelligence contrasting with his physical debility. When I look at my pretty Madeleine, once so gay, so caressing, so blooming, now white as death, her very hair and eyes seem to me to have paled; she turns a languishing look upon me as if bidding me farewell; nothing rouses her, nothing tempts her. In spite of all my efforts I cannot amuse my children; they smile at me, but their smile is only in answer to my endearments, it does not come from them. They weep because they have no strength to play with me. Suffering has enfeebled their whole being, it has loosened even the ties that bound them to me.

"Thus you can well believe that Clochegourde is very sad. Monsieur de Mortsauf now rules everything—Oh my friend! you, my glory!" she wrote, farther on, "you must indeed love me well to love me still; to love me callous, ungrateful, turned to stone by grief."

CHAPTER III
THE TWO WOMEN

It was at this time, when I was never more deeply moved in my whole being, when I lived in that soul to which I strove to send the luminous breeze of the mornings and the hope of the crimsoned evenings, that I met, in the salons of the Elysee-Bourbon, one of those illustrious ladies who reign as sovereigns in society. Immensely rich, born of a family whose blood was pure from all misalliance since the Conquest, married to one of the most distinguished old men of the British peerage, it was nevertheless evident that these advantages were mere accessories heightening this lady's beauty, graces, manners, and wit, all of which had a brilliant quality which dazzled before it charmed. She was the idol of the day; reigning the more securely over Parisian society because she possessed the quality most necessary to success,—the hand of iron in the velvet glove spoken of by Bernadotte.

You know the singular characteristics of English people, the distance and coldness of their own Channel which they put between them and whoever has not been presented to them in a proper manner. Humanity seems to be an ant-hill on which they tread; they know none of their species except the few they admit into their circle; they ignore even the language of the rest; tongues may move and eyes may see in their presence but neither sound nor look has reached them; to them, the people are as if they were not. The British present an image of their own island, where law rules everything, where all is automatic in every station of life, where the exercise of virtue appears to be the necessary working of a machine which goes by clockwork. Fortifications of polished steel rise around the Englishwoman behind the golden wires of her household cage (where the feed-box and the drinking-cup, the perches and the food are exquisite in quality), but they make her irresistibly attractive. No people ever trained married women so carefully to hypocrisy by holding them rigidly between the two extremes of death or social station; for them there is no middle path between shame and honor; either the wrong is completed or it does not exist; it is all or nothing,—Hamlet's "To be or not to be." This alternative, coupled with the scorn to which the customs of her country have trained her, make an Englishwoman a being apart in the world. She is a helpless creature, forced to be virtuous yet ready to yield, condemned to live a lie in her heart, yet delightful in outward appearance—for these English rest everything on appearances. Hence the special charms of their women: the enthusiasm for a love which is all their life; the minuteness of their care for their persons; the delicacy of their passion, so charmingly rendered in the famous scene of Romeo and Juliet in which, with one stroke, Shakespeare's genius depicted his country-women.

You, who envy them so many things, what can I tell you that you do not know of these white sirens, impenetrable apparently but easily fathomed, who believe that love suffices love, and turn enjoyments to satiety by never varying them; whose soul has one note only, their voice one syllable—an ocean of love in themselves, it is true, and he who has never swum there misses part of the poetry of the senses, as he who has never seen the sea has lost some strings of his lyre. You know the why and wherefore of these words. My relations with the Marchioness of Dudley had a disastrous celebrity. At an age when the senses have dominion over our conduct, and when in my case they had been violently repressed by circumstances, the image of the saint bearing her slow martyrdom at Clochegourde shone so vividly before my mind that I was able to resist all seductions. It was the lustre of this fidelity which attracted Lady Dudley's attention. My resistance stimulated her passion. What she chiefly desired, like many Englishwoman, was the spice of singularity; she wanted pepper, capsicum, with her heart's food, just as Englishmen need condiments to excite their appetite. The dull languor forced into the lives of these women by the constant perfection of everything about them, the methodical regularity of their habits, leads them to adore the romantic and to welcome difficulty. I was wholly unable to judge of such a character. The more I retreated to a cold distance the more impassioned Lady Dudley became. The struggle, in which she gloried, excited the curiosity of several persons, and this in itself was a form of happiness which to her mind made ultimate triumph obligatory. Ah! I might have been saved if some good friend had then repeated to me her cruel comment on my relations with Madame de Mortsauf.

"I am wearied to death," she said, "of these turtle-dove sighings."

Without seeking to justify my crime, I ask you to observe, Natalie, that a man has fewer means of resisting a woman than she has of escaping him. Our code of manners forbids the brutality of repressing a woman, whereas repression with your sex is not only allurement to ours, but is imposed upon you by conventions. With us, on the contrary, some unwritten law of masculine self-conceit ridicules a man's modesty; we leave you the monopoly of that virtue, that you may have the privilege of granting us favors; but reverse the case, and man succumbs before sarcasm.

Though protected by my love, I was not of an age to be wholly insensible to the triple seductions of pride, devotion, and beauty. When Arabella laid at my feet the homage of a ball-room where she reigned a queen, when she watched by glance to know if my taste approved of her dress, and when she trembled with pleasure on seeing that she pleased me, I was affected by her emotion. Besides, she occupied a social position where I could not escape her; I could not refuse invitations in the diplomatic circle; her rank admitted her everywhere, and with the cleverness all women display to obtain what pleases them, she often contrived that the mistress of the house should place me beside her at dinner. On such occasions she spoke in low tones to my ear. "If I were loved like Madame de Mortsauf," she said once, "I should sacrifice all." She did submit herself with a laugh in many humble ways; she promised me a discretion equal to any test, and even asked that I would merely suffer her to love me. "Your friend always, your mistress when you will," she said. At last, after an evening when she had made herself so beautiful that she was certain to have excited my desires, she came to me. The scandal resounded through England, where the aristocracy was horrified like heaven itself at the fall of its highest angel. Lady Dudley abandoned her place in the British empyrean, gave up her wealth, and endeavored to eclipse by her sacrifices _

*her_*

whose virtue had been the cause of this great disaster. She took delight, like the devil on the pinnacle of the temple, in showing me all the riches of her passionate kingdom.

Read me, I pray you, with indulgence. The matter concerns one of the most interesting problems of human life,—a crisis to which most men are subjected, and which I desire to explain, if only to place a warning light upon the reef. This beautiful woman, so slender, so fragile, this milk-white creature, so yielding, so submissive, so gentle, her brow so endearing, the hair that crowns it so fair and fine, this tender woman, whose brilliancy is phosphorescent and fugitive, has, in truth, an iron nature. No horse, no matter how fiery he may be, can conquer her vigorous wrist, or strive against that hand so soft in appearance, but never tired. She has the foot of a doe, a thin, muscular little foot, indescribably graceful in outline. She is so strong that she fears no struggle; men cannot follow her on horseback; she would win a steeple-chase against a centaur; she can bring down a stag without stopping her horse. Her body never perspires; it inhales the fire of the atmosphere, and lives in water under pain of not living at all. Her love is African; her desires are like the whirlwinds of the desert—the desert, whose torrid expanse is in her eyes, the azure, love-laden desert, with its changeless skies, its cool and starry nights. What a contrast to Clochegourde! the east and the west! the one drawing into her every drop of moisture for her own nourishment, the other exuding her soul, wrapping her dear ones in her luminous atmosphere; the one quick and slender; the other slow and massive.

Have you ever reflected on the actual meaning of the manners and customs and morals of England? Is it not the deification of matter? a well-defined, carefully considered Epicureanism, judiciously applied? No matter what may be said against the statement, England is materialist,—possibly she does not know it herself. She lays claim to religion and morality, from which, however, divine spirituality, the catholic soul, is absent; and its fructifying grace cannot be replaced by any counterfeit, however well presented it may be. England possesses in the highest degree that science of existence which turns to account every particle of materiality; the science that makes her women's slippers the most exquisite slippers in the world, gives to their linen ineffable fragrance, lines their drawers with cedar, serves tea carefully drawn, at a certain hour, banishes dust, nails the carpets to the floors in every corner of the house, brushes the cellar walls, polishes the knocker of the front door, oils the springs of the carriage,—in short, makes matter a nutritive and downy pulp, clean and shining, in the midst of which the soul expires of enjoyment and the frightful monotony of comfort in a life without contrasts, deprived of spontaneity, and which, to sum all in one word, makes a machine of you.

Thus I suddenly came to know, in the bosom of this British luxury, a woman who is perhaps unique among her sex; who caught me in the nets of a love excited by my indifference, and to the warmth of which I opposed a stern continence,—one of those loves possessed of overwhelming charm, an electricity of their own, which lead us to the skies through the ivory gates of slumber, or bear us thither on their powerful pinions. A love monstrously ungrateful, which laughs at the bodies of those it kills; love without memory, a cruel love, resembling the policy of the English nation; a love to which, alas, most men yield. You understand the problem? Man is composed of matter and spirit; animality comes to its end in him, and the angel begins in him. There lies the struggle we all pass through, between the future destiny of which we are conscious and the influence of anterior instincts from which we are not wholly detached,—carnal love and divine love. One man combines them, another abstains altogether; some there are who seek the satisfaction of their anterior appetites from the whole sex; others idealize their love in one woman who is to them the universe; some float irresolutely between the delights of matter and the joys of soul, others spiritualize the body, requiring of it that which it cannot give.

If, thinking over these leading characteristics of love, you take into account the dislikes and the affinities which result from the diversity of organisms, and which sooner or later break all ties between those who have not fully tried each other; if you add to this the mistakes arising from the hopes of those who live more particularly either by their minds, or by their hearts, or by action, who either think, or feel, or act, and whose tendency is misunderstood in the close association in which two persons, equal counterparts, find themselves, you will have great indulgence for sorrows to which the world is pitiless. Well, Lady Dudley gratified the instincts, organs, appetites, the vices and virtues of the subtile matter of which we are made; she was the mistress of the body; Madame de Mortsauf was the wife of the soul. The love which the mistress satisfies has its limits; matter is finite, its inherent qualities have an ascertained force, it is capable of saturation; often I felt a void even in Paris, near Lady Dudley. Infinitude is the region of the heart, love had no limits at Clochegourde. I loved Lady Dudley passionately; and certainly, though the animal in her was magnificent, she was also superior in mind; her sparkling and satirical conversation had a wide range. But I adored Henriette. At night I wept with happiness, in the morning with remorse.

Some women have the art to hide their jealousy under a tone of angelic kindness; they are, like Lady Dudley, over thirty years of age. Such women know how to feel and how to calculate; they press out the juices of to-day and think of the future also; they can stifle a moan, often a natural one, with the will of a huntsman who pays no heed to a wound in the ardor of the chase. Without ever speaking of Madame de Mortsauf, Arabella endeavored to kill her in my soul, where she ever found her, her own passion increasing with the consciousness of that invincible love. Intending to triumph by comparisons which would turn to her advantage, she was never suspicious, or complaining, or inquisitive, as are most young women; but, like a lioness who has seized her prey and carries it to her lair to devour, she watched that nothing should disturb her feast, and guarded me like a rebellious captive. I wrote to Henriette under her very eyes, but she never read a line of my letters; she never sought in any way to know to whom they were addressed. I had my liberty; she seemed to say to herself, "If I lose him it shall be my own fault," and she proudly relied on a love that would have given me her life had I asked for it,— in fact she often told me that if I left her she would kill herself. I have heard her praise the custom of Indian widows who burn themselves upon their husband's grave. "In India that is a distinction reserved for the higher classes," she said, "and is very little understood by Europeans, who are incapable of understanding the grandeur of the privilege; you must admit, however, that on the dead level of our modern customs aristocracy can rise to greatness only through unparalleled devotions. How can I prove to the middle classes that the blood in my veins is not the same as theirs, unless I show them that I can die as they cannot? Women of no birth can have diamonds and satins and horses—even coats-of-arms, which ought to be sacred to us, for any one can buy a name. But to love, with our heads up, in defiance of law; to die for the idol we have chosen, with the sheets of our bed for a shroud; to lay earth and heaven at his feet, robbing the Almighty of his right to make a god, and never to betray that man, never, never, even for virtue's sake,—for, to refuse him anything in the name of duty is to devote ourselves to something that is not _

*he_*

, and let that something be a man or an idea, it is betrayal all the same,— these are heights to which common women cannot attain; they know but two matter-of-fact ways; the great high-road of virtue, or the muddy path of the courtesan."

Pride, you see, was her instrument; she flattered all vanities by deifying them. She put me so high that she might live at my feet; in fact, the seductions of her spirit were literally expressed by an attitude of subserviency and her complete submission. In what words shall I describe those first six months when I was lost in enervating enjoyments, in the meshes of a love fertile in pleasures and knowing how to vary them with a cleverness learned by long experience, yet hiding that knowledge beneath the transports of passion. These pleasures, the sudden revelation of the poetry of the senses, constitute the powerful tie which binds young men to women older than they. It is the chain of the galley-slave; it leaves an ineffaceable brand upon the soul, filling it with disgust for pure and innocent love decked with flowers only, which serves no alcohol in curiously chased cups inlaid with jewels and sparkling with unquenchable fires.

Recalling my early dreams of pleasures I knew nothing of, expressed at Clochegourde in my "selams," the voice of my flowers, pleasures which the union of souls renders all the more ardent, I found many sophistries by which I excused to myself the delight with which I drained that jewelled cup. Often, when, lost in infinite lassitude, my soul disengaged itself from the body and floated far from earth, I thought that these pleasures might be the means of abolishing matter and of rendering to the spirit its power to soar. Sometimes Lady Dudley, like other women, profited by the exaltation in which I was to bind me by promises; under the lash of a desire she wrung blasphemies from my lips against the angel at Clochegourde. Once a traitor I became a scoundrel. I continued to write to Madame de Mortsauf, in the tone of the lad she had first known in his strange blue coat; but, I admit it, her gift of second-sight terrified me when I thought what ruin the indiscretion of a word might bring to the dear castle of my hopes. Often, in the midst of my pleasure a sudden horror seized me; I heard the name of Henriette uttered by a voice above me, like that in the Scriptures, demanding: "Cain, where is thy brother Abel?"

At last my letters remained unanswered. I was seized with horrible anxiety and wished to leave for Clochegourde. Arabella did not oppose it, but she talked of accompanying me to Touraine. Her woman's wit told her that the journey might be a means of finally detaching me from her rival; while I, blind with fear and guilelessly unsuspicious, did not see the trap she set for me. Lady Dudley herself proposed the humblest concessions. She would stay near Tours, at a little country-place, alone, disguised; she would refrain from going out in the day-time, and only meet me in the evening when people were not likely to be about. I left Tours on horseback. I had my reasons for this; my evening excursions to meet her would require a horse, and mine was an Arab which Lady Hester Stanhope had sent to the marchioness, and which she had lately exchanged with me for that famous picture of Rembrandt which I obtained in so singular a way, and which now hangs in her drawing-room in London. I took the road I had traversed on foot six years earlier and stopped beneath my walnut-tree. From there I saw Madame de Mortsauf in a white dress standing at the edge of the terrace. Instantly I rode towards her with the speed of lightning, in a straight line and across country. She heard the stride of the swallow of the desert and when I pulled him up suddenly at the terrace, she said to me: "Oh, you here!"

Those three words blasted me. She knew my treachery. Who had told her? her mother, whose hateful letter she afterwards showed me. The feeble, indifferent voice, once so full of life, the dull pallor of its tones revealed a settled grief, exhaling the breath of flowers cut and left to wither. The tempest of infidelity, like those freshets of the Loire which bury the meadows for all time in sand, had torn its way through her soul, leaving a desert where once the verdure clothed the fields. I led my horse through the little gate; he lay down on the grass at my command and the countess, who came forward slowly, exclaimed, "What a fine animal!" She stood with folded arms lest I should try to take her hand; I guessed her meaning.

"I will let Monsieur de Mortsauf know you are here," she said, leaving me.

I stood still, confounded, letting her go, watching her, always noble, slow, and proud,—whiter than I had ever seen her; on her brow the yellow imprint of bitterest melancholy, her head bent like a lily heavy with rain.

"Henriette!" I cried in the agony of a man about to die.

She did not turn or pause; she disdained to say that she withdrew from me that name, but she did not answer to it and continued on. I may feel paltry and small in this dreadful vale of life where myriads of human beings now dust make the surface of the globe, small indeed among that crowd, hurrying beneath the luminous spaces which light them; but what sense of humiliation could equal that with which I watched her calm white figure inflexibly mounting with even steps the terraces of her chateau of Clochegourde, the pride and the torture of that Christian Dido? I cursed Arabella in a single imprecation which might have killed her had she heard it, she who had left all for me as some leave all for God. I remained lost in a world of thought, conscious of utter misery on all sides. Presently I saw the whole family coming down; Jacques, running with the eagerness of his age. Madeleine, a gazelle with mournful eyes, walked with her mother. Monsieur de Mortsauf came to me with open arms, pressed me to him and kissed me on both cheeks crying out, "Felix, I know now that I owed you my life."

Madame de Mortsauf stood with her back towards me during this little scene, under pretext of showing the horse to Madeleine.

"Ha, the devil! that's what women are," cried the count; "admiring your horse!"

Madeleine turned, came up to me, and I kissed her hand, looking at the countess, who colored.

"Madeleine seems much better," I said.

"Poor little girl!" said the countess, kissing her on her forehead.

"Yes, for the time being they are all well," answered the count. "Except me, Felix; I am as battered as an old tower about to fall."

"The general is still depressed," I remarked to Madame de Mortsauf.

"We all have our blue devils—is not that the English term?" she replied.

The whole party walked on towards the vineyard with the feeling that some serious event had happened. She had no wish to be alone with me. Still, I was her guest.

"But about your horse? why isn't he attended to?" said the count.

"You see I am wrong if I think of him, and wrong if I do not," remarked the countess.

"Well, yes," said her husband; "there is a time to do things, and a time not to do them."

"I will attend to him," I said, finding this sort of greeting intolerable. "No one but myself can put him into his stall; my groom is coming by the coach from Chinon; he will rub him down."

"I suppose your groom is from England," she said.

"That is where they all come from," remarked the count, who grew cheerful in proportion as his wife seemed depressed. Her coldness gave him an opportunity to oppose her, and he overwhelmed me with friendliness.

"My dear Felix," he said, taking my hand, and pressing it affectionately, "pray forgive Madame de Mortsauf; women are so whimsical. But it is owing to their weakness; they cannot have the evenness of temper we owe to our strength of character. She really loves you, I know it; only—"

While the count was speaking Madame de Mortsauf gradually moved away from us so as to leave us alone.

"Felix," said the count, in a low voice, looking at his wife, who was now going up to the house with her two children, "I don't know what is going on in Madame de Mortsauf's mind, but for the last six weeks her disposition has completely changed. She, so gentle, so devoted hitherto, is now extraordinarily peevish."

Manette told me later that the countess had fallen into a state of depression which made her indifferent to the count's provocations. No longer finding a soft substance in which he could plant his arrows, the man became as uneasy as a child when the poor insect it is tormenting ceases to move. He now needed a confidant, as the hangman needs a helper.

"Try to question Madame de Mortsauf," he said after a pause, "and find out what is the matter. A woman always has secrets from her husband; but perhaps she will tell you what troubles her. I would sacrifice everything to make her happy, even to half my remaining days or half my fortune. She is necessary to my very life. If I have not that angel at my side as I grow old I shall be the most wretched of men. I do desire to die easy. Tell her I shall not be here long to trouble her. Yes, Felix, my poor friend, I am going fast, I know it. I hide the fatal truth from every one; why should I worry them beforehand? The trouble is in the orifice of the stomach, my friend. I have at last discovered the true cause of this disease; it is my sensibility that is killing me. Indeed, all our feelings affect the gastric centre."

"Then do you mean," I said, smiling, "that the best-hearted people die of their stomachs?"

"Don't laugh, Felix; nothing is more absolutely true. Too keen a sensibility increases the play of the sympathetic nerve; these excitements of feeling keep the mucous membrane of the stomach in a state of constant irritation. If this state continues it deranges, at first insensibly, the digestive functions; the secretions change, the appetite is impaired, and the digestion becomes capricious; sharp pains are felt; they grow worse day by day, and more frequent; then the disorder comes to a crisis, as if a slow poison were passing the alimentary canal; the mucous membrane thickens, the valve of the pylorus becomes indurated and forms a scirrhus, of which the patient dies. Well, I have reached that point, my dear friend. The induration is proceeding and nothing checks it. Just look at my yellow skin, my feverish eyes, my excessive thinness. I am withering away. But what is to be done? I brought the seeds of the disease home with me from the emigration; heaven knows what I suffered then! My marriage, which might have repaired the wrong, far from soothing my ulcerated mind increased the wound. What did I find? ceaseless fears for the children, domestic jars, a fortune to remake, economies which required great privations, which I was obliged to impose upon my wife, but which I was the one to suffer from; and then,—I can tell this to none but you, Felix,—I have a worse trouble yet. Though Blanche is an angel, she does not understand me; she knows nothing of my sufferings and she aggravates them; but I forgive her. It is a dreadful thing to say, my friend, but a less virtuous woman might have made me more happy by lending herself to consolations which Blanche never thinks of, for she is as silly as a child. Moreover my servants torment me; blockheads who take my French for Greek! When our fortune was finally remade inch by inch, and I had some relief from care, it was too late, the harm was done; I had reached the period when the appetite is vitiated. Then came my severe illness, so ill-managed by Origet. In short, I have not six months to live."

I listened to the count in terror. On meeting the countess I had been struck with her yellow skin and the feverish brilliancy of her eyes. I led the count towards the house while seeming to listen to his complaints and his medical dissertations; but my thoughts were all with Henriette, and I wanted to observe her. We found her in the salon, where she was listening to a lesson in mathematics which the Abbe Dominis was giving Jacques, and at the same time showing Madeleine a stitch of embroidery. Formerly she would have laid aside every occupation the day of my arrival to be with me. But my love was so deeply real that I drove back into my heart the grief I felt at this contrast between the past and the present, and thought only of the fatal yellow tint on that celestial face, which resembled the halo of divine light Italian painters put around the faces of their saints. I felt the icy wind of death pass over me. Then when the fire of her eyes, no longer softened by the liquid light in which in former times they moved, fell upon me, I shuddered; I noticed several changes, caused by grief, which I had not seen in the open air. The slender lines which, at my last visit, were so lightly marked upon her forehead had deepened; her temples with their violet veins seemed burning and concave; her eyes were sunk beneath the brows, their circles browned;—alas! she was discolored like a fruit when decay is beginning to show upon the surface, or a worm is at the core. I, whose whole ambition had been to pour happiness into her soul, I it was who embittered the spring from which she had hoped to refresh her life and renew her courage. I took a seat beside her and said in a voice filled with tears of repentance, "Are you satisfied with your own health?"

"Yes," she answered, plunging her eyes into mine. "My health is there," she added, motioning to Jacques and Madeleine.

The latter, just fifteen, had come victoriously out of her struggle with anaemia, and was now a woman. She had grown tall; the Bengal roses were blooming in her once sallow cheeks. She had lost the unconcern of a child who looks every one in the face, and now dropped her eyes; her movements were slow and infrequent, like those of her mother; her figure was slim, but the gracefulness of the bust was already developing; already an instinct of coquetry had smoothed the magnificent black hair which lay in bands upon her Spanish brow. She was like those pretty statuettes of the Middle Ages, so delicate in outline, so slender in form that the eye as it seizes their charm fears to break them. Health, the fruit of untold efforts, had made her cheeks as velvety as a peach and given to her throat the silken down which, like her mother's, caught the light. She was to live! God had written it, dear bud of the loveliest of human flowers, on the long lashes of her eyelids, on the curve of those shoulders which gave promise of a development as superb as her mother's! This brown young girl, erect as a poplar, contrasted with Jacques, a fragile youth of seventeen, whose head had grown immensely, causing anxiety by the rapid expansion of the forehead, while his feverish, weary eyes were in keeping with a voice that was deep and sonorous. The voice gave forth too strong a volume of tone, the eye too many thoughts. It was Henriette's intellect and soul and heart that were here devouring with swift flames a body without stamina; for Jacques had the milk-white skin and high color which characterize young English women doomed sooner or later to the consumptive curse,—an appearance of health that deceives the eye. Following a sign by which Henriette, after showing me Madeleine, made me look at Jacques drawing geometrical figures and algebraic calculations on a board before the Abbe Dominis, I shivered at the sight of death hidden beneath the roses, and was thankful for the self-deception of his mother.

"When I see my children thus, happiness stills my griefs—just as those griefs are dumb, and even disappear, when I see them failing. My friend," she said, her eyes shining with maternal pleasure, "if other affections fail us, the feelings rewarded here, the duties done and crowned with success, are compensation enough for defeat elsewhere. Jacques will be, like you, a man of the highest education, possessed of the worthiest knowledge; he will be, like you, an honor to his country, which he may assist in governing, helped by you, whose standing will be so high; but I will strive to make him faithful to his first affections. Madeleine, dear creature, has a noble heart; she is pure as the snows on the highest Alps; she will have a woman's devotion and a woman's graceful intellect. She is proud; she is worthy of being a Lenoncourt. My motherhood, once so tried, so tortured, is happy now, happy with an infinite happiness, unmixed with pain. Yes, my life is full, my life is rich. You see, God makes my joy to blossom in the heart of these sanctified affections, and turns to bitterness those that might have led me astray—"

"Good!" cried the abbe, joyfully. "Monsieur le vicomte begins to know as much as I—"

Just then Jacques coughed.

"Enough for to-day, my dear abbe," said the countess, "above all, no chemistry. Go for a ride on horseback, Jacques," she added, letting her son kiss her with the tender and yet dignified pleasure of a mother. "Go, dear, but take care of yourself."

"But," I said, as her eyes followed Jacques with a lingering look, "you have not answered me. Do you feel ill?"

"Oh, sometimes, in my stomach. If I were in Paris I should have the honors of gastritis, the fashionable disease."

"My mother suffers very much and very often," said Madeleine.

"Ah!" she said, "does my health interest you?"

Madeleine, astonished at the irony of these words, looked from one to the other; my eyes counted the roses on the cushion of the gray and green sofa which was in the salon.

"This situation is intolerable," I whispered in her ear.

"Did I create it?" she asked. "Dear child," she said aloud, with one of those cruel levities by which women point their vengeance, "don't you read history? France and England are enemies, and ever have been. Madeleine knows that; she knows that a broad sea, and a cold and stormy one, separates them."

The vases on the mantelshelf had given place to candelabra, no doubt to deprive me of the pleasure of filling them with flowers; I found them later in my own room. When my servant arrived I went out to give him some orders; he had brought me certain things I wished to place in my room.

"Felix," said the countess, "do not make a mistake. My aunt's old room is now Madeleine's. Yours is over the count's."

Though guilty, I had a heart; those words were dagger thrusts coldly given at its tenderest spot, for which she seemed to aim. Moral sufferings are not fixed quantities; they depend on the sensitiveness of souls. The countess had trod each round of the ladder of pain; but, for that very reason, the kindest of women was now as cruel as she was once beneficent. I looked at Henriette, but she averted her head. I went to my new room, which was pretty, white and green. Once there I burst into tears. Henriette heard me as she entered with a bunch of flowers in her hand.

"Henriette," I said, "will you never forgive a wrong that is indeed excusable?"

"Do not call me Henriette," she said. "She no longer exists, poor soul; but you may feel sure of Madame de Mortsauf, a devoted friend, who will listen to you and who will love you. Felix, we will talk of these things later. If you have still any tenderness for me let me grow accustomed to seeing you. Whenever words will not rend my heart, if the day should ever come when I recover courage, I will speak to you, but not till then. Look at the valley," she said, pointing to the Indre, "it hurts me, I love it still."

"Ah, perish England and all her women! I will send my resignation to the king; I will live and die here, pardoned."

"No, love her; love that woman! Henriette is not. This is no play, and you should know it."

She left the room, betraying by the tone of her last words the extent of her wounds. I ran after her and held her back, saying, "Do you no longer love me?"

"You have done me more harm than all my other troubles put together. To-day I suffer less, therefore I love you less. Be kind; do not increase my pain; if you suffer, remember that—I—live."

She withdrew her hand, which I held, cold, motionless, but moist, in mine, and darted like an arrow through the corridor in which this scene of actual tragedy took place.

At dinner, the count subjected me to a torture I had little expected. "So the Marchioness of Dudley is not in Paris?" he said.

I blushed excessively, but answered, "No."

"She is not in Tours," continued the count.

"She is not divorced, and she can go back to England. Her husband would be very glad if she would return to him," I said, eagerly.

"Has she children?" asked Madame de Mortsauf, in a changed voice.

"Two sons," I replied.

"Where are they?"

"In England, with their father."

"Come, Felix," interposed the count; "be frank; is she as handsome as they say?"

"How can you ask him such a question?" cried the countess. "Is not the woman you love always the handsomest of women?"

"Yes, always," I said, firmly, with a glance which she could not sustain.

"You are a happy fellow," said the count; "yes, a very happy one. Ha! in my young days, I should have gone mad over such a conquest—"

"Hush!" said Madame de Mortsauf, reminding the count of Madeleine by a look.

"I am not a child," he said.

When we left the table I followed the countess to the terrace. When we were alone she exclaimed, "How is it possible that some women can sacrifice their children to a man? Wealth, position, the world, I can conceive of; eternity? yes, possibly; but children! deprive one's self of one's children!"

"Yes, and such women would give even more if they had it; they sacrifice everything."

The world was suddenly reversed before her, her ideas became confused. The grandeur of that thought struck her; a suspicion entered her mind that sacrifice, immolation justified happiness; the echo of her own inward cry for love came back to her; she stood dumb in presence of her wasted life. Yes, for a moment horrible doubts possessed her; then she rose, grand and saintly, her head erect.

"Love her well, Felix," she said, with tears in her eyes; "she shall be my happy sister. I will forgive her the harm she has done me if she gives you what you could not have here. You are right; I have never told you that I loved you, and I never have loved you as the world loves. But if she is a mother how can she love you so?"

"Dear saint," I answered, "I must be less moved than I am now, before I can explain to you how it is that you soar victoriously above her. She is a woman of earth, the daughter of decaying races; you are the child of heaven, an angel worthy of worship; you have my heart, she my flesh only. She knows this and it fills her with despair; she would change parts with you even though the cruellest martyrdom were the price of the change. But all is irremediable. To you the soul, to you the thoughts, the love that is pure, to you youth and old age; to her the desires and joys of passing passion; to you remembrance forever, to her oblivion—"

"Tell me, tell me that again, oh, my friend!" she turned to a bench and sat down, bursting into tears. "If that be so, Felix, virtue, purity of life, a mother's love, are not mistakes. Oh, pour that balm upon my wounds! Repeat the words which bear me back to heaven, where once I longed to rise with you. Bless me by a look, by a sacred word, —I forgive you for the sufferings you have caused me the last two months."

"Henriette, there are mysteries in the life of men of which you know nothing. I met you at an age when the feelings of the heart stifle the desires implanted in our nature; but many scenes, the memory of which will kindle my soul to the hour of death, must have told you that this age was drawing to a close, and it was your constant triumph still to prolong its mute delights. A love without possession is maintained by the exasperation of desire; but there comes a moment when all is suffering within us—for in this we have no resemblance to you. We possess a power we cannot abdicate, or we cease to be men. Deprived of the nourishment it needs, the heart feeds upon itself, feeling an exhaustion which is not death, but which precedes it. Nature cannot long be silenced; some trifling accident awakens it to a violence that seems like madness. No, I have not loved, but I have thirsted in the desert."

"The desert!" she said bitterly, pointing to the valley. "Ah!" she exclaimed, "how he reasons! what subtle distinctions! Faithful hearts are not so learned."

"Henriette," I said, "do not quarrel with me for a chance expression. No, my soul has not vacillated, but I have not been master of my senses. That woman is not ignorant that you are the only one I ever loved. She plays a secondary part in my life; she knows it and is resigned. I have the right to leave her as men leave courtesans."

"And then?"

"She tells me that she will kill herself," I answered, thinking that this resolve would startle Henriette. But when she heard it a disdainful smile, more expressive than the thoughts it conveyed, flickered on her lips. "My dear conscience," I continued, "if you would take into account my resistance and the seductions that led to my fall you would understand the fatal—"

"Yes, fatal!" she cried. "I believed in you too much. I believed you capable of the virtue a priest practises. All is over," she continued, after a pause. "I owe you much, my friend; you have extinguished in me the fires of earthly life. The worst of the way is over; age is coming on. I am ailing now, soon I may be ill; I can never be the brilliant fairy who showers you with favors. Be faithful to Lady Dudley. Madeleine, whom I was training to be yours, ah! who will have her now? Poor Madeleine, poor Madeleine!" she repeated, like the mournful burden of a song. "I would you had heard her say to me when you came: 'Mother, you are not kind to Felix!' Dear creature!"

She looked at me in the warm rays of the setting sun as they glided through the foliage. Seized with compassion for the shipwreck of our lives she turned back to memories of our pure past, yielding to meditations which were mutual. We were silent, recalling past scenes; our eyes went from the valley to the fields, from the windows of Clochegourde to those of Frapesle, peopling the dream with my bouquets, the fragrant language of our desires. It was her last hour of pleasure, enjoyed with the purity of her Catholic soul. This scene, so grand to each of us, cast its melancholy on both. She believed my words, and saw where I placed her—in the skies.

"My friend," she said, "I obey God, for his hand is in all this."

I did not know until much later the deep meaning of her words. We slowly returned up the terraces. She took my arm and leaned upon it resignedly, bleeding still, but with a bandage on her wound.

"Human life is thus," she said. "What had Monsieur de Mortsauf done to deserve his fate? It proves the existence of a better world. Alas, for those who walk in happier ways!"

She went on, estimating life so truly, considering its diverse aspects so profoundly that these cold judgments revealed to me the disgust that had come upon her for all things here below. When we reached the portico she dropped my arm and said these last words: "If God has given us the sentiment and the desire for happiness ought he not to take charge himself of innocent souls who have found sorrow only in this low world? Either that must be so, or God is not, and our life is no more than a cruel jest."

She entered and turned the house quickly; I found her on the sofa, crouching, as though blasted by the voice which flung Saul to the ground.

"What is the matter?" I asked.

"I no longer know what is virtue," she replied; "I have no consciousness of my own."

We were silent, petrified, listening to the echo of those words which fell like a stone cast into a gulf.

"If I am mistaken in my life _

*she_*

is right in _

*hers_*

," Henriette said at last.

Thus her last struggle followed her last happiness. When the count came in she complained of illness, she who never complained. I conjured her to tell me exactly where she suffered; but she refused to explain and went to bed, leaving me a prey to unending remorse. Madeleine went with her mother, and the next day I heard that the countess had been seized with nausea, caused, she said, by the violent excitements of that day. Thus I, who longed to give my life for hers, I was killing her.

"Dear count," I said to Monsieur de Mortsauf, who obliged me to play backgammon, "I think the countess very seriously ill. There is still time to save her; pray send for Origet, and persuade her to follow his advice."

"Origet, who half killed me?" cried the count. "No, no; I'll consult Carbonneau."

During this week, especially the first days of it, everything was anguish to me—the beginning of paralysis of the heart—my vanity was mortified, my soul rent. One must needs have been the centre of all looks and aspirations, the mainspring of the life about him, the torch from which all others drew their light, to understand the horror of the void that was now about me. All things were there, the same, but the spirit that gave life to them was extinct, like a blown-out flame. I now understood the desperate desire of lovers never to see each other again when love has flown. To be nothing where we were once so much! To find the chilling silence of the grave where life so lately sparkled! Such comparisons are overwhelming. I came at last to envy the dismal ignorance of all happiness which had darkened my youth. My despair became so great that the countess, I thought, felt pity for it. One day after dinner as we were walking on the meadows beside the river I made a last effort to obtain forgiveness. I told Jacques to go on with his sister, and leaving the count to walk alone, I took Henriette to the punt.

"Henriette," I said; "one word of forgiveness, or I fling myself into the Indre! I have sinned,—yes, it is true; but am I not like a dog in his faithful attachments? I return like him, like him ashamed. If he does wrong he is struck, but he loves the hand that strikes him; strike me, bruise me, but give me back your heart."

"Poor child," she said, "are you not always my son?"

She took my arm and silently rejoined her children, with whom she returned to Clochegourde, leaving me to the count, who began to talk politics apropos of his neighbors.

"Let us go in," I said; "you are bare-headed, and the dew may do you an injury."

"You pity me, my dear Felix," he answered; "you understand me, but my wife never tries to comfort me,—on principle, perhaps."

Never would she have left me to walk home with her husband; it was now I who had to find excuses to join her. I found her with her children, explaining the rules of backgammon to Jacques.

"See there," said the count, who was always jealous of the affection she showed for her children; "it is for them that I am neglected. Husbands, my dear Felix, are always suppressed. The most virtuous woman in the world has ways of satisfying her desire to rob conjugal affection."

She said nothing and continued as before.

"Jacques," he said, "come here."

Jacques objected slightly.

"Your father wants you; go at once, my son," said his mother, pushing him.

"They love me by order," said the old man, who sometimes perceived his situation.

"Monsieur," she answered, passing her hand over Madeleine's smooth tresses, which were dressed that day "a la belle Ferronniere"; "do not be unjust to us poor women; life is not so easy for us to bear. Perhaps the children are the virtues of a mother."

"My dear," said the count, who took it into his head to be logical, "what you say signifies that women who have no children would have no virtue, and would leave their husbands in the lurch."

The countess rose hastily and took Madeleine to the portico.

"That's marriage, my dear fellow," remarked the count to me. "Do you mean to imply by going off in that manner that I am talking nonsense?" he cried to his wife, taking his son by the hand and going to the portico after her with a furious look in his eyes.

"On the contrary, Monsieur, you frightened me. Your words hurt me cruelly," she added, in a hollow voice. "If virtue does not consist in sacrificing everything to our children and our husband, what is virtue?"

"Sac-ri-ficing!" cried the count, making each syllable the blow of a sledge-hammer on the heart of his victim. "What have you sacrificed to your children? What do you sacrifice to me? Speak! what means all this? Answer. What is going on here? What did you mean by what you said?"

"Monsieur," she replied, "would you be satisfied to be loved for love of God, or to know your wife virtuous for virtue's sake?"

"Madame is right," I said, interposing in a shaken voice which vibrated in two hearts; "yes, the noblest privilege conferred by reason is to attribute our virtues to the beings whose happiness is our work, and whom we render happy, not from policy, nor from duty, but from an inexhaustible and voluntary affection—"

A tear shone in Henriette's eyes.

"And, dear count," I continued, "if by chance a woman is involuntarily subjected to feelings other than those society imposes on her, you must admit that the more irresistible that feeling is, the more virtuous she is in smothering it, in sacrificing herself to her husband and children. This theory is not applicable to me who unfortunately show an example to the contrary, nor to you whom it will never concern."

"You have a noble soul, Felix," said the count, slipping his arm, not ungracefully, round his wife's waist and drawing her towards him to say: "Forgive a poor sick man, dear, who wants to be loved more than he deserves."

"There are some hearts that are all generosity," she said, resting her head upon his shoulder. The scene made her tremble to such a degree that her comb fell, her hair rolled down, and she turned pale. The count, holding her up, gave a sort of groan as he felt her fainting; he caught her in his arms as he might a child, and carried her to the sofa in the salon, where we all surrounded her. Henriette held my hand in hers as if to tell me that we two alone knew the secret of that scene, so simple in itself, so heart-rending to her.

"I do wrong," she said to me in a low voice, when the count left the room to fetch a glass of orange-flower water. "I have many wrongs to repent of towards you; I wished to fill you with despair when I ought to have received you mercifully. Dear, you are kindness itself, and I alone can appreciate it. Yes, I know there is a kindness prompted by passion. Men have various ways of being kind; some from contempt, others from impulse, from calculation, through indolence of nature; but you, my friend, you have been absolutely kind."

"If that be so," I replied, "remember that all that is good or great in me comes through you. You know well that I am of your making."

"That word is enough for any woman's happiness," she said, as the count re-entered the room. "I feel better," she said, rising; "I want air."

We went down to the terrace, fragrant with the acacias which were still in bloom. She had taken my right arm, and pressed it against her heart, thus expressing her sad thoughts; but they were, she said, of a sadness dear to her. No doubt she would gladly have been alone with me; but her imagination, inexpert in women's wiles, did not suggest to her any way of sending her children and the count back to the house. We therefore talked on indifferent subjects, while she pondered a means of pouring a few last thoughts from her heart to mine.

"It is a long time since I have driven out," she said, looking at the beauty of the evening. "Monsieur, will you please order the carriage that I may take a turn?"

She knew that after evening prayer she could not speak with me, for the count was sure to want his backgammon. She might have returned to the warm and fragrant terrace after her husband had gone to bed, but she feared, perhaps, to trust herself beneath those shadows, or to walk by the balustrade where our eyes could see the course of the Indre through the dear valley. As the silent and sombre vaults of a cathedral lift the soul to prayer, so leafy ways, lighted by the moon, perfumed with penetrating odors, alive with the murmuring noises of the spring-tide, stir the fibres and weaken the resolves of those who love. The country calms the old, but excites the young. We knew it well. Two strokes of the bell announced the hour of prayer. The countess shivered.

"Dear Henriette, are you ill?"

"There is no Henriette," she said. "Do not bring her back. She was capricious and exacting; now you have a friend whose courage has been strengthened by the words which heaven itself dictated to you. We will talk of this later. We must be punctual at prayers, for it is my day to lead them."

As Madame de Mortsauf said the words in which she begged the help of God through all the adversities of life, a tone came into her voice which struck all present. Did she use her gift of second sight to foresee the terrible emotion she was about to endure through my forgetfulness of an engagement made with Arabella?

"We have time to make three kings before the horses are harnessed," said the count, dragging me back to the salon. "You can go and drive with my wife, and I'll go to bed."

The game was stormy, like all others. The countess heard the count's voice either from her room or from Madeleine's.

"You show a strange hospitality," she said, re-entering the salon.

I looked at her with amazement; I could not get accustomed to the change in her; formerly she would have been most careful not to protect me against the count; then it gladdened her that I should share her sufferings and bear them with patience for love of her.

"I would give my life," I whispered in her ear, "if I could hear you say again, as you once said, 'Poor dear, poor dear!'"

She lowered her eyes, remembering the moment to which I alluded, yet her glance turned to me beneath her eyelids, expressing the joy of a woman who finds the mere passing tones from her heart preferred to the delights of another love. The count was losing the game; he said he was tired, as an excuse to give it up, and we went to walk on the lawn while waiting for the carriage. When the count left us, such pleasure shone on my face that Madame de Mortsauf questioned me by a look of surprise and curiosity.

"Henriette does exist," I said. "You love me still. You wound me with an evident intention to break my heart. I may yet be happy!"

"There was but a fragment of that poor woman left, and you have now destroyed even that," she said. "God be praised; he gives me strength to bear my righteous martyrdom. Yes, I still love you, and I might have erred; the English woman shows me the abyss."

We got into the carriage and the coachman asked for orders.

"Take the road to Chinon by the avenue, and come back by the Charlemagne moor and the road to Sache."

"What day is it?" I asked, with too much eagerness.

"Saturday."

"Then don't go that way, madame, the road will be crowded with poultry-men and their carts returning from Tours."

"Do as I told you," she said to the coachman. We knew the tones of our voices too well to be able to hide from each other our least emotion. Henriette understood all.

"You did not think of the poultry-men when you appointed this evening," she said with a tinge of irony. "Lady Dudley is at Tours, and she is coming here to meet you; do not deny it. 'What day is it?—the poultry-men—their carts!' Did you ever take notice of such things in our old drives?"

"It only shows that at Clochegourde I forget everything," I answered, simply.

"She is coming to meet you?"

"Yes."

"At what hour?"

"Half-past eleven."

"Where?"

"On the moor."

"Do not deceive me; is it not at the walnut-tree?"

"On the moor."

"We will go there," she said, "and I shall see her."

When I heard these words I regarded my future life as settled. I at once resolved to marry Lady Dudley and put an end to the miserable struggle which threatened to exhaust my sensibilities and destroy by these repeated shocks the delicate delights which had hitherto resembled the flower of fruits. My sullen silence wounded the countess, the grandeur of whose mind I misjudged.

"Do not be angry with me," she said, in her golden voice. "This, dear, is my punishment. You can never be loved as you are here," she continued, laying my hand upon her heart. "I now confess it; but Lady Dudley has saved me. To her the stains,—I do not envy them,—to me the glorious love of angels! I have traversed vast tracts of thought since you returned here. I have judged life. Lift up the soul and you rend it; the higher we go the less sympathy we meet; instead of suffering in the valley, we suffer in the skies, as the soaring eagle bears in his heart the arrow of some common herdsman. I comprehend at last that earth and heaven are incompatible. Yes, to those who would live in the celestial sphere God must be all in all. We must love our friends as we love our children,—for them, not for ourselves. Self is the cause of misery and grief. My soul is capable of soaring higher than the eagle; there is a love which cannot fail me. But to live for this earthly life is too debasing,—here the selfishness of the senses reigns supreme over the spirituality of the angel that is within us. The pleasures of passion are stormy, followed by enervating anxieties which impair the vigor of the soul. I came to the shores of the sea where such tempests rage; I have seen them too near; they have wrapped me in their clouds; the billows did not break at my feet, they caught me in a rough embrace which chilled my heart. No! I must escape to higher regions; I should perish on the shores of this vast sea. I see in you, as in all others who have grieved me, the guardian of my virtue. My life has been mingled with anguish, fortunately proportioned to my strength; it has thus been kept free from evil passions, from seductive peace, and ever near to God. Our attachment was the mistaken attempt, the innocent effort of two children striving to satisfy their own hearts, God, and men—folly, Felix! Ah," she said quickly, "what does that woman call you?"

"'Amedee,'" I answered, "'Felix' is a being apart, who belongs to none but you."

"'Henriette' is slow to die," she said, with a gentle smile, "but die she will at the first effort of the humble Christian, the self-respecting mother; she whose virtue tottered yesterday and is firm to-day. What may I say to you? This. My life has been, and is, consistent with itself in all its circumstances, great and small. The heart to which the rootlets of my first affection should have clung, my mother's heart, was closed to me, in spite of my persistence in seeking a cleft through which they might have slipped. I was a girl; I came after the death of three boys; and I vainly strove to take their place in the hearts of my parents; the wound I gave to the family pride was never healed. When my gloomy childhood was over and I knew my aunt, death took her from me all too soon. Monsieur de Mortsauf, to whom I vowed myself, has repeatedly, nay without respite, smitten me, not being himself aware of it, poor man! His love has the simple-minded egotism our children show to us. He has no conception of the harm he does me, and he is heartily forgiven for it. My children, those dear children who are bound to my flesh through their sufferings, to my soul by their characters, to my nature by their innocent happiness,—those children were surely given to show me how much strength and patience a mother's breast contains. Yes, my children are my virtues. You know how my heart has been harrowed for them, by them, in spite of them. To be a mother was, for me, to buy the right to suffer. When Hagar cried in the desert an angel came and opened a spring of living water for that poor slave; but I, when the limpid stream to which (do you remember?) you tried to guide me flowed past Clochegourde, its waters changed to bitterness for me. Yes, the sufferings you have inflicted on my soul are terrible. God, no doubt, will pardon those who know affection only through its pains. But if the keenest of these pains has come to me through you, perhaps I deserved them. God is not unjust. Ah, yes, Felix, a kiss furtively taken may be a crime. Perhaps it is just that a woman should harshly expiate the few steps taken apart from husband and children that she might walk alone with thoughts and memories that were not of them, and so walking, marry her soul to another. Perhaps it is the worst of crimes when the inward being lowers itself to the region of human kisses. When a woman bends to receive her husband's kiss with a mask upon her face, that is a crime! It is a crime to think of a future springing from a death, a crime to imagine a motherhood without terrors, handsome children playing in the evening with a beloved father before the eyes of a happy mother. Yes, I sinned, sinned greatly. I have loved the penances inflicted by the Church,—which did not redeem the faults, for the priest was too indulgent. God has placed the punishment in the faults themselves, committing the execution of his vengeance to the one for whom the faults were committed. When I gave my hair, did I not give myself? Why did I so often dress in white? because I seemed the more your lily; did you not see me here, for the first time, all in white? Alas! I have loved my children less, for all intense affection is stolen from the natural affections. Felix, do you not see that all suffering has its meaning. Strike me, wound me even more than Monsieur de Mortsauf and my children's state have wounded me. That woman is the instrument of God's anger; I will meet her without hatred; I will smile upon her; under pain of being neither Christian, wife, nor mother, I ought to love her. If, as you tell me, I contributed to keep your heart unsoiled by the world, that Englishwoman ought not to hate me. A woman should love the mother of the man she loves, and I am your mother. What place have I sought in your heart? that left empty by Madame de Vandenesse. Yes, yes, you have always complained of my coldness; yes, I am indeed your mother only. Forgive me therefore the involuntary harshness with which I met you on your return; a mother ought to rejoice that her son is so well loved—"

She laid her head for a moment on my breast, repeating the words, "Forgive me! oh, forgive me!" in a voice that was neither her girlish voice with its joyous notes, nor the woman's voice with despotic endings; not the sighing sound of the mother's woe, but an agonizing new voice for new sorrows.

"You, Felix," she presently continued, growing animated; "you are the friend who can do no wrong. Ah! you have lost nothing in my heart; do not blame yourself, do not feel the least remorse. It was the height of selfishness in me to ask you to sacrifice the joys of life to an impossible future; impossible, because to realize it a woman must abandon her children, abdicate her position, and renounce eternity. Many a time I have thought you higher than I; you were great and noble, I, petty and criminal. Well, well, it is settled now; I can be to you no more than a light from above, sparkling and cold, but unchanging. Only, Felix, let me not love the brother I have chosen without return. Love me, cherish me! The love of a sister has no dangerous to-morrow, no hours of difficulty. You will never find it necessary to deceive the indulgent heart which will live in future within your life, grieve for your griefs, be joyous with your joys, which will love the women who make you happy, and resent their treachery. I never had a brother to love in that way. Be noble enough to lay aside all self-love and turn our attachment, hitherto so doubtful and full of trouble, into this sweet and sacred love. In this way I shall be enabled to still live. I will begin to-night by taking Lady Dudley's hand."

She did not weep as she said these words so full of bitter knowledge, by which, casting aside the last remaining veil which hid her soul from mine, she showed by how many ties she had linked herself to me, how many chains I had hewn apart. Our emotions were so great that for a time we did not notice it was raining heavily.

"Will Madame la comtesse wait here under shelter?" asked the coachman, pointing to the chief inn of Ballan.

She made a sign of assent, and we stayed nearly half an hour under the vaulted entrance, to the great surprise of the inn-people who wondered what brought Madame de Mortsauf on that road at eleven o'clock at night. Was she going to Tours? Had she come from there? When the storm ceased and the rain turned to what is called in Touraine a "brouee," which does not hinder the moon from shining through the higher mists as the wind with its upper currents whirls them away, the coachman drove from our shelter, and, to my great delight, turned to go back the way we came.

"Follow my orders," said the countess, gently.

We now took the road across the Charlemagne moor, where the rain began again. Half-way across I heard the barking of Arabella's dog; a horse came suddenly from beneath a clump of oaks, jumped the ditch which owners of property dig around their cleared lands when they consider them suitable for cultivation, and carried Lady Dudley to the moor to meet the carriage.

"What pleasure to meet a love thus if it can be done without sin," said Henriette.

The barking of the dog had told Lady Dudley that I was in the carriage. She thought, no doubt, that I had brought it to meet her on account of the rain. When we reached the spot where she was waiting, she urged her horse to the side of the road with the equestrian dexterity for which she was famous, and which to Henriette seemed marvellous.

"Amedee," she said, and the name in her English pronunciation had a fairy-like charm.

"He is here, madame," said the countess, looking at the fantastic creature plainly visible in the moonlight, whose impatient face was oddly swathed in locks of hair now out of curl.

You know with what swiftness two women examine each other. The Englishwoman recognized her rival, and was gloriously English; she gave us a look full of insular contempt, and disappeared in the underbrush with the rapidity of an arrow.

"Drive on quickly to Clochegourde," cried the countess, to whom that cutting look was like the blow of an axe upon her heart.

The coachman turned to get upon the road to Chinon which was better than that to Sache. As the carriage again approached the moor we heard the furious galloping of Arabella's horse and the steps of her dog. All three were skirting the wood behind the bushes.

"She is going; you will lose her forever," said Henriette.

"Let her go," I answered, "and without a regret."

"Oh, poor woman!" cried the countess, with a sort of compassionate horror. "Where will she go?"

"Back to La Grenadiere,—a little house near Saint-Cyr," I said, "where she is staying."

Just as we were entering the avenue of Clochegourde Arabella's dog barked joyfully and bounded up to the carriage.

"She is here before us!" cried the countess; then after a pause she added, "I have never seen a more beautiful woman. What a hand and what a figure! Her complexion outdoes the lily, her eyes are literally bright as diamonds. But she rides too well; she loves to display her strength; I think her violent and too active,—also too bold for our conventions. The woman who recognizes no law is apt to listen only to her caprices. Those who seek to shine, to make a stir, have not the gift of constancy. Love needs tranquillity; I picture it to myself like a vast lake in which the lead can find no bottom; where tempests may be violent, but are rare and controlled within certain limits; where two beings live on a flowery isle far from the world whose luxury and display offend them. Still, love must take the imprint of the character. Perhaps I am wrong. If nature's elements are compelled to take certain forms determined by climate, why is it not the same with the feelings of individuals? No doubt sentiments, feelings, which hold to the general law in the mass, differ in expression only. Each soul has its own method. Lady Dudley is the strong woman who can traverse distances and act with the vigor of a man; she would rescue her lover and kill jailers and guards; while other women can only love with their whole souls; in moments of danger they kneel down to pray, and die. Which of the two women suits you best? That is the question. Yes, yes, Lady Dudley must surely love; she has made many sacrifices. Perhaps she will love you when you have ceased to love her!"

"Dear angel," I said, "let me ask the question you asked me; how is it that you know these things?"

"Every sorrow teaches a lesson, and I have suffered on so many points that my knowledge is vast."

My servant had heard the order given, and thinking we should return by the terraces he held my horse ready for me in the avenue. Arabella's dog had scented the horse, and his mistress, drawn by very natural curiosity, had followed the animal through the woods to the avenue.

"Go and make your peace," said Henriette, smiling without a tinge of sadness. "Say to Lady Dudley how much she mistakes my intention; I wished to show her the true value of the treasure which has fallen to her; my heart holds none but kind feelings, above all neither anger nor contempt. Explain to her that I am her sister, and not her rival."

"I shall not go," I said.

"Have you never discovered," she said with lofty pride, "that certain propitiations are insulting? Go!"

I rode towards Lady Dudley wishing to know the state of her mind. "If she would only be angry and leave me," I thought, "I could return to Clochegourde."

The dog led me to an oak, from which, as I came up, Arabella galloped crying out to me, "Come! away! away!" All that I could do was to follow her to Saint Cyr, which we reached about midnight.

"That lady is in perfect health," said Arabella as she dismounted.

Those who know her can alone imagine the satire contained in that remark, dryly said in a tone which meant, "I should have died!"

"I forbid you to utter any of your sarcasms about Madame de Mortsauf," I said.

"Do I displease your Grace in remarking upon the perfect health of one so dear to your precious heart? Frenchwomen hate, so I am told, even their lover's dog. In England we love all that our masters love; we hate all they hate, because we are flesh of their flesh. Permit me therefore to love this lady as much as you yourself love her. Only, my dear child," she added, clasping me in her arms which were damp with rain, "if you betray me, I shall not be found either lying down or standing up, not in a carriage with liveried lackeys, nor on horseback on the moors of Charlemagne, nor on any other moor beneath the skies, nor in my own bed, nor beneath a roof of my forefathers; I shall not be anywhere, for I will live no longer. I was born in Lancashire, a country where women die for love. Know you, and give you up? I will yield you to none, not even to Death, for I should die with you."

She led me to her rooms, where comfort had already spread its charms.

"Love her, dear," I said warmly. "She loves you sincerely, not in jest."

"Sincerely! you poor child!" she said, unfastening her habit.

With a lover's vanity I tried to exhibit Henriette's noble character to this imperious creature. While her waiting-woman, who did not understand a word of French, arranged her hair I endeavored to picture Madame de Mortsauf by sketching her life; I repeated many of the great thoughts she had uttered at a crisis when nearly all women become either petty or bad. Though Arabella appeared to be paying no attention she did not lose a single word.

"I am delighted," she said when we were alone, "to learn your taste for pious conversation. There's an old vicar on one of my estates who understands writing sermons better than any one I know; the country-people like him, for he suits his prosing to his hearers. I'll write to my father to-morrow and ask him to send the good man here by steamboat; you can meet him in Paris, and when once you have heard him you will never wish to listen to any one else, —all the more because his health is perfect. His moralities won't give you shocks that make you weep; they flow along without tempests, like a limpid stream, and will send you to sleep. Every evening you can if you like satisfy your passion for sermons by digesting one with your dinner. English morality, I do assure you, is as superior to that of Touraine as our cutlery, our plate, and our horses are to your knives and your turf. Do me the kindness to listen to my vicar; promise me. I am only a woman, my dearest; I can love, I can die for you if you will; but I have never studied at Eton, or at Oxford, or in Edinburgh. I am neither a doctor of laws nor a reverend; I can't preach morality; in fact, I am altogether unfit for it, I should be awkward if I tried. I don't blame your tastes; you might have others more depraved, and I should still endeavor to conform to them, for I want you to find near me all you like best,—pleasures of love, pleasures of food, pleasures of piety, good claret, and virtuous Christians. Shall I wear hair-cloth to-night? She is very lucky, that woman, to suit you in morality. From what college did she graduate? Poor I, who can only give you myself, who can only be your slave—"

"Then why did you rush away when I wanted to bring you together?"

"Are you crazy, Amedee? I could go from Paris to Rome disguised as a valet; I would do the most unreasonable thing for your sake; but how can you expect me to speak to a woman on the public roads who has never been presented to me,—and who, besides, would have preached me a sermon under three heads? I speak to peasants, and if I am hungry I would ask a workman to share his bread with me and pay him in guineas, —that is all proper enough; but to stop a carriage on the highway, like the gentlemen of the road in England, is not at all within my code of manners. You poor child, you know only how to love; you don't know how to live. Besides, I am not like you as yet, dear angel; I don't like morality. Still, I am capable of great efforts to please you. Yes, I will go to work; I will learn how to preach; you shall have no more kisses without verses of the Bible interlarded."

She used her power and abused it as soon as she saw in my eyes the ardent expression which was always there when she began her sorceries. She triumphed over everything, and I complacently told myself that the woman who loses all, sacrifices the future, and makes love her only virtue, is far above Catholic polemics.

"So she loves herself better than she loves you?" Arabella went on. "She sets something that is not you above you. Is that love? how can we women find anything to value in ourselves except that which you value in us? No woman, no matter how fine a moralist she may be, is the equal of a man. Tread upon us, kill us; never embarrass your lives on our account. It is for us to die, for you to live, great and honored. For us the dagger in your hand; for you our pardoning love. Does the sun think of the gnats in his beams, that live by his light? they stay as long as they can and when he withdraws his face they die—"

"Or fly somewhere else," I said interrupting her.

"Yes, somewhere else," she replied, with an indifference that would have piqued any man into using the power with which she invested him. "Do you really think it is worthy of womanhood to make a man eat his bread buttered with virtue, and to persuade him that religion is incompatible with love? Am I a reprobate? A woman either gives herself or she refuses. But to refuse and moralize is a double wrong, and is contrary to the rule of the right in all lands. Here, you will get only excellent sandwiches prepared by the hand of your servant Arabella, whose sole morality is to imagine caresses no man has yet felt and which the angels inspire."

I know nothing more destructive than the wit of an Englishwoman; she gives it the eloquent gravity, the tone of pompous conviction with which the British hide the absurdities of their life of prejudice. French wit and humor, on the other hand, is like a lace with which our women adorn the joys they give and the quarrels they invent; it is a mental jewelry, as charming as their pretty dresses. English wit is an acid which corrodes all those on whom it falls until it bares their bones, which it scrapes and polishes. The tongue of a clever Englishwoman is like that of a tiger tearing the flesh from the bone when he is only in play. All-powerful weapon of a sneering devil, English satire leaves a deadly poison in the wound it makes. Arabella chose to show her power like the sultan who, to prove his dexterity, cut off the heads of unoffending beings with his own scimitar.

"My angel," she said, "I can talk morality too if I choose. I have asked myself whether I commit a crime in loving you; whether I violate the divine laws; and I find that my love for you is both natural and pious. Why did God create some beings handsomer than others if not to show us that we ought to adore them? The crime would be in not loving you. This lady insults you by confounding you with other men; the laws of morality are not applicable to you; for God has created you above them. Am I not drawing nearer to divine love in loving you? will God punish a poor woman for seeking the divine? Your great and luminous heart so resembles the heavens that I am like the gnats which flutter about the torches of a fête and burn themselves; are they to be punished for their error? besides, is it an error? may it not be pure worship of the light? They perish of too much piety,—if you call it perishing to fling one's self on the breast of him we love. I have the weakness to love you, whereas that woman has the strength to remain in her Catholic shrine. Now, don't frown. You think I wish her ill. No, I do not. I adore the morality which has led her to leave you free, and enables me to win you and hold you forever—for you are mine forever, are you not?"

"Yes."

"Forever and ever?"

"Yes."

"Ah! I have found favor in my lord! I alone have understood his worth! She knows how to cultivate her estate, you say. Well, I leave that to farmers; I cultivate your heart."

I try to recall this intoxicating babble, that I may picture to you the woman as she is, confirm all I have said of her, and let you into the secret of what happened later. But how shall I describe the accompaniment of the words? She sought to annihilate by the passion of her impetuous love the impressions left in my heart by the chaste and dignified love of my Henriette. Lady Dudley had seen the countess as plainly as the countess had seen her; each had judged the other. The force of Arabella's attack revealed to me the extent of her fear, and her secret admiration for her rival. In the morning I found her with tearful eyes, complaining that she had not slept.

"What troubles you?" I said.

"I fear that my excessive love will ruin me," she answered; "I have given all. Wiser than I, that woman possesses something that you still desire. If you prefer her, forget me; I will not trouble you with my sorrows, my remorse, my sufferings; no, I will go far away and die, like a plant deprived of the life-giving sun."

She was able to wring protestations of love from my reluctant lips, which filled her with joy.

"Ah!" she exclaimed, drying her eyes, "I am happy. Go back to her; I do not choose to owe you to the force of my love, but to the action of your own will. If you return here I shall know that you love me as much as I love you, the possibility of which I have always doubted."

She persuaded me to return to Clochegourde. The false position in which I thus placed myself did not strike me while still under the influence of her wiles. Yet, had I refused to return I should have given Lady Dudley a triumph over Henriette. Arabella would then have taken me to Paris. To go now to Clochegourde was an open insult to Madame de Mortsauf; in that case Arabella was sure of me. Did any woman ever pardon such crimes against love? Unless she were an angel descended from the skies, instead of a purified spirit ascending to them, a loving woman would rather see her lover die than know him happy with another. Thus, look at it as I would, my situation, after I had once left Clochegourde for the Grenadiere, was as fatal to the love of my choice as it was profitable to the transient love that held me. Lady Dudley had calculated all this with consummate cleverness. She owned to me later that if she had not met Madame de Mortsauf on the moor she had intended to compromise me by haunting Clochegourde until she did so.

When I met the countess that morning, and found her pale and depressed like one who has not slept all night, I was conscious of exercising the instinctive perception given to hearts still fresh and generous to show them the true bearing of actions little regarded by the world at large, but judged as criminal by lofty spirits. Like a child going down a precipice in play and gathering flowers, who sees with dread that it can never climb that height again, feels itself alone, with night approaching, and hears the howls of animals, so I now knew that she and I were separated by a universe. A wail arose within our souls like an echo of that woeful "Consummatum est" heard in the churches on Good Friday at the hour the Saviour died,—a dreadful scene which awes young souls whose first love is religion. All Henriette's illusions were killed at one blow; her heart had endured its passion. She did not look at me; she refused me the light that for six long years had shone upon my life. She knew well that the spring of the effulgent rays shed by our eyes was in our souls, to which they served as pathways to reach each other, to blend them in one, meeting, parting, playing, like two confiding women who tell each other all. Bitterly I felt the wrong of bringing beneath this roof, where pleasure was unknown, a face on which the wings of pleasure had shaken their prismatic dust. If, the night before, I had allowed Lady Dudley to depart alone, if I had then returned to Clochegourde, where, it may be, Henriette awaited me, perhaps—perhaps Madame de Mortsauf might not so cruelly have resolved to be my sister. But now she paid me many ostentatious attentions,—playing her part vehemently for the very purpose of not changing it. During breakfast she showed me a thousand civilities, humiliating attentions, caring for me as though I were a sick man whose fate she pitied.

"You were out walking early," said the count; "I hope you have brought back a good appetite, you whose stomach is not yet destroyed."

This remark, which brought the smile of a sister to Henriette's lips, completed my sense of the ridicule of my position. It was impossible to be at Clochegourde by day and Saint-Cyr by night. During the day I felt how difficult it was to become the friend of a woman we have long loved. The transition, easy enough when years have brought it about, is like an illness in youth. I was ashamed; I cursed the pleasure Lady Dudley gave me; I wished that Henriette would demand my blood. I could not tear her rival in pieces before her, for she avoided speaking of her; indeed, had I spoken of Arabella, Henriette, noble and sublime to the inmost recesses of her heart, would have despised my infamy. After five years of delightful intercourse we now had nothing to say to each other; our words had no connection with our thoughts; we were hiding from each other our intolerable pain,—we, whose mutual sufferings had been our first interpreter.

Henriette assumed a cheerful look for me as for herself, but she was sad. She spoke of herself as my sister, and yet found no ground on which to converse; and we remained for the greater part of the time in constrained silence. She increased my inward misery by feigning to believe that she was the only victim.

"I suffer more than you," I said to her at a moment when my self-styled sister was betrayed into a feminine sarcasm.

"How so?" she said haughtily.

"Because I am the one to blame."

At last her manner became so cold and indifferent that I resolved to leave Clochegourde. That evening, on the terrace, I said farewell to the whole family, who were there assembled. They all followed me to the lawn where my horse was waiting. The countess came to me as I took the bridle in my hand.

"Let us walk down the avenue together, alone," she said.

I gave her my arm, and we passed through the courtyard with slow and measured steps, as though our rhythmic movement were consoling to us. When we reached the grove of trees which forms a corner of the boundary she stopped.

"Farewell, my friend," she said, throwing her head upon my breast and her arms around my neck, "Farewell, we shall never meet again. God has given me the sad power to look into the future. Do you remember the terror that seized me the day you first came back, so young, so handsome! and I saw you turn your back on me as you do this day when you are leaving Clochegourde and going to Saint-Cyr? Well, once again, during the past night I have seen into the future. Friend, we are speaking together for the last time. I can hardly now say a few words to you, for it is but a part of me that speaks at all. Death has already seized on something in me. You have taken the mother from her children, I now ask you to take her place to them. You can; Jacques and Madeleine love you—as if you had always made them suffer."

"Death!" I cried, frightened as I looked at her and beheld the fire of her shining eyes, of which I can give no idea to those who have never known their dear ones struck down by her fatal malady, unless I compare those eyes to balls of burnished silver. "Die!" I said. "Henriette, I command you to live. You used to ask an oath of me, I now ask one of you. Swear to me that you will send for Origet and obey him in everything."

"Would you oppose the mercy of God?" she said, interrupting me with a cry of despair at being thus misunderstood.

"You do not love me enough to obey me blindly, as that miserable Lady Dudley does?"

"Yes, yes, I will do all you ask," she cried, goaded by jealousy.

"Then I stay," I said, kissing her on the eyelids.

Frightened at the words, she escaped from my arms and leaned against a tree; then she turned and walked rapidly homeward without looking back. But I followed her; she was weeping and praying. When we reached the lawn I took her hand and kissed it respectfully. This submission touched her.

"I am yours—forever, and as you will," I said; "for I love you as your aunt loved you."

She trembled and wrung my hand.

"One look," I said, "one more, one last of our old looks! The woman who gives herself wholly," I cried, my soul illumined by the glance she gave me, "gives less of life and soul than I have now received. Henriette, thou art my best-beloved—my only love."

"I shall live!" she said; "but cure yourself as well."

That look had effaced the memory of Arabella's sarcasms. Thus I was the plaything of the two irreconcilable passions I have now described to you; I was influenced by each alternately. I loved an angel and a demon; two women equally beautiful,—one adorned with all the virtues which we decry through hatred of our own imperfections, the other with all the vices which we deify through selfishness. Returning along that avenue, looking back again and again at Madame de Mortsauf, as she leaned against a tree surrounded by her children who waved their handkerchiefs, I detected in my soul an emotion of pride in finding myself the arbiter of two such destinies; the glory, in ways so different, of women so distinguished; proud of inspiring such great passions that death must come to whichever I abandoned. Ah! believe me, that passing conceit has been doubly punished!

I know not what demon prompted me to remain with Arabella and await the moment when the death of the count might give me Henriette; for she would ever love me. Her harshness, her tears, her remorse, her Christian resignation, were so many eloquent signs of a sentiment that could no more be effaced from her heart than from mine. Walking slowly down that pretty avenue and making these reflections, I was no longer twenty-five, I was fifty years old. A man passes in a moment, even more quickly than a woman, from youth to middle age. Though long ago I drove these evil thoughts away from me, I was then possessed by them, I must avow it. Perhaps I owed their presence in my mind to the Tuileries, to the king's cabinet. Who could resist the polluting spirit of Louis XVIII.?

When I reached the end of the avenue I turned and rushed back in the twinkling of an eye, seeing that Henriette was still there, and alone! I went to bid her a last farewell, bathed in repentant tears, the cause of which she never knew. Tears sincere indeed; given, although I knew it not, to noble loves forever lost, to virgin emotions—those flowers of our life which cannot bloom again. Later, a man gives nothing, he receives; he loves himself in his mistress; but in youth he loves his mistress in himself. Later, we inoculate with our tastes, perhaps our vices, the woman who loves us; but in the dawn of life she whom we love conveys to us her virtues, her conscience. She invites us with a smile to the noble life; from her we learn the self-devotion which she practises. Woe to the man who has not had his Henriette. Woe to that other one who has never known a Lady Dudley. The latter, if he marries, will not be able to keep his wife; the other will be abandoned by his mistress. But joy to him who can find the two women in one woman; happy the man, dear Natalie, whom you love.

After my return to Paris Arabella and I became more intimate than ever. Soon we insensibly abandoned all the conventional restrictions I had carefully imposed, the strict observance of which often makes the world forgive the false position in which Lady Dudley had placed herself. Society, which delights in looking behind appearances, sanctions much as soon as it knows the secrets they conceal. Lovers who live in the great world make a mistake in flinging down these barriers exacted by the law of salons; they do wrong not to obey scrupulously all conventions which the manners and customs of a community impose,—less for the sake of others than for their own. Outward respect to be maintained, comedies to play, concealments to be managed; all such strategy of love occupies the life, renews desire, and protects the heart against the palsy of habit. But all young passions, being, like youth itself, essentially spendthrift, raze their forests to the ground instead of merely cutting the timber. Arabella adopted none of these bourgeois ideas, and yielded to them only to please me; she wished to exhibit me to the eyes of all Paris as her "sposo." She employed her powers of seduction to keep me under her roof, for she was not content with a rumored scandal which, for want of proof, was only whispered behind the fans. Seeing her so happy in committing an imprudence which frankly admitted her position, how could I help believing in her love?

But no sooner was I plunged into the comforts of illegal marriage than despair seized upon me; I saw my life bound to a course in direct defiance of the ideas and the advice given me by Henriette. Thenceforth I lived in the sort of rage we find in consumptive patients who, knowing their end is near, cannot endure that their lungs should be examined. There was no corner in my heart where I could fly to escape suffering; an avenging spirit filled me incessantly with thoughts on which I dared not dwell. My letters to Henriette depicted this moral malady and did her infinite harm. "At the cost of so many treasures lost, I wished you to be at least happy," she wrote in the only answer I received. But I was not happy. Dear Natalie, happiness is absolute; it allows of no comparisons. My first ardor over, I necessarily compared the two women,—a contrast I had never yet studied. In fact, all great passions press so strongly on the character that at first they check its asperities and cover the track of habits which constitute our defects and our better qualities. But later, when two lovers are accustomed to each other, the features of their moral physiognomies reappear; they mutually judge each other, and it often happens during this reaction of the character after passion, that natural antipathies leading to disunion (which superficial people seize upon to accuse the human heart of instability) come to the surface. This period now began with me. Less blinded by seductions, and dissecting, as it were, my pleasure, I undertook, without perhaps intending to do so, a critical examination of Lady Dudley which resulted to her injury.

In the first place, I found her wanting in the qualities of mind which distinguish Frenchwomen and make them so delightful to love; as all those who have had the opportunity of loving in both countries declare. When a Frenchwoman loves she is metamorphosed; her noted coquetry is used to deck her love; she abandons her dangerous vanity and lays no claim to any merit but that of loving well. She espouses the interests, the hatreds, the friendships, of the man she loves; she acquires in a day the experience of a man of business; she studies the code, she comprehends the mechanism of credit, and could manage a banker's office; naturally heedless and prodigal, she will make no mistakes and waste not a single louis. She becomes, in turn, mother, adviser, doctor, giving to all her transformations a grace of happiness which reveals, in its every detail, her infinite love. She combines the special qualities of the women of other countries and gives unity to the mixture by her wit, that truly French product, which enlivens, sanctions, justifies, and varies all, thus relieving the monotony of a sentiment which rests on a single tense of a single verb. The Frenchwoman loves always, without abatement and without fatigue, in public or in solitude. In public she uses a tone which has meaning for one only; she speaks by silence; she looks at you with lowered eyelids. If the occasion prevents both speech and look she will use the sand and write a word with the point of her little foot; her love will find expression even in sleep; in short, she bends the world to her love. The Englishwoman, on the contrary, makes her love bend to the world. Educated to maintain the icy manners, the Britannic and egotistic deportment which I described to you, she opens and shuts her heart with the ease of a British mechanism. She possesses an impenetrable mask, which she puts on or takes off phlegmatically. Passionate as an Italian when no eye sees her, she becomes coldly dignified before the world. A lover may well doubt his empire when he sees the immobility of face, the aloofness of countenance, and hears the calm voice, with which an Englishwoman leaves her boudoir. Hypocrisy then becomes indifference; she has forgotten all.

Certainly the woman who can lay aside her love like a garment may be thought to be capable of changing it. What tempests arise in the heart of a man, stirred by wounded self-love, when he sees a woman taking and dropping and again picking up her love like a piece of embroidery. These women are too completely mistresses of themselves ever to belong wholly to you; they are too much under the influence of society ever to let you reign supreme. Where a Frenchwoman comforts by a look, or betrays her impatience with visitors by witty jests, an Englishwoman's silence is absolute; it irritates the soul and frets the mind. These women are so constantly, and, under all circumstances, on their dignity, that to most of them fashion reigns omnipotent even over their pleasures. An Englishwoman forces everything into form; though in her case the love of form does not produce the sentiment of art. No matter what may be said against it, Protestantism and Catholicism explain the differences which make the love of Frenchwomen so far superior to the calculating, reasoning love of Englishwomen. Protestantism doubts, searches, and kills belief; it is the death of art and love. Where worldliness is all in all, worldly people must needs obey; but passionate hearts flee from it; to them its laws are insupportable.

You can now understand what a shock my self-love received when I found that Lady Dudley could not live without the world, and that the English system of two lives was familiar to her. It was no sacrifice she felt called upon to make; on the contrary she fell naturally into two forms of life that were inimical to each other. When she loved she loved madly,—no woman of any country could be compared to her; but when the curtain fell upon that fairy scene she banished even the memory of it. In public she never answered to a look or a smile; she was neither mistress nor slave; she was like an ambassadress, obliged to round her phrases and her elbows; she irritated me by her composure, and outraged my heart with her decorum. Thus she degraded love to a mere need, instead of raising it to an ideal through enthusiasm. She expressed neither fear, nor regrets, nor desire; but at a given hour her tenderness reappeared like a fire suddenly lighted.

In which of these two women ought I to believe? I felt, as it were by a thousand pin-pricks, the infinite differences between Henriette and Arabella. When Madame de Mortsauf left me for a while she seemed to leave to the air the duty of reminding me of her; the folds of her gown as she went away spoke to the eye, as their undulating sound to the ear when she returned; infinite tenderness was in the way she lowered her eyelids and looked on the ground; her voice, that musical voice, was a continual caress; her words expressed a constant thought; she was always like unto herself; she did not halve her soul to suit two atmospheres, one ardent, the other icy. In short, Madame de Mortsauf reserved her mind and the flower of her thought to express her feelings; she was coquettish in ideas with her children and with me. But Arabella's mind was never used to make life pleasant; it was never used at all for my benefit; it existed only for the world and by the world, and it was spent in sarcasm. She loved to rend, to bite, as it were,—not for amusement but to satisfy a craving. Madame de Mortsauf would have hidden her happiness from every eye, Lady Dudley chose to exhibit hers to all Paris; and yet with her impenetrable English mask she kept within conventions even while parading in the Bois with me. This mixture of ostentation and dignity, love and coldness, wounded me constantly; for my soul was both virgin and passionate, and as I could not pass from one temperature to the other, my temper suffered. When I complained (never without precaution), she turned her tongue with its triple sting against me; mingling boasts of her love with those cutting English sarcasms. As soon as she found herself in opposition to me, she made it an amusement to hurt my feelings and humiliate my mind; she kneaded me like dough. To any remark of mine as to keeping a medium in all things, she replied by caricaturing my ideas and exaggerating them. When I reproached her for her manner to me, she asked if I wished her to kiss me at the opera before all Paris; and she said it so seriously that I, knowing her desire to make people talk, trembled lest she should execute her threat. In spite of her real passion she was never meditative, self-contained, or reverent, like Henriette; on the contrary she was insatiable as a sandy soil. Madame de Mortsauf was always composed, able to feel my soul in an accent or a glance. Lady Dudley was never affected by a look, or a pressure of the hand, nor yet by a tender word. No proof of love surprised her. She felt so strong a necessity for excitement, noise, celebrity, that nothing attained to her ideal in this respect; hence her violent love, her exaggerated fancy, —everything concerned herself and not me.

The letter you have read from Madame de Mortsauf (a light which still shone brightly on my life), a proof of how the most virtuous of women obeyed the genius of a Frenchwoman, revealing, as it did, her perpetual vigilance, her sound understanding of all my prospects—that letter must have made you see with what care Henriette had studied my material interests, my political relations, my moral conquests, and with what ardor she took hold of my life in all permissible directions. On such points as these Lady Dudley affected the reticence of a mere acquaintance. She never informed herself about my affairs, nor of my likings or dislikings as a man. Prodigal for herself without being generous, she separated too decidedly self-interest and love. Whereas I knew very well, without proving it, that to save me a pang Henriette would have sought for me that which she would never seek for herself. In any great and overwhelming misfortune I should have gone for counsel to Henriette, but I would have let myself be dragged to prison sooner than say a word to Lady Dudley.

Up to this point the contrast relates to feelings; but it was the same in outward things. In France, luxury is the expression of the man, the reproduction of his ideas, of his personal poetry; it portrays the character, and gives, between lovers, a precious value to every little attention by keeping before them the dominant thought of the being loved. But English luxury, which at first allured me by its choiceness and delicacy, proved to be mechanical also. The thousand and one attentions shown me at Clochegourde Arabella would have considered the business of servants; each one had his own duty and speciality. The choice of the footman was the business of her butler, as if it were a matter of horses. She never attached herself to her servants; the death of the best of them would not have affected her, for money could replace the one lost by another equally efficient. As to her duty towards her neighbor, I never saw a tear in her eye for the misfortunes of another; in fact her selfishness was so naively candid that it absolutely created a laugh. The crimson draperies of the great lady covered an iron nature. The delightful siren who sounded at night every bell of her amorous folly could soon make a young man forget the hard and unfeeling Englishwoman, and it was only step by step that I discovered the stony rock on which my seeds were wasted, bringing no harvest. Madame de Mortsauf had penetrated that nature at a glance in their brief encounter. I remembered her prophetic words. She was right; Arabella's love became intolerable to me. I have since remarked that most women who ride well on horseback have little tenderness. Like the Amazons, they lack a breast; their hearts are hard in some direction, but I do not know in which.

At the moment when I begin to feel the burden of the yoke, when weariness took possession of soul and body too, when at last I comprehended the sanctity that true feeling imparts to love, when memories of Clochegourde were bringing me, in spite of distance, the fragrance of the roses, the warmth of the terrace, and the warble of the nightingales,—at this frightful moment, when I saw the stony bed beneath me as the waters of the torrent receded, I received a blow which still resounds in my heart, for at every hour its echo wakes.

I was working in the cabinet of the king, who was to drive out at four o'clock. The Duc de Lenoncourt was on service. When he entered the room the king asked him news of the countess. I raised my head hastily in too eager a manner; the king, offended by the action, gave me the look which always preceded the harsh words he knew so well how to say.

"Sire, my poor daughter is dying," replied the duke.

"Will the king deign to grant me leave of absence?" I cried, with tears in my eyes, braving the anger which I saw about to burst.

"Go, _

my lord

," he answered, smiling at the satire in his words, and withholding his reprimand in favor of his own wit.

More courtier than father, the duke asked no leave but got into the carriage with the king. I started without bidding Lady Dudley good-bye; she was fortunately out when I made my preparations, and I left a note telling her I was sent on a mission by the king. At the Croix de Berny I met his Majesty returning from Verrieres. He threw me a look full of his royal irony, always insufferable in meaning, which seemed to say: "If you mean to be anything in politics come back; don't parley with the dead." The duke waved his hand to me sadly. The two pompous equipages with their eight horses, the colonels and their gold lace, the escort and the clouds of dust rolled rapidly away, to cries of "Vive le Roi!" It seemed to me that the court had driven over the dead body of Madame de Mortsauf with the utter insensibility which nature shows for our catastrophes. Though the duke was an excellent man he would no doubt play whist with Monsieur after the king had retired. As for the duchess, she had long ago given her daughter the first stab by writing to her of Lady Dudley.

My hurried journey was like a dream,—the dream of a ruined gambler; I was in despair at having received no news. Had the confessor pushed austerity so far as to exclude me from Clochegourde? I accused Madeleine, Jacques, the Abbe Dominis, all, even Monsieur de Mortsauf. Beyond Tours, as I came down the road bordered with poplars which leads to Poncher, which I so much admired that first day of my search for mine Unknown, I met Monsieur Origet. He guessed that I was going to Clochegourde; I guessed that he was returning. We stopped our carriages and got out, I to ask for news, he to give it.

"How is Madame de Mortsauf?" I said.

"I doubt if you find her living," he replied. "She is dying a frightful death— of inanition. When she called me in, last June, no medical power could control the disease; she had the symptoms which Monsieur de Mortsauf has no doubt described to you, for he thinks he has them himself. Madame la comtesse was not in any transient condition of ill-health, which our profession can direct and which is often the cause of a better state, nor was she in the crisis of a disorder the effects of which can be repaired; no, her disease had reached a point where science is useless; it is the incurable result of grief, just as a mortal wound is the result of a stab. Her physical condition is produced by the inertia of an organ as necessary to life as the action of the heart itself. Grief has done the work of a dagger. Don't deceive yourself; Madame de Mortsauf is dying of some hidden grief."

"Hidden!" I exclaimed. "Her children have not been ill?"

"No," he said, looking at me significantly, "and since she has been so seriously attacked Monsieur de Mortsauf has ceased to torment her. I am no longer needed; Monsieur Deslandes of Azay is all-sufficient; nothing can be done; her sufferings are dreadful. Young, beautiful, and rich, to die emaciated, shrunken with hunger—for she dies of hunger! During the last forty days the stomach, being as it were closed up, has rejected all nourishment, under whatever form we attempt to give it."

Monsieur Origet pressed my hand with a gesture of respect.

"Courage, monsieur," he said, lifting his eyes to heaven.

The words expressed his compassion for sufferings he thought shared; he little suspected the poisoned arrow which they shot into my heart. I sprang into the carriage and ordered the postilion to drive on, promising a good reward if I arrived in time.

Notwithstanding my impatience I seemed to do the distance in a few minutes, so absorbed was I in the bitter reflections that crowded upon my soul. Dying of grief, yet her children were well? then she died through me! My conscience uttered one of those arraignments which echo throughout our lives and sometimes beyond them. What weakness, what impotence in human justice, which avenges none but open deeds! Why shame and death to the murderer who kills with a blow, who comes upon you unawares in your sleep and makes it last eternally, who strikes without warning and spares you a struggle? Why a happy life, an honored life, to the murderer who drop by drop pours gall into the soul and saps the body to destroy it? How many murderers go unpunished! What indulgence for fashionable vice! What condoning of the homicides caused by moral wrongs! I know not whose avenging hand it was that suddenly, at that moment, raised the painted curtain that reveals society. I saw before me many victims known to you and me, —Madame de Beauseant, dying, and starting for Normandy only a few days earlier; the Duchesse de Langeais lost; Lady Brandon hiding herself in Touraine in the little house where Lady Dudley had stayed two weeks, and dying there, killed by a frightful catastrophe,—you know it. Our period teems with such events. Who does not remember that poor young woman who poisoned herself, overcome by jealousy, which was perhaps killing Madame de Mortsauf? Who has not shuddered at the fate of that enchanting young girl who perished after two years of marriage, like a flower torn by the wind, the victim of her chaste ignorance, the victim of a villain with whom Ronquerolles, Montriveau, and de Marsay shake hands because he is useful to their political projects? What heart has failed to throb at the recital of the last hours of the woman whom no entreaties could soften, and who would never see her husband after nobly paying his debts? Madame d'Aiglemont saw death beside her and was saved only by my brother's care. Society and science are accomplices in crimes for which there are no assizes. The world declares that no one dies of grief, or of despair; nor yet of love, of anguish hidden, of hopes cultivated yet fruitless, again and again replanted yet forever uprooted. Our new scientific nomenclature has plenty of words to explain these things; gastritis, pericarditis, all the thousand maladies of women the names of which are whispered in the ear, all serve as passports to the coffin followed by hypocritical tears that are soon wiped by the hand of a notary. Can there be at the bottom of this great evil some law which we do not know? Must the centenary pitilessly strew the earth with corpses and dry them to dust about him that he may raise himself, as the millionaire battens on a myriad of little industries? Is there some powerful and venomous life which feasts on these gentle, tender creatures? My God! do I belong to the race of tigers?

Remorse gripped my heart in its scorching fingers, and my cheeks were furrowed with tears as I entered the avenue of Clochegourde on a damp October morning, which loosened the dead leaves of the poplars planted by Henriette in the path where once she stood and waved her handkerchief as if to recall me. Was she living? Why did I feel her two white hands upon my head laid prostrate in the dust? In that moment I paid for all the pleasures that Arabella had given me, and I knew that I paid dearly. I swore not to see her again, and a hatred of England took possession of me. Though Lady Dudley was only a variety of her species, I included all Englishwomen in my judgment.

I received a fresh shock as I neared Clochegourde. Jacques, Madeleine, and the Abbe Dominis were kneeling at the foot of a wooden cross placed on a piece of ground that was taken into the enclosure when the iron gate was put up, which the count and countess had never been willing to remove. I sprang from the carriage and went towards them, my heart aching at the sight of these children and that grave old man imploring the mercy of God. The old huntsman was there too, with bared head, standing a little apart.

I stooped to kiss Jacques and Madeleine, who gave me a cold look and continued praying. The abbe rose from his knees; I took him by the arm to support myself, saying, "Is she still alive?" He bowed his head sadly and gently. "Tell me, I implore you for Christ's sake, why are you praying at the foot of this cross? Why are you here, and not with her? Why are the children kneeling here this chilly morning? Tell me all, that I may do no harm through ignorance."

"For the last few days Madame le comtesse has been unwilling to see her children except at stated times.—Monsieur," he continued after a pause, "perhaps you had better wait a few hours before seeing Madame de Mortsauf; she is greatly changed. It is necessary to prepare her for this interview, or it might cause an increase in her sufferings —death would be a blessed release from them."

I wrung the hand of the good man, whose look and voice soothed the pangs of others without sharpening them.

"We are praying God to help her," he continued; "for she, so saintly, so resigned, so fit to die, has shown during the last few weeks a horror of death; for the first time in her life she looks at others who are full of health with gloomy, envious eyes. This aberration comes less, I think, from the fear of death than from some inward intoxication,—from the flowers of her youth which ferment as they wither. Yes, an evil angel is striving against heaven for that glorious soul. She is passing through her struggle on the Mount of Olives; her tears bathe the white roses of her crown as they fall, one by one, from the head of this wedded Jephtha. Wait; do not see her yet. You would bring to her the atmosphere of the court; she would see in your face the reflection of the things of life, and you would add to the bitterness of her regret. Have pity on a weakness which God Himself forgave to

His Son when He took our nature upon Him. What merit would there be in conquering if we had no adversary? Permit her confessor or me, two old men whose worn-out lives cause her no pain, to prepare her for this unlooked-for meeting, for emotions which the Abbe Birotteau has required her to renounce. But, in the things of this world there is an invisible thread of divine purpose which religion alone can see; and since you have come perhaps you are led by some celestial star of the moral world which leads to the tomb as to the manger—"

He then told me, with that tempered eloquence which falls like dew upon the heart, that for the last six months the countess had suffered daily more and more, in spite of Monsieur Origet's care. The doctor had come to Clochegourde every evening for two months, striving to rescue her from death; for her one cry had been, "Oh, save me!" "To heal the body the heart must first be healed," the doctor had exclaimed one day.

"As the illness increased, the words of this poor woman, once so gentle, have grown bitter," said the Abbe. "She calls on earth to keep her, instead of asking God to take her; then she repents these murmurs against the divine decree. Such alternations of feeling rend her heart and make the struggle between body and soul most horrible. Often the body triumphs. 'You have cost me dear,' she said one day to Jacques and Madeleine; but in a moment, recalled to God by the look on my face, she turned to Madeleine with these angelic words, 'The happiness of others is the joy of those who cannot themselves be happy,'—and the tone with which she said them brought tears to my eyes. She falls, it is true, but each time that her feet stumble she rises higher towards heaven."

Struck by the tone of the successive intimations chance had sent me, and which in this great concert of misfortunes were like a prelude of mournful modulations to a funereal theme, the mighty cry of expiring love, I cried out: "Surely you believe that this pure lily cut from earth will flower in heaven?"

"You left her still a flower," he answered, "but you will find her consumed, purified by the forces of suffering, pure as a diamond buried in the ashes. Yes, that shining soul, angelic star, will issue glorious from the clouds and pass into the kingdom of the Light."

As I pressed the hand of the good evangelist, my heart overflowing with gratitude, the count put his head, now entirely white, out of the door and immediately sprang towards me with signs of surprise.

"She was right! He is here! 'Felix, Felix, Felix has come!' she kept crying. My dear friend," he continued, beside himself with terror, "death is here. Why did it not take a poor madman like me with one foot in the grave?"

I walked towards the house summoning my courage, but on the threshold of the long antechamber which crossed the house and led to the lawn, the Abbe Birotteau stopped me.

"Madame la comtesse begs you will not enter at present," he said to me.

Giving a glance within the house I saw the servants coming and going, all busy, all dumb with grief, surprised perhaps by the orders Manette gave them.

"What has happened?" cried the count, alarmed by the commotion, as much from fear of the coming event as from the natural uneasiness of his character.

"Only a sick woman's fancy," said the abbe. "Madame la comtesse does not wish to receive monsieur le vicomte as she now is. She talks of dressing; why thwart her?"

Manette came in search of Madeleine, whom I saw leave the house a few moments after she had entered her mother's room. We were all, Jacques and his father, the two abbes and I, silently walking up and down the lawn in front of the house. I looked first at Montbazon and then at Azay, noticing the seared and yellow valley which answered in its mourning (as it ever did on all occasions) to the feelings of my heart. Suddenly I beheld the dear "mignonne" gathering the autumn flowers, no doubt to make a bouquet at her mother's bidding. Thinking of all which that signified, I was so convulsed within me that I staggered, my sight was blurred, and the two abbes, between whom I walked, led me to the wall of a terrace, where I sat for some time completely broken down but not unconscious.

"Poor Felix," said the count, "she forbade me to write to you. She knew how much you loved her."

Though prepared to suffer, I found I had no strength to bear a scene which recalled my memories of past happiness. "Ah!" I thought, "I see it still, that barren moor, dried like a skeleton, lit by a gray sky, in the centre of which grew a single flowering bush, which again and again I looked at with a shudder,—the forecast of this mournful hour!"

All was gloom in the little castle, once so animated, so full of life. The servants were weeping; despair and desolation everywhere. The paths were not raked, work was begun and left undone, the workmen standing idly about the house. Though the grapes were being gathered in the vineyard, not a sound reached us. The place seemed uninhabited, so deep the silence! We walked about like men whose grief rejects all ordinary topics, and we listened to the count, the only one of us who spoke.

After a few words prompted by the mechanical love he felt for his wife he was led by the natural bent of his mind to complain of her. She had never, he said, taken care of herself or listened to him when he gave her good advice. He had been the first to notice the symptoms of her illness, for he had studied them in his own case; he had fought them and cured them without other assistance than careful diet and the avoidance of all emotion. He could have cured the countess, but a husband ought not to take so much responsibility upon himself, especially when he has the misfortune of finding his experience, in this as in everything, despised. In spite of all he could say, the countess insisted on seeing Origet,—Origet, who had managed his case so ill, was now killing his wife. If this disease was, as they said, the result of excessive grief, surely he was the one who had been in a condition to have it. What griefs could the countess have had? She was always happy; she had never had troubles or annoyances. Their fortune, thanks to his care and to his sound ideas, was now in a most satisfactory state; he had always allowed Madame de Mortsauf to reign at Clochegourde; her children, well trained and now in health, gave her no anxiety,—where, then, did this grief they talked of come from?

Thus he argued and discussed the matter, mingling his expressions of despair with senseless accusations. Then, recalled by some sudden memory to the admiration which he felt for his wife, tears rolled from his eyes which had been dry so long.

Madeleine came to tell me that her mother was ready. The Abbe Birotteau followed me. Madeleine, now a grave young girl, stayed with her father, saying that the countess desired to be alone with me, and also that the presence of too many persons would fatigue her. The solemnity of this moment gave me that sense of inward heat and outward cold which overcomes us often in the great events of life. The Abbe Birotteau, one of those men whom God marks for his own by investing them with sweetness and simplicity, together with patience and compassion, took me aside.

"Monsieur," he said, "I wish you to know that I have done all in my power to prevent this meeting. The salvation of this saint required it. I have considered her only, and not you. Now that you are about to see her to whom access ought to have been denied you by the angels, let me say that I shall be present to protect you against yourself and perhaps against her. Respect her weakness. I do not ask this of you as a priest, but as a humble friend whom you did not know you had, and who would fain save you from remorse. Our dear patient is dying of hunger and thirst. Since morning she is a victim to the feverish irritation which precedes that horrible death, and I cannot conceal from you how deeply she regrets life. The cries of her rebellious flesh are stifled in my heart—where they wake echoes of a wound still tender. But Monsieur de Dominis and I accept this duty that we may spare the sight of this moral anguish to her family; as it is, they no longer recognize their star by night and by day in her; they all, husband, children, servants, all are asking, 'Where is she?'—she is so changed! When she sees you, her regrets will revive. Lay aside your thoughts as a man of the world, forget its vanities, be to her the auxiliary of heaven, not of earth. Pray God that this dear saint die not in a moment of doubt, giving voice to her despair."

I did not answer. My silence alarmed the poor confessor. I saw, I heard, I walked, and yet I was no longer on the earth. The thought, "In what state shall I find her? Why do they use these precautions?" gave rise to apprehensions which were the more cruel because so indefinite; all forms of suffering crowded my mind.

We reached the door of the chamber and the abbe opened it. I then saw Henriette, dressed in white, sitting on her little sofa which was placed before the fireplace, on which were two vases filled with flowers; flowers were also on a table near the window. The expression of the abbe's face, which was that of amazement at the change in the room, now restored to its former state, showing me that the dying woman had sent away the repulsive preparations which surround a sick-bed. She had spent the last waning strength of fever in decorating her room to receive him whom in that final hour she loved above all things else. Surrounded by clouds of lace, her shrunken face, which had the greenish pallor of a magnolia flower as it opens, resembled the first outline of a cherished head drawn in chalks upon the yellow canvas of a portrait. To feel how deeply the vulture's talons now buried themselves in my heart, imagine the eyes of that outlined face finished and full of life,—hollow eyes which shone with a brilliancy unusual in a dying person. The calm majesty given to her in the past by her constant victory over sorrow was there no longer. Her forehead, the only part of her face which still kept its beautiful proportions, wore an expression of aggressive will and covert threats. In spite of the waxy texture of her elongated face, inward fires were issuing from it like the fluid mist which seems to flame above the fields of a hot day. Her hollow temples, her sunken cheeks showed the interior formation of the face, and the smile upon her whitened lips vaguely resembled the grin of death. Her robe, which was folded across her breast, showed the emaciation of her beautiful figure. The expression of her head said plainly that she knew she was changed, and that the thought filled her with bitterness. She was no longer the arch Henriette, nor the sublime and saintly Madame de Mortsauf, but the nameless something of Bossuet struggling against annihilation, driven to the selfish battle of life against death by hunger and balked desire. I took her hand, which was dry and burning, to kiss it, as I seated myself beside her. She guessed my sorrowful surprise from the very effort that I made to hide it. Her discolored lips drew up from her famished teeth trying to form a smile,—the forced smile with which we strive to hide either the irony of vengeance, the expectation of pleasure, the intoxication of our souls, or the fury of disappointment.

"Ah, my poor Felix, this is death," she said, "and you do not like death; odious death, of which every human creature, even the boldest lover, feels a horror. This is the end of love; I knew it would be so. Lady Dudley will never see you thus surprised at the change in her. Ah! why have I so longed for you, Felix? You have come at last, and I reward your devotion by the same horrible sight that made the Comte de Rance a Trappist. I, who hoped to remain ever beautiful and noble in your memory, to live there eternally a lily, I it is who destroy your illusions! True love cannot calculate. But stay; do not go, stay. Monsieur Origet said I was much better this morning; I shall recover. Your looks will bring me back to life. When I regain a little strength, when I can take some nourishment, I shall be beautiful again. I am scarcely thirty-five, there are many years of happiness before me,—happiness renews our youth; yes, I must know happiness! I have made delightful plans,—we will leave Clochegourde and go to Italy."

Tears filled my eyes and I turned to the window as if to look at the flowers. The abbe followed me hastily, and bending over the bouquet whispered, "No tears!"

"Henriette, do you no longer care for our dear valley," I said, as if to explain my sudden movement.

"Oh, yes!" she said, turning her forehead to my lips with a fond motion. "But without you it is fatal to me,—without _

*thee_*

," she added, putting her burning lips to my ear and whispering the words like a sigh.

I was horror-struck at the wild caress, and my will was not strong enough to repress the nervous agitation I felt throughout this scene. I listened without reply; or rather I replied by a fixed smile and signs of comprehension; wishing not to thwart her, but to treat her as a mother does a child. Struck at first with the change in her person, I now perceived that the woman, once so dignified in her bearing, showed in her attitude, her voice, her manners, in her looks and her ideas, the naive ignorance of a child, its artless graces, its eager movements, its careless indifference to everything that is not its own desire,—in short all the weaknesses which commend a child to our protection. Is it so with all dying persons? Do they strip off social disguises till they are like children who have never put them on? Or was it that the countess feeling herself on the borders of eternity, rejected every human feeling except love?

"You will bring me health as you used to do, Felix," she said, "and our valley will still be my blessing. How can I help eating what you will give me? You are such a good nurse. Besides, you are so rich in health and vigor that life is contagious beside you. My friend, prove to me that I need not die—die blighted. They think my worst suffering is thirst. Oh, yes, my thirst is great, dear friend. The waters of the Indre are terrible to see; but the thirst of my heart is greater far. I thirsted for thee," she said in a smothered voice, taking my hands in hers, which were burning, and drawing me close that she might whisper in my ear. "My anguish has been in not seeing thee! Did you not bid me live? I will live; I too will ride on horseback; I will know life, Paris, fetes, pleasures, all!"

Ah! Natalie, that awful cry—which time and distance render cold—rang in the ears of the old priest and in mine; the tones of that glorious voice pictured the battles of a lifetime, the anguish of a true love lost. The countess rose with an impatient movement like that of a child which seeks a plaything. When the confessor saw her thus the poor man fell upon his knees and prayed with clasped hands.

"Yes, to live!" she said, making me rise and support her; "to live with realities and not with delusions. All has been delusions in my life; I have counted them up, these lies, these impostures! How can I die, I who have never lived? I who have never roamed a moor to meet him!" She stopped, seemed to listen, and to smell some odor through the walls. "Felix, the vintagers are dining, and I, I," she said, in the voice of a child, "I, the mistress, am hungry. It is so in love, —they are happy, they, they!—"

"Kyrie eleison!" said the poor abbe, who with clasped hands and eyes raised to heaven was reciting his litanies.

She flung an arm around my neck, kissed me violently, and pressed me to her, saying, "You shall not escape me now!" She gave the little nod with which in former days she used, when leaving me for an instant, to say she would return. "We will dine together," she said; "I will go and tell Manette." She turned to go, but fainted; and I laid her, dressed as she was, upon the bed.

"You carried me thus before," she murmured, opening her eyes.

She was very light, but burning; as I took her in my arms I felt the heat of her body. Monsieur Deslandes entered and seemed surprised at the decoration of the room; but seeing me, all was explained to him.

"We must suffer much to die," she said in a changed voice.

The doctor sat down and felt her pulse, then he rose quickly and said a few words in a low voice to the priest, who left the room beckoning me to follow him.

"What are you going to do?" I said to the doctor.

"Save her from intolerable agony," he replied. "Who could have believed in so much strength? We cannot understand how she can have lived in this state so long. This is the forty-second day since she has either eaten or drunk."

Monsieur Deslandes called for Manette. The Abbe Birotteau took me to the gardens.

"Let us leave her to the doctor," he said; "with Manette's help he will wrap her in opium. Well, you have heard her now—if indeed it is she herself."

"No," I said, "it is not she."

I was stupefied with grief. I left the grounds by the little gate of the lower terrace and went to the punt, in which I hid to be alone with my thoughts. I tried to detach myself from the being in which I lived,—a torture like that with which the Torture punish adultery by fastening a limb of the guilty man in a piece of wood and leaving him with a knife to cut it off if he would not die of hunger. My life was a failure, too! Despair suggested many strange ideas to me. Sometimes I vowed to die beside her; sometimes to bury myself at Meilleraye among the Trappists. I looked at the windows of the room where Henriette was dying, fancying I saw the light that was burning there the night I betrothed my soul to hers. Ah! ought I not to have followed the simple life she had created for me, keeping myself faithfully to her while I worked in the world? Had she not bidden me become a great man expressly that I might be saved from base and shameful passions? Chastity! was it not a sublime distinction which I had not know how to keep? Love, as Arabella understood it, suddenly disgusted me. As I raised my humbled head asking myself where, in future, I could look for light and hope, what interest could hold me to life, the air was stirred by a sudden noise. I turned to the terrace and there saw Madeleine walking alone, with slow steps. During the time it took me to ascend the terrace, intending to ask the dear child the reason of the cold look she had given me when kneeling at the foot of the cross, she had seated herself on the bench. When she saw me approach her, she rose, pretending not to have seen me, and returned towards the house in a significantly hasty manner. She hated me; she fled from her mother's murderer.

When I reached the portico I saw Madeleine like a statue, motionless and erect, evidently listening to the sound of my steps. Jacques was sitting in the portico. His attitude expressed the same insensibility to what was going on about him that I had noticed when I first saw him; it suggested ideas such as we lay aside in some corner of our mind to take up and study at our leisure. I have remarked that young persons who carry death within them are usually unmoved at funerals. I longed to question that gloomy spirit. Had Madeleine kept her thoughts to herself, or had she inspired Jacques with her hatred?

"You know, Jacques," I said, to begin the conversation, "that in me you have a most devoted brother."

"Your friendship is useless to me; I shall follow my mother," he said, giving me a sullen look of pain.

"Jacques!" I cried, "you, too, against me?"

He coughed and walked away; when he returned he showed me his handkerchief stained with blood.

"Do you understand that?" he said.

Thus they had each of them a fatal secret. I saw before long that the brother and sister avoided each other. Henriette laid low, all was in ruins at Clochegourde.

"Madame is asleep," Manette came to say, quite happy in knowing that the countess was out of pain.

In these dreadful moments, though each person knows the inevitable end, strong affections fasten on such minor joys. Minutes are centuries which we long to make restorative; we wish our dear ones to lie on roses, we pray to bear their sufferings, we cling to the hope that their last moment may be to them unexpected.

"Monsieur Deslandes has ordered the flowers taken away; they excited Madame's nerves," said Manette.

Then it was the flowers that caused her delirium; she herself was not a part of it.

"Come, Monsieur Felix," added Manette, "come and see Madame; she is beautiful as an angel."

I returned to the dying woman just as the setting sun was gilding the lace-work on the roofs of the chateau of Azay. All was calm and pure. A soft light lit the bed on which my Henriette was lying, wrapped in opium. The body was, as it were, annihilated; the soul alone reigned on that face, serene as the skies when the tempest is over. Blanche and Henriette, two sublime faces of the same woman, reappeared; all the more beautiful because my recollection, my thought, my imagination, aiding nature, repaired the devastation of each dear feature, where now the soul triumphant sent its gleams through the calm pulsations of her breathing. The two abbes were sitting at the foot of the bed. The count stood, as though stupefied by the banners of death which floated above that adored being. I took her seat on the sofa. We all four turned to each other looks in which admiration for that celestial beauty mingled with tears of mourning. The lights of thought announced the return of the Divine Spirit to that glorious tabernacle.

The Abbe Dominis and I spoke in signs, communicating to each other our mutual ideas. Yes, the angels were watching her! yes, their flaming swords shone above that noble brow, which the august expression of her virtue made, as it were, a visible soul conversing with the spirits of its sphere. The lines of her face cleared; all in her was exalted and became majestic beneath the unseen incense of the seraphs who guarded her. The green tints of bodily suffering gave place to pure white tones, the cold wan pallor of approaching death. Jacques and Madeleine entered. Madeleine made us quiver by the adoring impulse which flung her on her knees beside the bed, crying out, with clasped hand: "My mother! here is my mother!" Jacques smiled; he knew he would follow her where she went.

"She is entering the haven," said the Abbe Birotteau.

The Abbe Dominis looked at me as if to say: "Did I not tell you the star would rise in all its glory?"

Madeleine knelt with her eyes fixed on her mother, breathing when she breathed, listening to the soft breath, the last thread by which she held to life, and which we followed in terror, fearing that every effort of respiration might be the last. Like an angel at the gates of the sanctuary, the young girl was eager yet calm, strong but reverent. At that moment the Angelus rang from the village clock-tower. Waves of tempered air brought its reverberations to remind us that this was the sacred hour when Christianity repeats the words said by the angel to the woman who has redeemed the faults of her sex. "Ave Maria!" —surely, at this moment the words were a salutation from heaven. The prophecy was so plain, the event so near that we burst into tears. The murmuring sounds of evening, melodious breezes in the leafage, last warbling of the birds, the hum and echo of the insects, the voices of the waters, the plaintive cry of the tree-frog,—all country things were bidding farewell to the loveliest lily of the valley, to her simple, rural life. The religious poesy of the hour, now added to that of Nature, expressed so vividly the psalm of the departing soul that our sobs redoubled.

Though the door of the chamber was open we were all so plunged in contemplation of the scene, as if to imprint its memories forever on our souls, that we did not notice the family servants who were kneeling as a group and praying fervently. These poor people, living on hope, had believed their mistress might be spared, and this plain warning overcame them. At a sign from the Abbe Birotteau the old huntsman went to fetch the curate of Sache. The doctor, standing by the bed, calm as science, and holding the hand of the still sleeping woman, had made the confessor a sign to say that this sleep was the only hour without pain which remained for the recalled angel. The moment had come to administer the last sacraments of the Church. At nine o'clock she awoke quietly, looked at us with surprised but gentle eyes, and we beheld our idol once more in all the beauty of former days.

"Mother! you are too beautiful to die—life and health are coming back to you!" cried Madeleine.

"Dear daughter, I shall live—in thee," she answered, smiling.

Then followed heart-rending embraces of the mother and her children. Monsieur de Mortsauf kissed his wife upon her brow. She colored when she saw me.

"Dear Felix," she said, "this is, I think, the only grief that I shall ever have caused you. Forget all that I may have said,—I, a poor creature much beside myself." She held out her hand; I took it and kissed it. Then she said, with her chaste and gracious smile, "As in the old days, Felix?"

We all left the room and went into the salon during the last confession. I approached Madeleine. In presence of others she could not escape me without a breach of civility; but, like her mother, she looked at no one, and kept silence without even once turning her eyes in my direction.

"Dear Madeleine," I said in a low voice, "What have you against me? Why do you show such coldness in the presence of death, which ought to reconcile us all?"

"I hear in my heart what my mother is saying at this moment," she replied, with a look which Ingres gave to his "Mother of God,"—that virgin, already sorrowful, preparing herself to protect the world for which her son was about to die.

"And you condemn me at the moment when your mother absolves me,—if indeed I am guilty."

"You, _

*you_*

," she said, "always _

*your self_*

!"

The tones of her voice revealed the determined hatred of a Corsican, implacable as the judgments of those who, not having studied life, admit of no extenuation of faults committed against the laws of the heart.

An hour went by in deepest silence. The Abbe Birotteau came to us after receiving the countess's general confession, and we followed him back to the room where Henriette, under one of those impulses which often come to noble minds, all sisters of one intent, had made them dress her in the long white garment which was to be her shroud. We found her sitting up; beautiful from expiation, beautiful in hope. I saw in the fireplace the black ashes of my letters which had just been burned, a sacrifice which, as her confessor afterwards told me, she had not been willing to make until the hour of her death. She smiled upon us all with the smile of other days. Her eyes, moist with tears, gave evidence of inward lucidity; she saw the celestial joys of the promised land.

"Dear Felix," she said, holding out her hand and pressing mine, "stay with us. You must be present at the last scene of my life, not the least painful among many such, but one in which you are concerned."

She made a sign and the door was closed. At her request the count sat down; the Abbe Birotteau and I remained standing. Then with Manette's help the countess rose and knelt before the astonished count, persisting in remaining there. A moment after, when Manette had left the room, she raised her head which she had laid upon her husband's knees.

"Though I have been a faithful wife to you," she said, in a faint voice, "I have sometimes failed in my duty. I have just prayed to God to give me strength to ask your pardon. I have given to a friendship outside of my family more affectionate care than I have shown to you. Perhaps I have sometimes irritated you by the comparisons you may have made between these cares, these thoughts, and those I gave to you. I have had," she said, in a sinking voice, "a deep friendship, which no one, not even he who has been its object, has fully known. Though I have continued virtuous according to all human laws, though I have been a irreproachable wife to you, still other thoughts, voluntary or involuntary, have often crossed my mind and, in this hour, I fear I have welcomed them too warmly. But as I have tenderly loved you, and continued to be your submissive wife, and as the clouds passing beneath the sky do not alter its purity, I now pray for your blessing with a clean heart. I shall die without one bitter thought if I can hear from your lips a tender word for your Blanche, for the mother of your children,—if I know that you forgive her those things for which she did not forgive herself till reassured by the great tribunal which pardons all."

"Blanche, Blanche!" cried the broken man, shedding tears upon his wife's head, "Would you kill me?" He raised her with a strength unusual to him, kissed her solemnly on the forehead, and thus holding her continued: "Have I no forgiveness to ask of you? Have I never been harsh? Are you not making too much of your girlish scruples?"

"Perhaps," she said. "But, dear friend, indulge the weakness of a dying woman; tranquillize my mind. When you reach this hour you will remember that I left you with a blessing. Will you grant me permission to leave to our friend now here that pledge of my affection?" she continued, showing a letter that was on the mantelshelf. "He is now my adopted son, and that is all. The heart, dear friend, makes its bequests; my last wishes impose a sacred duty on that dear Felix. I think I do not put too great a burden on him; grant that I do not ask too much of you in desiring to leave him these last words. You see, I am always a woman," she said, bending her head with mournful sweetness; "after obtaining pardon I ask a gift—Read this," she added, giving me the letter; "but not until after my death."

The count saw her color change: he lifted her and carried her himself to the bed, where we all surrounded her.

"Felix," she said, "I may have done something wrong to you. Often I gave you pain by letting you hope for that I could not give you; but see, it was that very courage of wife and mother that now enables me to die forgiven of all. You will forgive me too; you who have so often blamed me, and whose injustice was so dear—"

The Abbe Birotteau laid a finger on his lips. At that sign the dying woman bowed her head, faintness overcame her; presently she waved her hands as if summoning the clergy and her children and the servants to her presence, and then, with an imploring gesture, she showed me the desolate count and the children beside him. The sight of that father, the secret of whose insanity was known to us alone, now to be left sole guardian of those delicate beings, brought mute entreaties to her face, which fell upon my heart like sacred fire. Before receiving extreme unction she asked pardon of her servants if by a hasty word she had sometimes hurt them; she asked their prayers and commended each one, individually, to the count; she nobly confessed that during the last two months she had uttered complaints that were not Christian and might have shocked them; she had repulsed her children and clung to life unworthily; but she attributed this failure of submission to the will of God to her intolerable sufferings. Finally, she publicly thanked the Abbe Birotteau with heartfelt warmth for having shown her the illusion of all earthly things.

When she ceased to speak, prayers were said again, and the curate of Sache gave her the viaticum. A few moments later her breathing became difficult; a film overspread her eyes, but soon they cleared again; she gave me a last look and died to the eyes of earth, hearing perhaps the symphony of our sobs. As her last sigh issued from her lips,—the effort of a life that was one long anguish,—I felt a blow within me that struck on all my faculties. The count and I remained beside the bier all night with the two abbes and the curate, watching, in the glimmer of the tapers, the body of the departed, now so calm, laid upon the mattress of her bed, where once she had suffered cruelly. It was my first communion with death. I remained the whole of that night with my eyes fixed on Henriette, spell-bound by the pure expression that came from the stilling of all tempests, by the whiteness of that face where still I saw the traces of her innumerable affections, although it made no answer to my love. What majesty in that silence, in that coldness! How many thoughts they expressed! What beauty in that cold repose, what power in that immobility! All the past was there and futurity had begun. Ah! I loved her dead as much as I had loved her living. In the morning the count went to bed; the three wearied priests fell asleep in that heavy hour of dawn so well known to those who watch. I could then, without witnesses, kiss that sacred brow with all the love I had never been allowed to utter.

The third day, in a cool autumn morning, we followed the countess to her last home. She was carried by the old huntsman, the two Martineaus, and Manette's husband. We went down by the road I had so joyously ascended the day I first returned to her. We crossed the valley of the Indre to the little cemetery of Sache— a poor village graveyard, placed behind the church on the slope of the hill, where with true humility she had asked to be buried beneath a simple cross of black wood, "like a poor country-woman," she said. When I saw, from the centre of the valley, the village church and the place of the graveyard a convulsive shudder seized me. Alas! we have all our Golgothas, where we leave the first thirty-three years of our lives, with the lance-wound in our side, the crown of thorns and not of roses on our brow—that hill-slope was to me the mount of expiation.

We were followed by an immense crowd, seeking to express the grief of the valley where she had silently buried so many noble actions. Manette, her faithful woman, told me that when her savings did not suffice to help the poor she economized upon her dress. There were babes to be provided for, naked children to be clothed, mothers succored in their need, sacks of flour brought to the millers in winter for helpless old men, a cow sent to some poor home,—deeds of a Christian woman, a mother, and the lady of the manor. Besides these things, there were dowries paid to enable loving hearts to marry; substitutes bought for youths to whom the draft had brought despair, tender offerings of the loving woman who had said: "The happiness of others is the consolation of those who cannot themselves be happy." Such things, related at the "veillees," made the crowd immense. I walked with Jacques and the two abbes behind the coffin. According to custom neither the count nor Madeleine were present; they remained alone at Clochegourde. But Manette insisted in coming with us. "Poor madame! poor madame! she is happy now," I heard her saying to herself amid her sobs.

As the procession left the road to the mills I heard a simultaneous moan and a sound of weeping as though the valley were lamenting for its soul. The church was filled with people. After the service was over we went to the graveyard where she wished to be buried near the cross. When I heard the pebbles and the gravel falling upon the coffin my courage gave way; I staggered and asked the two Martineaus to steady me. They took me, half-dead, to the chateau of Sache, where the owners very kindly invited me to stay, and I accepted. I will own to you that I dreaded a return to Clochegourde, and it was equally repugnant to me to go to

Frapesle, where I could see my Henriette's windows. Here, at Sache, I was near her. I lived for some days in a room which looked on the tranquil, solitary valley I have mentioned to you. It is a deep recess among the hills, bordered by oaks that are doubly centenarian, through which a torrent rushes after rain. The scene was in keeping with the stern and solemn meditations to which I desired to abandon myself.

I had perceived, during the day which followed the fatal night, how unwelcome my presence might be at Clochegourde. The count had gone through violent emotions at the death of his wife; but he had expected the event; his mind was made up to it in a way that was something like indifference. I had noticed this several times, and when the countess gave me that letter (which I still dared not read) and when she spoke of her affection for me, I remarked that the count, usually so quick to take offence, made no sign of feeling any. He attributed Henriette's wording to the extreme sensitiveness of a conscience which he knew to be pure. This selfish insensibility was natural to him. The souls of these two beings were no more married than their bodies; they had never had the intimate communion which keeps feeling alive; they had shared neither pains nor pleasures, those strong links which tear us by a thousand edges when broken, because they touch on all our fibers, and are fastened to the inmost recesses of our hearts.

Another consideration forbade my return to Clochegourde,—Madeleine's hostility. That hard young girl was not disposed to modify her hatred beside her mother's coffin. Between the count, who would have talked to me incessantly of himself, and the new mistress of the house, who would have shown me invincible dislike, I should have found myself horribly annoyed. To be treated thus where once the very flowers welcomed me, where the steps of the portico had a voice, where my memory clothed with poetry the balconies, the fountains, the balustrades, the trees, the glimpses of the valleys! to be hated where I once was loved—the thought was intolerable to me. So, from the first, my mind was made up.

Alas! alas! was this the end of the keenest love that ever entered the heart of man? To the eyes of strangers my conduct might be reprehensible, but it had the sanction of my own conscience. It is thus that the noblest feelings, the sublimest dramas of our youth must end. We start at dawn, as I from Tours to Clochegourde, we clutch the world, our hearts hungry for love; then, when our treasure is in the crucible, when we mingle with men and circumstances, all becomes gradually debased and we find but little gold among the ashes. Such is life! life as it is; great pretensions, small realities. I meditated long about myself, debating what I could do after a blow like this which had mown down every flower of my soul. I resolved to rush into the science of politics, into the labyrinth of ambition, to cast woman from my life and to make myself a statesman, cold and passionless, and so remain true to the saint I loved. My thoughts wandered into far-off regions while my eyes were fastened on the splendid tapestry of the yellowing oaks, the stern summits, the bronzed foothills. I asked myself if Henriette's virtue were not, after all, that of ignorance, and if I were indeed guilty of her death. I fought against remorse. At last, in the sweetness of an autumn midday, one of those last smiles of heaven which are so beautiful in Touraine, I read the letter which at her request I was not to open before her death. Judge of my feelings as I read it.

Madame de Mortsauf to the Vicomte Felix de Vandenesse:

Felix, friend, loved too well, I must now lay bare my heart to you,—not so much to prove my love as to show you the weight of obligation you have incurred by the depth and gravity of the wounds you have inflicted on it. At this moment, when I sink exhausted by the toils of life, worn out by the shocks of its battle, the woman within me is, mercifully, dead; the mother alone survives. Dear, you are now to see how it was that you were the original cause of all my sufferings. Later, I willingly received your blows; to-day I am dying of the final wound your hand has given,—but there is joy, excessive joy in feeling myself destroyed by him I love.

My physical sufferings will soon put an end to my mental strength; I therefore use the last clear gleams of intelligence to implore you to befriend my children and replace the heart of which you have deprived them. I would solemnly impose this duty upon you if I loved you less; but I prefer to let you choose it for yourself as an act of sacred repentance, and also in faithful continuance of your love—love, for us, was ever mingled with repentant thoughts and expiatory fears! but—I know it well—we shall forever love each other. Your wrong to me was not so fatal an act in itself as the power which I let it have within me. Did I not tell you I was jealous, jealous unto death? Well, I die of it. But, be comforted, we have kept all human laws. The Church has told me, by one of her purest voices, that God will be forgiving to those who subdue their natural desires to His commandments. My beloved, you are now to know all, for I would not leave you in ignorance of any thought of mine. What I confide to God in my last hour you, too, must know,—you, king of my heart as He is King of Heaven.

Until the ball given to the Duc d'Angouleme (the only ball at which I was ever present), marriage had left me in that ignorance which gives to the soul of a young girl the beauty of the angels. True, I was a mother, but love had never surrounded me with its permitted pleasures. How did this happen? I do not know; neither do I know by what law everything within me changed in a moment. You remember your kisses? they have mastered my life, they have furrowed my soul; the ardor of your blood awoke the ardor of mine; your youth entered my youth, your desires my soul. When I rose and left you proudly I was filled with an emotion for which I know no name in any language—for children have not yet found a word to express the marriage of their eyes with light, nor the kiss of life laid upon their lips. Yes, it was sound coming in the echo, light flashing through the darkness, motion shaking the universe; at least, it was rapid like all these things, but far more beautiful, for it was the birth of the soul! I comprehended then that something, I knew not what, existed for me in the world,—a force nobler than thought; for it was all thoughts, all forces, it was the future itself in a shared emotion. I felt I was but half a mother. Falling thus upon my heart this thunderbolt awoke desires which slumbered there without my knowledge; suddenly I divined all that my aunt had meant when she kissed my forehead, murmuring, "Poor Henriette!"

When I returned to Clochegourde, the springtime, the first leaves, the fragrance of the flowers, the white and fleecy clouds, the Indre, the sky, all spoke to me in a language till then unknown. If you have forgotten those terrible kisses, I have never been able to efface them from my memory,—I am dying of them! Yes, each time that I have met you since, their impress is revived. I was shaken from head to foot when I first saw you; the mere presentiment of your coming overcame me. Neither time nor my firm will has enabled me to conquer that imperious sense of pleasure. I asked myself involuntarily, "What must be such joys?" Our mutual looks, the respectful kisses you laid upon my hand, the pressure of my arm on yours, your voice with its tender tones,—all, even the slightest things, shook me so violently that clouds obscured my sight; the murmur of rebellious senses filled my ears. Ah! if in those moments when outwardly I increased my coldness you had taken me in your arms I should have died of happiness. Sometimes I desired it, but prayer subdued the evil thought. Your name uttered by my children filled my heart with warmer blood, which gave color to my cheeks; I laid snares for my poor Madeleine to induce her to say it, so much did I love the tumults of that sensation. Ah! what shall I say to you? Your writing had a charm; I gazed at your letters as we look at a portrait.

If on that first day you obtained some fatal power over me, conceive, dear friend, how infinite that power became when it was given to me to read your soul. What delights filled me when I found you so pure, so absolutely truthful, gifted with noble qualities, capable of noblest things, and already so tried! Man and child, timid yet brave! What joy to find we both were consecrated by a common grief! Ever since that evening when we confided our childhoods to each other, I have known that to lose you would be death,—yes, I have kept you by me selfishly. The certainty felt by Monsieur de la Berge that I should die if I lost you touched him deeply, for he read my soul. He knew how necessary I was to my children and the count; he did not command me to forbid you my house, for I promised to continue pure in deed and thought. "Thought," he said to me, "is involuntary, but it can be watched even in the midst of anguish." "If I think," I replied, "all will be lost; save me from myself. Let him remain beside me and keep me pure!" The good old man, though stern, was moved by my sincerity. "Love him as you would a son, and give him your daughter," he said. I accepted bravely that life of suffering that I might not lose you, and I suffered joyfully, seeing that we were called to bear the same yoke—My God! I have been firm, faithful to my husband; I have given you no foothold, Felix, in your kingdom. The grandeur of my passion has reacted on my character; I have regarded the tortures Monsieur de Mortsauf has inflicted on me as expiations; I bore them proudly in condemnation of my faulty desires. Formerly I was disposed to murmur at my life, but since you entered it I have recovered some gaiety, and this has been the better for the count. Without this strength, which I derived through you, I should long since have succumbed to the inward life of which I told you.

If you have counted for much in the exercise of my duty so have my children also. I felt I had deprived them of something, and I feared I could never do enough to make amends to them; my life was thus a continual struggle which I loved. Feeling that I was less a mother, less an honest wife, remorse entered my heart; fearing to fail in my obligations, I constantly went beyond them. Often have I put Madeleine between you and me, giving you to each other, raising barriers between us,—barriers that were powerless! for what could stifle the emotions which you caused me? Absent or present, you had the same power. I preferred Madeleine to Jacques because Madeleine was sometime to be yours. But I did not yield you to my daughter without a struggle. I told myself that I was only twenty-eight when I first met you, and you were nearly twenty-two; I shortened the distance between us; I gave myself up to delusive hopes. Oh, Felix! I tell you these things to save you from remorse; also, perhaps, to show you that I was not cold and insensible, that our sufferings were cruelly mutual; that Arabella had no superiority of love over mine. I too am the daughter of a fallen race, such as men love well.

There came a moment when the struggle was so terrible that I wept the long nights through; my hair fell off,—you have it! Do you remember the count's illness? Your nobility of soul far from raising my soul belittled it. Alas! I dreamed of giving myself to you some day as the reward of so much heroism; but the folly was a brief one. I laid it at the feet of God during the mass that day when you refused to be with me. Jacques' illness and Madeleine's sufferings seemed to me the warnings of God calling back to Him His lost sheep.

Then your love—which is so natural—for that Englishwoman revealed to me secrets of which I had no knowledge. I loved you better than I knew. The constant emotions of this stormy life, the efforts that I made to subdue myself with no other succor than that religion gave me, all, all has brought about the malady of which I die. The terrible shocks I have undergone brought on attacks about which I kept silence. I saw in death the sole solution of this hidden tragedy. A lifetime of anger, jealousy, and rage lay in those two months between the time my mother told me of your relations with Lady Dudley, and your return to Clochegourde. I wished to go to Paris; murder was in my heart; I desired that woman's death; I was indifferent to my children. Prayer, which had hitherto been to me a balm, was now without influence on my soul. Jealousy made the breach through which death has entered. And yet I have kept a placid brow. Yes, that period of struggle was a secret between God and myself. After your return and when I saw that I was loved, even as I loved you, that nature had betrayed me and not your thought, I wished to live,—it was then too late! God had taken me under His protection, filled no doubt with pity for a being true with herself, true with Him, whose sufferings had often led her to the gates of the sanctuary.

My beloved! God has judged me, Monsieur de Mortsauf will pardon me, but you—will you be merciful? Will you listen to this voice which now issues from my tomb? Will you repair the evils of which we are equally guilty?—you, perhaps, less than I. You know what I wish to ask of you. Be to Monsieur de Mortsauf what a sister of charity is to a sick man; listen to him, love him—no one loves him. Interpose between him and his children as I have done. Your task will not be a long one. Jacques will soon leave home to be in Paris near his grandfather, and you have long promised me to guide him through the dangers of that life. As for

Madeleine, she will marry; I pray that you may please her. She is all myself, but stronger; she has the will in which I am lacking; the energy necessary for the companion of a man whose career destines him to the storms of political life; she is clever and perceptive. If your lives are united she will be happier than her mother. By acquiring the right to continue my work at Clochegourde you will blot out the faults I have not sufficiently expiated, though they are pardoned in heaven and also on earth, for _

      *he_*

is generous and will forgive me. You see I am ever selfish; is it not the proof of a despotic love? I wish you to still love me in mine. Unable to be yours in life, I bequeath to you my thoughts and also my duties. If you do not wish to marry Madeleine you will at least seek the repose of my soul by making Monsieur de Mortsauf as happy as he ever can be.

      Farewell, dear child of my heart; this is the farewell of a mind absolutely sane, still full of life; the farewell of a spirit on which thou hast shed too many and too great joys to suffer thee to feel remorse for the catastrophe they have caused. I use that word "catastrophe" thinking of you and how you love me; as for me, I reach the haven of my rest, sacrificed to duty and not without regret—ah! I tremble at that thought. God knows better than I whether I have fulfilled his holy laws in accordance with their spirit. Often, no doubt, I have tottered, but I have not fallen; the most potent cause of my wrong-doing lay in the grandeur of the seductions that encompassed me. The Lord will behold me trembling when I enter His presence as though I had succumbed. Farewell again, a long farewell like that I gave last night to our dear valley, where I soon shall rest and where you will often—will you not?—return.

      Henriette.

      I fell into an abyss of terrible reflections, as I perceived the depths unknown of the life now lighted up by this expiring flame. The clouds of my egotism rolled away. She had suffered as much as I—more than I, for she was dead. She believed that others would be kind to her friend; she was so blinded by love that she had never so much as suspected the enmity of her daughter. That last proof of her tenderness pained me terribly. Poor Henriette wished to give me Clochegourde and her daughter.

      Natalie, from that dread day when first I entered a graveyard following the remains of my noble Henriette, whom now you know, the sun has been less warm, less luminous, the nights more gloomy, movement less agile, thought more dull. There are some departed whom we bury in the earth, but there are others more deeply loved for whom our souls are winding-sheets, whose memory mingles daily with our heart-beats; we think of them as we breathe; they are in us by the tender law of a metempsychosis special to love. A soul is within my soul. When some good thing is done by me, when some true word is spoken, that soul acts and speaks. All that is good within me issues from that grave, as the fragrance of a lily fills the air; sarcasm, bitterness, all that you blame in me is mine. Natalie, when next my eyes are darkened by a cloud or raised to heaven after long contemplation of earth, when my lips make no reply to your words or your devotion, do not ask me again, "Of what are you thinking?"

*　　*　　*　　*　　*

Dear Natalie, I ceased to write some days ago; these memories were too bitter for me. Still, I owe you an account of the events which followed this catastrophe; they need few words. When a life is made up of action and movement it is soon told, but when it passes in the higher regions of the soul its story becomes diffuse. Henriette's letter put the star of hope before my eyes. In this great shipwreck I saw an isle on which I might be rescued. To live at Clochegourde with Madeleine, consecrating my life to hers, was a fate which satisfied the ideas of which my heart was full. But it was necessary to know the truth as to her real feelings. As I was bound to bid the count farewell, I went to Clochegourde to see him, and met him on the terrace. We walked up and down for some time. At first he spoke of the countess like a man who knew the extent of his loss, and all the injury it was doing to his inner self. But after the first outbreak of his grief was over he seemed more concerned about the future than the present. He feared his daughter, who, he told me, had not her mother's gentleness. Madeleine's firm character, in which there was something heroic blending with her mother's gracious nature, alarmed the old man, used to Henriette's tenderness, and he now foresaw the power of a will that never yielded. His only consolation for his irreparable loss, he said, was the certainty of soon rejoining his wife; the agitations, the griefs of these last few weeks had increased his illness and brought back all his former pains; the struggle which he foresaw between his authority as a father and that of his daughter, now mistress of the house, would end his days in bitterness; for though he should have struggled against his wife, he should, he knew, be forced to give way before his child. Besides, his son was soon to leave him; his daughter would marry, and what sort of son-in-law was he likely to have? Though he thus talked of dying, his real distress was in feeling himself alone for many years to come without sympathy.

During this hour when he spoke only of himself, and asked for my friendship in his wife's name, he completed a picture in my mind of the remarkable figure of the Emigre,—one of the most imposing types of our period. In appearance he was frail and broken, but life seemed persistent in him because of his sober habits and his country avocations. He is still living.

Though Madeleine could see me on the terrace, she did not come down. Several times she came out upon the portico and went back in again, as if to signify her contempt. I seized a moment when she appeared to beg the count to go to the house and call her, saying I had a last wish of her mother to convey to her, and this would be my only opportunity of doing so. The count brought her, and left us alone together on the terrace.

"Dear Madeleine," I said, "if I am to speak to you, surely it should be here where your mother listened to me when she felt she had less reason to complain of me than of the circumstances of life. I know your thoughts; but are you not condemning me without a knowledge of the facts? My life and happiness are bound up in this place; you know that, and yet you seek to banish me by the coldness you show, in place of the brotherly affection which has always united us, and which death should have strengthened by the bonds of a common grief. Dear Madeleine, you for whom I would gladly give my life without hope of recompense, without your even knowing it,—so deeply do we love the children of those who have succored us,—you are not aware of the project your adorable mother cherished during the last seven years. If you knew it your feelings would doubtless soften towards me; but I do not wish to take advantage of you now. All that I ask is that you do not deprive me of the right to come here, to breathe the air on this terrace, and to wait until time has changed your ideas of social life. At this moment I desire not to ruffle them; I respect a grief which misleads you, for it takes even from me the power of judging soberly the circumstances in which I find myself. The saint who now looks down upon us will approve the reticence with which I simply ask that you stand neutral between your present feelings and my wishes. I love you too well, in spite of the aversion you are showing me, to say one word to the count of a proposal he would welcome eagerly. Be free. Later, remember that you know no one in the world as you know me, that no man will ever have more devoted feelings—"

Up to this moment Madeleine had listened with lowered eyes; now she stopped me by a gesture.

"Monsieur," she said, in a voice trembling with emotion. "I know all your thoughts; but I shall not change my feelings towards you. I would rather fling myself into the Indre than ally myself to you. I will not speak to you of myself, but if my mother's name still possesses any power over you, in her name I beg you never to return to Clochegourde so long as I am in it. The mere sight of you causes me a repugnance I cannot express, but which I shall never overcome."

She bowed to me with dignity, and returned to the house without looking back, impassible as her mother had been for one day only, but more pitiless. The searching eye of that young girl had discovered, though tardily, the secrets of her mother's heart, and her hatred to the man whom she fancied fatal to her mother's life may have been increased by a sense of her innocent complicity.

All before me was now chaos. Madeleine hated me, without considering whether I was the cause or the victim of these misfortunes. She might have hated us equally, her mother and me, had we been happy. Thus it was that the edifice of my happiness fell in ruins. I alone knew the life of that unknown, noble woman. I alone had entered every region of her soul; neither mother, father, husband, nor children had ever known her.—Strange truth! I stir this heap of ashes and take pleasure in spreading them before you; all hearts may find something in them of their closest experience. How many families have had their Henriette! How many noble feelings have left this earth with no historian to fathom their hearts, to measure the depth and breadth of their spirits. Such is human life in all its truth! Often mothers know their children as little as their children know them. So it is with husbands, lovers, brothers. Did I imagine that one day, beside my father's coffin, I should contend with my brother Charles, for whose advancement I had done so much? Good God! how many lessons in the simplest history.

When Madeleine disappeared into the house, I went away with a broken heart. Bidding farewell to my host at Sache, I started for Paris, following the right bank of the Indre, the one I had taken when I entered the valley for the first time. Sadly I drove through the pretty village of Pont-de-Ruan. Yet I was rich, political life courted me; I was not the weary plodder of 1814. Then my heart was full of eager desires, now my eyes were full of tears; once my life was all before me to fill as I could, now I knew it to be a desert. I was still young,—only twenty-nine,—but my heart was withered. A few years had sufficed to despoil that landscape of its early glory, and to disgust me with life. You can imagine my feelings when, on turning round, I saw Madeleine on the terrace.

A prey to imperious sadness, I gave no thought to the end of my journey. Lady Dudley was far, indeed, from my mind, and I entered the courtyard of her house without reflection. The folly once committed, I was forced to carry it out. My habits were conjugal in her house, and I went upstairs thinking of the annoyances of a rupture. If you have fully understood the character and manners of Lady Dudley, you can imagine my discomfiture when her majordomo ushered me, still in my travelling dress, into a salon where I found her sumptuously dressed and surrounded by four persons. Lord Dudley, one of the most distinguished old statesmen of England, was standing with his back to the fireplace, stiff, haughty, frigid, with the sarcastic air he doubtless wore in parliament; he smiled when he heard my name. Arabella's two children, who were amazingly like de Marsay (a natural son of the old lord), were near their mother; de Marsay himself was on the sofa beside her. As soon as Arabella saw me she assumed a distant air, and glanced at my travelling cap as if to ask what brought me there. She looked me over from head to foot, as though I were some country gentlemen just presented to her. As for our intimacy, that eternal passion, those vows of suicide if I ceased to love her, those visions of Armida, all had vanished like a dream. I had never clasped her hand; I was a stranger; she knew me not. In spite of the diplomatic self-possession to which I was gradually being trained, I was confounded; and all others in my place would have felt the same. De Marsay smiled at his boots, which he examined with remarkable interest. I decided at once upon my course. From any other woman I should modestly have accepted my defeat; but, outraged at the glowing appearance of the heroine who had vowed to die for love, and who had scoffed at the woman who was really dead, I resolved to meet insolence with insolence. She knew very well the misfortunes of Lady Brandon; to remind her of them was to send a dagger to her heart, though the weapon might be blunted by the blow.

"Madame," I said, "I am sure you will pardon my unceremonious entrance, when I tell you that I have just arrived from Touraine, and that Lady Brandon has given me a message for you which allows of no delay. I feared you had already started for Lancashire, but as you are still in Paris I will await your orders at any hour you may be pleased to appoint."

She bowed, and I left the room. Since that day I have only met her in society, where we exchange a friendly bow, and occasionally a sarcasm. I talk to her of the inconsolable women of Lancashire; she makes allusion to Frenchwomen who dignify their gastric troubles by calling them despair. Thanks to her, I have a mortal enemy in de Marsay, of whom she is very fond. In return, I call her the wife of two generations.

So my disaster was complete; it lacked nothing. I followed the plan I had laid out for myself during my retreat at Sache; I plunged into work and gave myself wholly to science, literature, and politics. I entered the diplomatic service on the accession of Charles X., who suppressed the employment I held under the late king. From that moment I was firmly resolved to pay no further attention to any woman, no matter how beautiful, witty, or loving she might be. This determination succeeded admirably; I obtained a really marvellous tranquillity of mind, and great powers of work, and I came to understand how much these women waste our lives, believing, all the while, that a few gracious words will repay us.

But all my resolutions came to naught; you know how and why. Dear Natalie, in telling you my life, without reserve, without concealment, precisely as I tell it to myself, in relating to you feelings in which you have had no share, perhaps I have wounded some corner of your sensitive and jealous heart. But that which might anger a common woman will be to you—I feel sure of it—an additional reason for loving me. Noble women have indeed a sublime mission to fulfil to suffering and sickened hearts,—the mission of the sister of charity who stanches the wound, of the mother who forgives a child. Artists and poets are not the only ones who suffer; men who work for their country, for the future destiny of the nations, enlarging thus the circle of their passions and their thoughts, often make for themselves a cruel solitude. They need a pure, devoted love beside them, believe me, they understand its grandeur and its worth.

To-morrow I shall know if I have deceived myself in loving you.

Felix.

ANSWER TO THE ENVOI

Madame la Comtesse Natalie de Manerville to Monsieur le Comte Felix de Vandenesse.

Dear Count,—You received a letter from poor Madame de Mortsauf, which, you say, was of use in guiding you through the world,—a letter to which you owe your distinguished career. Permit me to finish your education.

Give up, I beg of you, a really dreadful habit; do not imitate certain widows who talk of their first husband and throw the virtues of the deceased in the face of their second. I am a Frenchwoman, dear count; I wish to marry the whole of the man I love, and I really cannot marry Madame de Mortsauf too. Having read your tale with all the attention it deserves,—and you know the interest I feel in you,—it seems to me that you must have wearied Lady Dudley with the perfections of Madame de Mortsauf, and done great harm to the countess by overwhelming her with the experiences of your English love. Also you have failed in tact to me, poor creature without other merit than that of pleasing you; you have given me to understand that I cannot love as Henriette or Arabella loved you. I acknowledge my imperfections; I know them; but why so roughly make me feel them?

Shall I tell you whom I pity?—the fourth woman whom you love. She will be forced to struggle against three others. Therefore, in your interests as well as in hers, I must warn you against the dangers of your tale. For myself, I renounce the laborious glory of loving you,—it needs too many virtues, Catholic or Anglican, and I have no fancy for rivalling phantoms. The virtues of the virgin of Clochegourde would dishearten any woman, however sure of herself she might be, and your intrepid English amazon discourages even a wish for that sort of happiness. No matter what a poor woman may do, she can never hope to give you the joys she will aspire to give. Neither heart nor senses can triumph against these memories of yours. I own that I have never been able to warm the sunshine chilled for you by the death of your sainted Henriette. I have felt you shuddering beside me.

My friend,—for you will always be my friend,—never make such confidences again; they lay bare your disillusions; they discourage love, and compel a woman to feel doubtful of herself. Love, dear count, can only live on trustfulness. The woman who before she says a word or mounts her horse, must ask herself whether a celestial Henriette might not have spoken better, whether a rider like Arabella was not more graceful, that woman you may be very sure, will tremble in all her members. You certainly have given me a desire to receive a few of those intoxicating bouquets—but you say you will make no more. There are many other things you dare no longer do; thoughts and enjoyments you can never reawaken. No woman, and you ought to know this, will be willing to elbow in your heart the phantom whom you hold there.

You ask me to love you out of Christian charity. I could do much, I candidly admit, for charity; in fact I could do all—except love. You are sometimes wearisome and wearied; you call your dulness melancholy. Very good,—so be it; but all the same it is intolerable, and causes much cruel anxiety to one who loves you. I have often found the grave of that saint between us. I have searched my own heart, I know myself, and I own I do not wish to die as she did. If you tired out Lady Dudley, who is a very distinguished woman, I, who have not her passionate desires, should, I fear, turn coldly against you even sooner than she did. Come, let us suppress love between us, inasmuch as you can find happiness only with the dead, and let us be merely friends—I wish it.

Ah! my dear count, what a history you have told me! At your entrance into life you found an adorable woman, a perfect mistress, who thought of your future, made you a peer, loved you to distraction, only asked that you would be faithful to her, and you killed her! I know nothing more monstrous. Among all the passionate and unfortunate young men who haunt the streets of Paris, I doubt if there is one who would not stay virtuous ten years to obtain one half of the favors you did not know how to value! When a man is loved like that how can he ask more? Poor woman! she suffered indeed; and after you have written a few sentimental phrases you think you have balanced your account with her coffin. Such, no doubt, is the end that awaits my tenderness for you. Thank you, dear count, I will have no rival on either side of the grave. When a man has such a crime upon his conscience, at least he ought not to tell of it. I made you an imprudent request; but I was true to my woman's part as a daughter of Eve,—it was your part to estimate the effect of the answer. You ought to have deceived me; later I should have thanked you. Is it possible that you have never understood the special virtue of lovers? Can you not feel how generous they are in swearing that they have never loved before, and love at last for the first time?

No, your programme cannot be carried out. To attempt to be both Madame de Mortsauf and Lady Dudley,—why, my dear friend, it would be trying to unite fire and water within me! Is it possible that you don't know women? Believe me, they are what they are, and they have therefore the defects of their virtues. You met Lady Dudley too early in life to appreciate her, and the harm you say of her seems to me the revenge of your wounded vanity. You understood Madame de Mortsauf too late, you punished one for not being the other,—what would happen to me if I were neither the one nor the other? I love you enough to have thought deeply about your future; in fact, I really care for you a great deal. Your air of the Knight of the Sad Countenance has always deeply interested me; I believed in the constancy of melancholy men; but I little thought that you had killed the loveliest and the most virtuous of women at the opening of your life.

Well, I ask myself, what remains for you to do? I have thought it over carefully. I think, my friend, that you will have to marry a Mrs. Shandy, who will know nothing of love or of passion, and will not trouble herself about Madame de Mortsauf or Lady Dudley; who will be wholly indifferent to those moments of ennui which you call melancholy, during which you are as lively as a rainy day,—a wife who will be to you, in short, the excellent sister of charity whom you are seeking. But as for loving, quivering at a word, anticipating happiness, giving it, receiving it, experiencing all the tempests of passion, cherishing the little weaknesses of a beloved woman—my dear count, renounce it all! You have followed the advice of your good angel about young women too closely; you have avoided them so carefully that now you know nothing about them. Madame de Mortsauf was right to place you high in life at the start; otherwise all women would have been against you, and you never would have risen in society.

It is too late now to begin your training over again; too late to learn to tell us what we long to hear; to be superior to us at the right moment, or to worship our pettiness when it pleases us to be petty. We are not so silly as you think us. When we love we place the man of our choice above all else. Whatever shakes our faith in our supremacy shakes our love. In flattering us men flatter themselves. If you intend to remain in society, to enjoy an intercourse with women, you must carefully conceal from them all that you have told me; they will not be willing to sow the flowers of their love upon the rocks or lavish their caresses to soothe a sickened spirit. Women will discover the barrenness of your heart and you will be ever more and more unhappy. Few among them would be frank enough to tell you what I have told you, or sufficiently good-natured to leave you without rancor, offering their friendship, like the woman who now subscribes herself

Your devoted friend,
Natalie de Manerville.

ADDENDUM

The following personages appear in other stories of the Human Comedy.

Birotteau, Abbe Francois   Cesar Birotteau   The Vicar of Tours

Blamont-Chauvry, Princesse de   The Thirteen   Madame Firmiani

Brandon, Lady Marie Augusta   The Member for Arcis   La Grenadiere

Chessel, Madame de   The Government Clerks

Dudley, Lord   The Thirteen   A Man of Business   Another Study of Woman   A Daughter of Eve

Dudley, Lady Arabella   The Ball at Sceaux   The Magic Skin   The Secrets of a Princess   A Daughter of Eve   Letters of Two Brides

Givry   Letters of Two Brides   Scenes from a Courtesan's Life

Lenoncourt, Duc de   Cesar Birotteau   Jealousies of a Country Town   The Gondreville Mystery   Beatrix

Lenoncourt-Givry, Duchesse de   Letters of Two Brides   Scenes from a Courtesan's Life

Listomere, Marquis de   A Distinguished Provincial at Paris   A Study of Woman

Listomere, Marquise de   Lost Illusions   A Distinguished Provincial at Paris   A Study of Woman   A Daughter of Eve

Louis XVIII., Louis-Stanislas-Xavier   The Chouans   The Seamy Side of History   The Gondreville Mystery   Scenes from a Courtesan's Life   The Ball at Sceaux   Colonel Chabert   The Government Clerks

Manerville, Comtesse Paul de   A Marriage Settlement   A Daughter of Eve

Marsay, Henri de   The Thirteen   The Unconscious Humorists   Another Study of Woman   Father Goriot   Jealousies of a Country Town   Ursule Mirouet   A Marriage Settlement   Lost Illusions   A Distinguished Provincial at Paris   Letters of Two Brides   The Ball at Sceaux   Modeste Mignon   The Secrets of a Princess   The Gondreville Mystery   A Daughter of Eve

Stanhope, Lady Esther   Lost Illusions

Vandenesse, Comte Felix de   Lost Illusions   A Distinguished Provincial at Paris   Cesar Birotteau   Letters of Two Brides   A Start in Life   The Marriage Settlement   The Secrets of a Princess   Another Study of Woman   The Gondreville Mystery   A Daughter of Eve

- 171 -

Also available from www.echo-library.com.

Honoré de Balzac   The comedié humaine.

Scenes from private life
Albert Savarus   Letters of Two Brides   A Daughter of Eve
Woman of Thirty   The Marriage Contract   A Start in Life
Modeste Mignon   Beatrix
Colonel Chabert With The Commission in Lunacy

Scenes from provincial life
Ursula (or Ursule Mirouet)   Eugenie Grandet
Eugénie Grandet (In French)
Pierrette   The Two Brothers   The Muse of the Department
The Jealousies of a Country Town
          An Old Maid   The Collection of Antiquities
The Lily of the Valley
Lost Illusions
          Two Poets   A Distinguished Provincial at Paris   Eve and David

Scenes from parisian Life
Scenes from a Courtesan's Life   The Thirteen   Father Goriot
Rise and Fall of Cesar Birotteau   Cousin Betty   Cousin Pons
The Lesser Bourgeoisie

Scenes from political life
An Historical Mystery   The Brotherhood of Consolation
The Deputy of Arcis

Scenes from military life
The Chouans

Scenes from country life
The Country Doctor   The Village Rector   Sons of the Soil

Philosophical studies
The Magic Skin   The Alkahest
The Physiology of Marriage   Petty Troubles of Married Life
Catherine De Medici   Seraphita

CPSIA information can be obtained at www.ICGtesting.com
Printed in the USA
LVOW100301270812

296060LV00001B/174/A